TRUTH ABOUT CATS & SPINSTERS

ANDREA SIMONNE

Liebe Publishing

Truth About Cats & Spinsters

By Andrea Simonne

Copyright © 2023 Andrea Simonne

All rights reserved. Published by Liebe Publishing

First Print Edition, March 14, 2023

ISBN: 978-1-945968-05-1

Edited by Hot Tree Editing: www.hotreeediting.com

Cover Design: LBC Graphics

CHAPTER ONE

~Leah~

Motorcycles in the night. That was how it started.

I'd barely fallen asleep and thought I was dreaming the hum of those engines. In my mind, I imagined a pride of lions thundering toward me under the cover of a night sky. Thick paws pounded the earth. One male lion moved ahead of the others, and when he spotted me in the distance, he roared. It wasn't long before the others joined him.

"Woo-hoo!"

"Fuck yeah!"

My eyes flew open.

Those aren't lions.

More yelling ensued as I lay in bed listening to the noise speeding by on the main road near my farm. *Who are these assholes?* Irritated, I grabbed my phone off the nightstand to check the time. It was after midnight.

They better not disturb my animals.

My cats meowed sleepily as I pushed the covers aside—three sets of golden eyes reflected the full moon outside.

"I'd better go check," I said to them. "Just in case."

By that point the motorcycles had turned into a distant buzz. I made my way downstairs to the living room and slid open the door for the back deck. The sound grew louder for an instant before fading off.

It was a warm August night, the air heavy with the scent of hay and livestock. My tall black rubber boots were nearby, and I slipped my feet into them and walked across the deck. I only wore panties and a short white camisole but figured it didn't matter. I wouldn't be outside long. The nearest neighbor was a good distance away, and my younger brother Shane, whose motorhome was parked on the other side of the barn, was tending bar at Walk the Plank tonight.

The ground was dusty as I clomped over to check on my girls.

When I reached the red-and-white barn, I found my dozen alpacas inside were happily cushed—sitting together in a cozy group. The barn doors were open on all three sides so they'd feel at ease.

I stepped back out, and my two guard llamas trotted over to greet me.

"Hello, ladies," I said, putting my hand over the wooden fence.

Phyllis, the friendlier of the two, sniffed and kissed my cheek. I laughed at her stinky breath before reaching out to pet her coat, rough beneath my hands. Her sister, Alicia, came close, and I petted her too.

Both animals were finally getting used to me. It had taken a while. When I'd bought this small farm a year ago, they could tell I was a dumbass who didn't know what I was doing.

I'd shocked my family. I'd even shocked myself. Within one month I'd quit my job in Seattle, moved back to Truth Harbor, and was living out here in the country.

Me. The girl who grew up in middle-class suburbia. Who dressed in high heels every day and had weekly manicures. The closest I'd ever been to an actual farm was a petting zoo. So what the hell was I thinking? Sure, I was a knitter who spun my own yarn and had daydreams of owning a farm.

But to actually do it?

I glanced over at the chicken coop. Soft clucks were coming from inside. In a few hours, my rooster, Cary Grant, would be crowing. I'd bought this place from a middle-aged couple who decided they were done farming and set off to travel the world.

It was an impulse. A crazy impulse, and, to be honest, I was barely making it. Every week there was a fresh crisis. My family still thought I'd lost my mind. They thought I should sell the place and go back to my normal life, back to my job in finance.

"It's been a year," my mom said. "Haven't you gotten it out of your system yet?"

Even my twin brother, Lars, thought it was a mistake. "A farm? Seriously, Leah, what were you thinking?"

Some days I worried they were right. That I'd bitten off more than I could chew, that I should give up and go back to my secure job and my weekly manicures.

Except then there were other days. The ones where I stood on my porch in the early morning, drinking coffee, quietly gazing out at my land, and a wave of exhilaration came over me.

I felt alive.

More alive than I ever had in my life.

It was a feeling I'd never gotten working in my cubicle analyzing stock valuations.

That feeling had kept me here.

"And, of course, you guys have too," I said to Phyllis, who made a soft huffing noise as I stroked her neck.

After a few minutes of petting them, both llamas trotted off to the barn. I leaned against the wooden fence rail enjoying the peaceful night, the way the full moon blanketed everything in a soft glow. Moments like these had been scarce in my former life, so I never took them for granted.

I wasn't going to think about how depleted my savings were, or how I needed money to buy more hay for winter. More firewood too. I'd been selling my fleece and handspun yarn, but it wasn't enough.

I looked up at the pale round orb in the sky. Some people liked to sunbathe, but I'd always liked to moonbathe.

It was what inspired the name I'd chosen for my farm and yarn business—Clarity Moon.

I tilted my face upward and took a deep breath, letting those moonbeams sink in. "We need rain," I said in a quiet voice. "It's costing more to take care of my animals and my land."

As I rested my forearms on the wooden fence rail, a silky breeze blew past, warm and inviting on my skin. My panties and camisole were just scraps of fabric. I might as well be wearing nothing.

The moon shone full and luminous. Close enough to touch. "I know you're listening," I whispered.

A peculiar energy hung in the air. Maybe I was crazy, but I swear I felt the moon's presence.

"One more thing." I gazed up at the night sky. "How about sending me a good man? I think I'm ready."

There was silence.

Another breeze blew past.

I shook my head and smiled to myself, embarrassed. I sounded like a weirdo out here talking to the moon. It was time to get back inside and get some sleep. I needed to be up at daybreak.

I strolled back toward the house, going over the list of chores in my head for the following morning. The sound of motorcycles broke the night's silence again, but I kept walking, figuring they'd pass on the main road like last time. But the engine noise grew louder.

With a jolt I realized they'd taken the turn onto the small road that led to my property.

What the hell?

The sound was moving directly toward me.

"Aaah!" I yelped in panic. I ran toward the house and barely had time to leap behind the arborvitaes near my front porch before two motorcycles came roaring into view. Their bright headlights shone on the exact spot where I'd been standing.

I pushed between the trees, surrounded by the aroma of pine, while bristly leaves poked my stomach and back. I tried my hardest not to think about spiders.

I peeked through the branches. Two motorcycles had stopped in my dirt driveway. A couple of guys looked around and then began yelling at each over the engines.

"Where is everybody? Is this the place?"

"How the hell should I know? I was following you."

They both turned their bikes off, and the night was quiet again with only the ping of metal cooling. One guy removed his helmet and stood while the other remained seated. They were each dressed in a combination of jeans and leather and had long bushy beards. The seated guy wore a bandana.

My heart hammered with fear as the guy standing swung a leg over his bike and lumbered up to my front door. He pounded on it with his fist. "Open up!"

I could barely believe this was happening. He wasn't far from my hiding spot, and for once, I was glad I'd forgotten to turn my porch light on. With the bright moon, I could see him well enough. He was big and heavyset with a bushy black beard. His meaty fist pounded my door like he was here to arrest me.

Despite my fear, I was getting pissed.

Who is this idiot? He better not break my door. If I weren't hiding in the bushes in my underwear, I'd give this belligerent asshole a piece of my mind.

Out of nowhere, the roar of a third motorcycle filled the air. It came sweeping around the corner and halted right next to the guy on the waiting bike. Sweat gathered in my armpits as I watched the two men talking, though I couldn't hear what they were saying over the engine noise and the incessant pounding.

The new guy turned his bike off. He removed his helmet, revealing a riot of long blond hair gathered in a low ponytail.

Meanwhile, Blackbeard had started ringing the doorbell as he pounded with his fist. Oddly, it sounded like music.

"Dean," the guy with the ponytail called out as he strode over. He was tall with long legs. "You crazy motherfucker, what are you doing?" He had a long beard too—blond, just like his hair—that went down to about mid-chest.

What is this? A beauty pageant for bearded bikers? Is there a swimsuit competition next?

The pounding and doorbell ringing stopped. "Josh? It's about damn time. I was starting to think I was lost."

"We should consider every day lost on which we have not danced at least once."

Dean snorted. "Well, I'll be happy to dance. Dance my ass off, even. But where is everybody?"

Josh chuckled. It was a sensual sound. Goose bumps rose on my skin. Low and masculine, that chuckle was doing something funny to me. My nipples hardened, and a pleasurable tingle started between my thighs. *My God.* I swallowed in horror. For some crazy reason, I was getting turned on.

I must be dreaming. It's the only explanation. And did that blond guy just quote Nietzsche?

I seriously considered the possibility that I was asleep. This was too surreal. I couldn't really be out here hiding in my underwear in the middle of the night watching a couple of bikers discuss Nietzsche on my front porch.

My eyes focused on the blond one again, Josh. He had broad shoulders and wore dark jeans, along with a faded motorcycle jacket. His hair hung all the way down his back. But this time I noticed something I hadn't before.

He was hot. Like super hot. But in a freaky outlaw sort of way.

"Dude, this isn't my house," Josh said, still chuckling.

"What?" Dean seemed startled. "No way. Are you kidding me?"

"I'm not kidding."

"Who the hell lives here?"

"I have no idea."

"Well, damn." He stroked his dark beard in contemplation. "Whoever they are, I guess they're not home."

"No shit." Josh laughed. "After all that pounding, you're lucky you're not staring down the barrel of a shotgun."

Dean glanced back at the house. "Guess we better get out of here before they decide to come home."

Both men turned to leave.

As it so happened, I *did* own a shotgun. Unfortunately, it was inside my hall closet where I couldn't get to it right then.

They walked past my hiding spot headed toward their motorcycles, and I let out a quiet sigh of relief.

As soon as they were gone, I planned to go inside my house, double-check all the locks, and sleep with that shotgun right next to me.

I gasped as something bit my leg. The sharp sting of a bug or spider.

My body shifted involuntarily, and I smacked my thigh, moving out from the shadow of the tree.

Dean didn't seem to notice anything, but Josh turned his head.

Oh shit.

He stopped walking.

I jumped back, but I could tell I wasn't fast enough, and that I'd made too much noise.

His eyes found me in the dark. I saw them widen with surprise, saw the way they flashed down to my body, to how I stood there in nothing but my skimpy panties, camisole, and black boots.

I couldn't believe I'd been discovered. Adrenaline poured into my veins like gasoline as I tried to figure out what to do.

Meanwhile, this hulking biker continued to stare at me.

The front door was locked, and the only way into the house was through the sliding glass door I'd left open in back.

Except there was a big problem.

In order to reach that door, I'd have to get past these two.

CHAPTER TWO

~Leah~

*S*hould I *make a run for it?*

I was panicking so hard my chest ached.

I mapped the shortest route to the back door in my mind. The two bikers were about fifteen feet away. The third one, still on his bike, appeared to be studying his phone. If I could somehow get past them, I might have a chance. If only I wasn't wearing these tall rubber boots.

Dean didn't seem to notice anything amiss and was talking to Josh about some party.

But Josh was still watching me.

His eyes were blue. Even at night, I could see their sharp color as we assessed each other.

I decided if he took one step closer, I'd take my boots off and throw them at him.

And then I'd run like hell.

Maybe they'd catch me. Maybe they wouldn't. But I wasn't going down without a fight.

I thought about my brother Lars, who was a deputy sheriff in town. He was the one who taught me how to use that shotgun. The one I wished I had in my hands right now. If anything happened to me, at least he'd make sure these assholes never saw the light of day again.

"Josh, what are you looking at?" the guy with the black beard asked. He began to turn in my direction.

I tensed, ready for a fight, lifting my right foot inside my boot so I could slip it off.

Josh laid a hand on his friend's shoulder and steered him toward the motorcycles. "It's nothing."

And then he looked back at me with a grin and winked.

My mouth dropped open.

Light-headed and breathless, I watched as the two men strode toward their bikes. I remained rooted to the spot, unable to take my eyes off them.

Moments later, in a roar of smoke and dust, all three were gone. Vanished into the night.

Almost like they were never there at all.

"ARE you sure you weren't dreaming?" Lars asked me the next morning as he stood near his silver pickup truck parked in front of my house. I'd just told him what happened.

"Of course I'm sure. Don't you think I know whether I'm awake or asleep?"

"Because it sounds like a dream to me." He rested his arm on the truck's rear gate. His short black hair shone under the hot sun as he reached down to shift some of the fencing supplies. "I mean, come on. A group of bikers came to your house in the middle of the night quoting Nietzsche?"

"Only one of them did that."

"And what were you doing this whole time?"

"Hiding in the arborvitae." I left out the part about being in my underwear.

"Why were you outside that late to begin with?"

"Checking on my girls, and then I was talking to the moon."

He chuckled. "You still do that?"

"Sometimes."

His dark eyes flashed over to me. "Face it, Leah. You were dreaming."

I bit my bottom lip. Maybe I was dreaming. The whole thing sure felt like a dream. A strange adrenaline-charged dream.

When that biker saw me, I thought for sure I was in real trouble. I remembered the way he'd grinned at me before he left. His teeth were straight and white, not what you'd expect for an outlaw.

I'd woken up this morning in bed with my shotgun next to me and an itchy red welt on my thigh that looked like a spider bite. If that was a dream, it was a very realistic one.

"I was *not* dreaming," I insisted. "I was wide awake."

Lars rubbed the back of his neck, then seemed to consider me. "All right, fine. I'll ask around. See if anyone's heard about a group of bikers causing trouble."

"Thank you. I'd appreciate that. And thank you for repairing my fence on your day off."

He grunted his reply and then motioned toward our younger brother's motorhome. "Isn't Shane helping?"

"I think so." I glanced over. "He's probably not awake yet. I think he has female company."

"I don't care. Go wake him up." Lars sounded irritable. He still thought my buying this farm was a mistake, and unfortunately, it had created a rift between us. At the same time, he felt obliged to help me, which only irritated him further.

I wish I could say I was superwoman and that I managed this place with no one's help, but that would be a lie.

Both of my brothers had helped. I'd tried to do everything on my own, and most of the time I'd managed fine, but after falling off the roof last winter and nearly impaling myself on a garden gnome, I'd accepted that certain jobs required assistance.

"I'm going to drive all this fencing over to your east pasture," Lars said, sounding impatient as he opened his driver's door. "Tell Shane to meet me there and bring his toolbox."

"Aye, aye, Deputy."

I heard him drive off behind me as I walked past the chicken coop and barn, heading over to Shane's thirty-two-foot motorhome. His blue truck was parked behind it, along with a red Camry I'd never seen before.

It was warm outside, and I could tell the day was going to be a scorcher. Luckily, my animals had plenty of shady spots. I reminded myself to check their water later.

Two lawn chairs and a stone firepit were set up next to the RV. It was the kind of fancy motorhome you imagined a nice retired couple driving around in as they lived out their golden years. Not a twenty-three-year-old guy who worked full-time construction and part-time tending bar. When he asked if he could park it on my property a few months ago, I said sure. I was happy to help.

Of course, he helped me too.

Not that he seemed to mind. Shane was the only one in our family who hadn't told me I should go back to my cubicle.

I knocked on the door. It was nine in the morning, but he'd closed the bar last night and probably didn't get home until after two.

I knocked again.

Finally, I heard movement inside.

A few moments later, the door swung open, and a pretty young blonde stood there. She wore one of my brother's wrinkled shirts, which appeared hastily thrown on.

"Hi," I said. "Is Shane awake yet?"

She nodded and moved back. "He's awake."

I walked up the wooden steps. Inside the motorhome was stuffy with the scent of fruity perfume and young lust. "Shane?" I called out.

He emerged tanned, shirtless, and barefoot from his bedroom at the back. "Shit. Sorry, Leah." He was holding a gray T-shirt and quickly slipped it on. "I forgot about the fence."

"Can you still help today?"

"Sure. No problem." He ran a hand through his bangs. His hair was layered and light brown with natural blond streaks throughout. My baby brother looked like a cute surfer. "Say, do you mind if Kayla here uses your shower? She has to get to work at the salon."

"I have to be there by ten thirty," she explained to me in a worried voice.

"Um, sure," I said, noticing the hickey on her neck. There were remnants of last night's makeup on her face, but other than that, her skin was dewy and perfect. I was only thirty-four, but somehow all of Shane's girlfriends made me feel like an old lady. This was the third one in two weeks who'd needed to use my shower.

"After the fence, I'm going into work," Shane said, taking a seat on the small couch, putting his socks and boots on.

"At the bar?"

He shook his head. "Matt needs some extra hands, so I told him I'd fill in at that big house by Treasure Lake."

"Lars says you need to bring your tools."

Shane nodded and stood up.

Kayla, who had disappeared into the bedroom, emerged now wearing a pink sundress and high-heeled sandals. She went over to my brother, who slipped his arm around her waist.

"Give us a kiss," he crooned.

"Will I see you again?" she purred.

"Sure. Of course you will."

I tried not to roll my eyes. Shane changed girlfriends as often as he did socks. In fact, those socks he'd put on were older than most of his relationships.

I waited as the two of them made kissy-face sounds to each other while saying goodbye.

After walking Kayla over to the house and showing her the facilities, I gave her a clean towel and wished her luck.

Since Lars had told me he didn't need my help with the fence, I decided to spend the rest of the morning cleaning out my chicken coop. Not a fun job, but a necessary one. I gave the chickens some of their favorite scratch to distract them, and all my birds came running over.

As I used a pitchfork to haul muck into a wheelbarrow, my mind kept going back to last night and those bikers—especially the blond one. It was bizarre how I'd gotten turned on. Was it the impending danger? Did my girl parts get confused? I mean, he was quoting Nietzsche, for God's sake. Who did that?

By the time I was done with the coop, it was nearly noon, and I was stinky and covered in sweat. My eight maidens and Cary Grant all seemed pleased as they clucked around inspecting things.

I took a break and sat down on the front porch steps with a glass of cold water. From the corner of my eye, I noticed something near the barn. I glanced over, but it was just a couple of my girls.

I took another sip of water and gazed out at the pasture. Peaceful, just the way I liked it.

Something by the barn caught my eye again. However, this time I saw a blue shirt disappear inside.

What the hell was that?

Alarm shot through me.

Did one of the bikers return?

I put my glass down, then got up and went inside the house. Recent events had me on edge. I should call Lars and Shane to come help, but they were in the east pasture. It would take time for them to get here. Instead I went to the hall closet and retrieved my shotgun.

I'd had enough and wasn't putting up with any more trespassers.

It was a small pump action made for women, and believe me, I knew how to use it. Lars had me practice at a gun range regularly. Thankfully, I'd never had any trouble, but I slept better at night knowing I could defend myself.

I kept the safety on as I headed out toward the barn, barrel pointed down. Walking as silently as I could, I peered around the barn door. My cat, Basil, wound himself around my legs and meowed. He didn't seem spooked.

A good sign.

Still on guard, I made my way deeper inside. It was a decent-sized structure with a large hay loft and plenty of space to comfortably house my animals. As I moved in farther, I saw the back of a blue T-shirt. Shoulder-length light brown hair.

I let my breath out with relief.

Not a biker but a kid. A little girl. She was watching a couple of my alpacas, who stood near their water trough. She looked to be about the same age as the kids I'd taught spinning and knitting classes to at the community center.

"What are you doing in here?" I asked.

The girl startled and spun around. Her eyes were large and dark. Except I'd gotten it exactly wrong.

It wasn't a girl but a boy. The long hair had thrown me.

"Can I help you with something?" I asked. "This is private property."

"I didn't mean any harm. I was only looking."

I blinked with surprise. The kid spoke with a British accent. "Who are you?"

He opened his mouth, but then his gaze dropped to the shotgun I was holding. Those dark eyes grew wide. They flashed up to my face again, and before I could stop him, he ran. Hightailed it right past me. Maybe I should have grabbed him, but it didn't occur to me.

"Hey, come back!"

But he kept on running. I strode outside to follow him and found the kid was already halfway across the pasture. I watched with admiration as he ran. Fast and steady with an even gait. Definitely a natural. Scrambling smoothly over the fence, he disappeared into a copse of trees that stood near the woods that bordered my property.

I glanced down at my shotgun and thought, *Smart kid. Never mess with an armed woman.*

CHAPTER THREE

~Leah~

I wished I'd left my gun inside the house. I'd rather not have scared the kid away but talked to him and found out who he was.

A few minutes later, after I'd put my shotgun safely back in the closet, Lars's silver truck pulled into the driveway next to my white one.

I walked outside to meet him. "You just missed it."

"Missed what?" He closed the driver's door.

"There was a kid here. He ran off into the woods."

My brother looked around.

"He was about ten years old. He was British."

Lars gave me a strange look. "How do you know he was British?"

"Because he spoke to me."

He walked around to the rear of the truck and opened it. "What did he say?"

"Nothing really. He was looking at my animals, but then he got scared and ran off."

He shrugged. "Probably just some neighbor kid."

"None of my neighbors have kids that age. And how do you explain the accent?"

"Maybe he was putting you on, or maybe he's friends with your Nietzsche bikers." His voice was dry. He pulled out the fencing supplies. "We should store these in the shed."

"Thank you for the repairs. I can make some lunch if you want to stick around."

"That's okay. I have to head out. I'm meeting someone later."

"A date?"

"Not really. Just a friend."

I could tell he didn't want to discuss it, so I didn't push further. Like me, my brother was single, but unlike me, he'd never been married—though I liked to pretend my horrible marriage never happened.

I helped carry everything over to the shed. Before he left, I gave him a couple of dozen eggs from my flock and a batch of chocolate chip cookies I'd made last night as a thank-you for his help. Once he was gone, I took a shower. My shoulders and arms ached from shoveling chicken poop and fresh straw all morning. The hot water felt like heaven.

When I was done, I made an egg salad sandwich for lunch and checked on the white alpaca fleece I'd dyed forest green recently. It came from my herd's spring shearing, and I'd never forget the way it felt seeing all those bags of raw fleece for the first time. Fiber from my own animals. I felt richer than a rock star.

I had an online shop where I sold my fleece along with the various yarns I spun. The owner of the local yarn store in Truth Harbor sold it as well.

I checked my online orders and was pleased to see three new ones. I liked to send purchases right away, so I went and pulled the skeins from my overstuffed shelves to be packed. Even before I had this farm, I was a spinner, so I'd always had a crazy amount of yarn. Every color and texture. Some women bought shoes, but my weakness was fiber.

Some of my dyed fleece was ready to spin, so I sat down at my wheel in the dining room, which I'd turned into a yarn den. I'd put hooks in the ceiling to hang some of the freshly spun skeins. It gave the room a colorful appearance.

Often when I spun, hours flew by, and today was no exception. It wasn't until a couple of my cats meowed for dinner that I looked at the time. I inspected the yarn I'd been working on. Satisfied things were in order, I put everything away so my seven cats couldn't get to it.

Yes, I had seven cats.

Three were mine from before I bought the place, and four were barn cats who already lived here. Those barn cats loved coming inside the house, and I was too softhearted to make them stay outside.

After putting out bowls of food, I went to give my girls their evening pellets. My alpacas and llamas had grass and fresh hay available at all times, but I supplemented their diet to be sure they stayed healthy. Plus, I had two—Lilith and Ruth—who were nursing, and they got some extras.

As I stood in the barn filling the trough with water, I watched everyone eat. There were grumbles as they bumped against each other, but nothing concerning. Rhiannon, the matriarch of the group, helped keep the peace.

Straw crunched behind me.

Surprised, I jerked my head around.

There was no one there, but my pulse kicked up a notch. I thought I'd heard a footstep.

I turned back to my animals, but then I heard the straw again, and this time I knew I wasn't alone.

Skin prickled on the back of my neck.

It might be that kid again. Maybe he was hiding.

But what if it's someone else?

I kept my breath steady and glanced around for a weapon. A pitchfork leaned against the wall nearby. I continued to fill the trough as I moved closer to pick it up.

Holding the pitchfork, I turned the hose off and pretended everything was normal as I walked out the west barn door. Instead of leaving, I sneakily slipped to the side of the structure so no one could see me.

I wasn't planning an attack, just wanted to see what I was dealing with. I hoped it was only the kid.

The pitchfork was there in case it wasn't.

It didn't take long for the trespasser to emerge from their hiding space. I heard straw underfoot again. The sounds of someone walking grew closer.

My grip tightened on the pitchfork's wooden handle.

A blue T-shirt and light brown hair emerged from the barn.

Thank God. Just the kid.

When he was about eight feet away, I called out to him. "Hey, what's your name?"

He spun around, and I could tell I'd startled him like earlier.

He opened his mouth, but then he saw the pitchfork I was holding.

Shit.

"It's okay," I said, taking a step toward him. I kept my voice gentle. "Let me put this down." I leaned the pitchfork against the barn. But when I turned around, it was too late. He was already running away.

"Come back," I shouted. "I just want to talk."

He kept going, following the same route as last time across the pasture. I glanced up at the sky. Blue and cloudless with a hint of orange. It was getting late, but there was still a good half hour of daylight left.

If I'd been wearing my boots, I wouldn't have even considered it. But as luck would have it, I had on a T-shirt, shorts, and sneakers.

I reached back to quickly tighten my ponytail.

Then I took a deep breath and followed after him.

———————

THE KID WAS FAST. I had to give him that. He made great time. Only, he didn't know it, but I was fast too. I ran track throughout high school and still ran most weekday mornings.

He had a good head start, but I was gaining on him.

After scrambling over the fence, he glanced back and seemed surprised that I was following.

"Wait up," I called out. "You're not in trouble."

All he seemed to hear was the word "trouble," because he turned and jumped to the ground. I watched him run toward the trees and knew from there he'd go straight into the woods.

Dammit. It would be harder to follow him into those woods.

I made my way to the fence and should have stopped. Instead I climbed it just like he did. When I glanced back at the pasture, Phyllis and Alicia were watching me with a combination of curiosity and concern. "Don't worry," I said before jumping to the ground. "I got this."

When I turned back toward the kid, he was zipping through the copse of deciduous trees like they weren't even there. It was obvious I'd lose him if I slowed down, so I pushed myself. I hadn't run this hard in a while, and it felt good.

I just made it past the trees when his blue shirt disappeared into the thick row of evergreens at the forest's edge. We were only about thirty feet from each other. As I ran closer, I hesitated. Was I really going to follow him into the woods?

He headed farther in and would be gone from sight within seconds.

I plunged after him.

I shouldn't have. My property line had already ended.

The vegetation was thick, and I was forced to slow down. I could make out flashes of blue to my left and continued to follow the kid steadily.

It was darker in the woods. The scent of earthy green things filled my nose. Soft pine needles covered the ground, and my sneakers dug into them with every step.

I should turn back.

The deeper we went, the stronger my inner voice told me to turn around and head home.

Life was different here. Peaceful yet foreboding. Untouched by man. I stepped over a fallen log, and something scurried away.

As the trees became thicker, it grew difficult to see. I hoped I didn't lose sight of the kid. I tried to judge which direction he was headed and was pretty sure we were moving south.

I racked my brain for who lived down there but couldn't think of anyone. The boy had to come from somewhere.

My pace slowed. It was getting darker. I thought I still saw movement ahead of me, but I wasn't sure.

By now my inner voice was berating me like a drill sergeant. It told me how stupid I was to follow that kid. It said I was lost in the woods and that I should have paid more attention to those documentaries where they showed people surviving on tree bark and rainwater.

I glanced around with a sinking feeling.

Shit.

It was fully dark out now. I had no idea where the kid was, and I had no idea where I was either.

How did I get myself into this mess? Did I take an idiot pill this morning? I thought those were vitamins.

I stopped moving and tried to get my bearings. The woods were mostly quiet, and the temperature had cooled considerably. I felt exposed in my T-shirt and shorts.

"Ow!" I slapped my arm at the sting of a mosquito. Another one bit my leg, and I slapped that too. Apparently they were calling all their buddies over for Leah's Happy Hour.

I rubbed my thigh as I pictured mosquitoes lined up on bar stools drinking my blood from tiny martini glasses. "She eats a lot of chocolate, doesn't she?" they said to each other with approval.

A growing hysteria was rising in me.

Stay calm. If that kid can find his way out of here, then so can you.

I took a deep breath to quell my panic and began moving forward again, slower than before but in the general direction of where I last saw him.

Images of search parties drifted through my mind. People discussing my odd disappearance with my face splashed across the local paper. Unfortunately, it was my driver's license photo—the camera had surprised me that day, and I wore a startled expression.

Surely my mom would give them a better picture of me than that? Maybe she was too upset to think clearly.

What a nightmare. I'd always told myself I'd learn survival skills. Why hadn't I ever done it?

I kept walking in silence and darkness, hoping I was still following that kid. For all I knew, I was going in circles.

But then I noticed something up ahead—a flicker of orange light. I headed toward it, and it wasn't long before I heard what sounded like voices in the distance. I kept going, eager to get out of the woods. Finally, I stood on the edge of a large grass clearing.

Thank God.

There was a house up ahead. A fire blazed with people gathered around it. The scent of woodsmoke drifted over as I stepped onto the grass and began walking toward the group. I figured I'd ask them to point me toward the main road.

It was dark out, so no one seemed to notice my approach. As I drew closer, I saw a couple of trucks in the driveway along with what must have been a half-dozen motorcycles.

I froze.

My gaze flew back to the fire. Sure enough, the guys all had beards and leather jackets. There were a few women sitting around too.

A bubble of hysteria formed in my chest. I couldn't believe it. I'd accidentally stumbled into the bikers' lair.

Slowly, I walked backward. At least no one had noticed me. Once I was close enough to the woods, I ran back inside.

Okay, fine. No big deal. I tried to catch my breath. *I'll just circle around to the front. I can still find the main road.*

It was gloomy in the woods, and I could hear myself panting as I moved steadily, keeping the tree line to my left. Things were going great, swimmingly even—

A twig snapped behind me.

I jerked my head around.

Even though my eyes had adjusted to the dark, it was difficult to see. Slivers of moonlight shone into the wood's canopy, illuminating branches.

It was probably just the kid out there, right? That made sense. I took a deep breath to call out, but my inner voice told me to stop.

I shut my mouth.

Yes, I listened to that inner voice for a change. It seemed to know what it was talking about.

I continued walking, stepping over fallen logs and twisted tree roots. It was like traversing an obstacle course. The forest seemed ominous and unwelcoming as I tried to keep track of where I was in proximity to the house.

Another twig snapped behind me. I turned my head toward the sound. At first I thought it was nothing but my jangly nerves.

But then I saw him.

Except it wasn't the kid.

My pulse skyrocketed. I could just make out the shape of a lone figure in the distance. More twigs snapped as the figure took a step toward me. Moonlight fell over him, and I gasped.

He was covered in... fur.

My head shook in disbelief as my brain tried to make sense of what I saw. It couldn't be. It just *couldn't*. But there he was.

A whimper escaped my throat. I broke out in a cold sweat.

And then I bolted.

In a blind panic, I ran as fast as I could through the thick woods, the underbrush scratching my bare legs, my mind racing. The Pacific Northwest was full of stories about these large humanlike creatures who lived in the woods, but that was all they were. Made-up stories. Nobody believed they were real.

There were crashing sounds behind me, and with terror, I realized he—it—was chasing me.

I was being chased through the woods by a Sasquatch.

CHAPTER FOUR

~Leah~

I *have to reach the road.* That was my one pervasive thought. *Or maybe I should run back toward the bikers. Dealing with outlaw bikers is probably better than a Sasquatch, right?*

To be honest, I wasn't sure.

So I kept running. Fear pumped through my veins, fueling me. My thigh muscles burned with exertion as I tried to maneuver through the heavy vegetation. My sense of direction felt askew, and I worried whether I was even headed toward the road anymore.

There were noises behind me that sounded like a yell. Was the creature bellowing at me?

With surreal panic, I ran faster, pushing myself as hard as I could, but then the unthinkable happened. My foot snagged on a tree root.

I cried out with alarm as I went down. Hard.

My hands flew out to brace the fall. Pain exploded through my body.

I gasped as the wind got knocked from my lungs, my mouth filling with dirt. I coughed and sputtered, trying to get up.

The creature was still behind me, hurtling through the trees, moving closer with each giant step.

I scrambled onto my back, but I wasn't fast enough. To my horror, it was looming right over me.

It must have been at least eight feet tall and covered in thick variegated fur.

My mind went blank with terror. I could see no way out of this crazy situation.

I thought of my farm. Would my animals miss me? My mom and Lars would surely sell the place. They'd be delighted to get rid of it. I hoped the new owners were nice and would still let the barn cats inside the house.

The Sasquatch appeared to be studying me. I decided to kick it in the nuts if it came any closer, then had a strange thought. *What if it doesn't have any nuts?*

"It's you again," the creature above me said in a deep voice.

I blinked at it with surprise. The Sasquatch was speaking. It could speak English.

"I remember you from last night."

I was confused. "Wha... what?"

"You were that chick hiding outside in your underwear."

I stared up at it.

The creature bent down and, before I knew it, was kneeling beside me. "Hey, are you okay? I didn't mean to scare you. Are you hurt?"

"You're not a Sasquatch."

It chuckled. A low rumble that made me feel funny. "No, honey, I'm not. I've been called a lot of things but never that."

I swallowed and tried to catch my breath.

"What's wrong with her?" There was someone else there with a British accent. He was looking over the creature's shoulder. "Is she going to be okay?"

"You were right to come get me, Little D. I think she's okay, but we scared her."

"Sorry," the accented voice said to me, and I realized it was the kid from earlier.

My mind began to clear. It was dark out, but up close, I could see what I was dealing with. It wasn't a Sasquatch at all but one of the bikers from last night. The blond one.

He was covered in hair, not fur. There was a lot of it too. His mess of curls framed his face like a mane and then fell down around his shoulders. And, of course, there was that long beard.

"Can you stand up?" he asked. "We should get you to the house."

I tried to stand, but my whole body ached. Then a muscular arm slipped around my waist, nearly lifting me off the ground. We walked slowly out of the woods together.

As we approached the fire, people noticed us.

"Who's that?" a guy with a bushy black beard asked. I recognized him from last night. He was the asshole who pounded on my door.

"I found her in the woods. She fell down," the non-Sasquatch told everyone. "I'm going to take her inside and clean her up."

I heard more curious mutterings as people watched us walk toward the back of the house.

"Leave it to Josh to find a hot chick roaming the forest!" some guy said with a laugh.

In a daze, I took in my surroundings. The house was large and built in a log cabin style. I could just make out a small lake a short distance away. We went in through some French doors in back, then through a living room and down a long hallway. There were moving boxes stacked everywhere. It smelled faintly of a recent meal with curry.

I followed him into a fancy bathroom. It was large and done in lavender and white tiles.

"Have a seat," he said, pointing toward a wooden bench. "There's a first aid kit in here somewhere."

I sat down, still looking around. The kid was with us, too, watching me with keen interest.

My adrenaline had worn off and was replaced with anger. "Why were you chasing me?" I demanded to know. "You scared me half to death."

The guy sat on the floor to my right and opened the first aid kit. "Put your legs out. Let me clean up some of these scratches for you."

I did as he asked and saw my legs were a mess, both of them scratched up. My right knee was oozing blood.

"You didn't answer my question."

He took out some antibacterial spray. "This might sting a little."

"Ouch!" I sucked in my breath as he sprayed both legs.

"Sorry."

"That hurts," I muttered.

He glanced up at me, and I saw the hint of a smile.

"What are you, a sadist?"

He seemed to consider this. "No, I can't say I am." Reaching into the box, he pulled out a packet of sterilized cloth, tearing it open. "We should clean the dirt off these scratches and then spray some more."

I bit my lip and saw he was right. I braced myself for more pain as he began wiping, but he was surprisingly gentle.

The three of us were silent as he worked on getting my wounds clean.

I took the opportunity to study him under the bathroom light. He wore a brown sweater and dark jeans. His blond hair hung down to his waist. His beard was mostly dark blond, as was the hair on his knuckles where he held the cloth. Fingernails were short and clean. No wedding ring, I noticed.

"Let me ask you something," he said. He had a nice speaking voice. Nearly hypnotic. The guy should do commercial voiceovers. "You want to know why I chased you in the woods, but why were you following Damian?"

There was an edge of mistrust to his question.

I glanced over at the kid, who must be Damian. "I found him in my barn a couple times today. The second time he was hiding. I wanted to know where he came from."

He flashed a look at the kid. "Is that true?"

Damian sighed. "It's true, but I swear I didn't mean any harm." He turned to me. "Your animals are amazing. They look right out of *Star Wars*."

I smiled. They sort of did. "I tried to talk to you, but you kept running away."

"You had a shotgun."

"Only the first time."

The guy stopped, and his expression turned thunderous. "What the fuck?"

"I wasn't pointing it at anyone," I said. "It was at my side with the safety on."

"But then you had a pitchfork the second time, didn't you?" Damian continued in his posh accent. "I didn't want to be stabbed either."

"I wasn't going to stab you with a pitchfork. I only had it there in case it was somebody else."

"Oh really? Like who?" Damian asked.

I leveled my gaze on the guy who'd been cleaning my wounds moments ago. Our eyes met. He seemed taken aback at my silent message. "*Me?*" He pointed at himself. "You were going to use a pitchfork on *me?*"

"Look, I keep having intruders on my property. First you and your biker friends, then this kid."

His brows rose. "So that was your place?" He took a moment and then nodded. "You're right. I apologize for that incident last night. My friends got lost. Luckily, I wasn't far behind."

"That guy nearly broke my front door with all his pounding."

"I'll be happy to replace it."

"Forget it." I sniffed with indignation.

He turned to the kid. "Damian, you need to apologize too. You were trespassing."

I studied them both. They sure had good manners for a bunch of bikers. Plus, why did this kid have a British accent? And how could they afford this super-nice house? Maybe they were rich bikers. Was there such a thing?

"I'm sorry," the kid said. He seemed dejected. "I shouldn't have done that."

I considered him. I didn't get the sense he was a bad kid. "Next time just come to my front door," I told him. "I'll give you a tour, okay?"

His entire demeanor brightened. "You will?"

"Sure. I'll introduce you to my girls."

"What are they called? The smaller ones." He seemed energized now. "I've never seen anything like them before."

"The large ones are llamas, and the smaller animals are alpacas. They're very sweet and gentle, unless you get them angry." I gave him a look. "Then they spit."

His brows rose. "They spit?"

I nodded. "Mostly at each other, but sometimes at people."

"I'll try not to get them angry then."

I chuckled. "Best if you don't."

The guy appeared to be taking my measure. "What's your name?"

"Leah."

"I'm Josh, and this is Damian."

I nodded, glancing between the two of them. Damian must be his son, though they didn't look much alike. "Nice to meet you both."

There were footsteps outside the bathroom door, and a very pretty woman with shoulder-length brown hair entered. "There you guys are. We're going to make s'mores. Do you want to join us?"

Damian shot up from the floor. "I do!"

Josh turned his head toward the woman. "Thanks, Nalla. I'll be out there in a minute."

She glanced at me, but didn't say anything before leaving the room with Damian.

That meant Josh and I were alone.

He went back to cleaning the dirt off my wounds. I shifted position, suddenly aware of our close proximity and how strange all this was.

I studied my battered legs. "Why were you chasing me?" I asked again.

"I was trying to help." His smooth voice echoed in the near-empty bathroom. "Damian said you followed him into the woods but never emerged. He was worried you were lost."

Obviously I *was* lost, but I wasn't about to admit it.

He glanced at me, a smile tugging on his mouth. "Did you really think I was a Sasquatch?"

I scoffed. "Of course not."

His eyes met mine, and I could see the humor in his.

"I fell down."

"Uh-huh."

"I was dazed and confused."

"Sure." But I could tell he wasn't buying it. "Can I ask you one more question?"

"What?" I eyed him warily.

"Why were you hiding outside in your underwear last night?"

CHAPTER FIVE

~Josh~

S he squirmed at my question. Maybe I shouldn't have asked it, but I was too damn curious.

That image of her last night had stayed with me well after we'd ridden off on our bikes. A gorgeous brunette hiding in the shadows wearing nothing but panties, a skimpy little top, and those tall black boots.

It had been quite a sight.

I'd seen a lot of crazy things over the years. I'd caught women hiding in the back seat of my car. Women hiding in my hotel room. I'd even had them jump out of closets or sneak into my shower after a concert. Some wore sexy lingerie while others were naked. During our recent tour in Australia, I found two chicks dressed in snakeskin leather hiding under my hotel room bed.

Over the years, I mostly sent them away.

Mostly.

Back in my twenties, I occasionally indulged myself, but I was thirty-five now and getting too old for that shit.

Of course, Leah here hadn't been hiding in the bushes for me. She'd been hiding *from* me. A big difference and, I had to admit, a refreshing change of pace.

In fact, I suspected she didn't know who I was.

"I was just checking on my animals," she said. "After all the noise you guys made, I wanted to make sure they were okay."

"And your husband lets you run around like that?" I didn't know why I asked, but I wanted to know if she was taken.

"I don't have a husband, so I don't need anyone's permission." There was a fierceness in her words that belied the faint blush on her cheeks.

She had pretty skin. If I had to guess, she was close to my age. Long-legged and athletic. Her dark hair was pulled back in a pony-tail. Her brown eyes were defiant.

"Guess you weren't expecting company, huh?"

"No, I wasn't."

I nodded and finished cleaning her wounds. She soldiered through the sting of more antibacterial spray, her gaze on me the whole time. I bandaged the larger scratches and then started putting everything back in the kit.

"Thank you." She peered down at her legs. "I appreciate you helping me."

"You're welcome."

"Even though it's *your* fault I fell down."

I paused what I was doing. "Are you serious?"

"If you hadn't been chasing me, I wouldn't have tripped and fallen in the first place."

"I see. So I should have let you stay lost in the woods."

"I wasn't lost." There was a stubborn set to her jaw. "Not exactly. I would have found my way out eventually."

"Listen, I didn't mean to scare you, but I had no idea you'd think I was a *Sasquatch*." I chuckled at the word. I couldn't help myself. It was absurd.

The blush on her cheeks grew deeper. "I knew you weren't really a Sasquatch. It's just that it was dark, and you're so big and hairy."

"*Hairy?*" I laughed. "Don't you mean *furry?*"

A smile played around the edges of her mouth. "What can I say? It was an honest mistake."

I ran a hand over my beard. Admittedly, I'd let it grow pretty damn long since our last tour. And my hair was nearly down to my ass. *But a Sasquatch?* "Guess I've been called worse," I said, getting up off the floor.

Hell, the truth was I'd been called plenty worse.

Those dark eyes of hers watched me as I put the first aid kit away. With Damian here, I figured we'd be using it soon enough.

"Can I borrow your phone?" she asked, standing up. "I don't have mine, and I need to get home."

"I can give you a ride. I mean, we're neighbors."

She went quiet and seemed to consider my offer. "All right. Thank you."

"Let's go out back again. I need to tell people I'm leaving."

We headed down the hallway, past all the moving boxes I had yet to deal with. I could pay someone to unpack it for me, but I wanted to do it myself. This was my first time buying a house, and I wanted the experience of living like a normal person for once.

It was cooler when we stepped outside. Everyone was gathered around the firepit, which had a large blaze going.

"Josh," Dean called over. His noticed the woman beside me. "And I see you've rescued a damsel in distress."

I glanced at Leah. She was watching him with an irritated expression.

"Her name's Leah," I said to him. "And it turns out you owe her an apology."

"Me? What did I do?"

"It's her door you were beating on last night."

"No shit. That was your place?" He seemed chagrined. "Damn. Sorry. I got lost and went to the wrong house."

Leah gave a brief nod. "I appreciate the apology. Just don't let it happen again."

There were a few raised brows at her tone. A couple people chuckled. I glanced at Leah and saw she meant it.

Firelight flickered over her features. There was something about her that caught my interest. She wasn't beautiful, although she was attractive. It was her defiance. I liked how she didn't take shit from anyone.

Tendrils of music began in me, starting the way they always did. Sometimes it was notes or a simple melody. Other times lyrics. And then sometimes, like now, it was just a feeling. But I knew that feeling.

I wondered whether I should take Leah home on my bike. The wind whipping over us both as we enjoyed the ride, her arms tight around my waist.

But then I shut that down quickly. "Let me grab the keys to my truck. I'll be right back."

Sometimes it was best to ignore the music.

When I returned, Damian was standing next to Leah, both of them eating s'mores.

"Here, Dad, I saved one for you." He handed it to me in a wrinkled paper napkin that was still warm.

"Thanks."

"Can I come along with you and Leah?" he asked. There was chocolate smeared on his face. His hands too. I was glad Charlotte agreed to let him stay with me for the summer. He needed a break. Hell, we both did.

"Of course." I took a bite of the s'more. A smoky sweetness filled my mouth.

"Maybe I could see more of her animals tonight," he said eagerly.

Leah licked chocolate off her fingers. I tried to ignore it, but couldn't look away.

"It's getting late tonight," she said to Damian. "How about I give you a tour in a few days?"

"Monday?" he asked eagerly.

"Let's do Tuesday instead."

"All right, Tuesday. You won't forget, will you? Promise?"

The desperation in his voice pained me. I knew Charlotte had a habit of promising him things and not following through.

"No, I won't forget," Leah said. "You can come by anytime. I'll be home all day."

"Brilliant!"

"I'll be right back," I said. "I'm going to tell people we're leaving."

I walked over to where Nalla and Dean stood near the fire. He had his arm around her waist. When I told them I was taking Leah home, Nalla's amber eyes flashed over to her. I sensed disapproval, though I must have imagined it.

"Of course." She smiled gently at me. Nalla had been a big help with Damian the past couple weeks, and I appreciated it.

"I'll make sure these hoodlums don't get too out of control," Dean said with a grin.

I headed back over to join Damian and Leah. We walked around to the front of the house, where my brand-new black pickup was parked.

"Nice truck," Leah said once we'd climbed inside the cab.

The sharp new-car smell surrounded us. I turned the engine over and listened with approval as it rumbled to life.

"Thanks. I just got it." I shifted into Reverse and backed out of the driveway. Driving was a pleasure I'd nearly forgotten about. I'd never owned a truck before. I felt like a kid behind the wheel and had an impulse to blow the horn and floor the gas pedal.

"If you don't mind my asking, what is it you do for a living?" Leah asked as I headed out toward the main road.

"What I do?" I glanced at her.

She nodded, and the cab went silent.

Even Damian seemed stunned. "You don't know who my dad is?" He sounded incredulous. "He's the lead—"

"I work in the music industry," I said, cutting him off before he told her who I really was. I wasn't sure why I didn't want her to know. Not like she wouldn't find out eventually. "I'm a... songwriter."

"Really?" She turned to me. "You must be a successful one."

"I do all right."

"What kind of songs do you write?"

I shrugged. "Mostly rock music. Different projects."

It wasn't untrue. I was a songwriter. And not just for East Echo. I'd written songs for other bands too. I even wrote one for a superhero movie last year.

"Anything I would have heard?"

"Probably not. Is this your turn?" I changed the subject on purpose. "I'm still trying to figure out these back roads."

"No, it's the next one."

I noticed how Damian was staying silent. He knew the score. He'd dealt with how invasive the press could be, how they wouldn't give you a moment's peace, and he'd been with me on more than one occasion when I was accosted by screaming fans.

In truth, fame wasn't always as great as people made it out to be. When you were forced to deal with it a long time, it wore on you.

Don't get me wrong. I wasn't complaining about success. But there were drawbacks to it as well. Times when I had to fight for my privacy. It was the main reason I bought a house out here in the sticks.

"That's the turn coming up on the right," Leah said, pointing. "It's just a narrow private road."

"Yeah, I remember it now." I looked over at her, and our eyes met. Obviously it wasn't the only thing I remembered.

She glanced away.

Regardless, I saw her in my mind's eye. That thin top and those silky white panties. I had a feeling that image of Leah hiding in the shadows was going to stay with me a long time.

"So, what is it *you* do?" I asked, trying to shake off last night's mental picture. "Do you manage this farm alone?"

"I'm a spinster."

"A what?" I glanced at her, figuring I must have misheard.

"Spinster," she repeated.

She seemed serious. "I don't think people use that term anymore." I wondered if this was some kind of local thing. People in small towns were sometimes old-fashioned, but surely things weren't that far behind in Truth Harbor. "You're not really a spinster."

"Of course I am. I enjoy it."

I glanced at her again and wondered if Leah wasn't playing with a full deck. She had recently thought I was a Sasquatch.... "You're not old enough to be a spinster."

"Sure I am."

"Isn't a spinster an old woman who's never been married?" Damian asked from the back seat.

"I think so," I replied.

And that's when Leah grinned. She put her hand up. "I'm just messing with you guys. I love saying that."

"What do you mean?" I parked my truck in front of her house next to a white one that must be hers.

She turned to us both. "A spinster used to be the term for a woman who spun wool into yarn. A lot of those women were unmarried, so that's how the word's meaning changed over time."

"Is that right?" I stroked my beard. "I didn't know that."

Damian leaned forward eagerly. "So, you spin wool?"

She nodded. "I do. I'm a fiber artist, and I spin wool from my animals."

"Wow, that's so cool."

"You're an artist?" My beard stroking stopped. In the darkened cab I could just make out her features. There was a light perfume coming off her that I hadn't noticed before, and I liked it.

She nodded. "I have a shop online where I sell my yarn, fleece, and some of my knitting too."

I started to say, "That's nice," but what came out instead was "You'll have to show me sometime."

She didn't respond and instead reached for the door handle. I got the sense she wanted to get away from me.

"See you Tuesday," Damian called out as she climbed out of the truck.

"I'll be here," she said to him and then closed the passenger side.

My truck's high beams shone on her as she walked over to the front porch, her dark ponytail swishing with each step. I tried to ignore how long and shapely her legs were. How good her ass looked in those shorts when she moved.

I forced myself to stop watching and studied her front porch instead.

My life was a mess of complications right now, and there was no room for romantic entanglements. The biggest complication being Charlotte—Damian's mom and my ex-girlfriend.

CHAPTER SIX

~Josh~

As soon as Leah opened the front door to her house, I put my truck in Reverse. She waved at us before going inside, and I felt Damian waving from the back seat.

"Do you really think she spins her own wool?" he asked as I pulled onto the main road.

"Sure. It makes sense why she keeps those alpacas and llamas."

"That's totally fucking awesome."

I shook my head. "Don't swear like that."

"But everybody at the house does it. Why can't I?"

"Because you're a kid, and it's not right." I thought back to my own childhood, to the way my younger brother, Jeremy, and I swore all the time. We thought we sounded badass when all we really sounded was pathetic. My mom shouldn't have allowed it. Except she basically let us run wild.

That was the hardest part about parenting Damian. I didn't have a fallback. I couldn't use my own childhood to guide me, and instead I'd had to learn everything brand-new.

He asked more about spinning wool as we drove back to the house. Damian was bright with a curious nature. He had a bold streak, too, something that could be good or bad depending on how it manifested.

Charlotte tucked him away in a boarding school in England, one her family approved of, and one for which they happily paid all the expenses. I told her I'd happily pay all the expenses to keep him out of it, but she couldn't be deterred.

And now that she and I weren't together anymore, I suspected she was glad he wasn't around. He interfered too much with her lifestyle.

Luckily, he seemed to be doing just fine at the school. I'd been flying back and forth so I could be there during his breaks. Charlotte's family had made noises about it at first, but they couldn't deny that I was a father to Damian in every way that counted.

Blood or no blood.

"I can't wait for Leah to show us her farm," he said. "It's so different from Granny's."

Charlotte's mother, Philomena, lived in the English countryside and raised horses. She had a large stable and was part of the British peerage. I had to agree it was pretty different.

"Granny mostly has horses," he continued. "Except for Winston."

"Who's Winston?"

"The goat."

"Hmm, I must have missed that."

"I can't wait to go to Leah's on Tuesday. Maybe she'll even let us feed her animals." He sounded excited.

I grinned to myself. The fact was Damian and I were a couple of city boys thrust into country living. "Maybe you'll get lucky, Little D. She might even put you to work."

LATER THAT NIGHT, after Damian went to bed, I asked everyone if they could cool it with the swearing.

"No one in Damian's family has admitted it out loud," I said, poking a stick at the fire, "but this is a test that he's staying with me this summer."

"Sure, of course we will." Dean eyed the group in his gruff way. He knew all about the situation with Charlotte and the adoption. "We'll make sure everybody keeps their language nice and clean."

"I appreciate it. I don't want to send him back to England teaching people all the new curse words he's learned."

There were nods and chuckles of agreement.

Glancing around, I could see my houseguests were cozy and relaxed. Everybody gathered around the fire—most of them with romantic partners.

I was the lone wolf in the pack.

It had to be this way.

The house had plenty of bedrooms for everyone, and there was even a small guesthouse by the lake. It was one of the reasons I'd bought the place. Besides the secluded area, I was thinking about turning that guesthouse into a recording studio.

The air smelled like woodsmoke, and when I gazed up at the sky, there were more stars than I'd seen in a long time.

"Sympathy for the Devil" played from the speakers. It must have been one of Nalla's playlists. She liked that old music. I liked it, too, though I was more of a Zeppelin fan myself.

I had to admit, I was enjoying my new house. I wanted this to be my home. Someplace I could relax and unwind. A place Damian could also call home and come to whenever he wanted.

Something made me glance over at Nalla and Dean, and I was surprised to discover she was watching me. Dean sat beside her, stroking her arm. He was drinking a beer, talking to Ranger, one of our sound engineers, about the video we'd shot for the new single.

She smiled, and I gave her a quick one in return. Ever since I met her in Seattle a couple weeks ago, she'd been trying to mother Damian and me. She meant well, so I didn't stop her. I figured she was one of those people who enjoyed it.

I leaned back in the lounge chair and put my feet up. Closed my eyes, listening to Mick Jagger's seductive vocal play at being the devil. I could only hope to have a career as influential and long-lasting as Mick's. He was a rarity.

My mind drifted back to the truck ride earlier. Back to Leah's long legs and those little shorts she wore. Her sassy history lesson about spinsters.

But then I stopped myself.

If Charlotte got wind that I was even thinking about another woman, there'd be hell to pay, and it would come at the cost of my son. It didn't matter that we'd split up a year and a half ago.

"You look tired," a female voice purred.

My eyes opened to find Nalla standing over me.

"Scoot over a little." She nudged my legs aside. "Let me join you."

I moved to give her some room on the chair. In truth, I wished she'd stayed over with Dean since this was the only quiet moment I'd had all day. Except I didn't want to hurt her feelings.

"What are you thinking about?" she asked, taking a seat facing me. "You look so deep in thought."

I shrugged. "Nothing much."

Her eyes lingered on my face, her brown hair falling in waves around her shoulders. She was an attractive woman, and I could see why Dean liked her.

"You can tell me." Her voice was soft and inviting. "I'm always curious about what goes on in that mysterious brain of yours."

"It's not that mysterious." I wondered if I should ask her to take Damian to see Leah on Tuesday. Might be best to avoid temptation. But then I decided I was being ridiculous. It would be fun to take him there.

"Sympathy for the Devil" ended, and "Paint it Black" started. Apparently it was a Rolling Stones kind of evening.

"*Now* what are you thinking about?" Nalla wanted to know. She lightly pressed her fingers to my forehead. "You always get a line right there."

"I was thinking about Mick Jagger." My gaze drifted over to the fire. "The guy's had one hell of a career. I hope I'm lucky enough to be making music into my seventies."

She moved her hand to my leg. "Of course you will be. You're a genius."

"Don't say that. In fact, I prefer you didn't."

"But you are," she insisted. "A musical genius. Everybody knows it."

I didn't reply. This was my main complaint about Nalla. She was over the top with her praise toward me. I disliked sycophants, and I'd learned early on to weed them out of my life. I kept telling myself she meant well. Plus, Damian seemed to like her, and she was Dean's girlfriend.

She began to stroke my leg. I shifted position, forcing her to move her hand. "I'm just a normal person who's damn good at what they do." Unfortunately, I knew it wouldn't make any difference. Nalla had that starry-eyed look some people got around me.

She sighed. "You're so modest. That's one of the other things I admire about you."

"Modest?" I snorted. "I don't think so." Modesty wasn't a trait people associated with me.

"When I first met you, I thought you'd be conceited," she went on. "Totally arrogant. But you're not at all."

I had to laugh. "Are you kidding? Of course I'm conceited."

Strutting across stage, flaunting my sexuality, I'd been called conceited by practically anyone who'd ever seen me perform, especially the press.

"*Joshua Trevant, lead singer for East Echo, is an arrogant tease who enjoys brandishing his sex appeal like a weapon—but there's no doubting his talent."*

That was one of my favorites. A reporter for *Billboard* wrote it after we played Madison Square Garden the first time.

Of course, Joshua Trevant onstage was a character I'd made up. But there was plenty of me in that character.

"You're not," she said. "You're like the perfect man, always so kind and generous."

I could be a holy terror to work with too. I had no patience with people showing up late or drinking themselves into oblivion around me. That didn't always go over well in the land of rock-n-roll. It was part of what had caused all the problems between me and Rhys.

She leaned closer, her hand on my leg again. I suspected Nalla may have had a few drinks herself. "I think you're amazing," she whispered. "Even before we met, I knew we'd hit it off."

"Thanks," I replied, getting uncomfortable. Dean was sitting only a few feet away.

Her eyes stayed on me, and there was something hungry in them.

"It's probably best if you go back to your man," I said.

She blinked a few times and seemed to catch herself. She drew back. "I'm sorry. I don't know what's gotten into me."

"That's okay, sweetheart." I eased her hand off my leg. "I think you've had a little too much wine."

She nodded. "That must be it."

"It's been a long day."

She gave me a coy smile. "I'd appreciate it if you kept this between the two of us."

"Sure, of course," I said. "There's nothing to keep."

CHAPTER SEVEN

~Leah~

As usual, it was a busy Saturday. After chores, I'd gone into town to mail my yarn orders and then stopped at the local farmers co-op to pick up some feed for my girls. It had intimidated me the first time I'd gone into the co-op, surrounded by all the real farmers. I felt like such a phony. It didn't help that people were standoffish toward me.

"I just heard Leslie and Rhonda have some pregnant Angoras," Naomi said as we waited in line together to have our orders rung up. She and her husband, Tim, were neighbors of mine and had, thankfully, never been standoffish. They were friends with the couple who'd sold me my farm, and I appreciated how welcoming they were.

My ears perked up at this news. I'd mentioned to Naomi once how I'd like to add Angora goats to my livestock.

"You should give them a call. I'm guessing those kids are going to go quick."

I nodded. "Thanks for the info."

I was excited as I loaded the feed into the back of my truck. Angora goats were sheared twice a year instead of once and produced a lot of fiber.

Of course, my mom and Lars would freak out if they heard I was planning to add more animals. They thought I had too many already. When I initially bought my farm, it came with a small flock of sheep, but I sold them to focus on my alpacas. Angora goats could be a profitable addition.

Once I got home, I took a quick shower and then sat down on the toilet seat lid to examine my scratched-up legs. I thought about Josh as I put on fresh antibacterial spray. How he'd tended to me. It had been sweet and sort of sexy even. I probably shouldn't have given him such a hard time, but I'd been embarrassed and out of my element.

I wondered if he was married, and where Damian's mother was. He didn't wear a wedding ring, but some guys didn't.

Oh my gosh. I shook my head and laughed. *Am I really having romantic notions about a biker dude with so much hair that I mistook him for a Sasquatch?*

I got up and grabbed fresh shorts and a T-shirt. I had company coming over this evening and still needed to clean the house.

When six o'clock rolled around, I heard a car approaching. Opening the front door, I stepped outside just as a green Jeep convertible rounded the corner, pulling up next to my truck. The driver had a head of curly red hair that blew around her like a crimson cloud. In the passenger seat was a curvaceous pregnant woman who wasn't showing yet, and sitting behind her was a cool blonde.

My two besties—Claire, the pregnant one, and Theo, the ginger— both waved at me. The blonde in the back seat was Isabel, a friend Claire and I knew from high school.

"Come on inside." I waved everyone over. "Did you bring the hair color?"

Claire held up a plastic bag.

We had these coloring sessions every couple months or so. I painted tint on Claire's hair to give her blonde highlights while she covered the silver streak that ran in the front of mine.

Initially we did it ourselves to save money, but Claire, who'd married a zillionaire recently, could afford the best salon in the city. Ironically, she still preferred I do it. Mostly our hair coloring sessions had become a fun social event.

The three of them followed me into the house. We usually did our hair in the kitchen, so that was where I headed. I pulled out glasses for the sangria I'd made and the ingredients for mini pizzas.

Except when I looked behind me, there was nobody there. The small group had gathered near the front window, watching something outside.

"What are you guys doing?" I asked, walking over.

"Admiring your little brother," Claire said with a grin.

"He sure is nice-looking." Theo adjusted her tortoise-shell glasses. "How old is he again?"

I peered out the window. Shane was by the barn moving bales of hay. He must have just gotten home from work. The hay was delivered a few days ago, but I hadn't had time to move it yet. "Twenty-three," I said.

"So young," Claire sighed. "And so handsome. I remember when he was just a kid."

"Is he still living in that RV he bought with his lottery money?" Theo asked.

"He's still in it." I glanced over at my brother moving the bales two at a time. He made quick work of it and was a lot faster than I was.

"Your brother won the lottery?" Isabel asked. "I didn't know that."

I nodded. "About a year ago. Not millions or anything. A couple of hundred grand." My parents assumed he'd use the money for college, but he had other plans. "Shane used part of the money to buy that motorhome and then traveled all around the United States for six months."

"Wow, really? That sounds cool."

"It was pretty cool," I agreed. When he came back from his trip was when he'd asked if he could park his RV here.

Shane must have sensed he was being watched because he turned toward the house.

He grinned and waved at us.

Everyone waved back.

"Are you guys hungry?" I asked. "I got the ingredients for mini pizzas." We usually had mini pizzas or tacos at our hair coloring parties. "I also made sangria."

The four of us went into the kitchen.

"I brought these beauty face masks for us to try," Isabel said, pulling out a bunch of packets from her purse. "The chef at work said they're amazing." Isabel worked at a popular diner in town called Bijou's.

The radio was still playing in the background while I mixed the color for Claire's hair. Theo and Isabel began cutting up ingredients for the pizzas. Before I started, I poured everyone a glass of sangria. For Claire, I'd made a virgin batch.

"This is really tasty," she said after the first sip. She was sitting in a kitchen chair. "What's in it?"

"Everything except the wine and triple sec. I used grape and orange juice instead."

"I still can't believe you got pregnant on your honeymoon." Theo glanced up from chopping tomatoes. "You seriously beat the odds."

Claire smiled and put a hand over her still flat stomach. She was only three months along. "I know. It's so exciting. Philip and I are thrilled."

"It's pretty great," I agreed.

She tilted her head downward as I painted the color on the back of her hair. "Oh my gosh, what happened to your legs?"

"That's an interesting story." I told everyone about the bizarre events of the last couple of days. At first they gawked, then cracked up when I described my encounter with a Sasquatch.

Claire made a face. "I think a houseful of bikers sounds scarier than a Sasquatch."

"That's what I thought, too, but they seem okay. The house they're staying in sure is nice."

She picked up a carrot stick from the nearby veggie tray. "I wonder where they came from," she mused, crunching on a carrot. "I haven't seen any bikers around town."

Isabel sucked in her breath. "I just remembered something. A group of guys with long beards came into the café a couple days ago."

I dipped the brush into the bowl of hair color. "Were they on motorcycles?"

"I don't know. I was in the kitchen, but someone told me about them."

"Maybe they're just tourists here for the summer." Theo moved the chopped tomatoes into a bowl.

"Do bikers go on vacation like regular people?" Isabel asked.

Theo shrugged. "Sure, why not? I'm guessing they want to get away from it all just like the rest of us."

Claire laughed. "Truth Harbor—top destination for outlaws who want to relax."

Theo pretended to be a radio announcer. "Tired after another hard day of knocking off liquor stores? Come join us for some fun in the sun."

"Actually, I don't think they're tourists," I said. "There were moving boxes in the house." I told them how Josh said he worked in the music industry.

"Music industry?" Claire's brows shot up. "Is he famous?"

"I doubt it. I didn't recognize anybody."

Shortly after I finished painting tint on Claire's hair and she put the dark color on mine, Shane came in the front door. "Don't mind me, ladies," he said with a grin. "I'm just here to take a shower."

"Are you hungry?" I asked. "There are mini pizzas. Feel free to make yourself one."

"That sounds good. I might grab one of those afterward."

He disappeared down the hall, and all three of my friends leaned over to watch him walk away.

"I don't think he has a bad angle anywhere," Isabel murmured once he was out of earshot.

Claire shook her head. "I keep reminding myself that Leah and I used to babysit him, but it's not helping."

"He's such a dish." Theo took a sip of sangria. "Does he have a girlfriend?"

I snorted. "More like *girlfriends*. It seems like he's got a new one every week."

I heard the shower turn on in the bathroom.

"I'm sure he's just a young guy having some fun," Claire said. "No harm in that."

"I suppose not. None of the women ever seem to complain."

"I wouldn't complain either." Isabel gave a sly grin.

"Ugh. Please." I put my hand up. "This is my baby brother we're talking about. Let's not go there."

"Your *cute* baby brother," Claire said. "Ooh, turn up the radio. I love this new East Echo song." She began singing with the music.

Since I was nearest, I reached over and cranked the volume. I liked this new song of theirs too. It had a catchy melody for the chorus. "La la la dee da dum." The lyrics talked about the reason and madness of love.

After making our pizzas, the four of us took our plates and moved to the living room. It had been a few weeks since we'd seen each other, so we relaxed and caught up on what was happening in our lives.

By the time we finished eating, I heard the shower turn off, and my brother emerged from the bathroom. I worried he might come out with only a towel, but thankfully, he wore jeans and a T-shirt.

"The ingredients are still on the counter if you want to make yourself a pizza," I told him.

Isabel got up, holding her empty glass. "Or I'm happy to make one for you," she said with a smile. "I'm getting myself more sangria anyway."

He ran a hand through his damp bangs. "Thanks, Isabel. I'd appreciate that."

Claire patted the space beside her on the couch. "Come talk to me, Shane. I want to hear all about your traveling adventures."

He ambled over and sat next to Claire.

Theo turned toward him. "I want to hear about them too."

"Well, what would you guys like to know?" He leaned back and made himself comfortable. The center of attention—like always.

My baby brother didn't just win the state lottery. He won the life lottery. Eleven years younger than Lars and me—our mom was forty when she had him—he was a surprise baby, so cute and sweet-natured, that everybody fell in love with him from day one.

I glanced out the window. "I should go check on my animals and put their feed out," I said, getting up. "I'll be back in a few minutes."

It was another warm evening, and as I walked toward the barn, I heard the roar of motorcycles pass by on the main road again. I frowned to myself. I enjoyed my peace and quiet and hoped these new neighbors weren't going to become a nuisance.

I wasn't gone long, but when I returned to the house, everyone was wearing a lime-green beauty mask—including my brother. He had his head back on a cushion, feet up on the coffee table with green goop smeared all over his face. He even had cucumber slices on his eyes.

I laughed at the sight. "Shane, I didn't know you'd become one of the girls."

He lifted a cucumber and grinned at me. "I'm just trying to fit in."

"I have to get a picture of this. I think the guys you work with might like to see it."

"Ha ha." He closed his eye and put the cucumber back in place. "You're hilarious."

I glanced over at Claire. "We should go wash the color out of your hair."

She nodded and then turned to my brother as she got up. "Don't say another word until I get back. I need to hear the full story before I can offer advice."

"Advice about what?" I asked as we went into the kitchen to use the sink.

"Shane's having romance problems."

"Really? I haven't heard anything about it."

"Apparently he likes someone, but she's not interested."

"Please." I snorted. "He likes someone new every single day of the week."

"I guess this one's different. She won't go out with him."

Claire put her head into the sink, and I began washing the color from her hair. If some girl was playing hard to get with my brother, she was on the right track. "Who is she?"

"Someone he met at the library."

"The *library*? What was Shane doing at the library?" My brother had a lot of great qualities, but being a book reader wasn't one of them.

Claire shrugged. "He didn't say."

After washing her color out, I washed my own out, too, then wrapped a towel around my head and joined the others in the living room.

"She won't take me seriously," Shane was telling everyone. "She thinks I'm a player, that I'm involved with too many women. I'm not sure what I can do."

There were sympathetic murmurs.

"What's her name?" I asked, surprised I hadn't heard any of this before.

"Her name's Martha. I really like her, but she won't give me the time of day."

Claire combed her fingers through her wet curls. "Maybe she has a boyfriend?"

"She doesn't."

"You should let her get to know you better," Theo said. "Don't come on too strong."

He scratched his head. "You think so?"

Isabel nodded. "I agree with Theo. Just take it slow. Be friends with her first."

"I guess I could do that."

I listened but didn't bother to comment. They were all forgetting one thing about my baby brother. He *was* involved with too many women.

WHEN TUESDAY ROLLED around I went about my usual routine, keeping an ear out for any approaching vehicles. I'd never admit it, but I took a little extra care with my appearance today, even putting on makeup, which I never bothered with while doing chores.

Not that I was interested in Josh. Please. That would be ridiculous. Even if you shaved all that hair off, he still worked in the music industry. A songwriter, he'd said. That was too close for comfort.

My ex-husband, Derek, was a musician. He'd been the lead singer for a punk band. I met him when I went away to the East Coast for college. I'd been dazzled by how edgy and poetic he was. His band was mostly struggling, but I didn't care. It was my first time away from home, and dating someone like that had felt so exciting that we eloped after only knowing each other two weeks.

Big mistake.

It didn't take long for reality to set in, and for my edgy, poetic husband to turn into a mentally abusive asshole. There were drugs and other women involved. The whole thing lasted less than four months.

Not exactly a great romance.

So I'd learned my lesson about the allure of bad boys.

Despite all that, my nerves were on edge as I drank my coffee that morning. As the day went on, I wondered—even hoped—that Damian would come alone. After all, he knew how to get here just fine.

When noon came and went, I told myself they probably weren't going to show up. Musicians were notoriously unreliable.

By two o'clock there was still no sign.

As it drew closer to four, I was rolling my eyes.

Typical. I shouldn't be surprised.

At five, I went into the kitchen to start dinner and shook my head with disgust. Josh was obviously just another musical flake, and in this case, it was even worse because there was a kid involved. I hoped drugs and alcohol weren't involved too.

The sad truth was that most of the musicians I'd known were self-absorbed jerks.

I stood in the kitchen cutting up vegetables for the penne pasta I was making for dinner, still complaining to myself, when I heard a car engine outside.

Probably just Shane coming home from work.

When I went over to the window, my pulse shot up. There was a shiny black truck headed toward my house.

Seriously?

I strode through the living room, yanked open the front door, and stood on the porch waiting as the truck pulled up next to mine. Josh was behind the wheel wearing a pair of mirrored aviators. My pulse skittered. He looked good. Too good. When he emerged from the driver's side, he put his hand up to wave, but I didn't wave back. He was wearing leather flip-flops, a fitted white T-shirt, and a skirt.

Yes, that's right. A skirt.

His long hair was gathered back in a low ponytail like that first night I saw him.

My eyes traveled down to the skirt again. I couldn't stop staring at it. It was black with a gray batik print and fell just below the knee with an asymmetrical hem.

It should have looked ridiculous. It wasn't even a utility kilt but an actual skirt. Like the kind women wore.

But it didn't look ridiculous. It looked straight-up hot.

A strange panic filled me.

The rear passenger door opened, and Damian jumped to the ground. There was a bounce in his step as he walked toward the house.

"I hope this is okay," Josh said, strolling up to me. "I know it's late."

CHAPTER EIGHT

~Leah~

"It is late," I said with my arms crossed.

Josh walked closer and took off his sunglasses, placing them on top of his head. Dazzling blue irises. The whites of his eyes glowed with good health. I could tell when someone was drunk or stoned, and Josh was neither.

"Yeah, about that." He stroked his beard and seemed chagrined. He wore a colorful chunky bracelet on his wrist along with a silver bangle. "I apologize for the time. Can we still get a tour?"

A part of me was tempted to say no. It would be an easy way to get rid of him. I glanced down at Damian, who appeared to be holding his breath with anticipation.

"It's fine." I motioned them both inside the house. "I just need to turn the stove off."

They followed me into the kitchen, where I had a pot of salted water at a near boil. I turned off the burner.

"Smells good in here," Josh commented, taking in his surroundings.

"It's the garlic bread in the oven. I was just making dinner."

He nodded. "Sorry to interrupt. Damian's mom called from LA and then his grandmother from the UK. It's been a busy afternoon on FaceTime."

"Is that your wife?" I cringed at my nosy question, but I was curious.

He shook his head. "I'm not married. She's my ex-girlfriend."

"When can I see the animals?" Damian asked. "I also want to see how you spin wool."

Josh put his hand on Damian's shoulder. "Slow down, Little D. Let's give Leah a chance to take care of things, especially since we showed up during dinner."

I smiled at Damian. "We can go out to the barn soon. I'll give you a proper introduction to everyone."

"Cool!"

I liked his enthusiasm. I got so much grief from my family about this place that it was a pleasure to have someone share in my joy for a change. Reaching across, I put the oven temperature to warm.

"Do you guys want anything to drink?" I tried to appear relaxed. I could sense Josh watching me, and it was making me self-conscious.

"We don't want to put you to any extra trouble."

"It's no trouble." I walked over and swung the fridge door open. "There's ice water, soda, or juice."

"What kind of soda?" Damian came and stood beside me.

"There are a couple of Cokes." I didn't actually drink the stuff but kept it on hand for Lars, who had a love affair with cola.

"I'll have a Coke," he said eagerly.

"I don't think so," Josh intervened.

Damian turned to him with a pleading expression. "Why can't I have a Coke?"

"Because it's too late in the day. If you drink that now, you'll be bouncing off the walls all night."

"That's not true."

"Yes, it is." Josh's tone made it clear they'd dealt with this before.

"How about apple juice?" I turned to Damian. "It's from a local farm and fresh-pressed."

He gave a dubious sigh. "I *suppose* that will have to do." His words sounded comically regal with his accent.

"Trust me, Harry. You'll like it."

He gave me a strange look. "My name isn't Harry. It's Damian."

"I know, but you sound just like Harry Potter."

"I do?" He appeared to consider this. "I don't believe we sound alike at all."

"I'm American, so most British accents sound the same to me."

This seemed to surprise him. "Really? Is that true?" He turned to his dad for confirmation.

"For the most part," Josh admitted. "But I've spent enough time in England that I can tell the difference."

"Well, I've never been to England," I told him.

Damian's eyes widened. "You've never been?" Except he pronounced it "bean."

I grabbed three glasses from the cabinet. "I've never had the opportunity. Though I've always wanted to see London."

"You must come visit then. It's brilliant." Damian began to list all the places he wanted to show me as I poured each of us a glass of apple juice. "That's not to say I don't like America," he stated quickly. "I do enjoy it here."

I handed them each a glass, and they took a sip. "What do you think?"

"It's good," Josh said.

"I like it very much," Damian agreed.

"It comes from my neighbors' Naomi and Tim's apple orchard. They grow over ten varieties and throw a harvest party every year."

"We're having a party this weekend," Damian stated. "It's for both our birthdays on Saturday." He grinned up at his dad, who grinned back.

"You two have the same birthday?" I asked.

"We do." Josh licked some juice off his lower lip. "August 11. A couple of Leos."

"How old will you be?" I asked Damian.

"Eleven."

"Really? Eleven on the eleventh. And what about you?" I looked at Josh.

He smirked and took another swig from his glass. "I'll be thirty-six."

"You're two years older than me." I wasn't sure why I was announcing it. "But my birthday's not until April." He was studying me, and it increased my nervousness, so I turned away. I felt strangely breathless around him.

"You should come to our party on Saturday," Damian said to me. "It's going to be kickass."

"Damian." Josh's voice had a mild reprimand. "We discussed this. No more swearing."

"That's not *really* swearing," Damian insisted.

"It most definitely *is*."

"No, it isn't."

"Let's ask Leah what she thinks." Josh turned to me, and I fell under the spotlight of his gaze.

Both of them waited expectantly, so I sighed and looked down at Damian. "Sorry, I agree with your dad. It's definitely swearing."

He stuck his lip out and seemed bummed but then brightened. "Hey, can I see your animals now?"

I laughed at his mercurial mood change. "Sure, let's go to the pasture."

We put our glasses down and went out to see my girls. I brought a bag of sliced carrots cut into small pieces to give as treats. I introduced Rhiannon—the alpha female of the herd—and Martina to them. Damian giggled as they nibbled a piece of carrot from his hand. Both animals hummed and were friendly. A few more alpacas came over to join us, and I explained to Damian how alpacas were very intelligent and knew their own names. I also explained how to pet them.

"Try not to touch their faces." I said. "They don't like that, but it's fine to pat their neck or body." I demonstrated by running my hand down Rosalie's furry neck before I gave her a piece of carrot.

Josh was taking pictures with his phone.

"Would you like to feed them too?" I asked him, offering the open bag.

He took a piece of carrot and held his palm out to Lilith, one of the nursing mothers, watching with interest as she gently took it.

"I'm so happy we were able to come today." Damian grinned as he fed some carrot to Ruth. "This is totally mega."

Josh asked if I'd take a picture of the two of them together, his fingers brushing mine when he handed me his phone. I tried not to notice it. They stood beside each other smiling, and I snapped a few photos.

Afterward, I walked them both around to see the rest of the farm while answering Damian's endless stream of questions.

"And you manage this all by yourself?" Josh asked as Damian went over to pet two of the barn cats.

"Basically." I explained how my brothers helped occasionally, and that my younger brother lived in the RV on the other side of the barn.

He nodded, studying me.

I wondered if I seemed like a hick to him. I even had a brother living in a motorhome out back. Maybe I should pull out a corncob pipe and a banjo.

But what do I care what this guy thinks? He's just some biker dude covered in hair.

Though I had to admit, I was noticing things about him, things I hadn't noticed before.

Like he had great bone structure beneath all that hair. His long beard was neatly trimmed, and his mess of blond curls was clean and well cared for. There was something sexy about the way he moved too. Fluid and self-assured.

Let's face it, he was seriously hot. Even in that skirt. Especially in that skirt. No wonder my girl parts went haywire that first night. They were going haywire right now.

I kept getting whiffs of his scent—lemongrass with a light musk that could only be his skin. I kept leaning toward him, hoping for another whiff.

He was obviously a great dad too. I could tell he and Damian were in sync with each other.

"So, it's just you, huh?" Josh's blue eyes rested on me, and there was a skittish quiver in my stomach. I waited for him to say more, but he didn't. Instead his phone started buzzing, and he pulled it out from the side of his skirt—which apparently had a pocket. Staring at the display, he frowned. "Sorry, I have to take this." He turned and walked off. "Yeah, what now?" he said in an irritated tone. "This is bullshit, Rhys."

I strained to hear more, but he was already out of earshot.

I went over to Damian, who was petting one of the two crias—my baby alpacas—and asked if he'd like to see how I spun yarn.

"Hell yes, I would!"

"I thought you weren't supposed to swear?" I said, keeping my voice light as we walked back toward the house.

"'Hell' isn't really a swear word," he informed me. "It's a place."

"Hmm, I'd say that depends on how you use it."

He shrugged and didn't seem to think the conversation merited further discussion. I figured he was at that age where kids liked to test their boundaries.

The tripod was still set up in the dining room from when I'd filmed a spinning video for my YouTube channel yesterday, so I moved it to the side. I grabbed one of my baskets of fleece and then sat down at my wheel.

Damian stood beside me, and I explained the different parts to him. He listened with interest. Spinning was often associated with girls, but I'd come to believe that was a cultural thing. The few boys I'd had in my classes had all been enthusiastic about learning, and Damian was no exception.

I stood up and gave him a turn and had him practice treadling for a bit—making the wheel go in one direction only. After that I guided him in drafting, and soon he was spinning his own yarn. Unsurprisingly, it was bumpy and uneven.

"Don't worry," I said. "Like anything, it takes practice."

He nodded, still spinning with enthusiasm, his tongue pushed to the corner of his mouth as he concentrated. Three of my cats came over to watch, and he glanced down at them, commenting that I seemed to have a lot of cats. I told him there were seven in all.

"That's awesome!" He stopped spinning and bent over to pet them. "I wish I had seven cats." It was obvious Damian loved animals.

I glanced outside the window, searching for Josh, who was still on his phone, pacing the gravel drive in front of my house. He didn't look happy.

I gave an internal eye roll.

Musicians and their drama.

I remembered it well from my horrible marriage to Derek. He and his bandmates thrived on emotional chaos. There was always some soap opera happening.

"What's this?" Damian asked. He'd gotten up and wandered over to the cabinet where I kept more of my supplies.

"That's a drop spindle."

"What's it for?"

"It's for spinning without a wheel. Here, I'll show you."

I pulled some fiber from the basket. There was already some leader yarn attached to the drop spindle, so I sat down in a chair and showed him how to park and draft, adding more fiber to get the spindle set up. Finally, I stood and started spinning.

"Cool!" he exclaimed. "Can I try?"

"Of course." I stopped it and handed the drop spindle over, showing him how to pinch the fiber as he got it started again.

"This is mega!"

As we stood there together, the front door opened and closed.

Damian called out, "Come watch me, Dad. I'm in here spinning yarn!"

Lemongrass and musk drifted over as Josh came into the room. The phone call had obviously upset him, but he seemed able to put it aside. He listened with interest as Damian explained everything I'd been showing him.

"This is called a drop spindle," he told his dad. "And guess what else? Leah has seven cats!"

Josh considered me, raising an eyebrow. "Seriously?"

I shrugged. "I'm a spinster *and* a cat lady."

There was a flash of white when he chuckled. What a great sound. When our eyes met again, pleasure shot through me, and my face grew warm.

No wonder I'd mistaken Josh for a Sasquatch. I couldn't put my finger on it, but there was something otherworldly about him.

He went back to watching his son. "That's great, Little D. We should get going soon. We've taken up enough of Leah's time."

"Aw, really? I wanted to see her animals again."

"Don't worry," I told Damian. "You can come back anytime you want. I don't mind."

"You don't? Can I come again next week?"

"Sure, just have your dad text me first to make sure I'm here."

"That's real nice of you." Josh pulled his phone out. "We appreciate it. What's your number?"

I rattled it off for him.

"Can Leah come to our birthday party on Saturday?" Damian asked him.

Josh glanced at me. "If she wants to."

"You must come!" Damian insisted. "It's going to be kicka—" He stopped himself. "Totally bangin'."

I saw Josh smile and shake his head at him before he turned to me. "If you decide you'd like to come by Saturday, the party starts around five. I'll text you the address." There was a teasing note in his voice. "Unless you'd like to find your way through the woods again."

I rolled my eyes. "I better not. I don't want to run into any more mythical creatures."

He grinned. "By the way, how are your legs doing?"

We both looked down at them. "They're healing."

"Good," he murmured in that smooth baritone.

"You know, you have a great voice," I blurted. "If you wanted to, I'll bet you could do commercials selling lotions and bath salts."

Josh's brows crinkled with humor. "You think I could sell lotions and bath salts?"

"Sure, why not?"

His turned to his son. "We should head out now, Little D. Make sure you thank Leah."

Damian put everything down on the coffee table and came over to me. He was all proper and polite. "Thank you for inviting me today."

"No problem."

"And I *do* hope you'll come to our party on Saturday."

CHAPTER NINE

~Leah~

The next day, after my morning run and my chores, I went into town for groceries. I grew a lot of my own vegetables, but there were still plenty of essentials I had to buy.

Like chocolate.

I placed a bag of semisweet chips in my cart. Contemplating the shelf, I reached over and grabbed two more bags—one for eating and two for baking cookies to bribe Shane and Lars.

After paying and loading the bags into the passenger seat of my truck, I made a pit stop at the local yarn shop. I chatted with Stevie, the owner, and bought Damian a drop spindle as a birthday gift. I'd decided I'd stop by their party on Saturday to say happy birthday and give him his present.

Heading home, I was still thinking about yesterday, and still trying to make sense of Josh. It felt like there was something about him I was missing.

To my surprise, I saw a strange blue minivan parked in front when I arrived.

I pulled up beside it. *This is weird.* I got out, wondering who it belonged to, when a friend of my mom's appeared from behind my house.

"Hi, Leah," she said, waving at me with a big smile. "Great place you've got here. Good bones. Is that a creek out back?"

"It is." I was confused. "What are you doing here, Linda?"

"I'll have to add 'waterfront' to the property listing. A lot of people will like that."

"To the what?" I stared at her. She wore a loose flower-print dress and dark sandals. Her blonde hair was cut into a shoulder-length bob.

"I think you're going to have a lot of interest," she continued. "And the animals come with the place, right?" She put her hand up to shield her eyes from the sun as she studied me.

I was getting a sick feeling. "What are you talking about?"

"I guess your mom didn't tell you I was coming by today." She laughed lightly. "She called and said you were interested in putting your farm on the market."

"*Excuse me?*" I just remembered that Linda was a real estate agent.

"I think you've chosen a good time to sell. Prices in Truth Harbor have been rising lately. Do you have time to sit down and go over the paperwork?"

My pulse pounded in my ears. "I don't know what my mom told you, but I am *not* selling this farm."

"You're not?" She seemed surprised but then smiled reassuringly. "Don't worry. I know the process can be overwhelming, but you're in excellent hands. Some realtors charge high commissions, but ours are quite reasonable." She began to spout off numbers and percentages going into a well-worn sales pitch.

"Sorry, but you need to *leave*," I said, interrupting her midsentence as she'd started telling me how devoted she was to her clients. "I have a lot to do today. This property is *not* for sale."

"Are you sure about that? Camilla told me to come by."

"It sounds like you were misinformed." I picked up my groceries from the back seat and shoved past her.

"Wait, let's discuss this some more." She chased after me. "Let me give you my card and give you a chance to think it over."

I didn't want her card, but as I unlocked the front door, she stood there holding it out like a religious zealot. It was obvious she wasn't going away, so I snatched it from her hand.

"Believe me, I can get you an excellent price," she continued. "Maybe you're not ready now, but when you are ready, call—"

I slammed the door shut.

This was too much. I was shaking with fury. My mom thought my buying this place was a mistake, another one of my "crazy" impulses, but she was wrong.

I dumped the groceries on the kitchen counter and then rummaged through my purse for my phone.

She answered on the second ring.

"Sorry, sweetheart, I can't talk now. I have a meeting in two minutes."

"How *could* you?" I tried not to sound hysterical. "How could you send a real estate agent to my house without even discussing it with me?"

"I take it Linda came by? Good. We need to get you out of that place."

"I can't believe you'd do that!"

"Leah, I had to step in. We can't have you wasting any more time and money on a losing venture. It's for your own good."

"I'm not selling. How many times do I have to say it?" My voice pitched higher, and to my annoyance, I sounded like a petulant teenager.

"You need to calm down."

"And you need to stop sending realtors to my house!"

She sighed. "Let's not get into this right now. I have two students who were caught skipping class."

My mom was the local high school principal. You can imagine how fun that was growing up.

"*Fine*. But I'm furious at you. You had no right to do that."

I could hear her speaking to someone else in the room, directing them to get some type of paperwork. "We'll discuss this later" was all she said before hanging up.

I was still fuming, so I went over to the freezer, pulled out a bag of frozen chocolate chips, and shoved a fistful into my mouth, letting the sugar soothe me.

My phone was on the counter. I picked it up and did the one thing I always did when I was angry at my mom. I called Lars to vent. It was an impulse from years of us being close, but as soon as he answered the phone, I knew I'd made a mistake.

"What is it, Leah?"

A small piece of my heart crumbled. Lars used to answer the phone happy to hear from me, but now he always sounded annoyed.

"Mom's friend Linda, the real estate agent, just showed up here out of the blue. Apparently Mom told her I wanted to sell my farm! Can you believe that?"

"What did she say?"

"The same old thing. That I made a mistake buying it to begin with. She couldn't talk long because she was having some kind of meeting at school."

He gave an irritated grunt. "That's not what I meant. What did Linda say?"

"Who cares?" The angry knot in my stomach tightened. "I can't believe she'd do this to me. She's gone too far."

Lars remained silent. Too silent.

"Oh my God." I slapped my hand to my forehead. "You knew about this, didn't you?"

"Mom ran the idea past me."

"Thanks for the warning."

"She's only looking out for your best interest."

"Just stop it. Both of you." My throat tightened. It threatened to close up, and I took a deep breath. "How could you? What's happened between us? You're never on my side anymore."

"Not on your side? Who just repaired your fence on my day off?" He gave another irritated grunt.

"I'm not selling my farm. I don't care what either of you say."

"You should listen to reason. It's not too late to get out from under that mess."

"What mess?" I glanced around my kitchen, which *was* a bit of a mess. "Are you talking about my *home*?"

I sensed his impatience. "You should call Linda. Maybe you can at least get back the money you paid for that place."

I rolled my eyes.

"It's too much for you to manage on your own and you know it."

"Geez, I had no idea I was such an imposition. Next time I'll do the repairs myself."

"Give me a break. Fixing that fence would have taken you hours."

"I don't care." I stopped and lowered my voice, unable to hide the hurt in it. "I thought you were okay with helping me occasionally."

"I *am* okay with helping you."

I snorted. "Only because you wanted things to look good for a realtor."

He sighed. "I knew you'd get like this. You're in over your head. Face it."

"I'm not in over my head." A part of me wanted to cry that my mom and Lars weren't on my side, but the other part of me was so furious I wanted to scream. It's like the more they pushed me to give up, the more I wanted to push back and prove them wrong.

"I don't know what possessed you to buy that property to begin with. It was a dumb impulse."

"Don't say that. I love Clarity Moon Farm."

"It's been over a year now," he went on as if I hadn't spoken. "Time to sell that mistake." This was another thing. My mom and Lars never referred to my farm by its name. "Cut your losses while you still can. I know you're bleeding money."

I *was* losing money, but I wasn't about to admit *that* out loud. I sold my yarn and animal fleece, but it wasn't enough to cover the bills right now. I had plans, though. Big plans. I was going to increase my herd, offer a wider selection of fleece, and I was also planning to expand my yarn business.

"You could probably get your old job back," he said. "At least you didn't burn that bridge."

I thought of my old job, sitting in my tiny cubicle as each day bled into the next. Gray and colorless.

Running this farm was hard work—I wasn't going to lie—but there hadn't been a single morning where I hadn't woken up with a sense of purpose. Of rightness.

I caught a glimpse of my animals grazing peacefully out in the pasture. They relied on me to take care of them, and that was exactly what I planned to do.

CHAPTER TEN

~Leah~

The next evening, I sat in my truck with the gift-wrapped drop spindle in the passenger seat beside me.

I pulled the visor down and stared at myself in the mirror. *Should I have put on more makeup? What does one wear to a biker party? I* had on jean shorts, a navy T-shirt, and flip-flops.

Sighing, I pushed the visor back up.

It had been dark the night Josh drove me home, and I'd been too emotional to pay attention to the route, so I followed Google Maps. I was glad he texted the address because I nearly missed the turn putting me on a narrow paved road.

After about half a mile, I finally saw a black metal gate ahead, opened wide with cars and motorcycles lined in front.

More people than I expected.

I could hear music drifting over from the house when I got out. My flip-flops smacked against the asphalt as I made my way past a

Range Rover and two Escalades. There were also several expensive motorcycles.

As I got closer, I noticed Josh's black truck parked in front of the open garage. A couple of muscular guys stood there talking, both dressed in dark clothes. They watched me closely as I walked past but didn't say anything. They looked like security, but who had security for a birthday party?

Rock music played, and I recognized Pearl Jam's "Even Flow." The house was even nicer than I remembered. A real beauty, done in a fancy log cabin style with plenty of windows to let in the light. The path to the front door had an intricate stone pattern.

I rang the bell, but with all the loud music, I couldn't even hear it. I waited, and after ringing it again with no response, I walked around back. It wasn't long before I saw a lot of people. They stood around with drinks in their hands talking. A quick scan told me the crowd was more dressed up than I expected.

I searched for a familiar face as I crossed the grass toward the stone patio. Nobody seemed to pay attention to me. Finally, I recognized the woman I saw here last time, the one who came into the bathroom while Josh was cleaning my scratches.

"Hi," I said to her. She was standing by a table laden with food that had balloons tied to the side. "I'm not sure if you remember me? I was here last week." I held up my gift. "I brought a present for Damian. Do you know where I could find him?"

She tilted her head in confusion. "I'm sorry, who are you?"

"We haven't officially met. I'm Leah." I put my hand out. "I own a farm nearby. I'm one of Josh's neighbors."

Her hand was cool as she brushed it against mine. "I'm Nalla," she murmured. She didn't smile, her amber eyes assessing me. I felt her take in my shorts, T-shirt, and flip-flops. I had to admit, she was stunningly beautiful. Very slender, with wavy brown hair that went just past her shoulders. She wore a gorgeous crocheted bustier that I was certain I could recreate, though I doubted I'd look as good in it as she did. It was designed to cover only her breasts while showing off the rest of her smooth skin. Like me, she wore jean shorts, though hers probably cost more than my last truck payment.

I felt like a hayseed standing in front of her. Self-conscious, I reached back to pat my messy bun.

"Oh, yes. You're the one with the farm."

I nodded. "I brought Damian a birthday present."

"I can take it. Are you just dropping it off?"

"Well, no, I wanted to say hello."

She put her hands out for the gift. "I'll tell him you said hello. It's no trouble."

"Actually, I'd prefer to tell him myself." I didn't know if she was clueless, rude, or intentionally trying to get rid of me. "Could you point me in the right direction?"

Her lips compressed, and I sensed disapproval. But why would she disapprove? But then she smiled at someone behind me.

"Hey, it *is* you," I heard from an earthy baritone over my shoulder. I turned to discover Josh standing there with a smile that could light up a room. My insides took a dip.

"Hi," I said in a breathy voice, then chastised myself for how dumb I sounded. "Happy birthday."

"Thanks. I'm glad you made it. I didn't know if you'd come by or not. Damian will be psyched you're here."

"I brought him a gift."

"That's real sweet of you."

Nalla stepped between us. "I was just taking her to find Damian. I know he'll be excited to see her." She turned to me. "He's been talking about your farm nonstop. Do you really have seven cats?"

I blinked in surprise at her complete one-eighty.

"You'll have to tell me more about it," she went on as if I were her best friend. "Let's go find Damian, and I can show you the table for the—"

"That's okay, Nalla, I'll take her," Josh interrupted. He rested his hand on my arm briefly. "C'mon, Little D will be happy you made it. He's inside the house playing foosball."

I followed Josh through the crowd. His blond curls were long and loose, with part of them twisted up into a knot in back. No skirt today. Instead he wore a tie-dyed T-shirt advertising a surf shop and a pair of faded jeans. They sure looked good on him. I tried not to stare at his ass. I could still feel the warmth of his hand on my arm from where he'd touched me a moment ago.

Geez, get a grip.

I didn't know what was wrong with me.

There was just something about him, something that got my insides fluttering.

For some reason, I glanced back at Nalla. I expected her to have moved on, but she remained in the same spot as before, staring at Josh with an intense expression.

As we made our way toward the house, a few people wishing Josh a happy birthday stopped us. He thanked them and then introduced me as his neighbor. People nodded and smiled. It turned out Nalla wasn't the only beautiful woman here. In fact, there were others just as stunning. Tall and thin as a blade of grass, most of them dressed in body-revealing clothes.

I was average height, and while I wasn't overweight, I'd always had an athletic body. My legs were long, but my shoulders were broader than I'd like.

Next to these women, I felt like a linebacker.

"Wow, you're, like, sooo lucky to have Josh as your neighbor," one of the women said to me, enveloping me in a cloud of astringent perfume. "I'd be down here every day asking for a cup of *sugar*—if you know what I mean." She gave a tinkling laugh before glancing sideways at Josh, who was speaking to some guy with black hair and a number of facial piercings.

I listened to her with uncertainty. Just like the other day, I felt like I was missing something about this situation.

A low masculine voice spoke in my ear. "Shall we go find Damian?"

I turned, and Josh was right there. So close. I could smell the lemongrass and musk, could see how his beard was pale blond in places while darker in others, how his cheeks were pink from the sun.

He touched my arm, and I could barely breathe. I swept my gaze over his wide shoulders to where his T-shirt met the hollow at his throat, and despite my wondering who the hell he was, I felt desire. A terrible desire.

He tilted his head. "What is it?"

"Nothing." It was my weakness for bad boys. Though I'd tried, I never could quite eradicate it.

"You have the same look on your face as when you thought I was a Sasquatch."

"To be honest, I don't know *who* you are."

Josh's brows rose at my tone, and then his expression grew serious, like he wanted to tell me something. He leaned closer. "Listen, Leah. I should explain more about my life to you."

"Leah!" I heard a familiar kid's voice.

I turned to see Damian running toward me like a giant puppy. "I'm so happy you came! See, Dad, I told you she would."

Josh nodded. "You were right."

"Is that for me?" Damian asked about the gift I was holding.

"Happy birthday," I said, handing it to him, touched by his enthusiasm.

He took it cheerfully. "Thank you. We're going to open them all later. Come watch me play foosball! Our team is beating everybody!"

He led me across the patio and through French doors into the house. There were still stacks of moving boxes, though not as many. Various prints hung on the walls. Art that looked avant-garde and expensive. A few surfboards took up most of another wall.

I stood to the side and watched Damian play foosball, feeling awkward. There were more kids. Some of them played with Damian while the younger ones ran around the room. A guy with a blue mohawk held the cutest little red-haired girl as he cheered on the foosballers.

"Damn, my manners are complete shit," Josh said to me. "Can I get you a drink?"

"Sure. I'll take a beer, if you have one."

He left, and I resisted the urge to watch him walk away. When I glanced around, I wasn't the only one. Practically every woman in the room had their eyes on Josh.

When he returned with a bottle of cold beer, I took it gratefully, since it gave me something to do with my hands. To my surprise, he remained at my side, and I could sense people observing us.

A few minutes later, there was some kind of commotion by the French doors in back. It drew everyone's attention. I peered over. As far as I could tell, it was all centered on some guy with pale skin and dark, shoulder-length hair.

I sensed Josh stiffen beside me. "Fuck," he muttered. "I don't believe this."

He watched the guy with a frown. A woman with short platinum hair appeared, and Josh's frown only deepened. The couple was smiling and waving at everyone. They seemed like quite the glamorous pair. Tall and lanky, there was something familiar about the dark-haired guy.

When he saw Josh, he grinned and put his hand up. "Happy birthday, dude."

"Rhys," Josh called out over the music and general noise. "I didn't think you'd show. Glad you could make it."

Rhys gave Josh a Cheshire grin. "Didn't want to miss one of my oldest friend's birthdays."

The woman beside him wasn't smiling anymore and seemed uncomfortable.

The sea of people parted as Josh left my side and went over to hug Rhys. More people crowded into the room, everyone watching the two of them.

I had to pee and left to go find the same fancy bathroom as last time. Afterward, I opened the door, then paused. The hallway continued on to the right, and I was curious what was down there.

It was noticeably quieter as I moved farther into the house. I could still hear music thumping. There were more doors, but I didn't open them.

As I explored, I discovered a small alcove with a spiral staircase that led upward. I wanted to climb it but knew that was too much. What if they caught me?

Just being a helpful neighbor and making sure your attic's insulation is up to code.

There were some double doors off to the right. I tried to open one, and it led into a large room. A piano stood near the windows in back along with a couple of acoustic and electric guitars. There was even a drum kit. It smelled smoky-sweet, like someone had burned sandalwood incense recently.

Okay, Josh is definitely a musician.

There were more moving boxes and some kind of recording equipment off to one side with a long black leather couch that sat against the wall. A coffee table in front of it had papers and electrical cords on it.

Most of the room was windows. Large floor-to-ceiling panels that let in the evening light and looked out onto the surrounding woods and lake. I walked across the thick carpet to admire the view.

This place is incredible.

CHAPTER ELEVEN

~Leah~

Eventually I left the beautiful view from the music room and made my way back out to the party. When I got there, people were already eating cake, and Damian was opening his presents. Josh was off to the side taking pictures. I watched Damian open a number of gifts, and when he got to mine, I could tell he was delighted. He insisted on showing everyone how a drop spindle worked, so I went over and helped him. I felt a lot of curious stares. Luckily, I'd included roving with the spindle so he could start spinning right away.

Afterward, I accepted a slice of cake and then stood off to the side, figuring I'd leave soon.

As I stood there, a gorgeous woman with red hair came up to me. She was the mother of the little girl I'd noticed earlier. "I haven't seen you around before," she said with a smile. "I'm Salem."

She seemed friendly enough, so I introduced myself, wondering how she fit in with this crowd.

"So, I have to ask you." She leaned in closer. "Is it true that you're one of Josh's neighbors?"

I nodded and told her I owned a small farm nearby, had fiber animals, and spun my own yarn.

"Wow, that's fantastic. I'm a knitter, too, though I just started." She rolled her eyes and laughed. "I've been trying to make socks for Sasha, my daughter, but mostly I'm just making a tangled mess."

I shrugged and swallowed a bite of chocolate cake. "I could show you sometime, if you want."

"Really?" She seemed thrilled. "That would be amazing."

"Sure." I took another bite. The cake was delicious. "So, how do *you* know Josh?"

She leaned against the wall where we were standing. "Oh, my husband works for him."

"Really? Doing what?"

"He's mostly in charge of the crew when they're on the road. He makes sure everyone stays on task and out of trouble." She smiled and shook her head. "Apparently it's not easy. Last time he had to bail three of the younger guys out of jail."

I stopped eating and tried not to show my shock. "Jail?"

"Of course, now they all laugh about it." She shook her head. "I guess boys will be boys, huh?"

"I guess so." I wanted to ask her who this crew was and why they were in jail but wasn't sure how to phrase it.

Who the hell is *Josh?*

A moment later, her little daughter ran up to her followed by her husband—the guy with the blue mohawk.

She introduced him as Dax, and he nodded at me. Apparently they had to get going, so we exchanged numbers.

After they left, I decided to leave too. I looked around for Damian and Josh to say goodbye. I didn't see them in the house, so I went outside. It was dark out now, and the party had thinned considerably.

As I searched, the guy with the black beard, the one who banged on my door with his fists that first night, came up to me.

"It's Leah, right?"

I nodded. "That's me."

"I'm Dean."

He was a big bear of a man with dark hair pulled back into a thick ponytail. He had on loose jeans and a black T-shirt. Colorful tattoos covered each arm.

"I wanted to apologize again for that night when I pounded on your door. I hope I didn't scare you."

Despite his intimidating appearance, I sensed a surprising gentle quality about him. His apology seemed heartfelt.

"It's okay," I said. "I'm over it."

"Really? You sure?" He didn't seem convinced. "Because I felt like a real asshole after that happened. Do you want me to pay for a new door?"

"That's not necessary. There was no harm done."

He considered this and stroked his beard. "Okay, then let me at least get you something to drink."

"Actually, I was just leaving. I'm looking for Damian and Josh to say goodbye."

"Don't go yet," he insisted. "Stay a little longer. What can I get you—white wine?"

This guy was like a big teddy bear. "Why do you assume I'm drinking white wine?"

"I don't know. Classy women like you always drink white wine."

I laughed, and he was grinning now too. At first I thought he had brown eyes, but on closer inspection, I realized they were a deep blue. Beneath that bushy black beard, he was handsome.

"So tell me, what are you having?" he asked again, and I could see I wasn't going to get rid of him unless I agreed to let him do something nice for me.

"You can get me a beer. I guess I'm not as classy as you thought."

"Oh, you definitely are. What kind of beer?"

"It doesn't matter."

"Nope. Tell me what kind."

"Pale ale, if you have it."

"Perfect choice." He grinned. "Go have a seat by the fire, and I'll bring it to you."

I glanced over at the firepit, which had a good-sized blaze going.

"Go on now," he said, motioning me toward it. "Relax by the fire, and I'll get you that pale ale."

I figured, *What the heck?* I did as he asked and headed toward the fire. There was a small group of people already there. A few chairs were open, so I sat down in one of them. To my surprise, I was right across from that lanky guy everyone had made such a fuss about earlier—Rhys.

He held a guitar in his hands and had his eyes closed, mindlessly playing some intricate melody. There were a few quiet conversations, but most people were relaxing and watching the flames.

I let myself relax too. A pungent grassy scent hung in the air, and I realized somebody was smoking weed. It mingled with the smell of wood burning, giving me a contact high.

Instead of worrying about it, I leaned back in my chair. It was a warm summer night. I should probably head home soon but wasn't compelled to at the moment.

Two more people approached the fire. My pulse jumped when I saw one of them was Josh.

Dean came over and handed me a pale ale. "Here you go, Leah. Let me know if you want anything else, okay?" He grinned and went over to take the empty seat between Josh and Rhys.

Nobody spoke at first. Rhys was still playing the guitar, and I recognized Led Zeppelin's "Babe I'm Gonna Leave You." Josh took a sip from a bottle of beer but remained quiet, just gazing at the flames as they illuminated his handsome features. He wore a couple of chunky rings on his fingers. I should look away. I knew I should, but instead I let my eyes wander all over. He was straight-up beautiful.

When I reached his face again, it was a jolt to discover he was watching me.

He held my gaze.

The fire crackled.

I turned my head as nervous energy danced through me.

"So here we are," Josh said, his deep voice breaking the silence. "Three of us together at last. It's been a while."

I glanced over to see he was speaking to Dean and Rhys.

"It's a damn shame Terence isn't here," Dean murmured.

Josh nodded. "He's been traveling. Last I heard he was in Nepal."

"I miss that asshole."

"Yeah. Me too."

They were silent again.

Josh took another sip from his beer, and his attention shifted to Rhys. "So, why did you come here tonight?"

The guitar playing slowed. He wasn't playing Led Zeppelin anymore but something classical. "I came for your birthday. What else?"

"I don't know what else. You tell me."

The two men studied each other.

Rhys sighed. "We have history, Josh. A lot of it."

"You're right, we do. I'm glad you haven't forgotten."

"Of course I haven't forgotten." And as if to prove it, he began to play something else on the guitar, something I recognized. It took me a moment to figure out it was Metallica's "Nothing Else Matters."

I couldn't help smiling. I'd always loved this song, and the guitar sounded perfect as he continued to play the melodic intro.

When he got to the part with the vocals, a mellow baritone began singing the lyrics. I glanced over and saw it was Dean. It turned out he had a nice voice. He continued singing, and then halfway through the first verse, another baritone joined him. Josh.

The two of them sounded amazing together.

I remained still, drawn in by the music. Soon the song shifted.

Dean sang the lower notes while Josh began singing the harmony, letting his voice soar.

I watched him in wonder. He could *really* sing.

When the second chorus finished and the focus went back to Rhys, Josh gazed out at the rest of us. He wore a sly grin. There was something about him. A magnetism. His eyes caught mine like earlier, and he held them just longer than was polite.

My cheeks grew as warm as those flames.

When they began singing again, Dean hit the low notes while Josh's voice rose up into the night sky. By the time they finished the song, I was flabbergasted.

Everyone clapped, and I joined them while some people hooted and whistled.

"Damn, I've always loved it when you guys cover that song!"

"Totally amazing."

"Let's hear some East Echo!"

"'Queen of Hearts'!"

Josh smirked. "Sorry, hard pass."

"'Truth in Madness' then," someone else said. "From the new album!"

Rhys began nodding and was already playing another song, one I recognized from the radio. It was an acoustic version of East Echo's "Truth in Madness."

I tapped my foot and took a swig of beer. It sounded great. Just like the original. These guys were really talented musicians.

Josh began to sing, and he did it perfectly. He had the same sexy growl as the lead singer from East Echo. He held his hand out, motioning his fingers around as if he were finessing each note.

When he got to the chorus and sang, "La la la dee da dum," I felt strange. A peculiar sense of unreality took hold of me.

Josh sounded good. *Too* good.

I glanced over at Rhys playing the guitar and then at Dean, who was slapping his thighs in a percussive way.

My head swam.

I finally understood why Rhys looked so familiar. Though I hadn't known his name, I'd seen pictures and videos of him. Of the entire band, in fact. I was in shock. Between the hair and long beard, I hadn't recognized Josh at all, but now I did. That was the reason he sounded so perfect.

Josh *was* the lead singer for East Echo.

I WAITED until they finished the song and then sprang up from my chair. I should probably get a hold of myself first, but I was too angry. I marched the short distance between us and stood in front of Josh, the fire hot against the backs of my legs.

He seemed surprised by my reaction. "Everything okay?"

"No, it's not okay." I glared down at him. "And guess what? You're a *fucking* asshole!"

Then I left. I was creating a scene, but I didn't care. Let him explain to the others why I was so pissed.

As I strode across the lawn, I felt someone coming up behind me. It was Josh.

"Slow down. Jesus, let me talk to you."

"Why? You've been lying to me this whole time!"

"No, I never lied. I misstated the truth a little, but I never lied."

I laughed without humor. "Are you even hearing yourself? Misstating the truth *is* lying!"

"You know what I mean. I meant to tell you tonight, but then I couldn't find you again after Rhys arrived. In fact, where did you go?"

"So this is *my* fault? *I'm* the idiot? You must have been having a good laugh at my expense."

I walked past the garage and saw a couple of thugs still standing around. Having security here made sense now.

Josh still followed me, and I had to admit, it was surreal being chased by a rock star. He followed me all the way to my truck, telling me how he made a mistake, that he should have been up front from the start.

"C'mon, honey, can't we start over?" He lowered his voice to a purr, and my stomach fluttered. He knew exactly what he was doing, except I wasn't falling for it.

"Don't call me 'honey,'" I snapped. "We barely even know each other. My name's Leah."

"Yeah... I know."

He went quiet after that. We both did. I already had my keys out, ready to go.

"Look, I made a mistake," he said. "I'm sorry. I should have been honest with you from the start."

I didn't respond.

He stood before me, his hand resting on my truck. "Three things cannot be long hidden: the sun, the moon, and the truth."

"So now you're quoting the Buddha?"

His brows went up, and I could tell I'd surprised him. He moved a step closer. "You're right, we barely know each other. So how about we get to know each other?" He lowered his voice. "Let's be friends."

I opened my truck's door. "Just fuck off. I don't want to be friends with you." I got inside and slammed it shut.

Josh stood there as I backed out, my headlights shining on him like a spotlight.

And seeing him like that, with his palms out asking for forgiveness, he looked exactly like what he was—a rock god.

CHAPTER TWELVE

~Leah~

I spent the next day brooding over what happened, feeling pissed off and foolish. I should have figured it out sooner, but how? Nobody at the party mentioned East Echo. In hindsight, a couple of people mentioned "the band," but I didn't know what they were talking about.

By the time Monday rolled around, I tried not to think about Josh anymore. About how angry I was or about how stupid and embarrassed he'd made me feel.

I drove into town and ran through my usual list of errands—the post office and then the yarn store. It pleased me to discover Stevie had sold all my skeins from last week. She told me she was getting great feedback from the local knitting community.

Before heading home, I decided to get a pick-me-up at a coffee shop in town called Polly's. Truth Harbor had an infamous past in that pirates smuggling liquor and other contraband once used the area. As a result, the town capitalized on its past for tourists. There were decorative fishing nets strung all over along with pirate flags and picturesque flower baskets. Many of the local stores and restaurants had taken on a pirate theme.

Polly's was one of them. There were stuffed parrots and bird-cages as part of the decor. The pastry case had treats with names like Jolly Roger Rum Balls and Saucy Jack's chocolate cake.

Luckily the place wasn't busy today, and there were only a couple of people standing in line. As I stood there staring at the pastry case and debating whether my ass needed another slice of chocolate cake, I heard the name Joshua Trevant mentioned.

I turned toward the two young women who stood directly in front of me. From what I could tell, they were asking the cashier if she knew whether Joshua Trevant from East Echo had moved to Truth Harbor.

The cashier only shrugged and said she had no idea. She took their order, and they both moved off to the side to wait.

I walked up next and ordered my usual skinny latte along with a slice of Saucy Jack's cake.

As the cashier left to take care of the orders, I waited beside the two women. One of them wore a white baseball cap with her blonde hair pulled into a ponytail. The other one had short dark hair and glasses.

They were still discussing Josh.

"I swear I heard he moved up here," the one with the glasses said. "Though he might be in a different town. We should try a few more. Someone has to know something."

"Hopefully we can find him. Otherwise, we'll be stuck here until the ferry tomorrow." Her friend sighed. "Maybe your source got it wrong, and he's in Seattle."

I was still angry at Josh, so I wasn't sure what made me speak to them. "So, you guys are fans of East Echo?" I asked.

They both turned to me. On closer inspection, they were a little older than I first thought and were probably around my age.

The two glanced at each other. "Yes, we're huge fans." The one with the glasses pushed them up on her nose. "Why?"

I shrugged. "No reason."

"Have you heard anything about Joshua Trevant moving to this area?" she asked.

I didn't answer right away, glancing toward the windows. The weather had cooled down, and it looked like it might rain. "I did hear something about that," I said offhandedly.

"Really?" The one with the glasses seemed keenly interested. "What have you heard? Because I heard he bought a house up here."

I nodded. "He did, actually."

Both women looked at each other and then at me again. "Have you seen him around town?"

"No, I've never seen him in town."

The cashier came over and gave the women their coffees. The blonde took a sip of hers, eyeing me over the rim. "So how *do* you know if he's here? Did someone tell you?"

"Not exactly." Like a lighthouse beacon that cautioned sailors away from the rocks, my inner voice spoke up. It issued a strong warning to shut my cakehole.

The two women studied me with eager expressions. They seemed like a couple of East Echo fans who'd come all the way from Seattle to meet their favorite lead singer. It was the dream of a lifetime for them, and who was I to stand in their way?

"He's my neighbor," I announced and watched as their eyes grew as round as drum cymbals.

"Your neighbor?" The blonde nearly choked on her coffee.

"That's incredible," her friend said. "So, have you met him?"

I nodded. "A few times."

The two of them seemed downright gleeful.

"Can you tell us where he lives?" The brunette put her cup down and got out her phone. "Even just the general area would be helpful."

"I can do better than that." I pulled my own phone out. "I can give you his address."

Both women wore smiles as bright and loud as an electric guitar solo.

Shouldn't Josh be happy to meet these adoring fans of his?

I brought up his text from last week, the one where he'd sent me his street address. By that point my inner voice had gone past the warning stage and was issuing a full-scale atomic meltdown. I ignored it because I was still pissed at Josh for lying to me.

Do not do this! Do not give these women Josh's address! Have you lost your freaking mind?

I held my phone out for them and watched as they both seemed giddy.

"Thank you," the one with the glasses said as she typed in the address. "You have no idea how great this is."

"Definitely!" The blonde nodded with agreement as she put the address into her phone as well. She brought up Google Maps on her screen. "Wow, this isn't even that far from here!" She glanced up at me. "And you're sure this is Joshua Trevant's home address?"

"I'm sure."

The two women continued gushing their thanks, but I told them to think nothing of it.

After they were gone, I took my skinny latte and slice of Saucy Jack's cake and sat down near one of the windows that looked out onto Main Street.

My inner voice was quiet now. I guess I'd shocked it into silence.

And that was when something weird happened.

Sitting there enjoying my latte and cake, I looked out the window, surprised to see the two women I'd just spoken to still on the sidewalk. I had imagined them driving over to where Josh lived, maybe even catching a glimpse of him, but instead they were outside talking to a couple of guys.

The four of them were standing in front of a white van that wasn't there before I came into Polly's. It had a dish antenna on top and the words "Channel 11 News" printed on the side.

My stomach dropped in alarm.

The chocolate cake tasted like alpaca manure in my mouth.

I continued to stare at the four of them and noticed they were chatting in a way that made it obvious they all knew each other.

I swallowed the goopy mouthful and tried to catch my breath.

Did I really just give two people from the press Josh's home address?

Oh my God. What have I done?

AS I DROVE HOME in a state of panic, I tried to tell myself everything was okay. They were only a small Seattle news station. It wasn't like I'd talked to one of the big networks. What was the worst they could do? Drive by his house and take pictures?

I tried to convince myself it was no big deal, but I knew in my gut it *was* a big deal. I'd betrayed Josh's trust.

What had I been thinking? Even if I thought they were fans, I never should have given out his address. It had been an impulse. A dumb, stupid impulse because I was angry at him for not being honest about who he was.

I should have kept my mouth shut.

The guilt ate at me. I desperately wished I could do it over again and not say anything. I finished my afternoon chores in a gut-wrenching haze.

By the time dinner rolled around, I'd almost convinced myself everything was fine.

I told myself they probably would have gotten his address anyway. I was sure they had other sources. Property records and such. All I really did was tell them something they could have figured out on their own.

Shane had messaged me an hour ago to let me know he'd be home for dinner since he wasn't working at the bar tonight. When he came by a little after six, I was relatively calm.

"Damn," he said. "Have you seen what's going on out there?"

"No, what do you mean?" I pulled out a loaf of fresh bread from the oven to go with the soup I'd made, figuring it would cool down enough to eat by the time we finished our salad.

"It's crazy. There's all kinds of traffic on the main road. I saw at least three TV news station vans."

"*What?*" I nearly dropped the hot bread.

He nodded. "Must be some kind of breaking story. Have you heard anything?"

I put the loaf on the cooling rack, accidentally burning my fingers. My heart pounded as I shook my head. "I haven't heard anything at all."

"Something big is going on. I should text Lars and see what he knows."

"Um... yeah. Good idea."

Tossing the fresh veggies from my garden into a salad, I took steady, even breaths as I tried to calm myself.

Shane was sitting at the table, typing a message into his phone. He still wore his work boots, though he'd taken his vest off.

I put the food on the table and sat down. "How was your day?" I asked, trying to act normal.

He poured ranch dressing over his salad before shoveling a forkful in his mouth. "Good." He nodded and chewed. "I think I'm getting more overtime this weekend."

"You've been working a lot of overtime lately."

"I'm saving money."

This surprised me. He still had a chunk of cash left from when he'd won the lottery, so I didn't think he needed money. "For what?"

He swallowed another mouthful of food. "I'm not entirely sure yet."

"You must have some idea." I forced down a piece of lettuce. I'd completely lost my appetite.

"I've been thinking about starting a business, or maybe buying into one."

My brows went up. This was the first I'd heard of it. "Really? That's great. What kind of business?"

He brushed his bangs back before reaching for his water glass. "I haven't decided yet. A restaurant or bar, or maybe a nightclub."

"Wow." I was stunned. There was obviously a lot more going on inside Shane's girl-crazy head than I gave him credit for.

"I'm trying to decide what would be smartest, you know?" He took a drink of water. "I've been going to the library and reading about different investment options."

I never thought I'd hear the words "investment options" or even "library" coming from him, but I was pleased. "I might be able to help," I said. I'd already helped him invest his lottery winnings, though in the end, he put most of it in a money market since he was worried about accessibility.

He nodded. "Thanks. Martha's actually been helping me a lot."

Ah. That explains the library visits.

"How has that been going?" I asked. "With Martha, I mean."

"All right, I guess." He smiled. "She sure is something. She's smart as hell. Except she still won't go out with me." He sighed and rubbed his chin. "Right now we're just friends."

"Well, that's a good place to start."

There was a strange whirring noise above us. Not quite an airplane but some kind of loud engine swooping over the house.

We both looked up.

"What was that?" My eyes went to the window, but I didn't see anything.

"That sounded like a helicopter. I've never heard one around here before."

"Me either."

Shane's phone buzzed on the table. He picked it up, and as he read the text, his mouth fell open. "Holy shit."

"What is it?"

"It's from Lars."

I picked at my thumbnail. I was still hoping this was all some kind of weird coincidence.

Shane laughed. "Damn. You're never going to believe this."

My gut twisted.

"The lead singer for East Echo just bought a house out here."

"Is that so?" I mumbled.

He nodded enthusiastically. "Apparently the band split up, and the press is having a field day. They've invaded Truth Harbor and are swarming the dude's house!"

Now I wanted to throw up. Or maybe faint. Was it possible to do both at the same time?

He put the phone down on the table. "Apparently we've got a rock star as one of our neighbors. Is that unreal or what?"

"Wait a minute. Did you just say the band split up?"

"Yeah, sucks, huh? I've always liked East Echo."

"But why are they splitting up?" I thought back to Saturday night. Obviously there'd been tension between Josh and Rhys, but I never got the impression they were breaking up the band.

He shrugged. "Lars didn't say. He just says it's been a real shit show and that everybody in town is going nuts."

Just as he said the word "nuts," another whirring engine swooped above us. We both got up from the table and headed for the front porch. Stepping outside, we could see a helicopter circling in the distance and then another one joining it.

"Hell, will you look at that! That must be where the dude lives. That's not far from here at all!"

"It's not," I agreed.

We both kept watching. It looked bad. I couldn't imagine what it was like there at the house.

Shane shook his head. "I feel kind of sorry for the guy. Lars said he hasn't been living here long. I wonder how the press figured out where his house was so fast."

"Who knows?" My voice had a strangled, high-pitched quality to it. "I'm sure they just looked at property records and such."

"Seems like it should be illegal to harass someone like that, even if they are famous."

I couldn't take my eyes off those helicopters. I imagined the swarm of newspeople and camera crews that were on the ground outside those black metal gates. How awful that must be.

And then I thought of something that made me feel a thousand times worse. It was bad enough that my stupid impulsiveness had brought this three-ring circus to Josh's door, but he wasn't the only one affected.

Damian was inside that house.

CHAPTER THIRTEEN

~Josh~

"How then?" I asked Dean for the tenth time. "How did these vultures figure out where I live?"

He sighed and shook his head. "I don't know, dude. But I don't think it's Rhys."

"Of course it's Rhys." I was furious. "He put out a press release that he's leaving the band, then leaked my address just to stick the knife in deeper."

"Maybe it was someone from the birthday party who leaked it."

"No." I shook my head. Almost everybody who came here Saturday had signed an NDA. More than half of them were part of our road crew. "We know those guys. They wouldn't give my address to anyone."

"I'm not talking about the crew. I'm thinking maybe it's one of the guests who came with them."

"But why? It doesn't make any sense. And on the same day as

that press release?" I rested my hands on the counter in front of me. "It was Rhys. That *motherfucker*."

Dean reached for his beer. "I still don't think so."

"It was him and Jane. I'll bet the two of them cooked this whole thing up right after they left here Saturday."

That birthday party had turned into a real mess. After Leah left in a fury, I'd been so pissed at myself that I'd come back in a bad mood and picked a fight with Rhys. I hadn't intended for it to get as bad as it did. Sometimes being in a band was like a marriage. Grudges and misunderstandings build up and become toxic.

Now Rhys said he was leaving over "creative differences." I had to roll my eyes. We'd been having creative differences since we started this band. Hell, our creative differences were what made us great to begin with, and he knew it.

"Have you heard anything from Terence yet?" Dean asked.

"I texted him but haven't heard back."

Our bass player was trekking somewhere in the Himalayas and probably had his phone turned off. He was in for an unpleasant surprise when he turned it on.

"Rhys is just being Rhys. He'll eventually cool down."

I shook my head. "I don't give a shit anymore. He's gone too far."

We didn't even have a manager, someone who could resolve this shit between us. Jane was supposed to be our manager until Rhys started sleeping with her.

Out of nowhere, I heard what sounded like a helicopter above us. I looked up. "Do you hear that?"

We both listened some more and then headed into the living room. The French doors were wide open, and Damian was standing outside on the back patio.

"Is that helicopter going to land in our backyard?" he asked, watching it.

I ran over and couldn't believe my eyes. The helicopter was hovering right over the grass. There was actually some asshole hanging out the side with a telephoto lens taking pictures.

"Sonofabitch!" I immediately jumped in front of Damian. "Get back inside the house, Little D."

Dean stood next to me, the two of us effectively blocking that piece of shit from taking any more photos of Damian.

"Jesus," Dean said. "Look at this prick. I hope he falls out and breaks his neck."

I nodded in agreement, though I was too enraged to speak. It was one thing to come here stalking me with their cameras but another thing to stalk my kid. I wanted to pull that fucker from his helicopter and beat him to a bloody pulp.

"Let's go inside," I said through gritted teeth. It took all my effort to stay calm.

I turned around, but not before I glimpsed Dean giving that photographer the finger.

Once we were inside, I locked the doors and pulled the curtains shut. I glanced around. "We're going to have to go through every room and close all the blinds and curtains."

"Why are they taking photos?" Damian asked.

"Because they're human garbage," Dean replied. "And because they don't have a shred of decency."

"Are they going to sell the pictures?"

It saddened me that he understood exactly what these paparazzi assholes were about. I put my hand on his shoulder. "Don't worry about any of this. Nobody's going to mess with us, understand? I won't allow it."

Damian nodded. "I know."

Dean shook his head in disgust. "I swear, calling these pricks vultures is an insult to *actual* vultures."

I walked around and began shutting all the blinds and curtains on the ground floor. Dean and Damian helped me. After we finished, we wound up back in the kitchen, where I was making Damian a peanut butter and Nutella sandwich.

Nalla, who'd apparently been napping upstairs, appeared. "Are you guys seeing all that commotion outside? There's a bunch of TV reporters and news stations gathered right outside the gate. I could see them from my window upstairs."

"Just ignore them," Dean said to her. "Eventually they'll get bored."

She walked out of the kitchen toward the living room. I was cutting Damian's sandwich in half when I heard what sounded like the French doors being opened.

Dean heard it too. We both ran into the living room. To my disbelief, Nalla was standing outside on the patio, waving at whoever was out there.

"Shit, get her inside," I yelled to Dean.

Damian came up and stood beside me. "What's she doing?"

Dean was already pulling her back and locking the doors again. Nalla's face was flushed and her eyes bright. I frowned to myself. That was not cool. And it better not happen again.

I watched as Dean patiently explained to her how this wasn't your normal press situation where we'd agreed to be interviewed. These people were leeches invading our privacy.

She pouted. "But I thought all press was good press."

He snorted. "Most definitely *not*." He glanced over at me. "Just so you know, there are two of them out there now."

"What do you mean?"

"Two helicopters."

I went over and pushed one of the curtains aside. Sure enough, there they were. "Unbelievable."

"Guess that explains why it's so loud," Dean said.

I continued to watch the assholes circling the area above my backyard. I'd dealt with plenty of paparazzi over the years, and I could honestly say I'd never felt this violated. I wanted to establish roots here, wanted to have a real *home* for the first time in my life.

"That's it," I announced. "I'm calling the cops."

"Really?" Dean seemed surprised. "Do you think they can help?"

"Who knows? But this is private property. I want these assholes dealt with. They should be able to do something."

I set up Damian with a movie and then called the local sheriff's department. I heard the receptionist's voice change when I told her who I was and what I wanted.

"We'll get someone out there right away," she said, sounding nervous. "And may I just say that I'm a huge East Echo fan."

"Thanks, that's nice to hear. How long do you think it'll take before someone gets here?"

"Oh, not long. I'll let them know immediately."

We hung up, and I hoped I hadn't made a mistake getting the law involved. In the past, cops had seldom been much help when dealing with invasive photographers. Over the years, we'd learned to handle them ourselves. At least I heard back from the private security firm I'd hired for the party on Saturday. Unfortunately, the soonest they could get anyone out here was tomorrow.

I felt tired. I ran a hand over my face and glanced at Dean. We'd been friends since high school, and he was one of the few people in the world I trusted completely.

"We still have to decide what to do about Rhys," he said. "Margo's been texting me. She says we need to control the 'narrative.'" He made air quotes with his fingers.

"I don't think we can do anything until we hear from Terence." Margo was our publicist. Jane should have been the one we were talking to, but we hadn't heard a single word from her. Some manager. The irony was I was the one who convinced the band to hire her. What a mistake that was.

About thirty minutes later, there was a call on the intercom. It was the deputy sheriff arriving. His police SUV sat in front of the large metal gate I'd had installed right after I bought the house. I walked out there myself to let him in. Reporters were crowded everywhere like sharks smelling blood in the water, yelling questions at me.

"Josh, what's going to happen now that Rhys has left the band?"

"Are you guys breaking up?"

"Is East Echo going to replace him?"

"Is it true you two are fighting over Jane Braxton, and that's why Rhys is leaving?"

The reporters backed off some to let the police vehicle pass through the gates when they opened. I stood and watched them close to make sure no one tried to slip inside.

My house has become a jail. There was probably a song in that. Then I thought of my younger brother, Jeremy, and felt guilty for thinking it at all.

A dude about my age with short dark hair and dressed in a sheriff's uniform of dark pants and a khaki button-down shirt stepped out of the police car.

"Deputy Sheriff Larson Kelly," he said, putting his hand out.

I gave it a firm shake. "Thanks for coming. As you can see, we've got a real situation here."

"That's quite a pack of reporters out there. I'm not sure if I've witnessed anything like it."

"You just missed the two helicopters that were here a minute ago."

The guy glanced up at the sky. "I don't see anything now."

"That's because they left when you arrived. I'm sure they'll be back as soon as you're gone."

He nodded. "I'm sorry you're dealing with this, truly I am. I'm not sure what you expect the sheriff's department to do about it."

I studied him with frustration. He had a patch on his shoulder and a metal badge pinned to his shirt, plus a gun belt on his waist. "How about you arrest all these people for invading my privacy?"

He shook his head. "Unfortunately, there's not much I can do. I can push them back some, but part of that road is public land. And the laws governing private airspace only go so far. You could try getting a court order, but that takes time." He considered me. "You're not going to like this, but your best bet is to vacate the premises for a while. Let things cool off."

"So I should let them chase me out of my own home? That's your solution?"

"I said you wouldn't like it. Eventually they'll leave, but it may require you leaving first."

———

THE NEXT MORNING, I discussed our options with Dean and Nalla. My biggest concern, of course, was keeping Damian protected from all this.

"We could leave like that cop suggested," Nalla said. "Maybe go back to Seattle."

Dean snorted. "Sounds to me like that guy was just trying to get rid of us. He probably thinks we're a nuisance."

I had to agree. The only thing that deputy sheriff accomplished was pushing the reporters back so they weren't right at the gate anymore. Frankly, I was pissed off at being told to leave.

I'd already thought of the outcome of us going back to the city. We could drive out of here or take the ferry, but either way the press would be right behind us. And then what? We'd be prisoners in whatever hotel we chose. "The problem," I said, "is they're going to follow us wherever we go."

"What about going to Leah's house?" Damian spoke up from over on the couch. I didn't know he was even paying attention to our conversation. "Nobody could follow us there."

"How do you mean?" I asked.

"We could go through the woods like I did before."

"That's an interesting idea, Little D, but we barely know Leah. I doubt she'd want us imposing on her." It pained me to think of how angry she'd been when she left here on Saturday. I knew it was a mistake not being up front with her, and I shouldn't have misled her like that.

"Leah's nice. I think she'd understand," he said.

"Let me think about it. We'll leave it as one of the options, okay?"

I told Dean and Nalla that I'd spoken to Jake, the head of the security team I'd hired for the birthday party, and he had some ideas as well. He said we could leave in separate vehicles, using alternate routes, trying to misdirect them from following us.

To be honest, it all sounded like a big headache. And in the end, what would it get us? We'd still be trapped in a hotel.

"Maybe we could leave the country," Nalla suggested. "Fly to Mexico or Costa Rica."

I shook my head. "I'm not allowed to travel with Damian until the adoption goes through." Charlotte had flown him to Seattle, where I'd met them at the airport. She'd gotten on another flight right afterward to Los Angeles.

My phone buzzed, and I checked it. I'd been getting calls all day but had been ignoring most of them. When I saw Damian's grandmother's name on the screen, my heart sank.

Shit. This couldn't be good.

I walked out of the room for privacy. I could still hear helicopters above the house and hoped she couldn't hear them through the phone.

"Hello, Philomena," I said, trying to sound cheerful. I was surprised once to learn that many of her family and friends called her "Lolo," a nickname I couldn't even imagine using.

I'd barely gotten the words out before she started speaking over me.

"*What* is happening there? I just saw a video of your *house*, the one my *grandson* is staying in, on the BBC." Her accent sounded sharp.

"We've been drawing some attention from the press," I explained carefully. "You might have heard about our guitar player, Rhys, that he's leaving the band. I've got it under control."

"Control? It appears to be a three-ring circus! I assume you're not allowing these horrid people to take photographs of Damian."

"Jesus, of course not." I told myself not to get offended, that she was only looking out for her grandchild. "Listen, I know it looks bad with all these reporters hanging around, but I'm handling it."

"You most certainly better be. Now let me speak to Damian."

"Sure."

I went and found him in the other room in front of the big flatscreen. I handed him the phone and hung back, hoping this conversation went well. He sounded like his normal upbeat self. Thankfully, he didn't mention anything about that helicopter hovering in our backyard yesterday, or the ones currently flying overhead.

"I *am* having fun, Granny, honestly." He paused. "Right now? I'm playing a video game."

I cringed, hoping she wasn't critical of that.

"I know, I know. I'm perfectly *fine*," he insisted. "Oh, and you *must* get some alpacas. They could keep Winston company. They're totally mega!"

I listened as he explained about Leah's farm and all the animals and her cats. He described his birthday party and playing foosball with the other kids here. Eventually he looked around for me, then held the phone out. "She wants to speak to you."

I took it with concern. "Yes?"

"Have you heard from my daughter?"

"No." Not that it surprised me. Since we split up last year, Charlotte seemed to have gotten more self-involved than ever.

"Maybe Damian should come home and stay with me, at least until this whole business is resolved."

I rested my hand on top of my head and paced out of the room. "Please don't do that. He's fine. We're having a good time together."

She was quiet for a long moment. "Very well then. But see that he's shielded from those reporters and paparazzi. He doesn't need to be entangled in your musician problems."

After the phone call, it felt like I needed a stiff drink. I went into the music room and played the piano instead. The curtains were closed, which sucked since I enjoyed the view of the lake, but I did some of my vocal warm-ups and then sang a song from our recent album. I worked on something new that I'd been piecing together. I'd never had piano lessons and couldn't read music, but I could play most songs by ear.

As I played, I decided to make a stand. To stay in the house and wait out the vultures. *Fuck those assholes.* I wasn't going to let them chase me from my own home.

Suddenly I heard Damian shriek.

I jumped up and raced down the hallway. I found him in the kitchen with Dean and Nalla.

"You okay?" My heart pounded as I scanned him for signs of injury. He looked okay but scared. I hugged him to me. "What happened?"

"I was frightened. I wasn't expecting it to be there."

"Expecting what?"

Dean and Nalla were pointing up at the skylight. Letting go of Damian, I walked over to see what they were motioning at and was startled to see some kind of freaky metal device straight out of a science fiction movie sitting on top of the glass.

"Jesus Christ." I stared up at it in shock. "It's a drone."

Dean and I exchanged a disquieting look. The house had a number of skylights. Hell, there were two of them in my bedroom right over my bed.

"Maybe we can cover them," he said. "Jake's guys might be able to do it."

I stood there and shook my head. "This is insanity." I glanced over to Damian and knew we couldn't stay here any longer. *So much for making a stand.* We were like moths trapped in a jar. My heart felt leaden with disappointment. I'd spent a lifetime in hotel rooms, and it wasn't how I wanted Damian to spend his summer with me.

"Is it illegal to shoot down drones?" Dean asked. "Actually, who gives a shit if it's legal. I say we go outside and shoot them all."

I almost smiled. It sure would feel good to shoot those fuckers down.

But then I thought of the phone call I'd just had with Philomena.

I could only imagine what she'd say if she saw video footage of us running around outside like cowboys shooting down drones.

"We should probably start packing." I turned to Damian. "How about we go stay at a fancy hotel in Seattle and order room service? What do you say?"

"What about going to Leah's?"

"I don't see how that's possible, Little D. We barely even know her. She's not going to want us staying there."

"I'll bet you she wouldn't mind. She said I could come back and visit anytime I wanted."

"That's not exactly what she meant."

"Let's ask her. It's better than going to Seattle and staying in some boring hotel."

I sighed and glanced over at Dean, who, to my surprise, was nodding. "You think it's a good idea?" I asked him.

"I agree with Damian. It's worth a try. And it wouldn't be for long. Maybe a few days at most."

"All four of us?"

He shook his head. "Just you and Damian. Nalla and I can stay here. They're not interested in me. You and Rhys are the real story." He got a mischievous grin on his face and looked at Nalla. "Maybe we'll have some fun torturing those assholes. What do you say, baby?"

Except Nalla didn't look happy. She had a strange expression on her face. "I don't think Josh and Damian should stay with Leah."

"Why not?" Dean asked her.

"It's just a bad idea. We should all stay together."

"Believe me," Dean said, "once those pricks outside realize Josh isn't here anymore, they'll leave too."

Nalla seemed upset. "Let's all go to Seattle. I'd rather do that."

"Can't we just try Leah's first?" Damian asked me. "Can't we, Dad?"

I couldn't believe I was even contemplating it, especially after how pissed Leah was at me when she left here, but finally, I nodded. "All right, let's go there and see what she says."

CHAPTER FOURTEEN

~Leah~

It was early evening, and I'd been spinning for the past couple of hours, though I was so upset I kept making mistakes. As hard as I tried, I couldn't stop thinking about Josh and Damian.

Shane was in the living room playing video games. Eventually he came into the dining room and stood there brushing his hands against some of the colorful yarns I had hanging from the ceiling.

"What's for dinner?" he asked. "I'm hungry."

I smiled and shook my head. Shane was always hungry. "Aren't you going to work soon? I thought you had a shift at Walk the Plank."

"Not until later."

"There's leftover soup and bread from yesterday."

He seemed to consider this. "Maybe I'll just grab a bag of potato chips."

"Suit yourself." And then I cursed aloud when I accidentally drafted too thin and my fiber broke apart. It was the third time I'd done it in the last hour. I searched for the end of the yarn on the bobbin with frustration. I wasn't having a good day and should probably stop spinning, but I was stubborn and soldiered on.

As Shane rooted around in the kitchen, I heard what sounded like a knock on the front door. I paused my foot on the treadle.

That's strange. I hadn't heard a car engine approaching the house.

"Did you hear that?" I asked Shane. "It sounds like someone's at the front door. Can you go check?"

"What?" he called back.

The knock happened again. There was definitely someone out there.

"Never mind." I put my fiber down and got up. I glanced out the window, expecting to see Lars's police SUV or maybe his truck, but there was nothing.

When I got to the door, I peeked out the side window and was stunned to see Damian and Josh. When I opened it, the two of them stood there with the air of a couple of desperadoes. They were both carrying backpacks.

Damian grinned up at me. "We've come for a visit!"

"Hello, Leah," Josh said in that honeyed voice. He smiled, though he seemed uncomfortable.

I tried to hide my surprise. "It's nice to see you. Come... in."

They both entered the house at the exact moment that Shane came out from the kitchen with a bag of potato chips between his teeth. In his hands, he was juggling a can of onion dip, a jar of peanuts, a bag of cookies, and a Coke. His sun-streaked bangs were falling in his face.

He stopped walking. His eyebrows shot up as he stared at Damian and Josh, who were staring right back at him.

I sensed Josh grow tense. He glanced at me but didn't say anything.

"Who *are* you?" Damian asked loudly in his English accent.

"This is my brother, Shane," I told them.

By that point Shane had removed the chips from his mouth and was trying to puzzle this situation out.

"This is your brother?" Damian seemed delighted. "The one who lives out back in the caravan?"

"That's the one," I said.

Damian grinned from ear to ear. Clearly, he thought this was a brilliant development and saw my life as highly colorful.

Josh seemed to relax. He nodded toward Shane and introduced both himself and Damian, just giving their first names. "We're new neighbors. I moved in down the road recently."

"And you guys know Leah?" Shane asked him.

"We do."

Shane turned to me in confusion. "You never mentioned meeting any new neighbors." But then his eyes widened, and he seemed to put two and two together. He flashed back to Josh's long hair and the tattoos covering his forearms. "Holy shit! You're that dude from East Echo—the lead singer, am I right?"

Josh didn't reply at first but then nodded. "I am."

"It's awesome to meet you." Shane unceremoniously dumped all the junk food into the nearest chair. He brushed his bangs back before putting his hand out to Josh, who shook it. He shook Damian's as well. "Nice to meet you both."

"Can I see the inside of your caravan?" Damian asked. "Do you really live there?"

"I do live there. At least when I'm not living *here*." He chuckled. "But sure, you can see it sometime."

"So, how did you guys get here?" I asked the two of them. "I didn't see your truck or motorcycle parked out front."

"I led my dad through the woods," Damian explained. "We didn't want the vultures following."

"The vultures?"

"The *press*," Josh said. "We're having a situation with them at the house right now."

"Oh yeah, dude." Shane nodded. "We saw those helicopters. That's intense."

Josh began to describe the nightmare happening at his house, and the more he talked, the worse I felt. I swallowed, trying to get rid of the taste of shame in my mouth.

"It's kind of what brought us here," Josh said finally. "We were wondering if we could stay a day or two."

"*Here?*" My voice rose an octave. I didn't know what I was expecting when I saw them on the porch, but this wasn't it.

"Hell yes." Shane grinned widely. "Of course you can stay here."

"Just until this mess dies down." Josh was studying me, obviously waiting for my response. "I know this is crazy, and we barely know each other, but I'm sort of at my wit's end."

I took a moment to regroup. "You can stay," I said. "It's not a problem. I'm happy to help." More than happy if it eased my guilt, though I'd help them regardless.

Josh studied me. "You sure?"

"Of course she's sure," Shane interjected. "Leah would never turn away a neighbor in need."

"See, Dad?" Damian looked up from where he was sitting on the floor petting one of my cats. "I told you she wouldn't mind. What's this cat's name?" he asked me.

"That's Coriander."

Shane went back over to the chair to pick up all his snacks. "Do you guys want to play on the Xbox?"

"What games do you have?" Damian asked, getting up.

Shane handed him the bag of potato chips. "Everything." The two of them went into the living room. Josh followed but then hung back, looking at me.

Our eyes lingered, but I turned away. "Have you guys eaten dinner yet? It's nothing fancy, but there's leftover soup and bread from last night."

"We're good. We had something before we came here."

I nodded. Our last conversation flashed through my mind. The one where he'd asked to be friends, and I told him to fuck off.

He took a deep breath and moved closer. "You're probably still pissed at me, and I'll bet you're amazed I had the gall to show up here like this and ask such a huge favor."

"I'm not angry anymore," I said, being truthful. "But why did you lie to me about who you are?"

He massaged the back of his neck. "I've been asking myself the same question, and, to be honest, I'm not entirely sure. All I can do is apologize again for misleading you. I'm really sorry, Leah. I hope we can start over."

I nodded. "All right, let's start over."

A smile tugged on the corners of his mouth, and there was something catlike about his expression.

"What is it?" I asked.

"Well, now that we're staying here and starting over, I was just thinking about the first night I saw you. Do you run around like that a lot?"

My face grew warm as I remembered it too. The way I'd been hiding outside in the bushes half naked. "Of course not."

He gave me a flirtatious grin. "Too bad."

I could smell the lemongrass and musk. Could sense how he already brought a different masculine energy into my house. I liked cats a lot, but this was one cat I needed to keep my distance from.

"Let me show you the guest bedroom," I said. "It's just down the hall."

He was still smiling as he followed me.

I pointed out the bathroom and then led him into the bedroom. "It's only a full-size bed. It might be too small for you guys to share."

He nodded. "Let's give it to Damian. I'll take the couch."

Josh wandered over to look out the window, which faced the back of the house. There was a large grassy area surrounded by trees.

I had a surreal moment as I watched him study the yard. He wore a short-sleeved blue T-shirt layered over a white one with long sleeves. His blond hair was pulled back into a thick ponytail.

I thought about the life he must lead, filled with five-star hotels, buckets of money, and leggy supermodels.

"I guess this is a step down for you," I said. "Not exactly as nice as what you're used to."

He glanced over his shoulder at me. "Actually, I like it here. It reminds me of my grandparents' house."

"Really?"

"They didn't have a farm, but it was on acreage."

This surprised me. "Do you still visit them?"

He turned toward me and shook his head. "Nah, they passed away years ago."

"I'm sorry to hear that. Do you have other family?"

He seemed to weigh his response. "My mom and my younger brother."

I already knew about the mom since I'd read about her on his Wiki page, but I never saw anything about a brother. As I recalled, his mom had also been a singer, which was why she was mentioned.

"Are you guys close?"

"Not really." He began walking toward the door, and it was clear this wasn't a discussion he wanted to continue.

Back out in the living room, Shane and Damian were ensconced on opposite ends of the couch playing some video game. Damian was laughing like crazy.

"Dude," Shane called out when he saw Josh. "There's a third controller. You need to get in here and help me. Your son is merciless!"

Josh chuckled as he strode over and sat in the middle between them. He reached for some potato chips dumped in a plastic bowl. "Sounds good. Set me up."

I left to go make myself something to eat in the kitchen and could hear the three of them laughing and shouting and having a great time. I had to hand it to my baby brother. Very little fazed him or put him off his stride. Even having a rock star show up at the front door. Let's be real—it was just another day in his charmed life.

By the time Shane had to leave for work, the three of them seemed to have become best friends. Josh was asking him about his job at Walk the Plank, while Shane regaled him with stories. Meanwhile, Damian seemed content as he sat on the couch, smiling and petting two of my cats—Basil and Nutmeg. I'd given him the laser pointer earlier, and four cats had shown up to play with him.

Shane took a swig from his can of Coke. "Bro, we have live music every Tuesday night. You *have* to come by and check it out."

Josh nodded, taking this in. He was settled back on the couch with his long legs stretched out in front of him as he absentmindedly petted Nutmeg. "I just might do that."

I tried to picture Josh hanging out at Walk the Plank, and oddly, it wasn't that hard. He'd probably fit right in.

When Shane got up to go to work, Josh walked with him to the front door. "Listen, I know this probably doesn't need to be said, but I'd appreciate it if you didn't tell anyone I'm staying here."

"No worries, I got you. It's in the vault." Shane put his hand out, and the two of them did some kind of handshake and gave each other a brisk hug.

I watched them with amazement.

"Your brother Shane is all right," Josh said as he came back into the living room. He glanced over at Damian. "It's time for bed, Little D."

At this announcement, Damian began to protest strenuously, claiming he wasn't tired at all, that he needed to pet the cats some more, that they *needed* him to play with them for "their exercise."

Eventually he agreed to go brush his teeth, and Josh went with him. I got some sheets out for the couch and made it into a bed.

To be honest, my head was spinning. Part of the problem was that I couldn't stop staring at Josh. I'd sat in the living room with the three of them, pretending to knit when I was mostly ogling him.

As Josh helped Damian get ready for bed, I poured myself a glass of ice water and sat on the front porch. It had become one of my nightly rituals. I was determined to keep this place afloat but honestly didn't know if I'd be able to pull it off another year. I savored every moment of living the life of my dreams, even if it might not last.

"There you are," Josh said, stepping outside.

I turned my head, so deep in thought I hadn't even heard the front door open. "I'm just sitting out here moonbathing."

"Mind if I join you?"

I shrugged and tried to pretend my stomach wasn't already fluttering. "Sure."

He sat down in the chair next to me, and we both gazed out at the pasture and the barn, taking in the smell of hay as it wafted in on the night air.

We remained silent, but it was a companionable silence. I felt myself relax a little and appreciated that he was the kind of person who understood the value of quiet spaces.

Reaching down, I picked up my water glass and took a sip.

Josh turned to me. "Can I ask you something?"

I looked at him.

"What's moonbathing?"

I smiled and put my glass down. "It's just what it sounds like. I like to sit outside at night and soak in the moonlight."

He nodded. "You have a thing about the moon, huh? I noticed your farm is called Clarity Moon."

"When I bought this place last year, that's what I felt—clarity. So that's where the name came from." I took a deep breath. "I love it here, but it hasn't been easy. Not to mention my family's been totally against it from day one." I stopped talking. I couldn't believe I'd just told him that.

He seemed to absorb my words. "Your brother Shane's against it?"

"No, he's the only one who's not. I have another brother—my twin—and then my mom. Both of them have been pressuring me to sell."

"Why?"

"They say it's too much for me, and that I can't handle running this place on my own."

"But you *are* running it on your own, aren't you?"

I nodded. "My brothers help occasionally, but yeah, I am." I thought over my own words. The fact was I made it through the first year. Shouldn't that be a reason for celebration and not recrimination?

"I know this isn't any of my business, but you have to ignore them. Otherwise, they'll drag you down. Trust me, I've dealt with people like that."

"It's hard, though. They're my family. They care about me."

"I'm sure they do, but they're not seeing you for who you are."

My brows went up. "And who am I, exactly?"

"A badass."

"What?" I gave a startled laugh. "I've never been called *that* before."

He was smiling, but there was understanding in his gaze. Like maybe he got something about me that I wasn't seeing myself. "A serious badass."

"I don't think that's true."

"It's true." He said it like it was a fact. "I noticed it right after we first met."

I didn't know what to say. I thought about everything I'd been through this past year. Learning how to take care of my animals, I'd been bruised and trampled on. I nearly cracked a rib last winter when Alicia, who was still getting to know me, pinned me against the fence.

No matter how hard it got, and no matter how much my family tried to convince me to quit, I kept going. I was determined. Some-days I wondered if I was a masochist. I certainly didn't feel like a badass. Most days I felt like the furthest thing from it.

Josh leaned toward me in his chair. "You never told Shane I was your neighbor, did you?" His voice was low and confiding. "Even after you found out who I was."

"No, I didn't."

There was an emotion on his face I couldn't quite place. "I appreciate that, Leah. Most people would have told everyone they know."

I shifted uncomfortably. I didn't want him thanking me. Not when I caused this mess. I wondered if I should tell him I gave his address to the press. Confess that I'd made a giant, stupid mistake. "How do you think they found out where you live?" I asked instead, hoping he'd tell me it was property records. I was still clinging to that lifeline.

But his expression turned hard as he leaned back in his chair. "It was Rhys. That brooding, grudge-holding motherfucker." He rolled his eyes. "Heathcliff on the moors."

"What? How do you know it was him?"

"I just know. He's messing with me." He inhaled sharply. "I didn't think he could sink this low, but apparently I was wrong. We used to be as close as brothers, and now look at us."

I shifted in my seat. "What about property records? The media probably did a search. It wouldn't be that hard to get your address from those."

He shook his head. "The house isn't even in my name. It would be impossible."

I felt my lifeline sinking. "What do you mean, it's not in your name?"

"Lawyers set it up so it's layered within a few businesses and stays private." He shook his head with disgust. "So much for *that*. The whole world knows where I live now."

"They might have still figured it out. I'm *sure* it's not Rhys."

"You have a good heart, Leah." He smiled thoughtfully. "So you probably don't understand how vindictive people can be, especially when huge sums of money are involved."

And in that moment, I realized what the emotion on his face was, the one I couldn't quite place. It was something that, if I had to guess, he gave out rarely.

It was trust.

CHAPTER FIFTEEN

~Leah~

The thing about having a rooster is they crow in the early morning. They also crow in the afternoon and even at night. I'd gotten so used to waking up to the sound that I didn't even set an alarm clock anymore.

"What the hell is that *racket*?" Josh's voice grumbled from over on the couch.

The living room was still dark. I'd snuck past him, quietly, holding my running shoes in one hand, trying not to wake him up.

"That's my rooster, Cary Grant."

"Cary Grant?"

Since Josh was awake, I didn't have to be quiet anymore and went over and sat in the living room chair to put on my sneakers. "Just think of him as your friendly five o'clock wake-up call."

As soon I said this, Cary Grant crowed again. Loud and proud.

Josh put his arm over his eyes and chuckled. "A damn *rooster*. I don't believe it...."

I shouldn't have, but I took the opportunity to check him out. It was dark, but I could see him well enough. He'd been sleeping on his back with only the sheet tangled around him. It looked like he'd taken off the long-sleeved shirt from yesterday and only wore the short-sleeved blue one. His jeans were on the edge of the couch, and I had to wonder what he had on beneath the sheet.

He shifted position, and when his gaze found me in the dim light, I quickly averted my eyes. To my surprise, I noticed a black Kindle on the coffee table that must have been his.

"Is this really what time you start your day?" he asked, watching me tie my shoes.

I smiled, remembering back to when I first moved here and how getting up at this hour had seemed insane to me too. "I know it's hard to believe, but you get used to it."

He didn't reply, but I sensed skepticism.

"It's nice watching the sunrise," I explained. "There's something about it that centers you."

"Are you suggesting I get up at this merciless hour?"

"Only if you want to." I tied the laces on my second shoe and stood up. "I don't usually make coffee this early, but I can put the pot on for you if you'd like."

He shook his head. "That's all right. I'm not a big coffee drinker."

I still felt him observing me and tried not to feel self-conscious. I wore shorts with a hoodie over my sports bra. His gaze lingered on my legs. "It looks like those scratches are healing nicely."

"They are. I'm headed out now. Can I do anything for you?" I meant in the kitchen, but it came out sounding oddly sexual.

"Hmm, let's see...." His voice deepened while his eyes wandered lazily down my body. "What are you *willing* to do for me, honey?"

A surprising jolt of lust rocketed through me. I ignored it and put my hands on my hips. "How many women would you say you've flirted with in your lifetime?"

He shrugged. "I don't know, Leah. How many would *you* guess?"

"More than there are stars in the sky."

"That sounds about right."

"I don't mind if you stay here, but don't get the wrong idea about me, okay? I'm not a plaything or a toy."

"Damn." He grinned with approval. "There's that badass."

And it was then that something occurred to me. "There are a million women in the world who'd be thrilled to have you stay with them. Why did you come here?"

He considered my question while he scratched his jaw. Finally, he sighed. "The truth is... well, it's not an easy thing to admit, but I'm looking for something real specific." He turned to me with an earnest gaze. "I need some Sasquatch lovin'."

I opened my mouth and then burst out laughing. It was so silly and unexpected that it totally got me. I collapsed in the chair, cracking up.

Josh was laughing, too, but he kept on talking. "It gets lonely out there in the woods by myself. I need a big-footed gal to keep me company. At least a size twenty. Can you help me out?"

I wiped my eyes. "You're crazy."

He peered down. "Except now that I'm looking at your feet, I'm not so sure. They're kind of small. I don't think we're compatible."

I was still catching my breath when Damian came into the room.

"What's so funny?" he asked, rubbing the sleep from his eyes.

"Good morning, Little D." Josh sat up and made room for Damian to sit with him on the couch. "I was just teasing Leah a little bit."

Right then Cary Grant crowed again, and Damian's eyes lit up. "Is that a real rooster?"

"Very real," I said.

"Can I go see him?"

"Definitely. How about you help me with the chickens later when I get back from my run?"

He seemed delighted. "I would like that very much!"

Josh was puzzling over me. "Is that what you're doing now? Going for a run?"

I nodded and stood up. "I go every morning before my chores."

His eyes drifted down my body again, lingering on my legs, but then he abruptly looked away. It was almost like he'd caught himself doing something he wasn't supposed to.

———

WHEN I CAME BACK from my run, the two of them were sitting at the kitchen table. Damian was eating a bowl of cereal with a banana cut into it while Josh was finishing a piece of toast and drinking a mug of warm water with honey.

I popped a piece of bread in the toaster. "Warm water with honey? I have some vitamin C if you think you're catching a cold."

He shook his head. "I'm fine."

"It's for his voice," Damian told me, crunching on his cereal.

"His what?"

"It's what I drink before I go onstage," Josh explained. "But I've gotten so used to it, I just drink it all the time now."

I noticed he wore the same jeans as yesterday but with a different T-shirt. This one was black and advertised some band I'd never heard of called the Beaver Kings.

"I thought all rockers drank a quart of whiskey before going onstage," I said, thinking back to my ex-husband years ago.

He smirked. "Not the ones who still want to be able to sing when they're fifty." He took another sip from his mug. "This is exceptionally good honey. Where did you buy it?"

My sourdough toast popped, and I spread butter on it. "My friend Theo gave it to me. She's a beekeeper—an apiologist."

"What's an apiologist?" Damian asked.

"It's a kind of entomologist who studies honey bees."

"Do they sting her a lot?"

I shook my head. "Not as far as I know. I should take you there sometime. You can see her hives."

Damian grinned. "I'd like that."

"Does she sell her honey?" Josh asked. "I wouldn't mind buying a case of this stuff."

"She doesn't sell it, but she'd probably give you a jar."

I took a bite of my toast and began making a pot of coffee since Shane usually came by to fill his thermos before work. "I'm going to make scrambled eggs for my brother. Would either of you like some?"

Damian shook his head, but Josh nodded. "Thanks, I could eat some eggs."

As I set to work cracking shells, Damian got out the laser pointer and went into the living room to play with a few of the cats.

That left Josh and me alone in the kitchen.

I was still wearing my running clothes, which amounted to a pair of shorts and a sports bra. I typically took off my hoodie after I got heated during my run. Now I felt self-conscious again.

"So, how was your run?" he asked, as if he'd read my mind.

I glanced over my shoulder and thought I saw him staring at my ass, but I wasn't sure since he looked away so quickly. "Good. Nice and quiet."

"It *is* quiet living out here. Back at the house, it's been hard for me to sleep with all this silence."

I nodded. "I lived in Seattle before moving here, so I know exactly what you mean."

"You were a city girl?"

"All the way." I flipped the eggs with a spatula as they cooked in the pan. I told him how I used to own a condo downtown and worked in finance. "I dressed up and wore high heels daily."

"That's quite a change."

Just then I heard the front door open and figured it was Shane. To my surprise, I heard Lars's voice out in the living room. "I think my twin brother is here."

I could hear him asking Damian who he was, and Damian replying, "A friend of Leah's. Who are you?"

I turned the heat down on the eggs to go out there, but Lars came into the kitchen.

"I didn't even hear your truck," I said.

"There's a British kid playing with the cats in your living room." But then he stopped and appeared stunned when he saw Josh sitting at the kitchen table.

Josh seemed surprised, too, but nodded at him. "Officer Kelly."

My brows went up. "You guys know each other?"

Lars's gaze cut between the two of us. Me standing at the stove in my sports bra and shorts while Josh sat at the table with his tattoos and Beaver Kings T-shirt. It was innocent enough, but I already knew what Lars was thinking. After all, I'd once married a rock-n-roll bad boy.

"We've met," Josh said, and something in his voice told me the meeting hadn't gone well.

Lars was dressed in his uniform, though he wasn't wearing his gun belt. He seemed suspicious studying us, but then Lars always seemed suspicious.

I turned back to the stove. "Do you want some eggs?"

He didn't reply. Instead he and Josh were having a staring contest.

"How about coffee?" I asked him.

He looked at me. "*Exactly* how do you two know each other?"

I was wondering how to explain all this when I was saved by Shane walking into the kitchen. "Good morning, everyone. It sure smells good in here." Oblivious to the tension, Shane got himself a mug of coffee, dumped in cream and sugar, and sat down across the table from Josh.

"Josh is one of my neighbors," I said, stating the obvious.

I dished out the eggs and put a plate in front of each of them. Lars was still standing there like he was wishing he could arrest someone.

"Thank you *so* much, honey," Josh said in a seductive drawl. I suspected he wasn't flirting but doing it to irritate my brother.

"Well, I'm going to go change into my work clothes now," I announced and left the room. Too much testosterone. I figured the men could resolve their own issues.

After changing into some fitted jean overalls—they were very practical, and it was just a coincidence that they looked good on me— I redid my ponytail and debated whether I should put on makeup. Finally, I decided a little eyeliner and blush were acceptable. I may not be a supermodel, but that didn't mean I had to look rustic.

By the time I got back downstairs, Shane and Lars had already left for work. Damian was on the couch surrounded by three cats while he read from a Kindle. Josh was in the kitchen cleaning up after breakfast.

Yes, that's right. There was a rock star in my kitchen loading the dishwasher.

I stopped in the doorway as he placed my Saint Catherine—the patron saint of spinners—mug in the top rack.

What twilight zone universe have I entered?

I wished I could take a picture of this. It was too much. Without photo evidence, I doubted my future self would ever believe it happened.

He glanced up at me. "So that guy is your twin brother?"

"He is."

"That explains a lot."

I decided not to comment since I didn't want to get in the middle of whatever problem they seemed to have with each other. "Thanks for doing the dishes. I'm going to have Damian come outside and help me with the chickens."

Josh nodded. "Sounds good. I need to make a few phone calls, but I'd like to help around here too."

"Sure." I smiled. "I can find something for you to do."

CHAPTER SIXTEEN

~Josh~

Leah in those little running shorts. Those long legs. That athletic bra where I could see the outline of her breasts.

Damn.

What the hell?

When I agreed to come here, I figured it might be awkward, but I had no idea it would turn into some kind of sexual torture.

I couldn't give Charlotte any reason to back out of this adoption. None. Not until the papers were signed and Damian was legally my son. She'd been holding his adoption over my head for years, but it wasn't until I finally left her that she had her lawyers draw up the papers. She got her family involved. It was just another way for her to try to keep me on a leash, but we all agreed that after this summer, if things went well, then we'd make it legal.

It didn't matter that we broke up well over a year ago. If Charlotte found out I was involved with another woman, she'd stop everything.

So I'd been living like a monk for quite a while. I'd accepted it. Hell, I turned down three offers at my birthday party. It didn't bother me a bit.

Except here I was, loading the dishwasher in Leah's kitchen, feeling like a horny teenager while I tried to stop thinking about her ass.

It was her defiance that had my number. I'd always been partial to a woman who knew her own mind, who didn't back down from a challenge, and Leah was definitely that.

I began my phone calls as I paced the living room. I called Philomena first. She didn't answer, so I left a brief message to let her know Damian and I were staying on a friend's farm. Hopefully the farm part made it sound wholesome. I figured I should let Charlotte know, too, so I called her next. She answered on the second ring.

"Hello, Josh," she said in her posh accent. "Everything all right with Damian?" She sounded rushed, like I'd caught her in the middle of something.

"Everything's fine. We're having a great time. I'm not sure if you heard about what's going on with the band. Rhys said he's leaving."

"Of course I heard. What else is new? Doesn't he say he's leaving every other month?"

This wasn't the first time Rhys had threatened to leave, though it was the first time he'd gone public with it.

"He's *such* a prima donna," she went on. "I'm certain you'll be better off without him."

"The reason I'm calling is because we're having a situation at the house. The press has been all over us. As a result, Damian and I are staying with some friends."

"Oh?" She paused. "*Who* is this?"

I could sense her antenna going up. She used to fly into jealous rages over the women who approached me, even if they were just fans. It was one of the many reasons I finally left.

"His name's Shane, and he has a much older sister named Leah." I was massaging the truth here, but what else could I do? Tell her we were staying with my sexy neighbor? "They live up the road from me. Shane's cool. I just wanted to let you know we weren't at the house."

She went quiet. It occurred to me that Damian might have already mentioned Leah to her.

"How long do you think you'll be staying there?"

"A few days. Just until things calm down."

"I suppose that's acceptable." She yawned. "Bloody jet lag. I should go. We're headed to Ziggy's new gallery."

"You're not in Los Angeles anymore?"

"No, I flew home with Malcom on Monday."

Malcom was a guy she'd been dating the past few months. He used to be the drummer in some British metal band. Apparently she didn't think it merited telling either me or Damian that she'd flown back to London.

"Too bad you aren't here." Her voice turned flirtatious. "There's a party happening later at the Experiment." The Experiment was a club we used to hang out at years ago. Full of pretentious assholes that I outgrew, but Charlotte never did.

"Do you want to talk to Damian?" I asked, thinking she might want to say hello.

"No, that's all right. We'll talk later. I need to get dressed."

After we hung up, I had a flashback of our lives together. We had some good times during the early parts of our relationship. I was getting over my heartache from an unexpected divorce, and Charlotte was attractive, wild, and needed a partner in crime. And to top it off, she had this really amazing kid. Damian was only two when I met him, but right away I felt a connection. Except while I got older and grew up, Charlotte stayed the same. If anything, her partying had gotten worse.

I tried calling Terence next, but he was still offline. I envied him in a way. Hiking through the Himalayas, enjoying the beauty and clean air, untouched by the current shit show we were dealing with.

There were messages from a few friends, and I texted to let them know we were fine.

Then I called Margo, who still insisted we make a statement, at least on our website. "Control the narrative," she kept repeating. Promoters were contacting her in a panic, and I told her to send them to Jane. Hell, we were still paying her to be our manager. Rhys hadn't said anything else publicly, but then he'd done enough damage.

I thought some more about Rhys. I'd tried calling him when the news first broke, but he didn't answer, and I didn't want to talk to a machine. But now in the light of day, after being forced from my home, I decided it might feel good to give him a piece of my mind. Unsurprisingly, the call went directly to voice mail.

"I hope you answer this message, you piece-of-shit coward. That's if you have the balls." I lowered my voice to a tone I only used for degenerates. "You want to be a dick and leave the band? Fine. Don't want to discuss it in person? Fine. But giving my address to the press when you *know* Damian is staying with me, and you *know* what this visit means, well, you can rot in hell for that, you sorry motherfucker."

I hung up.

I took a deep breath. I'd hoped getting that off my chest would make me feel better, but I couldn't say I felt any better at all.

I texted Dean and asked how things were going at the house. Then I slipped the phone into my front pocket and glanced out the side window. Leah and Damian were out by the chicken coop. He looked to be having a great time. I was glad one of us was. I could see Leah, too, in those fitted overalls she'd changed into.

I sighed to myself.

Time to be tortured some more.

I DECIDED the overalls were worse than the shorts. Some kind of soft denim that hugged her body and left little to the imagination. It didn't help that I had a great imagination.

"Look, Dad, I'm feeding the chickens!" Damian called out to me. He was tossing feed on the ground as all the chickens pecked at it. "They love it!"

I walked over. "I can see that."

"You're doing a great job," Leah told him. She was pushing a wheelbarrow from a shed over behind the coop. There were a couple of large bags inside of it.

I nearly offered to help her with it but knew she wouldn't like that. And she was obviously strong enough to manage on her own.

After feeding the chickens, Leah showed Damian how to get eggs from inside the coop.

I hung back because my phone buzzed with a text from Terence. I was glad to hear from him. He said he thought Rhys was just being a dick but wasn't serious, and that he was going to try and talk to him. I told him to do whatever he wanted, but at this point, I was done.

I decided to update Dean, but as I stood there with the phone in my hand, I got the strangest sensation. Kind of like I was being stalked. I glanced around but didn't see anyone, just a few chickens nearby pecking at the ground.

I went back to my text but then got that sensation again. This time when I looked up, I yelled as a big, puffed-up bird started flapping its wings and attacking me. It rushed at me in a flurry of brown feathers and clawed feet.

"Jesus Christ!" I kicked my legs and arms out. I didn't want to hurt it, but I didn't want to get hurt myself.

"*Cary Grant!*" I heard Leah shout as she ran over. "Get away from him!"

At the sound of her voice, the rooster—which was what I now realized it was—seemed to calm down. It backed off, and the flapping stopped.

"Are you okay?" she asked me with concern. She glanced back at the rooster, who was strutting away. His crown stood up high, as bright red as the blood I hoped wasn't running down my leg.

"Yeah, I think so." I inspected my jeans and could see he'd torn a hole in them. On further inspection, he hadn't broken any skin.

"I can't believe he did that," she said, obviously bewildered. "He's never attacked anyone before."

"Are you all right, Dad?" Damian rushed over, looking worried. He was carrying a wicker basket full of eggs.

"I'm fine. Just kind of spooked me is all. I wasn't expecting karate moves from a rooster."

"Why would Cary Grant attack my dad?" he asked Leah.

She shook her head. "I don't know. Maybe he felt threatened for some reason. What were you doing?" she asked me.

"Nothing. Just standing here sending a text."

"Something must have riled him up. I'm really sorry."

"Don't worry about it. I'm fine." I looked over at Cary Grant, whose real name should have been Chuck Norris. He was on the side of the yard, standing near some bushes. "What did I ever do to you?" I called over to him. "Hell, we just met."

He ruffled his feathers, still eyeing me. Somehow I'd pissed off a damn rooster. Go figure.

Leah helped Damian put the fresh eggs in the kitchen, and after he had a glass of apple juice and a granola bar, the three of us went back outside. She took him over to some metal bins near the coop, then showed him how she needed them both refilled with the bags of chicken feed from the wheelbarrow. He helped her scoop the feed inside.

"I can do it myself," he told her. "You don't have to help."

"You sure?"

He nodded. "I can do it. I want to."

Some of the chickens came over, clucking and pecking where a few pellets had been dropped.

"Thanks, Damian. You're a huge help."

He shrugged, but I could see him smiling.

Leah and I walked over toward the barn together, bringing the wheelbarrow with us. She'd already asked me if I wanted to help lay down fresh bedding for her animals.

"You don't think that rooster would try to attack Damian, do you?" I asked, glancing back at the chicken coop.

"No, he's always been friendly with everyone. Believe it or not, you're the only person he's ever attacked."

I searched around warily but didn't see any sign of Cary Grant.

Once we got in the barn, she handed me a pitchfork and showed me how we needed to get rid of the old bedding and then lay down the fresh stuff. We made quick work of it. When we were ready for the new straw, I grabbed a bale from outside the barn, but Leah stopped me.

"That's not straw. That's hay."

I put the bale down. "There's a difference?"

"Hay is used to feed animals." She pointed up at the hayloft. "Straw isn't." She began explaining how hay was used as food, especially during the winter months, while straw was nonnutritious and used for bedding.

I stroked my beard as I listened to her.

In the morning sunlight, I had to say, she was damn pretty. Those rich brown eyes and that smooth skin. Her nose was long with a small point at the end. I remembered thinking she wasn't beautiful when we first met but decided I might have to revisit that opinion.

As she went into more details about different grasses and the nutrients in them, my mind wandered. I began to imagine us up there in that hayloft. Just the two of us. She was undoing the snaps on her overalls, pulling her T-shirt overhead, and smiling at me with a come-hither expression. I'd never done it in a hayloft and had a feeling I'd enjoy it, especially with her.

But then Leah stopped talking, and her expression turned to a scowl. For a second, I worried she could read my mind because our hayloft adventures had turned kind of dirty. Okay, a lot dirty. Let's just say she was making wild barnyard sounds while her thighs were pressed tight to my face.

Thankfully, she wasn't scowling at *me* but at something by the house.

I turned to see what she was looking at. There was a blue minivan pulling up in front, and we watched as two people got out. Some woman with blonde hair and a dude with a crew cut and a short-sleeved button-down shirt. They looked like they were selling something.

"Shit," Leah said, still scowling. She turned to me. "Stay here. Don't move."

And then she left.

Of course, I didn't listen and followed right after her. I'd never been good at taking orders.

"Who are they?" I asked.

"Realtors."

"What do they want?"

Leah didn't reply. She looked highly pissed.

As we walked up to the pair, I could see the woman's eyes widen at the sight of me. They traveled from my long hair and beard down to the ink on my arms. It wasn't recognition that I was the lead singer for a multi-platinum-selling rock band but concern that I might steal her purse.

"Hello." She forced a bright smile. She wore a shapeless flower-print dress with a white collar that looked like a napkin. "We just thought we'd stop by to say hello and see how things are going. This is my associate, Cal."

The guy nodded at us. "It's good to meet you." He put his hand out, but since Leah didn't take it, neither did I.

He pulled it back. "I thought we could go over some projections for your farm. I think you'll see the numbers are excellent. You stand to make a nice profit. In fact, and I don't want to get your hopes up—" He chuckled. "—but we *may* already have an interested buyer."

"Well, that's too bad because you're wasting their time," Leah said. "I have no intention of selling."

Cal and Napkin Lady glanced at each other. "As we understand it, you may not have a choice," he said. "That's why we're here. We'd like to help."

"I'm sure you would, but I don't need any help."

"Perhaps your husband has something to say about that." Cal turned to me like I might add something to this conversation. "I think you'll be excited when you see these figures."

Leah scoffed. "This isn't my husband."

"Who *are* you?" Napkin Lady asked me. She looked nervous but seemed curious too.

By that point I'd gotten the lay of the land and could see these people were vultures of a different feather. I crossed my arms and put on a menacing sneer. It was the same one I wore on the cover of *Rolling Stone* six months ago. I opened my mouth to tell this woman, "None of your goddamned business," but Leah started talking.

"This is my cousin," she said.

"Your cousin?" Napkin Lady seemed surprised. "Your mother never mentioned anything about a cousin visiting."

"He just arrived. His name's, um... ah...." Her voice faltered, and she nearly piloted that plane straight into a mountain. "Friedrich!" she said with triumph, landing it on a grassy field.

I gave Leah a sideways glance. *Friedrich? She couldn't have said Butch or Angus?* I increased my sneer. It wasn't easy being a tough motherfucker with a name like Friedrich, but I gave it my all.

"Nice to meet you," Cal said.

Napkin Lady nodded and tried to smile.

"I'm not selling my farm," Leah told them both. "Not today, not tomorrow, not ever. So I'd appreciate it if you'd stop coming by."

"Leah, there's no reason to act this way. We already know all about your difficulties." Napkin Lady leaned forward and lowered her voice to a stage whisper. "About your *financial problems*." She paused to let that sink in. "I don't mean to embarrass you in front of your cousin."

But that was exactly what she meant to do, and one look at Leah's stricken face told me she'd succeeded.

All right. Now I was pissed.

"That's enough," I growled. I gave them a menacing glare, except this one was real. "You both need to *leave*."

Napkin Lady seemed startled by my tone. "We're only here to offer our assistance."

"The hell you are."

Cal put on an air of concern. "I think you're misunderstanding our intentions."

"I don't give a shit about your intentions. Get the fuck out of here before I throw your sorry asses into that minivan myself."

I glanced at Leah. She was watching me with a stunned expression, but I was pretty sure I detected amusement.

"Well, there's no need for that kind of language!" Napkin Lady acted put out. Her arms fluttered around, and she reminded me of the chickens. "You really have no cause to speak to us like that! Maybe you don't know this, but I'm good friends with your Aunt Camilla."

"My *who?*" I nearly asked, then realized that must be Leah's mom. "You should be ashamed of yourselves," I said. "The two of you coming here and trying to strong-arm Leah. You guys are acting like a couple of assholes. Is that really who you want to be?"

By that point they were both climbing back into their minivan in a huff. They didn't respond to my words, but I knew they heard me.

After they drove off, I turned to Leah, who had a funny little smile on her face. "My mom's going to kill me when she finds out about this."

I shrugged. "Just blame it all on your cousin Friedrich."

CHAPTER SEVENTEEN

~Leah~

J osh seemed bewildered. "Of all the names you could have chosen, why the hell did you pick Friedrich?"

"It's from that night when I first saw you, when I was hiding."

His brows shot up. "You thought I looked like a *Friedrich*?" There was an expression on his face that wasn't quite horror.

I laughed. It felt good to laugh, especially after the stress of dealing with Linda. Josh was right. She brought that guy, Cal, here so the two of them could pressure me. "It's because you were quoting Nietzsche."

"I was?"

"The one about dancing every day at least once."

He stroked his beard. "I do remember that." He was eyeing me thoughtfully. "You recognized it, huh?"

"Of course."

"Have you read Nietzsche?"

I nodded. "When I was in college. I was into philosophy for a while."

"I never went to college."

I smiled. "Guess you were too busy fulfilling your destiny of being a rock star."

"I suppose. Except I don't believe in destiny.

"You don't?"

He shook his head. "The idea that things are predetermined? Nah, I don't believe that."

We went to find Damian and tell him it was time for lunch. He was over by the barn, playing with two of my cats, pulling a rope on the ground while they chased it.

He brought me over to show the bins of chicken feed, and I complimented him on his work. "Excellent job. You didn't spill any."

He grinned. "It wasn't that hard. Though I gave Agnes extra since she was staying beside me."

I'd noticed that Agnes had taken a shine to Damian. She was a friendly bird, and one of my favorites. "I think Agnes wants you to be her new sweetheart," I teased, and he rolled his eyes.

Luckily, Cary Grant was keeping his distance and didn't seem inclined to attack Josh again, though I noticed he was still watching him. Very odd.

For lunch, I made peanut butter and jelly sandwiches and got started with the ingredients for chili tonight in the pressure cooker.

"I guess this is probably a lot less fancy than what you're used to," I said, watching Josh take a bite of his sandwich.

He shook his head as he swallowed. "Why do you keep saying that?"

"Because I'm sure it's true."

Damian was eating his sandwich but asked me if he could have Nutella instead of jelly next time.

"Sure. I'll grab a jar when I go into town tomorrow."

"You act like I was born with a silver spoon in my mouth," Josh said. "Is that what you think?"

I took a bite of my sandwich and shrugged. "I guess it's because you're rich and famous, so I assume your life is glamorous."

He snorted. "You can see how glamorous it is. I've been chased from my own home."

I was chopping peppers and nearly sliced my finger at his words. The weight of my guilt, which I'd conveniently forgotten about all day, came rushing back. "You're right. I shouldn't make assumptions."

"Hell, I've been poor," he went on. "Dirt poor. My brother and I used to think Ritz crackers were a delicacy. We'd eat them with our pinkies sticking out like we were royalty."

"I like Ritz crackers," Damian said. "And *nobody* sticks out their pinkies when they eat. It isn't proper."

"Is that so?" Josh stuck out both pinkies as he took a bite of his sandwich. "You mean like this?"

Damian and I laughed.

He took another bite and chewed, still holding his sandwich in a prissy way. "What's so funny?" he asked, perplexed. He reached for his glass of water and took a sip, still sticking a pinky out at a perpendicular angle. "It makes the food taste better."

"You look like a tosser," Damian said.

"Perhaps I am one."

"Or maybe a Friedrich," I said.

Josh chuckled. "Guess I'm one of those too." He ate another bite of his sandwich, still acting silly. "You two should try it. You don't know what you're missing."

I put my knife down and picked up half of my sandwich. I stuck my pinky out and took a bite. "Wow, it really makes a difference. This sandwich tastes like champagne and strawberries."

Damian was shaking his head. "That makes no sense at all."

Josh nodded toward me with approval. "Leah's got the right idea."

"Come on," I said. "Maybe your peanut butter and jelly will taste like fancy chocolates."

Finally, Damian picked up his sandwich with both hands and stuck his pinkies out. He had a grin on his face while he bit into it.

"How is it?" Josh asked.

"It tastes mega. You were right."

"See? I told you."

After finishing out sandwiches with our pinkies out, I told them I needed to open the second pasture gate for my alpacas to come back to the barn and then planned to weed in my garden. "You guys don't have to keep helping," I said. "Don't feel obligated just because you're staying here."

"We want to help, don't we?" Josh said, looking at Damian, who was nodding enthusiastically.

"Okay, but prepare yourselves. You might be sore tonight."

I took them out to the first pasture, which was still green but grazed down enough that I'd begun using the second one for my girls. As we walked toward the gate, I explained a bit about the grasses alpacas and llamas ate and how they were environmentally friendly animals and didn't pull out the plants by the root but grazed on the surface.

Damian was goofing around, walking backward, while Josh looked warily toward the chicken coop. I realized I was boring them to death.

"See that gate down there?" I asked Damian.

He nodded. "I see it."

"I'll race you!" Then I took off running. Luckily, I'd put sneakers on before we left the house.

"Hey!" I could hear him shouting behind me.

I ran fast, but not too fast, and glanced back to see Damian approaching on my right. For a while we ran side by side. He kept a nice even pace and was saving himself for a burst once we were closer to the gate. The kid had good instincts. I even pondered letting him win but decided that wouldn't do him any favors.

As we got closer, he pushed himself ahead of me, and I let myself run faster too. I passed Damian easily and reached the gate well before he did.

"You beat me!" He seemed shocked. "Nobody ever beats me!"

"You're fast, but so am I. Plus, I'm experienced." I rested my hands on my hips as we stood there catching our breaths.

"I'm the fastest runner in my class."

"I believe it. You have natural talent." I held my hand up. "Don't clench your fists when you run, okay? Pretend you're holding an egg." I put my hand on my abdomen. "You want the power to come from your core."

As I was giving Damian more pointers, Josh came strolling up to us. "You guys looked good, but I didn't get a chance to race. Are you ready for another match?" He rubbed his hands together with a mischievous grin, eyeing me up and down. "You're pretty fast," he said. "For a girl."

"You *didn't* just say that."

He continued to grin. "Let's see if you can beat *me*."

"Bring it on."

"Are you racing, Little D?" Josh asked. "Or maybe you should stay and be the referee to make sure Leah doesn't cheat."

"Cheat? I don't cheat!"

"You'll notice if she tries to trip me or elbow me in the stomach, won't you?" He gave Damian a wink. "I want it to go on record."

I scoffed. "I won't need to do you bodily harm because you'll be too busy eating my dust."

He gave me a smug smile. "Big talk for a girl, but we'll see about that."

We decided to race down to the second fence post. Damian agreed to referee, which mainly comprised him saying, "On your mark... get set... go!"

Josh and I took off running. At first he was ahead of me, and I let him, figuring he could use up some of his reserve. After the halfway point, I sped up so we were neck and neck. It didn't surprise me he could run. He was obviously in great shape.

We stayed at an even pace, but as we got closer to the fence post, I let myself fly. I got there a solid four seconds before he did.

"Damn, you *are* fast," he said, laughing as he came up to the fence. He put his hand on it and took a minute to catch his breath.

I told him how I used to run track and then later marathons.

"That explains it. Now that I think about it, it was probably just luck that you beat me."

"Luck!" I acted indignant. "I don't think so."

"Yep, it was definitely luck," he teased, grinning at me.

I shook my head. Josh's cheeks were flushed, and it was difficult not to notice how gorgeous he was. His eyes matched the color of the sky. My gaze went to the Beaver Kings T-shirt, admiring the muscular body beneath it.

"I think we need another race," he said. "Let's see if you can still beat me *then*."

I laughed out loud. He had a way of tickling my funny bone. "What are you going to do? Keep racing me until I'm so tired that you win? As you may recall, this was my second race and only your first."

He scoffed. "That sounds like something only a loser would say."

"I'm not a loser. I just beat you!"

"But that was luck."

"Aaargh! Is it okay if I strangle you first?"

"Sure, honey. You can do *whatever* you want."

And there it was. That silky baritone. Those flirtatious blue eyes. My stomach dipped. I wish I could say I was immune to it, but I wasn't.

We raced again, and this time we both arrived to meet Damian at the same time.

"I'm pretty sure I won that," Josh said. "You were trailing way behind. It was pitiful, actually."

"You *wish*." I swallowed and bent over at the waist for a moment to recover. I was really pushing myself, but it felt good.

He had his hands on his hips and was pacing to cool down. "I don't *wish* anything. I know when I'm the winner, and I won."

I snorted. "In your crazy dreams, Friedrich."

"Leah's right, Dad," Damian said with a grin. "It was definitely a tie."

Josh grabbed his chest and pretended to be wounded. "What? Now my own son is against me?" He gave an elaborate mock sigh, then shrugged. "I guess we'll just have to race again."

"So that's your plan?" I said. "Race me until I'm dead from exhaustion."

"No loser talk. Are we racing again or what?"

I rolled my eyes, but like an idiot, I agreed. This time Damian raced with us. And, of course, this time Josh won.

"Congratulations," I said, panting as I rested against the fence. "You finally beat me. You win."

"Damn straight, I did. And to think it *only* took me three tries." He high-fived Damian. "Awesome job, dude."

After that, we did a few more races. Josh and I were so wiped that Damian won them all. He was delighted. I collapsed on the grass near the second pasture gate.

By that point a small group of my girls had gathered by the fence, watching us run. "Hey, girls," I called out.

They hummed in response.

Josh and Damian collapsed on the grass next to me.

"I wish I'd brought some water," I said. "I'm parched."

"Do they always make that sound?" Damian asked, rolling onto his stomach to watch them.

I nodded. "They're humming. It's how they communicate. They do it with each other and also with people."

He seemed to consider this. "So it's like they're talking?"

"It is. They make lots of other sounds too. They cluck, which is mostly friendly or sometimes concerned, and snort when they're irritated. They have warning calls, and if they get very upset, they scream."

He looked at me with wide eyes. "Have you ever heard them scream?"

"Only once. When they were sheared in May, Jade screamed the whole time." I felt sick at the memory, even though she was fine afterward. "It's a terrible sound."

"Does shearing hurt them?" Josh asked.

"Not at all. And it's over quick. The guys I hired did a great job."

Damian turned to me. "Do you have to shear them? Maybe they don't like it."

"You do have to shear them. What you're seeing now is them practically naked. They grow a lot of wool. It's very thick and heavy. It keeps them warm in the winter, but by spring, it's uncomfortable and can make them sick if you don't remove it."

He nodded, accepting this, and turned back to watching the alpacas.

"Hey, what are they doing?" Damian asked, sitting up. "They're running around and hopping in the air."

I turned my head back a little to see and smiled. "They're pronking."

"It looks like fun. Like they're playing!"

Josh rolled onto his stomach beside me and was watching them too. "I'd say they're definitely partying it up."

"They are," I acknowledged. "They do it sometimes for fun or before they go to sleep at night."

Damian jumped up and began skipping around the pasture, hopping in the air in imitation.

I laughed. "I think you're turning into an alpaca. Maybe they'll adopt you into the herd."

He went over by the fence to watch them more closely.

I tucked my arm beneath my head and turned back to gaze at the sky. White clouds feathered across the blue. I thought of how days like this would never have happened in my old life. I could never take a break in the middle of the afternoon to run outside and play.

As I lay there, I grew very aware of Josh beside me. He was still on his stomach, watching the alpacas and Damian over by the fence. His body was close, like the summer air.

"It's really relaxing here," he said. "Peaceful."

I took a breath and tried to find my center, but excitement stirred in me.

"So, what other philosophers have you read?" he asked, turning on his side. The scent of his sweat drifted over, and it smelled good.

I tried to bury this attraction to him, bury it deep, but it was hard. I couldn't remember the last time I'd felt such acute lust. My eyes went to his elegant fingers. He wasn't wearing as many rings as before, just a chunky silver one with a tiger's eye. I imagined those fingers touching me. "I've read Sartre and Simone de Beauvoir," I said, plucking the two from memory.

He nodded with approval. "Existentialism."

"Some Plato and Aristotle."

"The classics."

I moved onto my side so we were facing each other. "I've always really liked *Candide* by Voltaire. I think it still has meaning today with people blindly forcing reality to fit their idealism, even when it's false."

He stroked his beard. "I agree. It has relevance in a number of ways. Have you read any Hobbes or Locke?"

"Just a little. I also read some Schopenhauer, but it was hard going."

He chuckled. "Yeah, it's not easy to read. Did you get anything out of it?"

I thought about it. "Not much. Just that we live our lives chasing one want after another."

He gazed out at the pasture. "What do you think of that notion? Is it true? Do we spend our lives chasing *desire*?" His voice lowered.

Lying in the soft grass with him, sharing this moment, I was captured by desire. I should have gotten up or done something, but instead I let myself remain captured.

"Desire is a powerful thing," he continued. "It's a powerful motivator, and I often wonder if it's something that can be separated from our most basic self."

He went on talking about philosophy and desire, and I tried to listen. I did. Normally I enjoyed philosophical discourse, but I was too caught up in the dizzying spiral of my own desire. I understood how Josh enthralled millions of people all over the world. Everything seemed brighter when he was near. Electric. I took in the whole picture—the long hair, the tattoos, that bad boy mystique—and realized there was a lot going on beneath the surface. Behind all that glitz and glam was a fine mind.

His hand rested near me, and without thinking, I reached over and touched the tiger's eye on his ring.

He stopped talking.

I stroked the stone. "It's so cool. I wasn't expecting that."

"What were you expecting?" He kept his hand still for me. His tone wasn't the usual flirtatious one but something deeper.

"I thought it would feel warm because it looks like a flame."

He leaned toward me. "Only some flames burn you." I felt his gaze on me then, so intimate. The way he took in my face. I could barely breathe. The pull toward him was powerful, and I knew this was his thing. He was like gravity, drawing people into his orbit.

I swallowed, and though it wasn't easy, I turned away. I couldn't do this. I'd walked this path before, and I wasn't going to walk it again.

CHAPTER EIGHTEEN

~Leah~

After weeding in the garden, we each took turns showering. I had mine first because they both insisted, "Ladies first." Damian took his next, and then Josh went last. I was in the kitchen, making corn bread for the chili and chatting with Shane, who'd just gotten home, while Damian played video games in the living room.

I'd just gotten the cornbread in the oven when Josh came strolling into the kitchen fresh from his shower. He wore a pair of clean jeans and nothing else. My eyes wandered over his sculpted torso, trying not to stare.

When he walked up to me, he came close enough that—weirdly—I thought he was going to kiss me. *What? Why? Who?* I was so confused and blinded by lust, I nearly put my hand on his shoulder, but it turned out he was only reaching for a water glass.

After he got some water and stood in the kitchen talking to Shane, I discreetly checked him out. I couldn't help myself. He had one of those "just right" muscular bodies. Lean with the perfect amount of bulk. His skin was smooth, with a scattering of light hair on his chest and a tan that was fading. There were a bunch of tattoos —various images, but a surprising number of areas inscribed with words. I wanted to move closer, glide my fingers over his skin, and read them all. Read him like a book. There was a sun on his right pectoral, and when he turned for a moment to get more water, I saw a huge, intricate lion on his back covering his right shoulder.

A Leo. I remembered that.

I didn't have much ink myself. A crescent moon on my ankle and a yin-yang symbol on my upper back that I'd gotten in college. I'd since thought about getting a skein of yarn or a spinning wheel but hadn't gotten around to it.

Josh pulled his phone out. "Dean just texted me a video link and said we all need to watch it." He glanced up. "Let me grab my computer."

He returned with a sleek MacBook and Damian. He set the computer up on the kitchen counter, and the four of us watched a YouTube video open. A female newscaster's voice said, *"... fans all over the world were reeling from the surprise breakup of the popular band East Echo..."* The video showed Josh's house and a slew of reporters camped out in front of those familiar black gates.

I felt sick to my stomach seeing it.

As the newscaster stood in front of the gate still talking, you could hear some weird clanking noise in the background. Some guy was loudly singing "99 Bottles of Beer." It confused me at first, but then the video zoomed in, and we could see it was Dean dragging a bat along the metal fence as he sang in a booming voice. Occasionally he stopped, and when a reporter asked him a question, he held up his index finger, opened his mouth like he was going to answer, but then started singing again. For his grand finale, he stood in front of the main gate, dropped his pants, and mooned everyone. On his butt cheeks, written in black magic marker, were the words FUCK YOU.

At the sight of this, Josh and Damian howled with laughter.

The camera in the video tried to quickly pull away, fumbling, but Dean's pale ass with his message hung out there for all the world to see.

"Awesome! Who is that?" Shane asked, cracking up. Josh explained it was their band's drummer and one of his best friends.

"Dean was totally brilliant," Damian said, still laughing.

"That crazy bastard." Josh wiped his eyes. "That *was* brilliant."

"So, I take it Dean is still at the house?" I asked.

Josh nodded. "He and his girlfriend, Nalla, are staying there. He said he wanted to torture the press. I should have known he'd come up with something good."

My brows went up with surprise. "Nalla is Dean's girlfriend?" My eyes went back to the screen, which was frozen on Dean's FUCK YOU butt cheeks.

Josh was watching me. "What? You don't like Nalla?"

I didn't know what to say, except that Dean deserved better. "I guess I don't really know her very well."

He nodded, but it was obvious he'd noticed my distaste.

———

THE NEXT DAY, after my run and morning chores, the three of us piled into my truck and headed into town. Josh wore jeans, one of Shane's plain gray T-shirts, a safety vest, and an empty tool belt. It was meant to be a disguise. There was also an extra hard hat Shane loaned him sitting on the back seat next to Damian.

"So, how do you feel?" I asked Josh once we were on the highway. "Like a construction worker?"

He glanced down at his outfit. "More like a member of the Village People."

"You look real enough."

"Do I?" Josh turned to me, his expression deadpan, and then, without warning, he burst out singing "Macho Man."

It caught me off guard. I glanced back at Damian, who was grinning and already clapping his hands to the beat. Clearly, he was used to this sort of thing.

Josh sounded fantastic. Big surprise there, but it was jarring to be reminded of his talent, like I'd somehow forgotten who he was.

He kept singing. It was a warm sunny day, so we had the windows rolled down. Damian and I both joined in when he sang the chorus.

It felt like a party. Like we were celebrating life.

Josh moved to the rhythm. Occasionally he slid a hand down his torso and gave me an eye smolder. He was only joking around, but it was strangely arousing.

When the song finished Damian and I clapped and hooted.

"How do you even know the lyrics to that?" I asked Josh.

"You'd be surprised how many songs I know the lyrics to."

"Let's do another one," Damian said from the back seat. "How about Queen?"

Josh chuckled. "You don't want to hear any East Echo?" He glanced at me. "You probably don't know this, but Damian is a *huge* Queen fan."

"I'd *love* to hear some East Echo," I blurted. "How about 'Ritual of You' or 'Silver Days'?" I felt giddy at even the thought of hearing Josh sing those songs. "'Silver Days' is actually my favorite."

"No, I want to hear *Queen!*" Damian said from the back.

Josh grinned. "And did I mention he's a bigger Queen fan than an East Echo fan?"

"Let's flip for it," I said, unwilling to give up that easily. "Do either of you have a coin?"

"I think I might." Josh pulled out his wallet that connected to a chain on his belt loop.

As he sifted through it, a part of this felt surreal. Was I really going to hear Josh sing one of my favorite East Echo songs from the passenger seat of my truck?

Once he found a quarter, Damian called heads, and when Josh flipped it, unfortunately, I lost.

"Sorry, Leah," he said, then turned behind him. "All right, Little D, which Queen song am I singing?"

"'Don't Stop Me Now,'" Damian said immediately.

Josh grinned at me. "That's *his* favorite."

I loved Queen, too, so it wasn't like this was a tragedy, but still.

I felt Josh's gaze on me. "I'll sing 'Silver Days' for you sometime."

"You *will*?" I tried not to gawk.

"Of course. Just remind me."

He began to sing "Don't Stop Me Now," and, no surprise, it sounded amazing. Different from Freddie Mercury, but very cool, and with his own style. When I glanced over at Josh, he had his hand in front of himself, his fingers dancing through the air as he sang.

Once the song picked up in tempo, I heard Damian join in, bouncing around with his seat belt on. I sang, too, and by the time we arrived downtown, the three of us were dancing in our seats as we sang our hearts out.

We finished the last verse just as I pulled into a parking spot in front of the post office.

"Wow, perfect timing," I said, glancing over at Josh. "That sounded incredible. If you ever need a side hustle, you could always join a Queen tribute band."

"I'll keep it in mind."

We got out of the truck, and I gathered my packages from the back seat. "Do you want the hard hat?" I asked him, holding it up.

"Nah." Josh was standing on the sidewalk, adjusting the tool belt and the neon vest. "Leave it. I'm not sure I want to carry it around." He gave me a wry grin before slipping on his sunglasses. "I *might* start to feel ridiculous."

The three of us walked into the post office. Damian was in front of me, looking like an average kid with jeans and a striped T-shirt. His shoulder-length hair was the only thing kind of unusual about him. Luckily, there was no line. I recognized the woman, Jennifer, at the counter since I came here every week.

She smiled and asked how my day was going, though I could see her watching Josh, who had wandered over to examine the stamps for sale on the wall.

"It's been good," I said.

"Is that your boyfriend?" she whispered, still staring at him. "He's cute." This was one of the bad things about living in a small town. Everybody felt entitled to know everything about you. "I don't think I've ever seen him in here before."

I didn't want to lie to people and almost told her he was a friend.

"Actually, he looks sort of familiar." She was still studying him. "Is he new in town?"

"He's my cousin from Seattle."

Damian came over and stood next to me. He glanced around as if he'd never been inside an American post office, which he probably hadn't.

"You can take a sucker if you want," Jennifer said to him with a smile.

He looked at her.

She picked up the jar filled with candy, still smiling, and offered it to him. "Go on, take one. Don't be shy."

He brightened. "Thank you." He reached for a grape Tootsie Pop. "That's very kind of you." Except I saw her give him a double take. I realized it was his accent. He may look like a normal kid, but that English accent wasn't normal—not in Truth Harbor, anyway.

"Well, we'd better get going!" I said. "Lots of errands to run." I called over to Josh, "Come on, Friedrich!"

Once we were outside again, Josh wanted to stop at the truck and drop off his tool belt. "It's too much wearing this," he said, tossing it in the back seat. "Also, I want to be called Diesel from now on, or maybe Fang."

"Fang? What are you, my vampire cousin?"

"I need a name that has some badassery to it."

"Sorry, Friedrich, but we have bigger problems than that. Damian's accent is going to give him away every time he opens his mouth." I looked over at Damian, who was licking his sucker while examining a parking meter. "Can you speak with an American accent?" I asked him.

He looked at me like I was crazy. "Why would I ever want to do that?"

"So people don't guess who you are."

His eyebrows rose. "Oh." He paused and tilted his head. "I suppose I could try."

We headed down the sidewalk while I attempted to coach Damian on how to speak English with an American accent. I gave him a few sentences to repeat. Apparently it wasn't easy, and he kept turning it into a mangled Southern accent.

Josh shook his head, skeptical of the whole thing. "He sounds like a cowboy on crack."

"Can you say, 'I drink water every day'?" I asked Damian.

He repeated it slowly and then faster, but every time it sounded Southern, except strange and chewed up.

"I take it back," Josh said. "He sounds like a cowboy who's been kicked in the head by his horse too many times."

By that point the we were cracking up as Damian hopped down the sidewalk repeating, "I driiink waaater evereee daaay," in the worst exaggerated American accent possible.

"Hmm," I said. "Maybe it's best if you stick with being English after all."

As we wandered through town, we stopped in a couple of stores —a comic bookstore and a store called Treasure Chest with all sorts of fun odds and ends. Josh tried on a pair of glasses that gave him huge crossed eyes. All three of us put them on and took selfies together. A variety of soaps and lotions were for sale with names like "Butt Cleanser" and "Velvet Vagina." I nearly bought a pair of Wonder Woman socks that had a cape on the back.

"Uh-oh, I think you need this, Leah." Josh held up a book. On closer inspection I saw it was a knitting how-to using the hair that cats shed.

"Is that for real?" I laughed and took it from him. After flipping through it, I could see that it was, indeed, for real.

We kept browsing the store. I was glad we'd come inside. What a treasure trove.

When I looked through the voodoo dolls section, something caught my eye.

"Oh my gosh. I *have* to get this for you," I told Josh.

"What is it?" He came up and stood behind me. We were alone together in a small alcove.

When I turned around to show him, he was right there. So close. My pulse jumped. I should have backed away, or he should have, but neither of us moved.

I took a deep breath, inhaling his scent. "Lemongrass," I murmured. "That's what you always smell like."

"It's my soap. A friend of mine makes it." He considered me. "Do you like it?"

"I do."

He took a step closer and leaned down, putting his face near my neck, not quite touching me. My breath caught. I closed my eyes as a dizzying wave of desire swept over me.

"Mmm, you smell good too," he whispered in my ear. "Coconuts."

I was out of my depth. Way out. The waters were closing in.

He pulled back, and we gazed at each other while my stomach did cartwheels.

What a terrible mistake this attraction was, but what could I do? I was a mere mortal dealing with a rock god. Though that wasn't the whole story. Let's face it—I'd be attracted to Josh if he was pumping gas at the corner station.

"So, what is it you want to buy me?" he asked in a low voice.

I held up the small doll so it was right next to my face, and he burst out laughing.

It was a Sasquatch.

His teeth flashed white as he smiled with approval. "Looks like I have my own action figure."

"Apparently you do."

In that moment, Damian came up to us. He said he'd found some items he'd like to buy as gifts. "These are for Mum." He held up some earrings that looked like coffee cups with lids on them. "And these are for Granny." He showed us some women's socks that had pictures of teacups all over them.

Josh studied them both. "Nice job, Little D. I think they'll like those a lot."

He grinned. "Mum is always drinking coffee, and Granny is always drinking tea!"

We went over to the cash register, which was manned by a young guy in his twenties. Josh paid for the gifts, along with a deck of magic cards, juggling balls, and a few other items Damian wanted. There was also the book he'd shown me earlier.

"Are you buying that for me?" I asked.

"I am," he said. "I'm looking forward to that sweater you'll be knitting me with cat hair."

The guy behind the register kept staring at Josh. "Dude, do I know you?"

"Nah, I don't think we've met."

"You sure? Because you look familiar."

"Pretty sure."

I stepped up next to Josh. "This is my cousin, Friedrich," I said to the guy behind the register. "He's from Germany. Have you ever heard of the Ironman Triathlon?"

The guy nodded. "I sure have. Damn, dude, did you win that?"

"No, he didn't win that," I said. "But he won the Bigfoot Marathon, which is almost as famous."

The guy seemed confused. "I don't think I've ever heard of that one."

"Well, he came in last place, but *we* still consider him a winner." I patted Josh's shoulder and could feel him shaking beside me with either fury or laughter. "We're hoping by the third race he finally wins it for real. Fingers crossed!"

Once we paid for our stuff and were back on the sidewalk, Josh turned to me. "*Last* place? You couldn't have said *first* place?"

"But you *were* last place, remember? *I* was first place."

"Also, I want to be called Bruno. Or Talon. I'd be happy with either of those."

I sniffed. "The name Friedrich has plenty of badassery. Are you guys forgetting Freddie Mercury?"

Damian and Josh stopped walking.

"What?"

"Freddie Mercury's real name was Farrokh Bulsara," Damian informed me.

I tilted my head. "Are you sure?"

Josh grinned. "We're sure."

We walked past a store that sold nothing but cozy sweaters, and I wavered at the door.

"You want to buy a sweater when it's this warm out?" Josh asked.

I sighed. "I've been trying to figure out a way to get to know the owner. It would be cool if her knitters used my yarn."

Josh nodded but was looking around at all the street decorations. "Is it my imagination, or is there an inordinate amount of pirate stuff here?"

I gave him a strange look and laughed.

"What's so funny?"

"You really don't know?"

"Know what?"

"We're a pirate town."

He appeared confused, so I explained to him how Truth Harbor once had a lot of pirate activity. "Some people say pirates built this place. That's our thing. There's even a pirate museum."

Josh seemed amazed and delighted. "Damn, seriously? I sure chose the right place to buy a house."

"You really had no idea?"

He shook his head. "But it suits me just fine. In that case, I should be Captain Razor Blade. Just call me Razor for short."

I rolled my eyes. "Give it up, Friedrich."

Damian's face lit up as he saw something across the street. "Is that a sweets shop? Can we get some chocolate?"

Uh-oh.

The shop he was talking about—Scallywag Sweets—was owned by Delores. She was a good friend of my mom's and also the town's biggest gossip.

CHAPTER NINETEEN

~Leah~

I wanted to stop them from going into Scallywag Sweets, but Damian had already grabbed Josh's arm and was pulling him across the street. I dragged myself behind them, hoping Delores wasn't working today.

The two of them entered the shop, and I was immediately surrounded by the sugary smell of candy.

The place was a paradise for kids or any person with a sweet tooth. There was a display case with chocolate truffles, caramels, and fudge. Jars lined the walls filled with colorful sweets like gummy bears and taffy.

There were a few people inside, and unfortunately, Delores was manning the counter.

She waved at me, and I waved back. Josh and Damian were already busy browsing. I wandered around, looking at the various displays. Damian had gotten a small shopping basket and was filling it with candy.

"Slow down, Little D," Josh said. "We're not buying the whole store." Though Josh was putting more stuff into the basket than Damian was. "Gummy worms. Damn, I love those. I'd better get some gummy colas for Dean too. What can I get you?" he asked me.

I shook my head. "I'm fine."

He gave me a look. "I'm going to get you something anyway, so you might as well tell me what you like."

"All right, fine. I'm partial to the rocky road fudge."

Damian struggled to open one of the jars filled with taffy, and Josh went over to help him.

By that point the store had cleared out, and I walked up to the display case. Delores smiled at me as she put some items away. "It's good to see you, Leah. How is your mom? I need to call her soon."

"She's fine." I asked after her family, and we chatted a bit. Her son was a lawyer in Seattle now, but we went to high school together.

Josh and Damian came and stood next to me with their basket of sweets. "We *must* get some chocolates as well," Damian said. "Perhaps I should buy some for Mum and Granny."

Delores seemed puzzled. She took in both of them and then looked at me. "Are you three together?"

"We are," I said. "This is—" I was going to say "a friend of mine," but Josh spoke up.

"I'm her cousin Friedrich, but you can call me *Spike*." He gave me a smug smile, daring me to argue.

I wanted to tell him it didn't matter.

"Cousin?" Delores was confused. She'd known my mom since second grade and knew all my cousins. All two of them. Both female.

She glanced at us, then focused on Josh. He had his sunglasses on top of his head and stood there all sexy with his blond hair and colorful ink, and despite wearing that neon safety vest, he still managed to look glamorous.

"Oh my goodness." She sucked in her breath. "You're that singer, aren't you? The one everyone is making a fuss about."

I groaned.

Josh's brows shot up to his hairline.

Damian was pointing at the display case. "Could we get some of the chocolate fudge?" he asked her. "And some truffles as well?"

"You certainly can, young man," she said, moving over to where he was pointing. She asked him what flavors he wanted and began pulling out the trays for them. I heard her asking him where he was from, and he told her England.

Josh looked at me.

"Delores is a good friend of my mom's," I explained.

Damian turned to us. "Shall we get some fudge for Dean and Nalla?" he asked his dad.

"Definitely. Pick out whatever you think they'd like."

Eventually the candy was on the counter, and Delores began ringing it all up. "Is it true you bought a house here in Truth Harbor?" she asked Josh.

"It is."

"How long do you plan to stay?"

He stroked his beard. "To be honest, my plans were to settle here for a long while. I've never owned a house before."

Delores stopped what she was doing and stared at him. "Really?"

Even I was staring at Josh. How was that possible?

He explained how he'd always rented or lived with someone. "I moved here because I wanted to have a real home for the first time in my life." He glanced down at Damian. "A place for me and my son."

Delores's face softened. "Well, of course you do. Truth Harbor is a wonderful place to live and raise a family. Everyone deserves that."

"It's been difficult with all the press. They've been hounding me and won't leave us alone."

I saw her expression change to concern. "I've heard those reporters are parked right in front of your house and that they even have helicopters flying overhead."

"It's true. They even have drones spying on us. We've basically become prisoners." He shook his head. "Damian and I had to sneak out through the woods so they wouldn't see us."

"That's terrible." She glanced down at Damian. "No one should have to live that way, even if you are famous. It's not right."

Josh met her eyes. "I'd appreciate it if you wouldn't tell anyone you saw me here in town, especially not with Leah."

She nodded. "Oh, don't worry. I won't say a word."

"Thank you, Delores."

"And don't you worry about anything else either. We take care of our own around here." She smiled and winked at him. "You're one of us now, Spike."

———

"DO you think Delores will tell anyone she saw me?" Josh asked later as we were driving back home. I'd finished my last errand of buying groceries—which Josh insisted on paying for. I tried to argue, but he wouldn't take no for an answer and handed the cashier a hundred-dollar bill before I could stop him. "Your cousin, Viper, is really generous," the cashier had said with a smile.

"I think Delores is going to tell everyone in town that she saw you in her sweets shop," I said. "She's the biggest gossip I know."

"Really? *Fuck.*" He rubbed his brow in frustration. "I'm sorry, Leah. Damian and I will leave immediately."

"What?" I felt jolted at the thought of them leaving already and realized I enjoyed having them around. "Why do you need to leave?"

"Because the vultures will be circling your house by nightfall. Once they realize we're not there, hopefully they'll go away quickly."

"Oh." I waved my hand. "Don't worry about that. There's no way Delores will tell anyone you were with *me*."

"She won't?"

"Not a chance." *Although she'll probably tell my mom. That's going to be an interesting conversation.* I was surprised I hadn't heard from her about that fiasco with Linda yesterday. "Like I said before, she's a good friend of our family's. Plus, you heard what she said—you're one of us now."

"What did she mean by that?"

"It means she's got your back. In fact, she's a good person to have on your side. She's really popular and knows everybody."

He stroked his beard in contemplation. "I feel like I'm learning how to live in a new culture."

I laughed. "Small towns are definitely their own culture."

Shane showed up for dinner, and then afterward, Damian called his grandmother in England. I could hear him teasing her about the gifts he got her, and that she'd just have to "wait and see" what they were. He was a great kid, and I had to admit I'd grown really fond of him.

I sat in the living room with everyone and knitted. By nine o'clock my eyes were closing, and I announced I was going to bed. Shane and Damian were playing video games, dipping into the open bags of candy on the coffee table, while Josh was doing something on his computer.

I was so tired that I basically fell asleep when my head hit the pillow.

When I woke up, my room was dark, and I felt disoriented. I'd been having a sexy dream about Josh biting my neck and insisting I call him Fang.

I wasn't sure what woke me, but then I heard it. Cary Grant. He was giving a distress call.

Shit! I jerked up in bed.

Fumbling around in the dark for my jeans, I shoved my legs into them, then checked the time. It was just after midnight.

Cary Grant gave another distress call. By the time I made my way downstairs, I was in a full panic.

The living room light was still on, and Josh was awake. He was dressed and still on his computer but got up when he saw me. "I take it that's not a good sound."

I quickly pulled my hair into a ponytail. "It means there's some kind of predator out there messing with my chickens." I glanced at the couch. Shane was lying on it, fast asleep. "You know, you can kick my brother out if you need to go to bed."

"I wasn't sleepy yet. I'm used to staying up late."

I went to the hall closet and got out a flashlight and my shotgun, which I kept on a high shelf. Josh watched me but didn't say anything as I checked to make sure the gun was loaded. I wondered if I should wake up Shane, but he looked so peaceful. He'd been working so much overtime lately, and he probably needed his sleep.

"I'm coming with you," Josh said. "Let me just check on Damian."

"I can do it alone." But he was already walking off, so I waited.

Cary Grant had quieted, and I didn't know if that was a good or a bad sign.

Josh came back into the room. "He's sound asleep."

We both glanced at my brother and were thinking the same thing. Damian wouldn't be alone in the house.

"Let's go," he said, taking the flashlight from me.

I grabbed the house keys and locked the front door. Living in the city so many years had taught me to be cautious.

It was a beautiful night. Warm with a lush breeze. You could see a blanket of stars overhead.

We were both silent as we made our way toward the coop. When we were almost there, Cary Grant started his alarm call again.

"Shit!" I looked at Josh, and his eyes were wide. He put his finger to his lips, and I nodded. We crept up slowly. It was difficult to see anything since I hadn't fully adjusted to the dark yet, but I was certain I saw movement out there.

"I'm going to turn on the flashlight," he whispered.

A round spotlight shone on my chicken coop, illuminating the two large raccoons who were trying to break in like bank robbers.

"*Hey!* Get away from there!" I yelled.

The next few moments were pandemonium as Cary Grant

started crowing in alarm and the raccoons ran, tripping the motion detector lights. In the melee, they grew confused and, instead of running in the opposite direction, began running right toward us.

"Dammit!" I pulled my gun up, adrenaline bursting through me. Most people thought raccoons were cute, but I'd seen them get vicious.

I was ready to shoot when Josh threw something at them. I didn't know what it was at first, but there was a squeal, and it was obvious he'd hit one of them. When he shone the flashlight again, I could see it was the small metal bucket I used to feed my chickens. The raccoons were both running away from us toward the barn.

I put my gun down, relieved I didn't have to fire.

"Wow, that was close," I said, catching my breath. "I nearly shot one of them. They were coming right at us!"

"I know." He put his hand on his chest and grinned. "I have to admit my heart is pounding."

"Mine too. Did you see them? They were trying to open the door to the coop. I'm going to have to padlock it."

He nodded. "I saw it."

"I'm glad you threw that bucket. I'd rather not kill a raccoon if I don't have to."

"I hope you're not going to have a recurring problem."

I licked my dry lips. "Me either. We'll have to go check the barn, but first let me lock up the coop."

"Do raccoons kill and eat chickens?" he asked, walking over with me.

"They do. I had a terrible problem with them when I first moved in, and they slaughtered all my birds. They killed both of my neighbor's cats too."

He waited for me while I grabbed the padlock that I usually left open on the coop and made sure it was secure. I could hear some clucks from inside but nothing alarming, and Cary Grant had quieted —a good sign.

"I wonder why those motion detector lights didn't go on earlier," he said, surveying the area. "I'll check them for you tomorrow and see why they're malfunctioning."

We headed toward the barn. "At least they won't mess with my alpacas or llamas. Hopefully my cats are all hiding."

At the barn, Josh grabbed a pitchfork and helped me search for the raccoons, pushing aside bales of straw and looking into empty stalls. My alpacas were all crushed together outside. Phyllis and Alicia trotted over, and I introduced them to Josh.

He patted Phyllis's neck. "I heard you mention before that these are guard llamas."

"They protect the herd by chasing off predators." I peered around. "Hopefully the raccoons have taken off."

It was in that moment that I heard a creak above us in the hayloft.

We both looked up. It could just be the structure settling. Barns made all kinds of creaking noises—at least this one did, since it was made of wood.

"They probably aren't up there," I said. The hayloft looked like a black cave. "I should check it to be sure."

I decided it would be too awkward holding my gun. Josh and I both grabbed a short piece of lumber as protection. He still had the flashlight.

"I should go first," he said.

"There's no need to be chivalrous."

"I'm bigger and stronger than you, Leah. If they come at me, I'll have a better chance of fighting them off."

I couldn't argue with his logic. On the other hand, I didn't want him to get injured. "Just be careful. I don't want the whole world angry at me because their favorite singer is in the hospital."

He smiled, and his face took on that flirty expression. "Am I *your* favorite singer?"

"Maybe." I pretended indifference. "I suppose you're in the top one hundred."

He snorted. "I feel honored."

Josh started up the ladder, and I waited until he'd gone up a few rungs before following. When he got near the top rung, he stopped and clicked on the flashlight, shining it around. "I don't see any sign of them up here."

He continued climbing, and I followed, hoisting myself over the edge. The scent of dusty hay tickled my nose. There were piles of it all over the floor and bales stacked along the side. Josh was standing in the middle of the loft, shining the light around.

I stood up, but as I started walking toward him something snagged my foot. I tried to right myself, but before I knew it, I was stumbling forward.

"Aaah!" I gave a shriek and reached out, falling right on Josh, taking us both down onto a pile of hay. I heard him grunt when we landed.

Instantly we were plummeted into darkness. He must have dropped the flashlight, and it turned off.

For a moment neither of us moved or said anything. I was basically lying on top of him.

"Are you all right?" he asked.

"I'm really sorry. I tripped over something." My senses felt heightened in the dark. His smell was so near. He shifted his body beneath mine, large and muscular. I was enjoying the feel of him, and it took me a moment to realize I should get up. "I didn't hurt you, did I?" I asked.

"No." His voice sounded different. Deeper. "I'm not hurt."

I started to move away, but then his hand slid down my back and stopped me. I went still. Maybe it was the darkness emboldening me, but instead of moving off, I moved up so I was centered on top of him.

Both his hands were on me then, sliding down to my waist, resting on my hips. Neither of us spoke, but we were both breathing unsteadily.

"Leah," he said softly.

I brought a hand to his face. I couldn't see a thing, but I felt so many textures. Bristly, hard, and then soft as my fingers found his beard, jaw, and finally his mouth.

His grip on my hips tightened.

Maybe it was because we'd just escaped danger, or maybe it was the acute lust I'd been fighting for days, but I couldn't stop myself. I kissed him.

He immediately groaned, definitely on board, opening his mouth to me while his arms pulled me in closer.

Desire flooded my veins. *So good.* It was like denying myself a luscious dessert and finally tasting that first bite.

One of his hands cupped my ass, squeezing, while the other one held my back.

The first kiss turned into another with more tongue, the darkness somehow making it more intimate and exciting.

I explored the muscular planes of his body while we continued making out and moving against each other. His hands were all over me. Something hard and male pushed at my stomach, and I moaned into his mouth. This seemed to inflame him even more. Our hot breath mingled with the smell of hay, but then out of the blue, something changed.

Josh broke the kiss. "I can't," he said, panting against my cheek.

I blinked into the darkness with confusion. I hadn't expected this. "You can't?" I tried to catch my breath.

He swallowed. "I want to. *God,* you have no idea how much. But it's complicated."

Slowly, I sat up in a daze, still aroused. My whole body was sensitive, and my mouth felt swollen. I didn't know what to do. I attempted to get off him, but he stopped me, holding me in place. "I'm in the process of adopting Damian. I can't fuck that up." He began to tell me how Charlotte, his ex-girlfriend, has been holding this over his head for years, how if she got one whiff that he was involved with another woman, she'd stop the adoption.

I was quiet taking all this in. I'd assumed Damian was his biological son. It was clear Damian considered Josh his dad.

"If she's your ex-girlfriend, why would she care if you're with someone else? Can't you just do as you please?"

TRUTH ABOUT CATS & SPINSTERS   165

He blew his breath out. "I wish it were that simple. But it's not."

It was strange to be having this conversation in the dark, as I could barely see his face. I could hear the emotion in his voice, and this obviously meant a lot to him.

"I've been living like a monk for months without a problem," he went on. "And then I come here, and after only two days around *you*, I'm losing my mind."

I'd been losing my mind, too, but his admission woke me up. All the reasons I needed to stay away from Josh came rushing back.

"It's all right," I said. "We just had a moment of weakness. I can't get involved with you either." I could tell he wanted to know more, but I stopped the conversation. "We should probably get back to the house."

I lifted my body off his, and this time he let me go. I sat beside him. He sat up, too, but then leaned toward me, his hand groping my thigh.

I jumped, startled. "Hey, what are you doing?"

"Sorry." He chuckled softly. "I'm looking for the flashlight. I thought this is where I dropped it."

We both searched around in the hay. I discovered a long cylindrical object and pulled it out. "I found it."

I turned the light on, creating a spotlight on the bales stacked near us. I turned it toward him, and it felt strange to see each other. Almost like all that groping in the dark never happened.

He met my gaze. His pupils were huge. His eyes lowered to my mouth, and for a second it looked like he was going to kiss me.

He licked his bottom lip and abruptly turned. "We should head back now."

"We should," I agreed.

The corner of his mouth kicked up in a smile. "Guess there aren't any raccoons up here after all."

CHAPTER TWENTY

~Josh~

I needed a cold shower. Hell, I needed twenty cold showers. And maybe a stiff drink.

I could barely sleep all night. Just kept thinking about Leah upstairs in her bed, wondering if she was asleep or awake, if she was thinking about me at all. At least I didn't have to wonder what she felt like because now I knew.

Damn good.

That's how.

I couldn't believe we'd been going at it in the hayloft off all places. That hayloft was my favorite fantasy, and I had to turn it down.

Unbelievable.

I ground my palms into my eyes, trying to force sleep. Not that it mattered.

By morning light, I was exhausted. Cary Grant was crowing his heart out when I heard Leah slip past me for her run. I didn't say anything and kept my eyes shut, not wanting to see her in those shorts and that little sports bra. Though, at this point, she could wear a circus tent, and I'd still be in trouble.

I got up and considered making myself coffee. I rarely drank it since the caffeine wasn't good for my voice. Instead I settled for my usual warm water and honey.

Today was Saturday, but I discovered life on a farm didn't have weekends. At least not in the usual sense. It reminded me of being on the road, where even your days off were on. Animals had to be fed and cared for in the same way that lighting and sound equipment had to be moved.

While Damian fed the chickens, I checked the motion detector lights by the coop, trying to figure out why they hadn't worked correctly last night. After examining them, I realized the sensor was dirty. I cleaned it, and it worked right as rain.

Cary Grant was still stalking me. That bird hated my guts. He glared at me the whole time.

"I helped save your crazy ass last night," I told him. "The least you could do is thank me."

Leah and I had been avoiding each other all morning. Or mostly she was avoiding me, but I needed to keep my distance too.

I missed our banter. She was a lot of fun and never had any trouble keeping up with me or took my jokes the wrong way. It was something I'd had to be careful about with other women. They always took me too seriously.

I chuckled, thinking about her telling that guy yesterday that I came in last place in the Bigfoot Marathon. I'd nearly burst out laughing. She was quick on her feet, in more ways than one.

True to her badass self, she was neither impressed nor intimidated by me. I might have rattled her a little when I started singing "Macho Man." Luckily, it didn't take her long to get into the vibe.

Shane showed up for lunch, which was good since it helped ease some of the awkwardness between us. We ate tuna sandwiches and potato chips. Damian wanted to know if he could see the inside of Shane's RV.

"Sure," Shane said. "As long as your dad doesn't mind."

I shrugged. "I don't see a problem."

Leah swallowed a bite of food. "I wonder if you should clean it up a little first," she said to her brother with an amused expression. "Make sure none of your visitors have left anything behind."

Shane chuckled. "I'll make sure."

I assumed the visitors they were talking about were women. Leah had mentioned something about it the other day, calling her brother "girl crazy."

After lunch, I asked Leah if I could help her with anything, but she brushed me off. Damian left with Shane, so I sat alone on the front porch with my phone and answered the hundred messages I'd gotten over the last two days. I saw my brother, Jeremy, had tried to call and felt a wave of guilt. Nothing from my mom, of course—big surprise there. Nothing from Rhys either. It was mostly friends, promoters, and reporters. I texted or emailed a few people back. I wasn't much in the mood to talk to anyone.

I'd been at it for about an hour when I heard a car approaching. I glanced up and watched a small light green SUV park next to Leah's truck. A stocky woman with shoulder-length steel-gray hair got out. She wore slacks, a beige blouse, and a determined scowl.

She didn't seem to notice me at first but then paused when she got to the first porch step. We studied each other. There was something formidable about her, and I felt a strong urge to apologize, though I didn't know why or what for. I just assumed I was in trouble.

"You must be Friedrich—my long-lost nephew."

My brows went up, and I wasn't sure how to respond. Luckily, Leah came jogging over.

"Hi, Mom. I didn't know you were stopping by today."

The woman turned. "Hello, sweetheart."

They gave each other a brief hug. Leah was about the same height as her mom, but beyond that, they didn't look much alike.

Her mom nodded toward me. "Aren't you going to introduce me to your guest? It isn't every day I encounter a *rock star*." She used the term "rock star" in the same tone she might have used the word "scoundrel."

I noticed Leah's demeanor had shifted in front of her mom, and she seemed less the badass I knew, more unsure of herself. "This is Josh Trevant. He's one of my neighbors."

"*Just* a neighbor, huh?" Her mom came walking up the steps to me. She put her hand out, and I took it. She had a solid grip. Disconcertingly, her eyes were the same rich shade as Leah's. They didn't sparkle like Leah's, but were stern. "I'm Camilla."

"It's nice to meet you," I said.

She nodded. "So what exactly is going on here?" Her hard gaze moved between the two of us.

"Josh and his son, Damian, are staying here for a few days," Leah said.

The steel mama stared at me. "A hotel's not good enough for you? I'd think a *rock star* could afford the best."

"Mom!"

"A hotel is plenty good enough," I said. "But Leah here was kind enough to welcome us into her home."

The scowl was still there, but then her expression softened. "How old is your son?"

"Eleven."

"And where is he now?" She surveyed the area.

"Shane's giving him a tour of his RV."

I almost detected a smile but couldn't be sure. She went back to studying me. "Are you romantically involved with my daughter?"

Damn, this woman doesn't beat around the bush.

Leah and I glanced at each other.

"No," I said. "We're just friends."

"Good. Let's keep it that way."

I should have been offended, but instead I felt nostalgic. It had been a long time since someone told me to stay away from their daughter.

Leah let out a frustrated noise. "This is *too* much. I just told you Josh and Damian are my guests." She began to tell her mom about all our problems with the press, the helicopters, and the drones, and how no one should have to live like that.

Her mom listened, but I could tell she wasn't impressed.

She took a seat next to me on the porch and began asking more questions. They were all posed as polite small talk, but they had meat on the bone. None of them were if I was married or asked anything that couldn't be found on the internet, so I figured she'd done her homework. Instead she wanted to know exactly how Leah and I met, and exactly why I'd chosen to settle in Truth Harbor.

"It's far enough from the city that it offered privacy," I explained, "yet close enough that I can still travel to Seattle if I need to." I didn't offer the other reason, which was that it was close enough that I could visit Jeremy on a regular basis.

"And what about now? Your privacy is blown. Are you still planning to stay?"

Leah had come up and was standing on the porch, shifting around. She seemed uncomfortable. "He probably hasn't decided yet what he's doing."

Actually, I had been pondering it. "For now, yes, I intend to stay. I'm hoping things will be all right once the attention dies down."

Leah's mom absorbed my words. "And what about your son? Will he be staying? I understand he's British."

I guess she didn't dig deep enough or else she would have read about Charlotte. "No, he goes to boarding school in England. He'll be staying with me mostly during the summer months."

I sensed Leah watching me with compassion.

The phone in my pocket buzzed. I wondered if I should ignore it, then realized it might be Jeremy again, so I pulled it out. To my surprise, it was Rhys.

"Excuse me," I said, standing up, "but I have to take this."

The steel mama didn't like that. She frowned. I was preemptively ending her interrogation, but there wasn't much I could do.

I walked off the porch and answered the phone, glancing back to see Leah and her mom arguing.

"Well, color me surprised," I said to Rhys with scorn. "I'm surprised you have the balls to call me back."

"Fuck you. And fuck all your accusations. I just thought you should know I'm not the one who leaked your address to the press."

"Of course you didn't."

"What the hell, man? Do you think I'm a monster? I'd never do something like that."

There was something in his emphatic tone that brought back a memory. It was of the two of us in the early days. Flat broke and living in a ratty motel in Seattle that smelled like the inside of an ashtray. Somehow I'd caught a wicked flu and could barely talk, much less sing. As I lay in bed, feverish and out of my mind, Rhys came into the room and placed a bottle of orange juice on the night-stand, then unceremoniously dumped a bunch of cold medicine, vita-mins, and herbal remedies on the bed. Apparently he'd shoplifted a whole damn pharmacy. He told me he'd even asked the pharmacist what would help before he stole it all.

"How do you explain the timing then?" I asked. "You announce you're leaving the band, and the next thing I know my house is swarming with vultures."

"You really think I'd do something to screw up your adoption? I might be pissed at *you*, but I'd never do anything to hurt Damian."

"Then who the hell gave them my address?"

"I have no idea, but it wasn't me. This has been your problem all along, you stubborn prick. You make up your mind about something and then won't listen to reason. So go fuck yourself."

He hung up.

I stared at my phone, and then I slid it back into my pocket. I'd been sure Rhys had been the one who leaked my address, but now I wasn't so sure. It was true what he said. I couldn't see him doing something that would hurt Damian.

———————

I'D HAD my conversation with Rhys behind the house, so I walked back around to the front. When I got there, Leah was on the porch alone. Camilla's car was still here.

"Where's your mom?"

"Over talking to Shane and Damian." She was sitting in the same chair her mom had been in. Instead of her usual bright energy, though, she seemed dejected.

I sat down next to her. "Everything okay?"

"Sure, I'm fine." She faced me. "I'm sorry my mom was so rude, especially the way she was asking all those questions."

"Don't worry about it. I've dealt with worse than that."

"I shouldn't let her get to me." She examined her hands. "She's not an easy person to get along with."

"What is it your mom does for a living?" I asked, curious.

"She's a high school principal."

My eyes widened. "*Fuuuck.* Seriously?"

Leah laughed. "You should see your expression."

"Damn. No wonder the hairs on the back of my neck stood up when I met her."

"She can be intimidating."

"I nearly started apologizing to her and didn't even know what I was apologizing for."

"She has that effect on people."

I went silent and considered Leah. She looked pretty sitting out here in the golden sunlight. "You two don't look much alike."

"I take after my dad."

"And what does he do? Is he a paid assassin?"

She began laughing all over again. "Oh my gosh." She wiped tears from her eyes. "You really know how to tickle my funny bone."

"I figure he must be a tough dude."

She smiled. "He's a retired banker and lives in Mexico."

"Mexico?"

"My parents got divorced when I was a teenager, and afterward he moved down there. He lives on the Baja coast with his girlfriend."

"Do you see much of him?"

"Once a year or so, he flies up. Before I bought the farm, I used to fly down. We're not really that close." She glanced at me. "What about your mom? Do you get along with her?"

I snorted. "We get along just fine as long as we don't talk to each other."

Leah nodded with understanding.

"She lives in Hawaii. I bought her a house there a few years back."

Her brows went up. "Wow. You bought her a house in Hawaii?"

I shrugged. "It's what she wanted." I couldn't believe I was telling Leah any of this. I rarely talked about my mom. Even Charlotte knew very little.

"She's also a singer, right?"

I nodded. "Used to be. I don't know what she's doing now. And as long as she leaves me out of it, I'm good."

"You don't want to try to have a relationship with her?"

"Nah." I shook my head. "That ship sailed a long time ago."

"That's too bad. What about your brother?"

I shifted in my chair. There was no way I was discussing Jeremy with her or anyone. I leaned forward. "Listen, I've been thinking. Maybe we should talk about what happened between us last night."

She studied me. "There's nothing to discuss. We had a moment, that's all. Let's forget about it."

I should have been happy with that. I definitely needed to forget about it. But for some reason, I wasn't happy. The problem was I liked Leah. "I don't want things to be awkward between us."

"Me either."

"You'd tell me if we were overstaying our welcome, right?"

She sat up straight. "This is because of what my mom said, isn't it? Don't listen to her. She doesn't speak for me."

"It's partly that, but I have to admit, she has a point. We've been here three days now. I don't want to take advantage of you."

"You're not taking advantage of me. I'm happy to help." For a moment it seemed like she wanted to say more but didn't. Instead she chewed her bottom lip.

My eyes went to her mouth, remembering the lush feel of it last night. I averted my gaze. "I'm going to walk down to my house tomorrow and check on things. See what the situation is." I scanned the area. "I don't see any helicopters today."

"Maybe they've finally given up."

It was then I heard voices and saw Damian walking with Leah's mom and Shane from the direction of his motorhome. The three of them appeared to be having a lively conversation. The steel mama was laughing and looked nothing like the stern-faced interrogator she'd been earlier.

By the time they reached us, I could hear Shane teasing his mom. "Of course I didn't eat it. I barely recognized what it was. Might have been an old shoe."

She smiled. "Next time I'm bringing my new improved meatloaf. You'll see."

"What's a meatloaf?" Damian asked.

"Trust me, you don't want to know," Shane told him. "At least not my mom's recipe. She may as well call it burnt loaf."

Their mom laughed some more. I glanced at Leah, who watched the two of them with a wry expression.

Eventually their mom left, hugging Shane and Damian goodbye. "It's nice to meet you, young man."

She nodded her goodbyes at me and Leah.

After she was gone, Damian began to describe Shane's RV and how it was totally brilliant, and that I should buy one, and we could live in it. "That way the vultures would never know where we are. It's like a house you can move!"

I smiled at the thought of us living on the road like that. It occurred to me that Damian had never been inside our tour bus since we only used it in the States. He'd be impressed. Once the adoption went through, it would be fun to bring him along for a leg of our next US tour.

And that was when it hit me.

There wouldn't be a next US tour, or any tour.

If Rhys left the band, then it was all over. We'd never replace him with another guitar player. Hell, I wouldn't want to. Each of us brought our own talents to this group, and despite the way Rhys and I argued, I couldn't deny the sonofabitch was a brilliant musician.

It occurred to me that I probably shouldn't have been so quick to tell Terence I was done. I could be a stubborn bastard. Maybe it was time we all sat down and tried to hash this thing out. If only we weren't stuck with Jane as our manager. I'd love to fire her, but that would only make things worse with Rhys.

Shane had to leave for his job at the bar, so the three of us were on our own for the evening. We played cards, ate popcorn, and had a pretty decent time. When I finally got Damian to bed, he fell asleep quickly, as usual. All this fresh air and activity was good for him.

Out in the living room, I was going to put sheets on the couch but saw Leah had already done it for me. There was something on my pillow, and when I walked over to see what it was, I had to chuckle. It was the Sasquatch doll from the other day. She must have bought it when I wasn't looking.

I went outside and found her sitting on the front porch again. Moonbathing, as she liked to call it.

"Looks like I have a visitor on my pillow," I said, taking the seat next to her. "Kind of resembles my aunt June, except her beard's longer."

Leah laughed lightly.

"Aunt June looks awfully comfortable." I leaned toward her and lowered my voice. "I might have to find another bed tonight."

Our eyes met, and lust shot straight through me. White-hot. I had an image of the two of us rolling between her bedsheets. Leah's long legs wrapped around my back. Moans of ecstasy coming from us both.

Jesus, I need to quit flirting with her.

I was the one playing with fire.

I shifted position in the chair to hide the hard-on now plaguing me.

"Just remember," she said with a smile, "the barn is always available to you."

"I'll keep that in mind." I tried to smile back, but my eyes had gone to her legs propped up on the porch rail. I'd always been a leg man. They were long and shapely, crossed at the ankles. She had a tattoo of a crescent moon on her left one.

I took a deep breath, then watched as she sipped from a bottle of beer.

"Feel free to get yourself one," she said. "Or you can share mine."

She offered it me, and I nearly pressed it against my forehead. Instead I brought it to my mouth. She usually drank ice water, and I suspected her mom's visit today had something to do with this beer. "Are you okay?"

She accepted the bottle back and took another swig. "I've been better."

"Your mom seemed like a different person with your brother."

She shrugged. "That's because he's her favorite."

I didn't like hearing this. "Parents shouldn't have favorites."

"I don't mind. Shane is everyone's favorite. Lars and I are used to it."

That didn't sound right to me, but every family had its own dynamics. "Can I ask you a personal question?"

She considered me. "So you want to get personal?"

"What exactly are your financial problems? Are you in danger of losing your farm?"

She paused and then blinked a few times. "Oh my God. You're not going to offer me money, are you?"

"Of course not." Although to be honest, I had thought of it. I'd earned more than I could spend in two lifetimes and tended to be generous.

"Okay, good." She seemed to relax.

"Are you in financial trouble?"

"Things are tight," she admitted. "My farm is earning less than it costs to run, but it gets better every month. I have big plans in the works." She told me she planned to buy some Angora goats, and that she was on the waiting list to sell eggs, vegetables, and fiber at the local farmers market. "I'll do whatever it takes to keep this place going."

"And that's why your mom and brother want you to get rid of it?"

She nodded. "They want me to go back to my cubicle where it's safe." Her eyes filled with defiance. "But I don't care if it's safe. I'm not going back."

"Then don't. You were made for bigger things, Leah." I leaned closer. "Some people are too afraid to chase their dreams, but you and I aren't like that."

She didn't say anything for a few moments, then smiled. "So we're both badasses, huh?"

"Damn straight."

She continued to gaze at me, and there was an understanding between us. We recognized each other.

Her voice lowered. "I am not afraid. I was born to do this."

I tilted my head. "Is that a quote from someone?"

"Joan of Arc."

I nodded slowly. "I'll have to remember that one. I like it."

"You seem to know a lot of quotes," she commented.

I chuckled. "I have a strangely good memory for them. Quotes and song lyrics."

"I guess that makes sense considering what you do for a living."

I reached for the beer bottle in her hand and felt a rush when our fingers brushed against each other.

This was ridiculous. I felt like a schoolkid.

"Who called you earlier?" she asked. "It seemed important."

"Rhys."

Her eyes widened. "I hope that means you guys aren't breaking up the band."

"We'll see. He called to tell me he wasn't the one who leaked my address to the press." I took a swig of beer.

She seemed to go still. There was a worried expression on her face.

"What is it?"

She shook her head. "It's nothing."

"You look like you want to say something. Do you think he's lying to me?"

"No, I don't. I'm sure he's telling the truth." She fidgeted a little and brushed something from her leg. "Do you believe him?"

"I think so. The problem is I don't know who the hell leaked it then." I stared up at the moon in frustration while something hard and angry grew in my chest. "Somebody stabbed me in the back. And I'll tell you this much—when I find out who did it, they're going to wish they'd never met me."

CHAPTER TWENTY-ONE

~Leah~

After the conversation with Josh, I didn't sleep well at all. I'd been up half the night, angry at myself for not confessing that I was the one who gave his address to the press. I should have told him when he brought up Rhys. It was the perfect time, but of course, I chickened out.

So much for being a badass.

When I finally got up and went downstairs the next morning to put on my running shoes, I discovered Damian and Josh were not only awake but wanted to join me.

"I want to run with Rosalie, Martina, and Eva," Damian said eagerly

I smiled at him. It warmed my heart that he already knew the names of my girls.

Josh yawned from where he was sitting on the couch. "And I'm only joining you maniacs because I don't want to be left out of all the fun."

His hair was pulled back into a guy version of a messy bun. While Damian wore regular athletic shorts and a T-shirt, Josh wore jeans and the black Beaver Kings shirt I'd washed for him yesterday.

Cary Grant crowed as we stepped outside. The morning air was cool, and the sun was just rising when we started our run. I loved the swish of rainbow color that happened when everything changed from night to day.

I didn't usually bring water but brought a few bottles this time, along with some chopped apples for Damian to feed my alpacas.

"I can carry that," Josh said, motioning to my small backpack.

I shooed him away. "I got this. Besides, we already know you'll need all your strength to keep up with me, Friedrich."

He snickered, and I could tell he enjoyed being teased. Thankfully, we were back to our usual banter. Both he and Damian were naturally athletic, and while they didn't take running as seriously as I did, it pleased me to discover they kept up just fine.

As soon as Rosalie, Martina, and Eva saw us they galloped over. Damian laughed and was beyond delighted. He waved and called out hello.

When we reached the halfway point of our run, we took a break, and I got out the water bottles.

"It's amazing out here," Josh said, glancing around as he accepted the bottle. "I can't believe I'm saying this, but you're right about watching the sunrise. There's something energizing about it."

I nodded. "It centers me, and I feel ready to take on the day."

"Can we go pet the alpacas?" Damian asked.

We walked over to where Rosalie, Martina, and Eva were playing with each other near the fence. I got out the apple pieces for Damian, who giggled as Martina nibbled them from his palm. Josh and I fed some to Rosalie and Eva as well.

I leaned back against the fence and sighed. Did life get any better than this? I watched Josh's handsome profile as he fed another piece of apple to Rosalie and then petted her neck while she hummed at his touch.

I know exactly how you feel, Rosalie.

He turned to me. And we smiled at each other like a couple of fools in the early morning sunshine.

We were still smiling when Josh got a mischievous glint in his eyes. He put his water bottle on the ground, and then before I knew what was happening, he took a step forward and did a handstand right in front of me.

"Oh my God!" I sputtered, letting go of the fence. "What the heck are you doing?"

His whole body went straight up into the air as the muscles in his arms stood out, supporting his weight. His black T-shirt fell to his chest, revealing that beautiful washboard stomach. I stared at it. A dark blond happy trail led from his belly button into the waistband of what looked to be a pair of black boxer briefs.

Damian laughed when he saw his dad upside down but didn't seem surprised.

Meanwhile, I couldn't hide my astonishment. Even more so when Josh walked around on his hands. "Holy shit," I said. He was seriously fit.

After a few more seconds, he brought his legs down and gracefully righted himself. His face was flushed. He wore a cheeky grin, and when his eyes met mine, I knew he'd done it for *me*—that he was a boy trying to impress a girl.

A warm, tingling sensation filled my belly. It had been a long time since a boy showed off for me. "That was incredible. Do you do those often?"

"You've never seen us perform live?"

I shook my head. "I've always wanted to, but I never have."

"Damn, seriously? You're missing out, Leah. I do handstands on stage."

"Really?" I tried to act like that wasn't the hottest thing ever. Like my eyeballs weren't still burning from the sight of those abs. "That must be impressive."

He reached back to fix his hair, which had come loose. "Hell yeah, it's impressive. I'm basically a maniac. You'll have to come to a show sometime."

"I'd love to. You're in amazing shape. Even I can't walk on my hands."

He shrugged, but I could tell he enjoyed the compliment.

When we headed back, we were more playful with each other than ever. I kept telling myself to stop, but it was too much fun. It was all juvenile stuff. Josh pulled my ponytail, and I'd run in front to cut him off. I teased him about his man bun and told him he was the prettiest Sasquatch I ever saw.

He batted his eyelashes. "My daddy always says, 'Pretty is as pretty does.'"

We pulled Damian in on the fun and had a race where we all ran backward and then sideways. He won both times because Josh and I kept laughing and tripping over each other.

Once we were back at the house, I made chocolate chip pancakes for breakfast, arranging the chips in a smiley face for Damian.

"So who are the Beaver Kings anyway?" I asked once I sat down to eat. "I keep staring at your shirt, but I've never heard of them."

"You will. They're the first band we've signed to our own label. I'll have to play some of their music for you. It's kick-ass."

As we dug into our food, Josh reminded me that he and Damian were headed down to the house today to check on things and to see how Dean and Nalla were holding out.

"Could we invite them here for a visit?" Damian asked with a mouthful of pancake.

Josh put his mug down. "I don't know about that, Little D. Leah's already got her hands full with the two of us." He glanced at me.

"Do you really mind?" Damian turned to me with those big brown eyes.

"Why don't you invite them for dinner tonight?" I said on impulse.

"Really?" Damian grinned and bounced in his seat. "I can't wait to tell Dean. He's going to think it's mega meeting all your animals."

Josh studied me. "You sure you don't mind?"

"It's fine. I can grill up some burgers. I'll see if Shane wants to join us."

"That's real nice of you."

"What time do you think you guys will head down there?"

"Around noon, why?"

I told him I had a YouTube channel and planned to do a video today, so I needed to make sure I wasn't disturbed.

"No problem. We'll stay out of your way." But then he eyed me with interest. "You have a YouTube channel?"

"It's for my yarn business. I basically spin while I talk about fiber art and other related topics."

"Do you have a lot of followers?"

I snorted. "If you call nineteen people a lot of followers."

He stroked his beard but didn't say anything more.

After breakfast, I tackled my morning chores. As usual, Damian helped me with the chickens. I didn't see Shane around, and his truck wasn't here, so I texted him about tonight and asked if he could pick up some beer and burger buns in town.

As it drew closer to noon, I went back into the house. Josh had packed both his and Damian's backpacks and placed them by the front door. It felt strange seeing them. I knew most people were relieved when their guests left, but I'd enjoyed having them here. It occurred to me that if things were improved at the house, they might not come back at all.

"Hey, what's up?" Josh came over to me. He'd just taken a shower and looked good. He smelled good too. "Are you starting your video yet?"

I nodded. "In a few minutes. I usually do them in the dining room."

Just as I said this, the sound of an engine swooped over the roof. It was a helicopter.

Josh had been smiling, but his face fell. "Shit! What the hell is that?"

He strode toward the door, and I followed him outside, where we both stood on my front porch, watching as a helicopter made its way south.

"I don't believe this." He stared in the direction of his house with his mouth open. "I haven't seen one of those all weekend."

He looked pissed, but I felt a peculiar sense of relief wash over me. It turned to guilt when I glanced at him. "Maybe it won't be as bad as you think," I said, trying to be encouraging.

He scowled, still watching the helicopter in the distance. "This is bullshit." But then his eyes met mine and softened. "Looks like you might have company a little longer. Are you cool with that?"

I could have danced a jig, but I simply nodded. "Of course it's fine. You guys can stay as long as you need to."

He tilted his head. "You have a good heart, Leah. Not many people would put up with strangers staying with them like you have."

I felt embarrassed. "Thanks," I mumbled.

"You're generous and kind." He leaned toward me and lowered his voice. "And let's be honest. You're sexy as hell."

My eyes flashed to his face while my insides dipped.

He wore a flirty smile. "Guess I shouldn't have said that."

"Probably not."

He stepped closer. "Tell me, honey, what should I do?" He still wore that flirty smile, but then his expression grew serious, and when he spoke, his tone was thoughtful. "I amend my earlier comment. You're not just sexy, Leah. You're beautiful."

My eyes stayed on his. I didn't even know what to do with a compliment like this. I licked my lips. "Thank you."

The motion got his attention, and his looked at my mouth. He moved closer.

My heart pounded. I knew I should back away. I remembered us making out in the hayloft. I'd thought of it constantly. It felt like a dream, like it had never happened.

He reached up and gently tucked a piece of hair behind my ear. "I wish I could kiss you," he whispered. "I'd really love to kiss you right now."

My breath shook. "You'd better stop with all this sweet talk, Friedrich. I think my knees are going weak."

"Don't worry. I'll catch you if you fall."

We studied each other.

"We can't do this," I said. "You know we can't."

He inhaled deeply and then closed his eyes. "I know."

AFTER JOSH AND DAMIAN LEFT, I set up my phone on a tripod. I was still reeling from what just happened on the porch. My acute lust was turning into something else, and if I wasn't careful, I was going to fall for Josh.

That was the last thing I needed.

I smiled when I thought of that handstand earlier and of how much fun we had goofing around afterward. I'd had a great time with those two since they arrived.

Josh liked attention. There was no doubt about that. Unfortunately, my ex-husband also liked attention. It went hand in hand with being the lead singer for a band.

Derek wasn't fun like Josh. Josh was playful while Derek had been brooding. I couldn't even imagine Derek with a son. He'd never be as thoughtful and generous a parent as Josh. I shouldn't compare the two, but I couldn't seem to stop myself.

On the other hand, what did I really know about Josh? We met less than a month ago, and he could be hiding something dark as well.

I headed into the dining room. Every few weeks I did a live YouTube video. I was careful to get my spinning wheel and the batt I was using ready in advance. Most of my followers were locals, but a few were from the East Coast, and two were from the Midwest.

"Hi, everyone," I said as I started the live stream and took a seat behind my wheel. "I hope you're all doing well. I've got some beautiful snowy white alpaca roving I'll be working with today." I held up the batt for everyone to see, then pulled off a strip and got started. "This particular fiber comes from my alpaca Rhiannon—the matriarch of my herd and a very pretty lady. There are pictures of her on my website. I still have a few batts of this particular fiber for sale if you're interested. And, of course, it's all been hand carded by yours truly."

As I continued to talk about my alpacas and some of the fiber I'd been working with lately, I heard a sound in the other room. I figured it must be Shane. Luckily, I'd put a Do Not Disturb sign on the dining room door so he'd know I was videoing.

To my surprise, the door opened. I turned my head to tell Shane I was doing a live stream, but it wasn't Shane.

It was Josh.

My pulse shot up. "What are you doing? I thought you guys left."

He walked in, closing the door behind him.

"Wait!" I glanced at the tripod where my phone was capturing this whole thing. "I'm videoing right now, and it's *live*."

"Really? That's great. I just wanted to stop in and say hello." He waved at the camera and grinned. "Hello, everyone."

By that point I was gawking and didn't know what to do. "This is... uh... a friend of my mine. I mean, my cousin Friedrich!"

"Leah's only kidding. Call me Josh." He winked at the camera, where all nineteen women were probably gawking as well. I wondered if any of them recognized him. I hoped not.

Josh looked down at my spinning wheel with interest. "I've seen you do this, but I don't understand how it works. Is it difficult?"

"It's not difficult. It takes practice, though."

"Mind if I try?"

I was stunned. "Uh... sure, of course. You can try it out."

I had no idea what Josh was doing, but I got up and let him have the chair. He was taller than me, so we had to move it back a little.

He sat down and studied the spinning wheel. "I'm not going to prick my finger and fall into a deep sleep, am I?"

I glanced at my audience and raised a brow. The whole concept of Sleeping Beauty pricking her finger was a common annoyance.

"Because I might need a kiss if that happens," he said in a flirty tone. He looked directly at the camera and grinned. "Any volunteers?"

"Don't worry," I assured him. "There isn't anything that pointy on a spinning wheel."

He turned to me with surprise. "There isn't?"

"In the fairy tale, Sleeping Beauty pricked her finger on a spindle, but spindles aren't sharp, so it doesn't make sense. You might impale yourself on one if you really tried, but you'd have a hard time pricking your finger."

"Huh." He stared down at the wheel with a bemused expression.

"This is a flywheel anyway," I explained. "So there's no spindle."

"And all this time I thought spinning wheels were dangerous." He turned to me and murmured in a low voice, "I guess it's just the spinsters who are dangerous."

Our eyes caught. Attraction rippled through me, and I glanced away. I hoped my feelings didn't show since this was all being captured live.

For the next ten minutes, I explained the different parts of the wheel to Josh. He chuckled and swore a little as he made some bumpy yarn. "Damn, this is harder than it looks."

"You're doing fine," I said encouragingly. "It's your first time."

He worked at it a little longer, smiling, cracking jokes, and charming the hell out of all nineteen of my followers.

Eventually he thanked me for the experience, got up, waved goodbye to everyone, and left.

I blinked a few times at the oddness of it all. Finally, I sat back down and moved the chair closer. "All right, then," I said and took a deep breath. "Let's get back to our regularly scheduled video."

———

AFTER I FINISHED LIVE STREAMING, I checked through the comments. There were a few:

"He's cute! Is that your boyfriend?"

"Who is that? Damn, he's fine. He can spin with me anytime he wants."

"Holy hotness. Come to mama..."

"I'd be happy to kiss him whether he's awake or asleep."

"Have I seen him before? He looks familiar. What was his name again?"

That last comment gave me pause, but I decided not to respond. I wasn't sure what Josh was thinking crashing my live video, but hopefully it wouldn't be a big deal. It looked like only fifteen people actually watched it.

By late afternoon, I started getting ready for dinner. Shane texted and told me he'd stop in town after work to pick up beer and burger buns. I peeled potatoes and boiled them. While they were cooling, I went out and picked fresh lettuce and tomatoes from my garden.

Shane arrived, and I took the bags, thanking him for going to the store. While he took a shower, I prepped dinner. I was just ready to make potato salad when there was a knock at the front door.

When I answered it, I found Josh and Damian standing there, along with Dean and Nalla.

Josh's eyes met mine, and immediately we were grinning.

"Hey," he said.

"Hey, yourself." I tried to stop smiling. This was ridiculous. It had only been a few hours since we saw each other.

"We're back to torment you," he said in that silky baritone. "And we brought reinforcements."

"Great to see you again, Leah," Dean said. "This is for you." He handed me a round dish wrapped in multiple layers of foil.

I took it from him. "What is it?"

"A peach pie."

"That's really nice. Thank you."

Dean nodded and waggled his brows. "We figured we'd bring dessert."

I glanced at Nalla, who was standing beside him, but she only stared at me and said nothing.

I led them into the house and explained that I'd be grilling burgers on the back deck. Damian ran ahead when he saw my cats Storm and Coriander both lounging on the couch. He wore a backpack, and I asked if I could take it from him.

"All right," he said, shrugging it off. I shifted the pie to my left hand and placed his backpack behind the couch for now, figuring I'd put it in the guest room later.

Josh took his off, too, and that was when I noticed the large black case.

"You brought a guitar?"

"This way I can easily perform all the Queen songs that Damian demands." He glanced at me. "I haven't forgotten about singing 'Silver Days' for you."

"You haven't?"

"Of course not. You said it's your favorite, right?"

I nodded. "It is. I love that song."

"Well, then I'll have to make it happen."

CHAPTER TWENTY-TWO

~Leah~

"Can I get you guys something to drink?" I asked everyone as we all gathered in the kitchen. I put the pie on the counter. "There's beer, soda, water, and apple juice."

Dean and Josh both accepted a beer. Nalla took a bottle of water, and Damian had a root beer. "Shane's taking a shower," I said, "but he'll be joining us for dinner too."

Josh started to tell Dean about Shane and Walk the Plank, how they had live music once a week, and they needed to check it out sometime. I gave Damian one of the feathered cat toys, and he led Storm and Coriander outside to play in the backyard.

Nalla stood there silently with her arms crossed, leaning against the kitchen counter as she sipped her bottled water. She still hadn't said one word to me.

"So, how are things at the house?" I asked her, trying to make polite small talk.

She shrugged. Her hair was pulled back with a few tendrils loose around her face. She wore a tight gauzy top and jean shorts that showed off her slender frame.

"That video of Dean messing with the press was so funny," I said. "Did you help him with that?"

"Not really." She took a sip from her bottle. Her expression remained cool. Her amber eyes, rimmed with black eyeliner, were striking.

I'd barely put any makeup on and had only pulled my hair into a ponytail. "Well, we all thought it was hilarious."

She didn't reply and just looked around the kitchen like she was bored. I wondered what Dean saw in her. She was pretty but beyond that seemed snotty and rude.

I got out all the ingredients from the fridge so I could finish making potato salad.

Dean came over to me. "Hey, can I help?"

I looked at him with surprise. "Sure. I'm making potato salad, but I could use some help with the regular salad."

"Just tell what you want me to do. I'm all yours."

I told him the lettuce, tomatoes, and cucumbers were in the fridge, and if he could clean and toss everything together, that would be great.

While he washed his hands in the kitchen sink, I noticed Josh had gone outside and was watching Damian play with the cats, who were doing backflips in the air as they tried to catch the feathered toy.

Nalla noticed it too. Her gaze intent on Josh.

"I love peach pie," I said to her. "Are you the one who made it?"

"Dean made it." She stared at Josh through the window.

"Wow, so Dean likes to bake?"

"Excuse me" was all she said as she took her water bottle and left. A few moments later, I saw her outside talking to Josh about something. He glanced down at her, but I couldn't see his expression.

"Do you have a salad spinner?" Dean asked me.

"I do." I turned away from the window. "Let me grab it for you."

Dean and I stood next to each other in the kitchen, preparing food in a companionable way. I studied him from the corner of my eye, noticing he seemed quite comfortable. "Nalla said you made the pie?"

He nodded. "I hope you like it. Can't say I've ever made a peach pie, but Josh has a couple of peach trees on his property, and I figured I'd give it a shot."

"You like to cook?"

He chuckled and patted his belly. "Hell yeah. How do you think I got this fat?"

"A drummer who likes to cook," I mused. "You're a man of many talents."

"I always said if I weren't a drummer, I'd be a chef."

"Really?"

He chopped up a cucumber and added it to the salad bowl. "Crazy, huh?"

"I don't think so."

We chatted a bit about his cooking adventures with the band while they were on the road. He told me a story about making a huge meal for the entire crew using a hotel kitchen at two in the morning. "I think the employees thought wild monkeys had ransacked the place."

Dean was a big guy, and between the black beard and all the tattoos, he looked intimidating, but the more I talked to him, it was obvious my impression of him from Josh's birthday party was correct. He was a big softie.

As I was adding some dill to the potato salad on Dean's recommendation, Shane came into the kitchen. His hair was still damp, and he wore jeans and a faded *Planet of the Apes* T-shirt.

I made the introductions. Shane, of course, took meeting another rock star in stride. By now Josh and Nalla had come back into the kitchen. Nalla was smiling and seemed less aloof. She asked if there was anything she could do to help.

I glanced around at the food that Dean and I had just finished preparing. Damian was already taking napkins and paper plates onto the back deck. Josh was filling a pitcher with ice water.

"You could grab the burgers," I said. "They're in the fridge. There are some veggie burgers in the freezer too."

By the time we were all outside and I got the grill fired up, Dean came over to me. "Why don't you let me make the burgers? Josh told me how hard you work all day."

"You don't mind?"

"Not at all. Grab yourself a beer and take a load off. I got this."

In truth, I did like the idea of taking a break. I felt like I'd been going nonstop since this morning. "But you're my guest. I can't let you make dinner," I said with a laugh.

Dean rolled his eyes. "Woman, am I going to have to wrestle that spatula from your hand?"

"Let Dean do it," Josh said. "He's a good cook."

I chewed my lip and studied Dean. "As long as you really don't mind."

"Trust me, he doesn't mind," Josh said, pulling the empty chair next to him closer. "Come on over here, honey. Sit beside me and relax."

I shrugged. "All right, fine." I went over and sat next to Josh.

"I'll even let you share my beer," he said, handing me the bottle.

I felt a zing of pleasure when our hands touched. His expression was warm and inviting. He was like a gorgeous big cat. His mess of blond hair framed his face, and his muscular body looked graceful draped in that chair. I tried to remind myself that big cats were dangerous, but my inner voice said it wanted to pet this one.

I took a swig from the bottle and handed it back. "Thanks, Friedrich."

I watched him reach for a tortilla chip and dip it into some salsa. He was back to wearing multiple chunky rings on his long fingers, along with a few bracelets on each wrist. He'd changed clothes when he'd gone home, too, and had on thigh-hugging jeans and a blue tie-dye T-shirt that matched his eyes.

"Anytime, my little spinster."

Something made me glance at Nalla, and I discovered she was staring at me again. I smiled, but she didn't smile back. I wondered what her problem was. She obviously didn't want to be here.

I turned my attention back to Josh. "What on earth made you crash my live stream today? And then you told everyone your real name. I can't believe you did that."

He shrugged before popping a chip in his mouth. "I figured I'd shake things up a little. Get some attention for you."

"Well, I don't know about the attention part. Only fifteen people saw it."

"That's all right. How were the comments afterward?"

"Are you kidding? They were all about you. Everyone thought you were hot."

He gave a teasing smile and ran a hand down his body like he was posing for a camera. "That's because I *am* hot." He made a sizzling sound and touched a finger to his chest. "*Ow!*"

I laughed. I couldn't help it. I'd never met anyone so vain, yet so endearing about it, in my entire life.

Josh poked my shoulder and made another sizzling sound. "*Oooh!* Damn, woman, you're hot too." He poked various parts of my body, tickling me. "Holy shit, Leah. You're on fire!"

I giggled and poked him back. Pretty soon we were poking each other all over, making sizzling noises, and cracking up with laughter.

It was in the middle of all this flirtatious mayhem that I noticed Lars had appeared on the back deck. He watched us with a flat expression. It was a warm day, but a cloud appeared over his head, blocking the sun.

"Hi, Lars." I tried to stop giggling and swatted Josh's fingers away. "I didn't know you were stopping by."

"Good evening, Officer Kelly," Josh said in a casual tone. He'd stopped poking me, but I felt his hand on my lower back. Hidden from view, his fingers snuck beneath my shirt and drew lazy circles on my skin.

My breath caught. *What's he doing?* Erotic sparks danced through me, and I didn't dare look at him.

"Hey, bro," Shane said, glancing up from his phone. "Do you want to stay for dinner?"

My brother surveyed our group. He wore dark jeans and a blue button-down shirt with the sleeves rolled up. His short black hair appeared crisp and freshly cut. "I don't think I've met everyone here."

"This is our drummer, Dean," Josh said. "Along with his girlfriend, Nalla."

"Good to meet you." Dean put his hand out from where he was standing next to the grill. I saw my brother take in his appearance—his size, the ink, the long ponytail and crazy black beard, not to mention the pierced eyebrow. They shook hands.

Nalla didn't offer hers but gave him a watery smile.

Lars glanced over at Damian, who was running around the yard with the feather toy while four cats chased him.

"There's beer and soda in the fridge," I told my twin. "Help yourself."

Lars hesitated, like he wanted to say something but then thought better of it. "Thanks, I'll do that."

Josh was still drawing on my skin, and I knew I should make him stop. When I turned to him, those blue eyes were already watching me.

"What are you doing?" I whispered so the others couldn't hear.

He leaned close and put his mouth to my ear. "Trying to resist you and failing."

His words shimmered through me. My girl parts tingled, and I knew my panties were practically melting. This attraction between us was getting out of control.

"Let's moonbathe tonight," he murmured, and his tone made it sound illicit.

To make matters worse, I could sense Nalla watching us. She

seemed way too interested. There was something about her I didn't trust.

Lars came back with his Coke and took the empty seat directly across from me. "Sorry if I'm crashing your party. I didn't know you were having one."

"It's not a party. It's just a casual dinner."

He nodded and took a sip from his can.

"So, what are you up to today, Officer Kelly?" Josh asked. He'd stopped drawing circles, but I could still feel the warmth of his hand.

Lars glanced between the two of us, and it occurred to me that we were sitting way too close. I took a sip of Josh's beer and realized how all this must look.

"Not much."

"Catch any bad guys lately?"

Lars put his Coke down and stared at Josh.

Josh didn't move a muscle and stared right back.

Oh no. I did an internal eye roll. *Not this again.*

"What's that live stream thing you were talking about?" Dean asked me over his shoulder. He flipped the burgers. The smell of grilled meat wafted over. "Did you say you have a YouTube channel?"

I was relieved for the change of topic and hoped this would break up Josh and my brother's staring contest. I described my channel and the types of videos I posted. When I was done, Josh told Dean that spinning wheels didn't have anything pointy on them.

"They don't? What about Sleeping Beauty?"

"Apparently that part's bullshit."

Dean's brows rose. "Really?"

I glanced at Lars, and I could tell we both found it amusing that these two guys would know anything about fairy tales.

"Why do you guys know so much about Sleeping Beauty?" I asked.

Josh explained how Dax, the guy who managed their road crew, had his wife and baby girl visit on the last tour. "Dax's little girl was obsessed with that movie," he said, chuckling. "Kept playing it over and over."

Dean nodded. "I think all of us got sucked into it at one point or another."

I tried to imagine a bunch of rockers getting into a kid's fairy tale and couldn't visualize it.

Josh must have noticed my perplexed expression. "Being on the road is mostly mind-numbing boredom broken up by a few hours of intense excitement. Trust me, you search for any kind of distraction when you're bored."

Shane, who was texting on his phone, glanced up. "Hey, do you guys mind if I invite Martha to join us?"

"We don't want it to get out that Josh and Damian are staying here," I said.

"That won't be a problem. I'm sure she can keep a secret."

Josh listened to him with interest. "Wait, is this that woman you're into? The librarian?"

Shane nodded. "Yeah. I was thinking she might be okay with coming over if it's just a casual dinner with friends."

"Hell yeah, invite her over." He glanced at me. "You don't mind, do you?"

I shrugged. "Not if you don't."

Shane grinned. "Okay, I'm going to ask her."

Lars didn't seem surprised, so I guessed Shane must have told him about Martha.

I heard laughter in the grass and saw Damian still playing with the cats. Amazingly, all seven of them were there. "I can't remember the last time I've seen all of them together like that. He's like the cat whisperer."

Josh watched him too. "I'll have to get him a couple cats. That might be a nice surprise."

Nalla leaned forward and smiled. "That's a great idea. I'd love to help you find them."

He nodded but didn't say anything.

She was still watching him, and I wondered if she had a crush on Josh. There was something hungry in her gaze. But then why was she with Dean?

I glanced over at Dean still manning the grill. I hoped I was wrong.

Eventually the burgers were done, and Josh called Damian over. Just as Dean brought a plate of them to the table, a young Asian woman with long dark hair came around the corner of the house. She was about Shane's age and had a boy with her who looked to be close in age to Damian.

Shane waved at her, grinning, and then jumped up from where he was sitting. "That's Martha and her younger brother, Eddie."

He went over to greet them. They all came back to the table, and Shane introduced them to everyone. She was pretty but, surprisingly, not my brother's usual flashy type. She wore glasses and very little makeup. Instead of a short skirt and high heels, she had on jean shorts, a lavender tank top, and sneakers.

I got up to get them both folding chairs while everybody scooted around to make room. Shane placed the chairs beside his own.

Martha smiled as she took a seat. "It's so nice to meet all of you. Shane's told me so much about your farm. It's beautiful out here."

"Thank you," I said. "It's nice to meet you too."

Meanwhile, Shane had the sweetest smile on his face as he helped get her food and something to drink. My heart squeezed seeing my baby brother so enamored with a girl.

As we all talked and ate, my impression of Martha was a good one. She was smart and had a quick sense of humor, and it was clear she didn't put up with any nonsense. To be honest, she seemed more like someone I'd be friends with than Shane. It occurred to me that she'd be good for him. He could use a no-nonsense woman. From what I could tell, most of the ones he dated let him get away with everything.

During dinner, Dean and Josh told some funny stories about

being on the road. I never knew musicians traveled so much, but apparently they spent more time touring than anything else. I also noticed that Dean had the same FTMF tattoo on his forearm as Josh.

Lars was mostly quiet, listening. I couldn't tell what he was thinking, but I was glad he hadn't come here to cause trouble.

Nalla didn't say much either. Dean sat beside her and acted affectionate toward her, but she seemed more interested in what Josh and I were doing. Every time Josh joked around with me, she stared.

After dinner, Damian and Eddie left the table to play in the yard. Shane and Martha decided to set up the badminton net, and I started cleaning up the leftovers. To my surprise, Nalla helped me.

We brought paper plates inside to throw in the garbage, and I got out the plastic wrap to cover the leftover potato salad. She opened the fridge to put the condiments away.

"So how long have you been sleeping with Josh?" she asked.

I stopped what I was doing. "Excuse me?"

Nalla closed the fridge door and gave me a sly smile. "It's okay. It's just the two of us here. You can tell me."

"We're not sleeping together," I informed her. "We're just friends."

She wore a knowing expression. "Josh isn't capable of being friends with a woman. He always winds up sleeping with them."

I didn't know what to say to this, but I felt annoyed. "Well, we're not involved, so I guess you're wrong about that."

"You don't believe me?" She leaned against the counter. "Why do you think he and Rhys are having all these problems? It's because Josh slept with Jane behind his back."

I started loading dirty utensils into the dishwasher. "Who's Jane?"

"He hasn't told about her?" Nalla smirked. "I'm not surprised. She's the band's manager. She's also Rhys's girlfriend. Josh started out as just friends with her too."

I took in this information. Josh hadn't told me why Rhys wanted to break up the band, but I never pictured anything like this. It didn't fit in with the Josh I knew at all.

Nalla shrugged. "Look up Jane Braxton sometime and you'll see what I'm talking about." She smiled. "I'm just trying to be a friend here. I don't want to see you get hurt." Her skinny arms pushed away from the counter. "I'm going to go check on Dean."

She left the kitchen, and I finished loading the dishes and then wiped down the counter. There was a sick feeling in my stomach. I didn't like Nalla and didn't believe for one second that she wanted to "be a friend." On the other hand, this was exactly the kind of drama I'd dealt with when I was married to Derek. It felt way too familiar.

I glanced out the window and could see Josh playing badminton with Shane, Damian, and Eddie. They'd paired off into teams. He was graceful even playing a game like backyard badminton. My eyes went to those faded jeans and the way they hugged his thighs and ass. The pull of him was only getting stronger. Josh had a magnetism that was hard to resist. I could watch him all day.

Of course, millions of other people felt the same way. A disconcerting thought.

I heard a sound behind me and turned to see Lars walk into the kitchen.

"Hey," I said. "Are you taking off?"

He nodded. "I'm meeting someone."

My brows went up, and I smiled. "Do you have a date? Do tell."

Lars didn't smile back. He got a serious expression on his face. "What's going on between you and that guy? And don't tell me 'nothing.' I've got eyes."

"We're friends."

He tilted his head and gave me a look. "Are you sleeping with him?"

Geez, first Nalla and now Lars. Why did everyone think Josh and I were having sex? Of course, I knew exactly why. Our attraction had spilled over. We weren't coloring inside the lines anymore.

"No, it's not like that," I said.

"Nothing's happened?"

"Not really."

"What does that mean?"

I took a deep breath. "All right, we kissed." I decided that was plenty of information to share with my brother.

He studied me for a long moment and then shook his head. "I shouldn't have to tell you this, but you're making a big mistake. I know this guy's type, and so do you. He may be successful at what he does, but he's not someone you want to get involved with."

"What does that mean? You barely even know him." My inner voice asked me how well I knew Josh. After my conversation with Nalla, I was standing on less stable ground.

His dark eyes, so familiar, were concerned. "Didn't you learn anything from your horrible marriage?"

"That was a million years ago."

"Apparently not."

I shook my head. "Is this why you came here today? To give me grief about Josh?" And to think I was glad Lars hadn't come by to cause trouble. Then I realized the rest of it. "Mom sent you, didn't she?"

"I came here to see for myself what was going on. I was concerned, especially after she told me he cursed out Linda and her associate when they came here to talk to you about selling this place. Is that true?"

"Are you kidding me? They deserved it."

"Linda said he threatened them with bodily harm. Did they deserve that too?"

I laughed. "That's a wild exaggeration. And trust me, they were being assholes. They were trying to pressure me into selling."

Lars shook his head. "You're not thinking clearly. It seems like you haven't been thinking clearly since you bought this money pit."

I rubbed my forehead, trying to quell the headache I sensed coming on. "Let's not have this same dumb conversation again."

"Fine. But think about what I'm saying. I don't want to see you get hurt." It was weird to hear him saying the same thing Nalla had just said moments earlier. "My gut tells me that guy is trouble."

"I think your gut is wrong. Besides, I know what I'm doing."

"I hope so." He studied me. "Just do me a favor, Leah. Look before you leap this time."

CHAPTER TWENTY-THREE

~Josh~

"Damn, dude, so you and Leah are a thing, huh?" Dean was studying me. "I like her. She's cool."

We were standing on Leah's front porch. It was getting dark soon, and he and Nalla were getting ready to head back to the house through the woods. Nalla was inside using the bathroom.

Dean had downloaded a geographical app that Damian told him about. I'd nearly had a heart attack when Damian first brought me here. The woods were thick and dark. I mean, shit, he was only eleven. He laughed and showed me this app with a compass that gave his position on a map, but I didn't like it. I made him promise to never come here again without me.

"We're not a thing," I said. "We're just friends."

Dean raised a skeptical brow. "It's pretty obvious you're into her. You could barely take your eyes off her."

I stuffed my hands into my front pockets, embarrassed I'd been so obvious.

"I can't remember the last time I've seen you act that way with anyone, except maybe Lindsay."

Lindsay was my ex-wife from years ago. The last thing I wanted was a repeat of that scenario.

I shook my head. "You know my situation with Charlotte. She's got me by the short hairs."

"Do you really think she'd stop the adoption if she heard you were involved with someone?"

"I know she would."

Dean nodded. He'd spent enough time around Charlotte to know how temperamental she could be. "Yeah, it probably is best to play it safe. Except you and Leah looked awfully cozy. Does she understand you guys aren't a thing?"

"I've explained it to her. She knows the score." I may have explained it to Leah, but I wondered if I needed to explain it to myself again. I could barely keep my hands off her.

Dean chuckled. "I hope this adoption goes through soon so you can stop living like a Shaolin monk."

I grinned. We both grew up watching *Kung Fu* reruns. "You and me both, brother."

"Did you see that text from Terence? I think it's a good idea. Are you down with it?"

Nalla opened the front door and stepped onto the porch.

"Absolutely." I'd seen the text when I checked my messages after dinner.

"What are you guys talking about?" Nalla asked. She was surveying the area, rubbing her arms with an expression of distaste. "What's a great idea?"

"Terence thinks the four of us should rent a house somewhere and try to hash out our problems," Dean told her.

"Oh, you guys should definitely do that. It would be a shame if the band broke up forever."

"Do you know when Terence is flying back from Nepal?" I asked him.

"I don't think he's said anything yet."

I stroked my beard. I wondered how soon everyone would want to get together. Obviously I still had Damian to think of.

Dean looked down at Nalla. "Well, what do you say, baby? Should we bounce?" He glanced at me. "I'll keep you posted on what's going on at the house."

"Thanks, dude." We gave each other a hug. "Believe me, I appreciate everything you're doing."

Nalla stepped in close to me, so I felt obliged to hug her too.

"How much longer do you think you'll be staying here?" she asked, her hand still on my arm. "You should just come home with us tonight."

I took a step back so she'd have to let go of me. "Not much longer."

She got a pouty expression. "It's just that we really miss you. I don't know how you can even stand it here."

I cocked my head. "What do you mean?"

"Well, the whole place stinks. Haven't you noticed? It smells like cow shit."

Dean and I both laughed. "That's alpaca and llama shit," I said. "There aren't any cows."

"Whatever. You know what I mean." She wrinkled her nose. "It's gross."

I took a whiff of the evening air. "All I smell is hay."

"Same here," Dean agreed.

"Well, I can smell it. It feels like it's getting in my pores. It's probably not healthy for Damian either."

I gave her a look. "How's that?"

"Breathing in all this air polluted by farm animals. That can't be good for him."

"That's absurd." I felt annoyed. I'd noticed this more and more with Nalla. She could be irritating. "The air out here is cleaner than anywhere."

Dean laughed and put his arm around her shoulders. "Come on, my city girl. I guess we won't be buying a farm anytime soon." He gazed up at the sky, which was turning orange. "Looks like we might be walking through the woods in the dark after all. If you hear wolves howling, don't be alarmed. That's just us."

She smiled and shoved at Dean's chest. "I'm not a wolf."

He grinned at her. "But I am."

She rolled her eyes and laughed. She looked over at me, trying to catch my eye, but I pretended not to notice.

After I waved them off, I went around to the back of the house searching for Leah. She'd disappeared after dinner, and I worried maybe I'd offended her. Our chemistry together was hot, but I hoped she didn't think I was sending mixed signals.

I found Shane and Martha sitting next to each other on the grass in the backyard, watching Damian and Eddie play badminton. A Foo Fighters song drifted out from a nearby radio.

"Have you guys seen Leah?" I asked them.

Shane looked up at me. "Yeah, she said she's taking a shower and going to bed."

Disappointment thudded in my chest. I'd been looking forward to moonbathing with her. It wasn't like Leah to go to bed without saying good night, and now I felt certain something was wrong.

I stood for a moment watching Damian and Eddie play, though they were mostly goofing around. Eddie pretended to play guitar with his racket while Damian held his like a microphone, singing along with the radio.

That's my boy. I couldn't help smiling.

"Looks like those two have become friends," I said to Martha.

She nodded in agreement. "I'm glad I brought him. I think he already texted my mom to see if he and Damian could have a sleep-over sometime."

"Really?" I liked the idea of Damian making friends here. These were exactly the kind of roots I wanted for him. "I'm sure he'd enjoy that. Eddie is definitely welcome to stay with us once we're back at the house."

She nodded. "I'll let my mom know."

I noticed the way Shane and Martha were sitting close together. Shane kept gazing at her in a lovesick way.

Is that how I look with Leah?

Probably.

I was already feeling like a third wheel with these two and told them I was going inside.

It was quiet in the house. I figured I'd get my guitar out and maybe work on some songs. Once I was in the living room, my eyes kept going toward the staircase.

The one that led up to Leah's bedroom.

I debated it for about five minutes before deciding, *Fuck it.*

I'd never been upstairs in her house before since I hadn't any reason to be. When I arrived at the second landing, it was dim. There were three doors, and I had no idea which one was her bedroom. The floor creaked when I walked.

I knocked lightly on the nearest door. There was no answer, so I opened it to discover a bathroom.

All right, not that one.

I tried the next door, and this one turned out to be an office.

Third time's a charm.

My palms felt sweaty, and I wiped them on my jeans. It was weird being so nervous about a woman. I swallowed and knocked on the last door.

I waited.

There was still no response.

Is she asleep?

My pulse went up as I gripped the handle and turned the knob. This time when I opened the door, I found I was looking into a feminine bedroom. Leah was lying in bed, propped up on one elbow, studying her phone. The room was softly lit by a single lamp on her nightstand.

She still hadn't noticed me, so I knocked lightly on the doorframe.

She turned her head, her mouth opening as she pulled her earbuds out. "Josh?"

Our eyes met, and I felt the blood grow thick in my veins, felt every inch of that short distance between us. I knew I shouldn't be here, that I should leave, but instead I got a rush as I stepped inside her private space. Her perfume lingered in the air. It had been ages since I'd entered a woman's bedroom for the first time.

She didn't say anything, just watched me as I moved closer and sat on the edge of her bed. Her room wasn't frilly but definitely feminine, and I felt like an interloper.

For a long moment, neither of us spoke.

"Did I fuck up earlier?" I asked finally. "Is that what's happening? Are you pissed at me?"

She put her phone aside and sat up, keeping the covers around her legs. She wore a plain white camisole, and the coconut scent of her freshly showered skin was doing things to me, putting thoughts into my head.

"Why do you think that?"

"Because you left without saying anything. I thought we were moonbathing tonight."

She lifted her chin, and there was something wrong. I could see it on her face.

"What's going on? Talk to me."

"Tell me about Jane Braxton."

My brows went up, and my first response was anger, but I pushed that down. I wondered if this was what she'd been looking at on her phone. "There's nothing to tell. She's our band's manager."

"Did you sleep with her behind Rhys's back?"

"Jesus, where's this coming from?"

"Did you?"

"No, I didn't. Of course not."

"That's not what the news story I just watched said. It said you had an affair with her, and that's why Rhys is leaving the band."

"None of that's true."

She stared at me, and I saw skepticism. This was the problem when your life was fodder for the public, when people felt like they had the right to know things about you, personal things. They had no problem making shit up.

"Why are they saying it then?"

"Why do you think? Because it's juicy, and people like to hear juicy stories. It doesn't matter whether there's truth in it." I stared at her, feeling frustrated. "What are you going to believe? Some bullshit story on the internet or me?"

She leaned her head back against the wall. "I don't know what to believe."

"Are you kidding?"

She bit her lip and seemed uncomfortable. "I have to tell you something. I was married to the lead singer for a punk band in my early twenties."

My eyes widened. This surprised me.

"Except he was a serious asshole. He lied, drank too much, and played constant head games. I finally found out he was cheating on me and left."

"Damn, Leah, I'm sorry. That's messed up." I was pissed just hearing about it. I wondered who this prick was.

"It was a long time ago."

"And now you think it's happening again. You think I'm like that guy?"

She sighed. "It's hard not to make comparisons. Especially with all the drama, you know? There was always drama with him too. I felt like an idiot, like I should have known a guy like that would never be faithful."

"Well, that's not me. I've never cheated on a woman. *Ever.*" It was the ultimate irony that my ex-wife and Charlotte worried constantly that I'd stray. It destroyed both relationships. It was like neither of them seemed to grasp the most fundamental thing about me—that I was loyal. "Do you believe me?"

She searched my face, but it didn't take her long. I could see she grasped it. "I believe you."

"Good."

"I guess this friendship of ours has taken me by surprise."

"Yeah, me too." I thought back to when we were in that hayloft. I'd relived it a dozen times, most of them in the shower. "Is this why you said you couldn't get involved with me? Because your ex was a singer?"

She nodded and gave a wry smile. "It's a strange coincidence, don't you think?"

"Problem is you were with the *wrong* singer. I mean, could that guy even sing? Was he in your top one hundred like I am?"

She smiled. "Not even in my top one thousand."

I snorted. "See? So what number am I?"

She shrugged, her eyes flitting around the room. "High seventies. Maybe even high sixties."

I waggled my brows. "Is it... sixty-nine? Do I detect a hidden message?"

She laughed and kicked her leg against me. "You're an outrageous flirt."

"I know." I grew more serious. "It's my nature, and it's part of who I am onstage. Sometimes the two get mixed up together."

"Is that what this is between us?" she asked. "A flirtation?"

"It's more than flirting, Leah. I like you."

She didn't reply.

"Do you like *me*?" I felt oddly nervous asking. It reminded me of those few seconds right before I touched a microphone. People always knew who I was before they met me. If I was judged, it was based on what they knew about me as a musician. It was rare that I was simply judged as a man.

"I do," she said. "I like you."

"But do you *like* me, like me?"

She smiled. "You're hard to resist."

Those brown eyes pulled at me. Her mouth looked better than a bowl of ripe cherries. More than anything I wanted to kiss her. My chest ached thinking about how much I wanted it.

We gazed at each other. I knew there was a lovesick expression on my face, but I couldn't help it. Leah was something special.

"You've really done a number on me, honey," I said softly. "I've been in a terrible state from the moment I walked into your house."

"You have?"

"Staying here while wanting you and knowing I can't have you has been torture."

"Maybe that's all it is." She brought her knees up. "You're just chasing your desires. Moving from one want to the next."

"Except all I want is you."

My words lingered, filling the small space of her bedroom.

"Have I really been torturing you?" She tilted her head. "I had no idea."

"It's those running shorts every morning. Then at night I wonder what you're wearing to sleep."

"Well, now you can see." She motioned down at her body. "Not exactly a sexy nightie."

My eyes lingered on her little white top. "I prefer this. It reminds me of that first night I saw you." I thought about those tall black boots she'd been wearing. I wouldn't mind seeing her in that hot ensemble again.

She snorted softly. "An unforgettable experience."

"It sure was. Do you ever think about me when you're up here alone in your bed?"

"Maybe," she teased. "Sometimes."

I lowered my voice. "Could you do something for me?" My tone sounded gravelly to my own ears, coarse with the arousal I'd been fighting.

"What's that?"

"Show me the panties you're wearing."

She didn't move at first, but the air changed, and I knew she felt it too. Felt the way the energy shifted, how the lamp's light took on a sensual glow.

A long moment passed, and then, without a word, she slowly slid down the sheet from her hip so I could see. Light blue nylon with lace on top and a tiny little bow. I studied them, memorizing every detail for my next shower.

"Would you like to see more?" she asked, a throaty note in her voice.

All that flirting at dinner had clearly heated us both up. Her hands still held the sheet, and I knew I should say no. I should tell her this was enough, that this was all I needed, but it was far from all I needed.

"Yeah." I licked my lips with anticipation. "Show me the rest, honey."

She slid the sheet all the way down and brought her legs out. They were long and shapely, and I took my time admiring them. The little white top only went to her belly, so I could see more of the panties, could see that bit of dark hair beneath the lace.

"Would you do something for me now?" she asked.

I looked at her face.

"Take your shirt off."

I swallowed. *Fuck.* This was a dangerous game.

I glanced toward her bedroom window, hesitating.

"You're not shy, are you?"

I snorted. We both knew I was anything but shy.

Reaching behind myself, I pulled the shirt over my head and tossed it aside.

The expression of wanting on her face went straight to my dick. I was already straining against my jeans. I shifted on the bed, trying to ease the pressure, but it didn't help. My cock, my balls, everything ached.

"God, you're gorgeous." Her eyes roamed over me.

I smiled at the compliment.

"Maybe I shouldn't have said that." She was still staring at my chest. "Your ego is probably big enough already."

"Honey, my ego isn't the only thing about me that's big."

I wasn't sure how she'd react to that, but I saw the color rise to her cheeks. It gave her a pretty flush. Her cherry lips parted, and when she licked them, I nearly groaned.

"Then show me," she said. "I want to see."

"How about you show me something first?" My heart beat faster, though I told myself this was harmless. "Take your top off."

Leah's lips parted, her eyes as dark as India ink. She sat up, but then she got on her knees so she was right in front of me, only inches away. I watched as that little white camisole disappeared, revealing breasts that were small, pert, and luscious. Her nipples were like two pink candies I wanted to lick and suck.

"See anything you like?" she whispered.

My heart pounded like a bass drum.

So close, her coconut-scented body was so tempting.

Before I knew it, lust crashed through me like a train wreck. My hands reached out of their own volition, and I grabbed her hips, dragging her toward me.

Leah gasped.

I smashed my face against her breasts, immersing myself in the scent of her soft skin. Fuck, it was heaven.

"Goddammit," I growled, holding her in a firm grip. I couldn't stop myself. Her candy tits were right there, and I lavished them with my tongue, licking and sucking just like I wanted.

She moaned and squirmed toward my mouth, grabbing me, pulling me closer, yanking on my hair.

I slid one hand down between her thighs, knowing I shouldn't. An alarm bell blared inside my head, telling me to stop.

Her panties were soaked through the fabric. I groaned with pleasure at how wet she was for me. She trembled as I played with her, sliding my fingers along the outside for a bit before snaking them beneath the elastic.

"Josh," she whimpered, breathing hard, moving her hips. "Oh *God*."

I wanted to pull these panties off her, wanted to lick her until she came, until she screamed, until her juices were all over my face.

Fuck.

Instead I pulled back from her tits. "Give me your mouth."

She did what I asked, and I kissed her. Long and hard. Reckless with tongues and teeth.

I felt her hand on the outside of my jeans. She was trying to yank my zipper down. My cock ached and throbbed, but I pushed her hand away.

"Just you, honey," I said, panting. "Just taking care of you tonight."

Not entirely true because I wanted it too. I wanted to feel Leah shatter in my arms. I wanted it badly.

She gripped my wrist while I played with her, squeezing two fingers inside where she was hot and slippery. Moaning, she rode my hand as my fingers worked her over and my thumb circled her clit.

"That's it, honey," I gritted out, worried I was too close myself. "Give it to me. I want you to come so hard."

I felt her whole body grow tense as it went on, her hips moving in a rhythm, pushing against me. I closed my eyes, awash in the sounds, smells, and textures of her. My head swam. I wanted to fuck her, but this was erotic as hell.

She gripped me tight, and when she gasped aloud, I knew she was there. Her pussy tightened around my fingers, undulating in waves, while her hips thrashed and bucked. It was so damned hot. Hotter than shit that it was *Leah* moaning and writhing against me. The intensity was too much. It felt too *good*. I groaned and tried to stop myself, but it was beyond my control. I held her tight while stars burst in front of my eyes, and I exploded right along with her.

CHAPTER TWENTY-FOUR

~Leah~

I collapsed against Josh, my body vibrating all over from a crazy, intense orgasm. He held me tight and seemed to be recovering from something himself. "Did you just—"

"Come in my pants like a teenager?" He swallowed, breathing hard. "Yeah, I did."

I laughed softly.

"I can't believe how embarrassing this is."

His arm was still wrapped around my waist, and I stroked his face, then gently tugged his beard. "There's nothing to be embarrassed about."

I lay back on the bed, bringing him down with me. He came easily, and soon we were wrapped together, our hearts still pounding against each other.

He chuckled. "When I fantasized about us together, a pair of sticky boxer shorts was never part of that fantasy."

"You fantasized about us?" I felt a rush of delight.

"Constantly. Every time I take a shower. In fact, I'd like to borrow your coconut shampoo for my next appointment with Rosie."

"Who's Rosie?"

"Rosie Palm and her five daughters." He held up his hand.

I groaned and rolled my eyes. "That joke is so old. I can't believe you just made it."

"Sometimes for variety I meet with Lucy."

"Do I even have to ask?"

"Lefty Lucy and her five sisters."

I groaned again. "This is so cringy."

"Hey, I'm just telling it like it is. Rosie and Lucy have been my mistresses for quite a while now."

"Is that really true?" I reached over and played with his beard. "You haven't had anyone at all?"

He shrugged. "A couple one-night stands, but that was ages ago. Right after Charlotte and I split up, and before the adoption paperwork was brought into it." His expression turned serious.

"How long then?"

"Over a year."

"Wow." I was surprised. "I can see why you've grown so close with Rosie and Lucy."

He nodded, but his expression didn't change, and it was clear something troubled him.

"I'm not going to tell anyone you were in my bedroom," I assured him.

He nodded again but then closed his eyes and pinched the bridge of his nose. "This shit is *so* messed up. Choosing my son means choosing celibacy?" His voice shook. "The irony is it's not even about the sex. I'm fucking *lonely*."

My heart hurt hearing this. I wrapped my arms tighter around him. Josh was so funny and generous, and nearly always upbeat. He was like a magnificent lion being forced into a cage.

I had to wonder about Charlotte. What kind of person treated someone like this? Especially her son's father. Because it was obvious that was who Josh was, even if not legally.

"She's probably still in love with you," I said. "That's why she doesn't want you to be with anyone."

"That's not love."

"Maybe it is to her."

He shook his head. "You don't know her. She doesn't love me. She wants to possess me. It's ownership she wants."

I tried to imagine having Josh but then being forced to give him up. It would be terrible. She probably did still love him. "Who instigated the breakup? You or her?"

"I'm the one who left."

"Why?"

He blew his breath out. "Too many reasons to name."

I nodded, figuring he didn't want to get into it.

"What about you?" He drew back a little to look at me. "How is it you're not married or don't have a boyfriend? I can't figure it out. A woman as hot as you? It doesn't make any sense."

I smiled that he thought I was so "hot."

"I can be a handful," I admitted. "Plus, I get bored easily." It surprised me that I was being so honest, but I figured whatever this was between us was temporary, so what did it matter?

He chuckled. "I'll bet you are a handful."

"I think that's why I married Derek, because he was so intense, and I liked it."

"But then you got burned by that flame."

My eyes flashed to his. It was an insightful comment. It hadn't escaped my notice that Josh was intense too.

We studied each other in the soft light. His pupils were huge, nearly eclipsing the blue of his corneas.

"Come here, honey." He drew me in closer. "Kiss me some more before I have to leave your bedroom and turn back into a pumpkin."

I laughed lightly. "You should have been a comedian instead of a singer."

"Maybe I'll start doing stand-up at our shows. I can tell all my cringy jokes."

"I don't know. They might throw rotten eggs at you."

"That's all right. I've had worse thrown at me."

"Have you?" I pulled back. I couldn't tell if he was joking or serious.

He nodded. "I've had shit thrown at me lots of times. Years ago, we did a show in Detroit, and some chick in the audience threw a spiked high-heeled shoe right at my face. Nearly took my eye out." He turned his head and pulled his hair back so I could see the scar near his temple. "Three stitches, and I bled like a motherfucker."

My jaw dropped with outrage. "Someone did that to you? Did you find out who it was?"

"No clue. Figured she was either crazy or on drugs."

"That's horrible." I put my hand up to his cheek, then leaned in and kissed his scar. "I hope that doesn't happen often."

"Not so much nowadays, but things used to get wild."

I tried to imagine the life he'd led, so different from mine. I continued to caress his beard and jaw while he watched me, his eyes roaming my face.

"Damn, Leah. You really are beautiful."

"Thank you. I think you're beautiful too."

"Come closer," he whispered, sliding his hand down my spine. We were still skin to skin. "Let me taste that pretty mouth again."

I slipped both my arms around his neck, and we kissed some more. It was different from those hot, fevered ones earlier. These were slow and sensual. His mouth felt like sinking into a warm bath. When he rolled me onto my back, I enjoyed his weight, the smell and taste of him.

We went at it for a while, just kissing, except I giggled as his facial hair kept going up my nose.

"What is it?" he asked, smiling.

"It's your beard. It tickles." I pushed some of it aside. His beard was crazy, especially lying on my back.

"Is it too much?"

"I don't think I've ever kissed anyone with this much facial hair."

He nodded and seemed to consider this. "I've definitely never let it get this long before."

"It's not that I don't like beards. I love them."

"You do?"

"Of course. Beards are hot."

He smiled and kissed me again before moving to my neck, working some kind of magic there. My breath caught. I ran my hands down his muscular back, pulling him close.

Josh worked his way lower until he was at my breasts. "Look at you," he whispered. "So damn pretty all over."

I squirmed as he licked my nipples before gently sucking on them. I closed my eyes at the sensation. It felt so good. His mouth was making me tingle.

A door closed downstairs, and my eyes flew open.

Josh stopped what he was doing, and we both went on high alert, listening.

"It's probably Shane," I said. "I think that was the sliding door for the back deck."

Josh sat up. "Shit, I don't even know what time it is. I've probably stayed up here too long." He met my eyes. "I should go."

I nodded in agreement and sat up too. "You probably should."

He leaned in and kissed me again, then searched around for his T-shirt, slipping it back on. I did the same with my camisole.

When he stood up, I could see that he had a large erection in his pants.

"That's an impressive sight."

He put his hand on his waistband and made a strange face, then shook his leg. "Except I think these shorts are permanently glued to me."

"Ew...."

He chuckled. "It's your fault. You're too damn sexy."

"I guess I must be."

He put his hand out. "Come here, honey. One more kiss before I go take a shower and obsess about you some more."

I stood up, and he wrapped his arms around me. We hugged for a long moment before he bent down and kissed me softly. "See you later, my little spinster."

THE NEXT MORNING, Damian and Josh joined me on my run. Everything felt normal between Josh and me, though our eyes kept finding each other. We joked and flirted in our usual way, and then afterward, when we were alone in the kitchen, he came up behind me. I was cooking scrambled eggs when I felt him kiss the back of my neck.

My breath hitched. "You shouldn't do that," I whispered as his kiss sent erotic shivers down my spine.

"I know." That smooth baritone was low in my ear. I felt his hands on my hips. "It's just that you look so good."

After breakfast, I started my morning chores with the two of them helping me with the chickens. Damian fed them some scratch to distract them while Josh helped me clean out the coop.

"I think that rooster is stalking me again," he said, leaning against his shovel. He nodded toward Cary Grant, who was standing near some bushes about ten feet away.

When I glanced over, I could see Josh was right. The bird was fixated on him. "This is so weird. If things don't improve, we may have to try some rooster love."

"Rooster *love*?" Josh shivered with horror. "That doesn't sound like anything I want to be a part of."

I laughed. "It's something people do to calm down aggressive roosters. You hold them and pet their feathers—sweet-talk them until they finally get used to you."

He appeared skeptical. "And that works?"

"I don't know. I've never had to try it. I've only heard about it."

During lunch, I was checking my messages and realized I'd forgotten about a dinner date I had with Theo and Claire tonight. I texted them to let them know I'd be there.

"I'll be gone a few hours," I told Josh and Damian. "Shane will be here, so you guys can all hang out."

"Can we order pizza?" Damian asked. He was sitting at the table reading one of my books about alpaca farming of all things.

"It's up to your dad," I said. "But I'm sure Shane would be all over that."

"Who are you having dinner with?" Josh asked. His voice sounded casual.

"A couple of my girlfriends."

He nodded but didn't say anything more.

The rest of the afternoon was uneventful. After my regular chores, Damian helped me weed in the garden while telling me all about life at his boarding school in England. I listened with interest. It sounded like a fancy place. It was hard to imagine going to boarding school, but Damian seemed happy with it. Josh said he needed to make a few phone calls and had stayed back at the house.

When it got closer to dinnertime, I took a quick shower and put on a sundress with colorful earth tones that came to just above my knees. I was going to wear jeans but decided it would be fun to dress up a little. I blow-dried my hair and wore it down. My hair was naturally straight, but I used a flat iron to make it even straighter. I put on makeup and hoop earrings and, after a spritz of perfume, was feeling quite glamorous for a change.

By the time I got downstairs and was ready to leave, Shane, Josh, and Damian were standing in the kitchen discussing what kind of pizza to order.

"Are you going on a date?" Shane asked me.

"No, it's just dinner with Theo and Claire."

I felt Josh watching me.

Damian was telling Shane that he'd like corn on his pizza.

"Corn?" Shane gave him a strange look. "You can't put corn on pizza, dude. That's weird."

"It's not weird!" Damian laughed.

Josh was still studying me as I hovered in the doorway. He tilted his head. "Come here. I have something for you."

"What is it?"

He walked over to me instead. "Hold out your wrist."

I didn't know what he was talking about. I watched as he took off one of his bracelets—a silver beaded one. "Here, I think this will look good with your dress."

I glanced down at myself and realized he was right. "It's too big," I said. "It'll never fit me."

"It'll fit," he murmured. "It's adjustable."

I held my wrist out, and he gently slipped the bracelet on. After a few seconds of fiddling with it, he made it smaller.

He continued to hold my wrist, his thumb gently brushing my skin. "You look pretty," he said in a low voice so the others couldn't hear. "I like seeing you in a dress."

The thumb caresses were so erotic I could barely catch my breath. His blue eyes stared straight into mine, pinning me in place.

I could still hear Damian trying to convince my brother that corn tasted good on pizza.

"Tell him, Dad," Damian said with frustration. "He won't believe me."

Josh smiled and let go of my wrist. He turned toward Shane. "Yeah, it's actually really good. A lot of countries eat it that way."

"See!" Damian threw his hands up. "We *always* order it with corn back home."

"Really?" Shane scratched his chest. "That sounds crazy. I suppose we could order a pizza and put corn on it ourselves. I doubt they'd do it for us."

They were still hashing out the details when I waved goodbye and left.

I kept glancing down at the bracelet as I drove into town. I shook my hand around. It was heavier than it looked. On closer inspection, the whole thing was nicely made and probably expensive.

We were meeting at a Thai place, and since I was a few minutes late for dinner, Theo and Claire were already waiting for me.

I sat down and instantly knew something was up. "What?"

They both looked at me like I had antennae growing out of my head.

"You tell us," Claire said. She wore a blouse with a white camisole beneath it. You still couldn't tell she was pregnant.

Theo raised an auburn brow. "A certain rock star appeared in your last YouTube video."

My jaw dropped. "Wait, you guys watch my spinning videos?"

Claire laughed. "I do when one of my clients tells me Joshua Trevant is in it!" She ran a busy maid service with customers all over town.

"Please explain the situation to us," Theo said, lacing her fingers. "Especially the way you two looked... so comfortable."

"Yes, please do! How on earth do you know Joshua Trevant?" Claire asked with an incredulous expression. "I demand that you tell us this instant!"

Luckily, we were in a corner booth on a Monday night, and it wasn't busy, so no one had overheard our conversation.

"I'll tell you, but I have to swear you both to secrecy," I said, keeping my voice quiet.

They both nodded and leaned forward with interest.

I quickly explained the story to them, leaving out the part where I gave his address to the press and caused this fiasco to begin with. "He and Damian have been staying with me for about a week now."

"That's amazing," Claire breathed. "What's he like?"

"He's really nice. Both he and his son are great."

"So, what's going on between the two of you?" Theo wanted to know.

"Nothing." I hoped my cheeks weren't turning pink. I hated lying to my friends, but I had to protect Josh.

"Uh-huh," Claire said. "Have you actually watched that video?"

I shrugged. "Not really." Obviously I checked the stats on it afterward.

"It looked like you guys were flirting," Claire said. "You seemed to have a lot of chemistry."

"Oh, that's nothing." I waved my hand. "Josh is always flirting. I wouldn't read anything into it."

Theo studied me and leaned back in her seat. "A lot of the comments seemed to think you were his girlfriend."

"What comments?" I snorted. "There's like five in total."

Claire and Theo both raised their brows.

"Uh, I think you need to check again," Theo told me. "Because there are a lot more than five."

"There are?" I grabbed my phone from my purse and brought up the main screen. "How many?"

"Best if you just check it yourself," Theo said.

"That's a pretty bracelet," Claire commented. She took a sip of her water. "Is that new?"

"No, it's Josh's." I was still staring at my screen, waiting for YouTube.

"You're wearing his jewelry?"

"He thought it looked good with my dress."

I saw Claire and Theo glance at each other.

"It's just a bracelet," I said. "No big deal."

Finally the app opened, and I quickly navigated to my page. When I saw the number of views, I was confused. It said 10.3K, but that didn't make sense. Was there some mistake? But then I realized what it meant. "Oh my God! Over ten thousand people have watched this video?"

Theo nodded. "There are quite a few comments too."

I opened the link and sucked in my breath. There were over five hundred comments. Scrolling through them, I felt sick to my stomach, because Theo was right—a lot of them seemed to think Josh and I were a couple. *What if Charlotte sees these?*

"Are you okay?" Claire asked. "I thought you'd be happy. It looks like your live stream went viral. That has to be good for business, right?"

I nodded. "Sure." I usually checked my web store for orders daily but had been so busy and distracted that I haven't looked at it for a couple of days.

"What's going on?" she asked. "Are you worried people will invade your privacy?"

I couldn't tell them about Charlotte and the adoption. This was Josh's personal life, and I didn't feel right sharing it, even with my besties.

"I doubt you'll have a problem with the press," Claire said. "Last I heard they were running out of places to stay in Truth Harbor."

"What do you mean?"

"One of my clients, who owns a small bed-and-breakfast, said Delores has been encouraging fellow business owners to think of Josh as one of our own and to discourage the press from booking rooms. She says they're harassing him, and it has to stop."

"Wow... seriously?" I was stunned, and Josh would be too. Delores could move mountains when she wanted to. "People are actually going along with it?"

Claire nodded. "Some of them are. Is he really planning to stay here permanently?"

"That's what he says."

She smiled and shook her head. "I just can't get over this. I remember when you were so impressed after I met Philip. It's like the tables have turned."

It was true. I'd been very impressed when Claire met her husband. He co-owned the venture capital company I used to work for and was a financial genius.

"I can't believe you have a rock star as a houseguest," she mused. "Does he ever sing?"

I remembered how he sang in the truck that day we went into town. "Sometimes."

"Really? God, that's so hot. I'll bet he's super sexy all the time."

I thought of my acute lust and nodded. "Yeah, he pretty much is."

She laughed. "So there's really nothing going on between you two?"

I could feel Theo studying me as well. These women were my closest friends. I promised Josh I wouldn't tell anyone he'd been in my bedroom, and I owed him that much. "We flirt sometimes, but that's basically it."

"Too bad," Claire sighed. "He's gorgeous."

Luckily, we were interrupted by our server asking if we were ready to order dinner. We told him to come back in a few minutes.

As we studied our menus, I changed the subject and asked Claire and Theo how they were doing.

Claire told us the latest news with her pregnancy. She'd had an ultrasound recently, and everything looked great.

"That's wonderful," I said. "Do you know whether it's a boy or girl?"

She shook her head. "Philip wants to know, but I want to wait and see, so for now, we're holding off."

"I can't believe you don't want to know," Theo said. "That would drive me crazy."

"Me too," I agreed.

Claire rubbed her belly. "I just like the surprise of it. I think it'll be exciting to find out when they're born."

We talked some more about what being pregnant was like, and she told us about her morning sickness. I'd never been pregnant, and while I thought maybe I'd like to have a baby someday, it wasn't anything I felt urgent about.

"How are things with you?" I asked Theo. "Have you met your new neighbor yet?" She'd mentioned recently that someone had bought the land next to her property that had been vacant for years. It contained several acres and an abandoned farm.

Theo bristled. "No, I haven't, but his lawyer sent me a letter demanding I get rid of my beehives or else he was suing me."

"For what?" I gaped.

"He claims they're interfering with his property somehow. It's my land and my hives, though. So screw him."

Claire shook her head. "What an asshole."

"Indeed." Theo perused her menu. "The whole thing is absurd. I'm not going to worry about it."

"That reminds me, Josh is crazy about your honey. He called it exceptional and wanted to buy a case."

Theo smiled. "Well, my honey *is* exceptional, but I don't sell it."

"I know, I told him. Do you think it would be okay if I brought them both by sometime and they could see your beehives? I think Damian would especially love it."

"Sure, that's fine. Just text me, and we can set up a time when I'm home." Theo worked at the university's research facility just outside of town.

Claire leaned forward. "Do you mind if I come too? I'd love to meet Josh. Do you think he'd be okay with that?"

I shrugged. "I'm sure it would be fine, but I'll ask him."

She got an excited look on her face. "This is going to be so amazing. East Echo is my favorite band."

I nodded. East Echo was one of my favorites too. I knew Josh was a big deal, but somehow I saw him less as a rock star and more as a guy.

"I wonder how much longer he'll be staying with you," Claire said.

"I don't know. Obviously I value my privacy." But even as I said it, there was a part of me that wasn't at all ready to see them go.

CHAPTER TWENTY-FIVE

~Leah~

It was just after nine when the dinner with Theo and Claire ended. I rolled my truck window down on the way home, taking in the warm evening air. When East Echo's "Silver Days" came on the radio, I laughed with delight and sang right along with it:

"Silver days shine so bright
All that I needed
I found in you...
Silver days pure as a morning
Make every night
burn hot and true..."

I kept glancing down at Josh's bracelet as I sang. The feel of it against my skin had kept me connected with him throughout dinner, and I wondered if that had been his intention.

The sky was blue with streaks of gold when I pulled up to Clarity Moon Farm, driving past the sign I'd hand-painted with pride just after I moved in. Despite all the grief I got from my mom and Lars, I knew in my heart this place was special and worth fighting for. I just wished I could get them to see it.

Walking up the front porch steps, I could hear Josh, Shane, and Damian laughing even before I opened the door. Once inside, I discovered them sprawled on the living room couch. Pizza boxes sat on an end table, a variety of cats lounging nearby, while the three of them laughed like hyenas as they played a video game.

Of course, none of that surprised me.

What surprised me was the green goo smeared all over Josh's and Shane's faces.

What the heck? "Is that the face mask Isabel brought over a few weeks ago?"

"Yeah, it is." Shane was staring at the screen and hammering at his video game controller.

The coffee table was littered with snacks—chips, salsa, bean dip, and a jar of olives with a spoon in it. There were a couple of beers, and Damian was drinking a Coke.

Talk about male bonding.

"I'm just worried for the female population," I said. "Aren't you two pretty enough?"

Josh grinned and gave me a flirty eye smolder. "I can *never* be pretty enough. My beauty has no limits."

"Where's your masculine pride then? Are you guys going to give each other perms next?"

"Hey, I got plenty of masculine pride," Shane said.

"Maybe you'd like to pick out nail polish colors." I couldn't resist teasing them. I definitely had to take pictures. This was too funny not to capture.

"Just ignore her," my brother told Josh as he manipulated his controller. "She doesn't know what she's talking about."

"No worries." Josh grinned at me. And even with the green goop on his face, my stomach took a dip. He spoke in that silky baritone. "As Leah very well knows, I don't embarrass easily."

Our eyes lingered, and I smiled. He was talking about last night.

"'Cause you gotta trust me, bro," Shane said. "This face mask is bitchin'."

I glanced over at Damian. "Where's his beauty mask?"

"I don't want that disgusting stuff on my face." Damian scowled. He was staring at the screen, too, working his controller, his tongue pushed into the corner of his mouth. "Maybe when I'm a proper geezer."

"He's right," Shane said. "Little dude doesn't need it."

"I paint my fingernails occasionally," Josh commented, holding his hand up to look at. "Usually black or sometimes violet."

"Awesome." Shane nodded.

Josh's fingers were as masculine as the rest of him. He wore a couple of chunky rings. I tried to imagine his fingernails painted black or violet. Instead of turning me off, it had the opposite effect. It turned me way the hell on.

And then I realized something had changed. He looked different. "Oh my gosh, you cut your beard!"

His hand went to his chin, and he grinned at me. "I trimmed it. Figured it was time."

My pulse quickened since I knew why he did it.

"You should try the pizza," Shane said, glancing over at me. "We put a can of corn on it. I couldn't believe it, but that stuff is *good*."

"Really?" I'd never had corn on pizza. "I'm full from dinner, but I'll try a slice tomorrow."

I took a few photos with my phone while Shane and Josh grinned at the camera for me like two green-faced aliens.

Afterward, I took my sandals off, slipped into my tall black rubber boots, and clomped out to the chicken coop and then the barn to check on everyone. The guys said they'd take care of my evening chores, and I was sure they did fine, but I couldn't resist seeing for myself.

As far as I could tell everything looked good. The chickens were nestled and locked up cozy inside their coop. Thankfully, the raccoons had kept their distance, and Cary Grant hadn't made any more alarm calls.

My alpacas relaxed in the nearest pasture, sitting in two groups, still close to each other. I'd noticed lately that Suki had become a second alpha while Rhiannon was still primary. I figured I'd monitor that, though so far everything seemed peaceful. Watching my alpacas over the last year, I'd learned they had complicated social dynamics just like people.

Rosalie, Martina, and Eva got up and came over when they saw me.

I leaned against the fence and petted their long necks while they hummed sweetly. I noticed Martina's bottom incisors were getting long. It was probably time to trim them. Pippa's and Lucy's also needed to be trimmed.

My attitude when I took over the farm had been that happy and stress-free alpacas made for healthy animals, and so far I'd been relieved to discover that was true.

"How was your dinner?"

I turned to find Josh walking up the path in that graceful way of his.

"You washed off your beauty mask," I said.

He came and stood next to me by the fence and ran a hand over his face. "So what do you think? Am I any prettier?"

I pretended to study him. He was absurdly gorgeous and knew it. "Hmm... I think you may need a second application, Friedrich."

"Dammit. And here I was hoping to impress you."

"I like the beard." It was trimmed neatly and seemed blonder. It showed off more of his bone structure. "You look handsome."

He ran a hand over his jaw. "Thanks. I figured it was time to blend in with the humans again. Not that I've forgotten my Sasquatch roots."

"I should hope not."

We studied each other, and I sensed we were both uncertain how to handle this relationship that was obviously developing between us.

He reached out to stroke Rosalie's neck. "You never answered my question. How was dinner?"

"Actually, there's something I need to talk to you about. I didn't want to alarm you when I got home, but we may have a problem."

He stopped petting Rosalie and turned to me with concern. "What kind of problem?"

I had my phone on me, so I brought up YouTube to show him. "Remember that live stream you made a guest appearance on? Well, it's gone viral."

His brows rose. "Seriously?" Then he grinned. "That's awesome."

"I don't know if it *is* awesome. Apparently a lot of people who watched it think I'm your girlfriend." I handed my phone to him so he could see the posts himself.

He studied the screen for a few seconds before opening the comments.

"I'm worried Charlotte will see it and get the wrong idea," I said. "There are over ten thousand views."

Josh was still smiling as he scrolled through them. "A number of these talk about the yarn and fleece you sell." He glanced at me. "Have your sales gone up?"

I nodded. "They have." I'd checked my numbers in the parking lot before I'd driven home. "They've tripled."

"Fantastic."

"You're not worried about Charlotte?"

He handed my phone back. "Don't take this the wrong way, but ten thousand views is nothing. If we don't get at least a few million within twenty-four hours of dropping a new song or video, our publicist is ready to kill herself."

"So you don't think Charlotte will see it?"

He shook his head. "I doubt it. Plus, I was just helping a friend. Nothing more."

I blew my breath out. "Okay, because I was worried."

He smiled softly. "You have such a good heart, Leah. I'm amazed

I met you. Sometimes it feels like everybody wants something from me, but you don't want anything. You don't know how rare that is."

I tried to smile back. I wished I was as innocent as he thought I was. I needed to tell him I was the one who caused this fiasco with the press.

"What is it?" he asked, noticing my expression. "Are you still worried? Because I don't think that video is a problem. I wouldn't have done it if I thought it would be."

"No, it's not that." I gazed out at the pasture. The two cria, Neo and Simon, were pronking before bedtime as their mothers looked on. It was so sweet. "I need to tell you something." I took a deep breath, trying to summon the courage. I imagined Josh's face when I told him I'd betrayed his trust. It would hurt him. And that was the last thing I wanted.

And then I had a strange thought.

Why did I have to tell him? I mean, how would he ever know?

I glanced at him as he watched me with growing concern.

I'd simply made a dumb mistake. I doubted Josh would see my giving his home address to a couple of reporters as simply a dumb mistake. He'd be angry and upset. My inner voice reminded me I was normally a trustworthy person, and it wasn't like this would ever happen again.

"My friend Theo said we could go see her beehives," I told him. "I think Damian would like them."

"Sure. That sounds good." He was still watching me. "Is that all you wanted to tell me?"

"My friend Claire wanted to know if she could meet you." I smiled sheepishly. "She's a huge East Echo fan. Would you mind if she joined us?"

"Of course I don't mind. I'd like to meet your friends."

I nodded. "Okay, thanks. That's nice of you."

He studied me for a moment longer but didn't say anything. Finally, he glanced over his shoulder. "I should head back to the house and make sure Damian takes a shower before bed. I let him have a Coke, so hopefully he's not bouncing off the walls all night. Are you walking back with me?"

I shook my head. "I'm going to stay out here a little longer."

"Are we moonbathing later?"

I couldn't stop the stupid grin on my face. "Okay."

"I'll meet you on the porch." Then, to my surprise, he stepped closer. I got a whiff of lemons and clean sweat. "I know I shouldn't do this," he whispered, "but I'm going to anyway."

Then he leaned down, and with soft lips, he kissed me.

I WALKED along the perimeter of the pasture for a while until the golden sky darkened. When I'd lived in the city, it was unsafe to walk alone at night, so this was one of my special pleasures now.

I needed to think things over. Because something was happening between Josh and me, something deeper than friendship, and I didn't know what to do about it.

He lived in a different world than I did. He may be staying here, but this was just a temporary stop for him, and I needed to remember that.

Eventually I made my way toward the house. As I approached it, I could see him already sitting on the porch waiting for me, his legs resting on the side rail.

I walked up the steps, and my heart skipped a beat at the way he was looking at me. "Come here, little girl. Why don't you sit on Santa's lap and tell me what you want for Christmas?"

I bit my lip and moved closer. "It's not Christmas yet."

"Santa doesn't care whether or not it's Christmas. He just wants you to sit on his lap."

I laughed lightly. "You're terrible."

As soon as I stepped close enough, he swooped his arm around me so I fell onto him. "There. That's better," he murmured.

Instantly I was surrounded by Josh's warmth. His delicious scent.

I slipped my arm around his neck, and a girlish excitement pulsed through me. Being around him did feel like Christmas.

"The things that we love tell us what we are," he said softly, our faces close.

I stroked his newly shortened beard, thrilled to have this kind of familiarity with him. "I don't recognize that quote. Who is it from?"

"Thomas Aquinas." He gazed out at the pasture. "I was just thinking about you and Clarity Moon Farm while I waited here. This place is a reflection of you."

"It was my dream for a long time."

"I'm glad you get to live your dream, Leah. That's very cool."

I nodded, then thought about how he had just quoted Thomas Aquinas. *Who the heck does that?* "Why is it you never went to college?" I asked, curious, still playing with his beard. "It seems like something you would enjoy."

He shrugged and then reached down for his bottle of beer. "It's like you said before. I was too busy being a rock star. Or trying to be one back then." He took a swig and offered me the bottle.

"I could totally see you as a scholar," I mused. I took a sip and handed it back. "You could always take classes now for fun."

"For fun?" He gave me a strange look. "I barely graduated high school."

"That's hard to believe. You're so bright and articulate."

Josh snorted. "Trust me, that's not how the school saw it. They were glad to see the back of me."

"Weren't there any classes you liked?"

"Not really." He ran his thumb over the bottle's label. "I suspect I have one of those attention disorders."

"You do? Like ADHD?"

He nodded. "Pretty sure."

"But you seem to concentrate just fine."

"I've learned to deal with it over the years. I've also built my life so I only have to focus on things I enjoy. School was a big problem for me."

I thought about this. "Where were your parents? Couldn't they have helped?"

"My dad split when I was a kid, and my mom's parenting style was to let Jeremy and me do whatever the hell we wanted." He took another sip of beer. "The only guidance came from my grandparents, but they weren't around enough since we moved a lot."

"Who's Jeremy? Is that your brother?"

Josh went still, then nodded. "Yeah, that's my little brother."

"What does he do?"

Instead of answering, he put the beer back down and reached for my hand. He slipped his fingers through mine and stroked my thumb. I studied his handsome profile and remembered how he'd told me he was lonely. It must be weird to be adored by millions of people, all of them strangers.

I rested my head against his shoulder. "You don't have to tell me anything if you don't want. I should stop being nosy."

"It's just complicated is all. I don't normally talk about this with anyone. I never even told Charlotte about Jeremy."

"You never told her you have a brother?"

"She knows I have a brother but not the situation."

I remained quiet, listening. We both fell silent. I could hear his soft breathing. Could feel the weight of the moment.

"The truth is he's one of the reasons I moved here." His thumb still stroked mine. "It's close enough that I can see him again."

"He lives out here?"

"Not exactly." He paused and took a deep breath. "Jeremy's in prison."

I lifted my head to look at him.

His eyes met mine. "Armed robbery."

"Shit."

"I know. It's fucked-up. And it's all my fault."

"How could that be your fault?"

He wore a pained expression. "Because I left him behind. Hell,

I'm the one who practically raised him. I should have stayed and looked after him, but I wanted to be a rock star."

"That's not your fault."

"It is. He'd gotten in with a bad crowd, but I didn't do anything. At least not enough. It was right around the time the band started to get noticed, and I should have dropped everything to help him, but I didn't."

"Where was your mom in all this?"

"I just told you. She didn't give a shit—too self-involved."

"You can't blame yourself. People make their own decisions. Their own choices in life. Didn't Kant say that? That we have the freedom to choose what's right over what's wrong?"

He shook his head. "He also would have said I had a duty to come to my brother's aid. My help could have steered Jeremy's life in a different direction."

I watched a moth flitter and land against the porch rail, shimmering as it reflected the moonlight.

"Believe me, I've thought this through," Josh went on. "And I live with the guilt of it every day."

"How come you never told Charlotte he was in prison?"

"Because I knew she'd use it against me somehow." He sighed. "I think I was embarrassed too. The only people who know about it are the guys in the band and my ex-wife, since she was around when it happened."

"But you just told me."

His voice softened. "Yeah, honey, I did."

"Why did you do that?"

He squeezed my hand. "Because I trust you, Leah."

CHAPTER TWENTY-SIX

~Leah~

The next morning, I told Josh and Damian that I had an unpleasant chore today, and they didn't have to help if they didn't want to.

"I need to clean out the herd's latrine areas," I said. "It's overdue. I should have done it days ago."

"What are latrine areas?" Damian asked.

"It's where the alpacas and llamas use the bathroom. There are two of them, one in each pasture. It's like a big litter box."

Damian's eyes widened.

Even Josh seemed apprehensive. "And this has to be done today? It's pretty hot outside."

I nodded. "Like I said, I should have done it already. You guys don't have to help. It's a gross task."

"I'll help," Josh said. He turned to Damian. "How about you supervise, Little D? You can do it from a distance."

Damian nodded and seemed relieved.

I turned to Josh. "We basically have to scoop all the alpaca beans into a wheelbarrow and then move them to the compost area."

"Beans? Is that what their sh—poop is called?" he asked.

I nodded. "It's because they look like black beans."

Damian made a face. "That's disgusting."

I smiled. "Are you sure I can't make you a nice bowl of alpaca beans for a snack?"

He grabbed his throat with great fanfare and pretended to retch.

"Don't worry. I won't sneak any into your burrito when I cook dinner tonight."

His expression turned comically alarmed.

Once we got back to the house, I pulled out Shane's rubber boots for Josh to wear so he didn't ruin his expensive sneakers.

"I sometimes wear a bandana on my face," I said, grabbing a couple from the laundry room. "Their droppings normally don't smell that bad, but the whole area is stinkier when it's this hot out."

Once we got to the first latrine, I groaned at the number of manure piles. "I should have done this days ago. There aren't usually this many." I gazed out at the pasture. "I hope they haven't started using another area to poop."

Damian had already found a shady spot and switched between watching us and goofing off on his phone. Apparently he'd been texting with Eddie, his new "best mate."

Josh waved his hand in front of his face. "Damn, you're right about the smell. It's not exactly perfume."

I pulled the bandanas from my pocket and handed him the red one. "Here, for your fiery nature."

He accepted it and tied it on his face while I put on a pink one. Then we both got to work shoveling all the beans into a wheelbarrow before rolling them one load at a time to the compost area. Even with the scarf, the smell of animal droppings and urine was nearly over-powering. Not that it stopped Josh from cracking endless jokes and making me laugh the whole time.

"Thanks for helping me," I said. "Having you here makes a chore I hate almost fun."

"That's all right. I like being with you."

"Me too." I glanced over at him. "This isn't exactly ideal, though, is it?"

"Are you kidding? This is as romantic as it gets. You and me shoveling a mountain of alpaca shit on a day that's hotter than a thousand suns."

"Who needs a candlelit dinner or a walk on the beach when we have all this?" I motioned at the giant litter box we were standing in.

"Exactly." But then he gave me an eye smolder. "Although I'd prefer the two of us naked between cool sheets—if you know what I mean."

And just like that, standing knee-deep in alpaca manure, Josh turned me inside out.

Unfortunately, he was right about the day being hotter than a thousand suns. It was ninety degrees, but it felt like a million. Between the odor, the flies, and the general disgusting nature of the task, it couldn't be over soon enough.

We were both sweating as we finished the first latrine area and headed for the second one. Josh had his hair pulled back into a ponytail. His face was flushed, and strands of blond hair stuck to his neck as he wiped his forehead with the back of his hand.

We'd both pulled our bandanas down, and I couldn't seem to drag my eyes away from him. Except every time I snuck a peek, he was doing the same thing with me. We'd been at it all day. This connection between us had grown even stronger since he told me about his brother last night.

I motioned down at the black-and-white plaid shorts he was wearing as he pushed the wheelbarrow. "So, how come I haven't seen you in a skirt since you've been staying here?"

"A skirt?"

"You wore one when you visited that first day with Damian." I walked beside him, carrying two shovels and a rake. "Don't you remember?"

"Ah, that's right. A friend of mine designs those and sent me a few to try out. What did you think?"

"I'd never seen a guy wear an actual skirt before. It was kind of sexy."

He smirked. "Of course, most men don't look as good in a skirt as I do."

I rolled my eyes even though it was true. "Does your ego have any limits at all?"

He chuckled. "Not really."

"I don't know how you get away with it, but somehow you do."

He gave me a mischievous grin. "It's because I'm so damn lovable."

Luckily, the second latrine area didn't appear to be as full as the first one, so it was a tad less disgusting. Josh set the wheelbarrow nearby, and we both pulled our bandanas back up to get started.

"What was your ex-wife like?" I asked, stepping around some of the manure. "You haven't said much about her."

His brows rose. "You want to talk about my ex-wife? *Now?*"

"What better way to pass the time? I already told you about my marriage. It's only fair that you spill the beans about yours." I motioned to the ground. "So to speak."

He snorted. "I guess it is appropriate that I'm shoveling shit while I discuss it."

I began raking a large pile of droppings together. "What was her name?"

"Lindsay."

"How long were you two married?"

"About a year, though we were together for a year before we got married." He dug his shovel into the hill I'd created, lifted it out, and dumped the droppings into the wheelbarrow. I watched his arm muscles flex, enjoying myself. "There's really not much to tell," he went on. "It was a long time ago. We were both young and foolish. Or

I was foolish, since I honestly thought I'd found the woman I was going to spend my life with."

"So what happened?" His tone was cavalier, but I sensed something deeper.

"She couldn't bring herself to trust me. The band started getting more press, and there was a lot of attention on us." He wiped his brow. "She constantly worried I was going to cheat on her."

"But you didn't cheat, so what was the problem?"

"She just couldn't let it go. It sucked."

"And that's why you guys broke up?"

"There was more to it. She was trying to get pregnant and for some reason couldn't. She took it as a sign that we shouldn't be together and left."

"Just like that?"

He nodded. "Basically." He stopped raking and gazed out at the pasture. "I guess I wasn't enough for her."

I raked a large clump of beans. "I'm sorry to have to say this, but she sounds like an idiot."

"We were just young is all. I don't think it was meant to be."

"I thought you didn't believe in destiny."

He snorted. "I don't. And I can tell you this much—I'm *never* going through that again."

"How can you be so certain?"

"Because I'm never getting married again."

"You might change your mind. What if you fall madly in love?" I had a teasing note in my voice, but when I glanced over at him, I saw he was serious.

"Being in love once was enough for me." He stuck his shovel into a pile of fresh manure, then emptied it into the wheelbarrow.

"Do you still have feelings for Lindsay?"

He shook his head. "I've been over that for a long time. But I haven't forgotten how much it messed me up. That's not happening again."

His statement struck me as bizarre. "You really plan to never fall in love again?"

"Nope. Never."

"But how can you control that? You *can't* control it."

"Of course I can."

"Weren't you in love with Charlotte?"

"I cared for her. I was always faithful to her, but no, I was never in love with her." He paused. "Obviously I love Damian. I'd die for that kid, but that's completely different."

There was something about the way he was talking and his expression. "You're like a wounded lion with a thorn in his paw."

"A thorn?" He scoffed. "More like scars from a gunshot wound."

It saddened me to think of someone as passionate and bighearted as Josh never falling in love again. "I think you're making a mistake. That's a terrible way to live the rest of your life."

"What about you?" He was studying me now. "How many guys have you been in love with since your marriage to that talentless asshole?"

I opened my mouth to respond to his question, but nothing came out. I didn't have an answer.

Josh was watching me. "That many, huh?"

It was sad but true. I hadn't been in love since Derek. "I just haven't met anyone yet."

"Are you sure about that? Who was the last guy you dated?"

"Neil. He's a large animal vet who comes out to the farm when I need help."

"And what's wrong with him?"

"Nothing. He's a great guy." There wasn't a thing wrong with Neil. He was handsome and fun to be around. "I liked him a lot."

"Uh-huh."

"What's your point with all this?"

"It just makes sense to me now why a woman like you isn't married or tied down." He stopped what he was doing and stared at me. "You and I are more alike than you think, Leah."

I didn't say anything to that. Maybe we were alike, and maybe I had been holding back, but I knew there was one way we were different, because a nervous part of me suspected I was already falling in love.

And that I was making the same crazy mistake all over again.

THE THREE OF us headed back to the house. I took a shower first and then went into the kitchen to get dinner started while Josh took his shower. Damian lay in the hammock in the backyard with two cats nearby as he read more about alpaca farming. He explained to me how he planned to talk his granny into buying some alpacas and wanted to make sure he knew how to take care of them.

I had to smile. He was a great kid, and I wondered if his grandmother would go along with it. Damian seemed a lot like Josh in that he had a relentless quality and didn't give up on things easily. Something told me he might just talk her into buying a small herd.

While I was getting dinner ready, I heard Shane's truck outside. I noticed he'd been working less overtime lately. He probably enjoyed having two new buddies here to hang out with. It was strange, but Josh and Damian staying here had been the highlight of my summer.

"Hey, what's up?"

I'd been gazing out the window and turned to find Shane entering the kitchen, sweaty and wearing his dusty work boots. "Whew, it sure is a hot one out there." He opened the fridge. "What are you making for dinner tonight?"

"Mexican food."

"Awesome." He got some water and a jar of salsa. I watched him grab a bag of tortilla chips and then take a seat at the kitchen table. "Anything new happening?"

"You're eating those now? We're having burritos soon."

"This is just an appetizer." He dug a chip into the salsa and then popped it in his mouth.

I shrugged and went back to sorting beans—pinto beans—for the pressure cooker. "Josh and I finally cleaned the latrine areas today. It was totally gross. I shouldn't have put it off for so long."

Shane nodded. It wasn't exactly a task he relished either. But then he paused and looked at me. "Wait, did you just say you made Josh help you clean the latrine areas?"

"Well, I didn't *make* him. He offered to help."

"And you let him?" Shane chuckled and shook his head. "The dude's a rock star, Leah. Literally. And you've got him out there shoveling alpaca shit."

"So what? Like I said, Josh wanted to help."

At that moment, the rock star himself breezed into the kitchen. "Did someone say my name?" He wore clean jeans and another surfboard company T-shirt. His damp hair was long and flowing down his back.

"You always think someone is saying your name, don't you?" I teased, even though I had just said it.

He moved closer and brushed his fingers along my hip before lightly caressing my ass. My breath caught. I wore a pair of cloth shorts, and the heat from his hand felt like it was scalding me. I quickly glanced at Shane, but luckily he hadn't noticed and was still eating his chips and salsa.

"That's because someone usually *is* saying my name," he said with a playful grin.

He looked so handsome and delicious. I wanted to reach out for him, but obviously I couldn't. Instead we grinned at each other like a couple of goofballs.

Finally, he turned toward Shane. "How was work, bro?" He walked over, and they gave each other some kind of fist bump handshake thing.

"Good." Shane nodded. He began describing the house they were currently working on. Apparently it belonged to the head coach for Seattle's football team. Josh listened with interest as he sat down and shared Shane's chips and salsa.

My phone buzzed on the counter. To my surprise, it was a text from Salem—the woman I'd met at Damian and Josh's birthday party. She said they were spending the next few days in Truth Harbor and wanted to know if I could still teach her how to knit socks.

"Would you mind if Salem came here?" I asked Josh. I explained how I'd just gotten this text and the offer I'd made.

He sucked salt off his thumb. "Dax's wife? Is he coming with her?"

"I think so. It sounds like they're up here for a short vacation." Truth Harbor turned into a tourist town during the summer months.

"Sure. It would be great to see them."

I texted Salem back, and we set up a time for them to drop by. After I finished getting things going for dinner, I went into the dining room to work on spinning. I still couldn't believe I'd sold triple my usual amount from that single YouTube video. I stayed at my wheel for about an hour until I heard the pressure cooker beeping.

We ate dinner outside on the back deck. Damian was so worried that I'd added alpaca beans to the burritos that he was ready to have me swear on a bible that I didn't.

I laughed. "Do you really think I'd add something that gross to our food?"

"I just want to be totally sure. And everyone knows you can't lie if you swear on a bible."

"I'm eating them too," I pointed out.

"That's true." He appeared to think it over. "Okay, I've decided I trust you."

Josh watched this exchange with amusement.

"Do people eat Mexican food in the UK?" Shane asked, spooning guacamole onto his plate.

I listened as Josh and Damian explained how they do eat Mexican food, but it wasn't as ubiquitous as it is here in the States.

"Indian food is probably the nearest comparison," Josh said. "You can get that everywhere just like Mexican food here."

After dinner the guys did the cleanup, which let me get back to my wheel. I had some clean fleece that I'd hand carded and was spinning from the cloud when Josh came in and stood in the doorway watching me.

I glanced up, but he seemed content, so I just went back to what I was doing.

He wandered around the room, examining the shelves with all the skeins separated by color and weight. "Did you create all these yourself?" he asked.

"Most of them."

"I don't know much about yarn, but this stuff looks amazing."

"Thank you," I said, pleased at the compliment.

He hung out a little longer and then left. A few minutes later, I heard a guitar in the living room. Shane and Damian were, of course, playing some video game. Josh fiddled with the tuning and then started singing "Muddy Riches," an older East Echo song. It had a bluesy feel to it, and his voice sounded great. I smiled to myself, listening as I spun.

When he finished that one and started "Ritual of You," I felt like I was having an out-of-body experience.

I could hear the sound effects from the video game, could hear Josh's honeyed vocals singing one of my favorite East Echo songs. It didn't feel real. *Is this actually my life now?*

It was right then that I had a moment of clarity. Just like the one I'd had when I bought my farm. I decided I was going to enjoy whatever came next between Josh and me. Even if it was temporary. Even if it broke my heart. In life there were some journeys worth taking no matter the cost.

Whatever happened between us, I was going to enjoy the ride.

LATER THAT NIGHT, I found him on the porch as usual waiting for me, sipping a glass of water. He put it down.

"Come here, my little spinster," he said, smiling as he pulled me onto his lap.

There wasn't any pretense between us anymore. I snuggled against him and slipped my arm around his neck. It was still warm out, and when I looked up at the night sky, I could see the moon shining down, giving us its blessing.

I closed my eyes.

"What is it?" His deep voice rumbled.

"Sometimes I talk to the moon," I admitted, turning to him. "When I'm out here alone. That's what I was doing that first night you saw me."

He leaned his head back against the chair, lazily caressing my leg. "And what were the two of you discussing?"

"Secrets I don't share with anyone." I slid my fingers over his shoulder and down his arm, enjoying the solid feel of him. "I asked it to bring me a good man. I told it I was ready."

"And here I am."

His eyes were shining, and mine were too. I brought my hand up to stroke his jaw.

"I wonder what secrets I'll be telling you tonight," he whispered, our faces close. "Guess you've become my moonlight."

I didn't even know how it started. If he kissed me or I kissed him. All I knew was our mouths were together, our tongues sliding over each other. He tasted so good. So right. Like that first sip of moonshine. Like I was falling fast, tumbling into space.

"Damn, honey," he breathed. "You've got me in such a tailspin I can't tell which way is up or down." He squeezed my hip. "I wish I didn't want you so much. I can't remember the last time I felt this good with someone, when it was so easy."

I smiled. "Even shoveling alpaca beans together was a joy."

"Even that."

I played with his hair. "Shane told me I shouldn't have asked you to do that since you're this big rock star and all. Do you think that's true?"

"Leah, I'd shovel shit with you any day of the week."

"Listen to you. Such romantic whisperings."

He chuckled. "I *am* a songwriter after all."

"I know. I heard you earlier. It sounded wonderful, but how come you didn't play 'Silver Days'?"

He stroked my back. "Because I'm saving that one for you. I thought I'd sing it out here tonight."

My breath caught. I didn't even know what to say. By the expression on his face, he knew I was struggling to put words together.

"Shall I sing it now?" he asked softly.

I nodded.

And so he did.

CHAPTER TWENTY-SEVEN

~Josh~

"When it begins, it's you and me
Heard your laugh and the world spun free
Waited so long for our time in the light
Dreamed of your smile and knew you might
Tell me you're ready, and I'll give you the sky
Because I know why
I know why...
Silver days last forever
Silver days shine so bright
All that I needed
I found in you...
Silver days are pure as a morning
Because silver nights
burn hot and true..."

. . .

IT HAD BEEN a long time since I sang to a woman. Just the two of us on a moonlit night. I let myself play with the melody. The truth was I wanted to impress Leah, wanted to show her what I could do. There were plenty of things in life I couldn't do, but this wasn't one of them.

I was a damn good singer.

Her dark eyes were on me the whole time. Every word. I moved from chest to head voice and back, pulling it in and then opening up. When I finally finished, she remained still and quiet.

"Wow," she breathed. And then her mouth was on mine, kissing me, hot and hard. A bonfire in my arms.

It wasn't the first time a woman had gotten excited hearing me sing, but it felt like the first time. It was satisfying in a way I couldn't quite explain. Everything about Leah felt different and new.

"I guess you liked that, huh?" I asked, catching my breath when we came up for air.

"I've always loved that song. Did you write it?" Her voice sounded throaty and intimate.

I nodded. "It's one of mine. Rhys added the bridge, but I wrote the rest."

"I love it. What inspired you?"

I smiled to myself. I got asked this question a lot—by fans and reporters. People always wanted to know where our songs came from. "It's from this fantasy I had when I was younger where I imagined my perfect life. I always called it my silver days."

"Have you ever had your silver days?"

I shook my head and shifted in the chair a little, trying to ease my hard-on. This beautiful woman in my lap wasn't making it easy. I reached down for the water. "Like any fantasy, it's not real."

"But maybe it could be someday."

"I suppose." For a moment I remembered how badly I used to want it, how it had been hard for me to accept that it was just a mirage.

"What's it like to be able to sing like that?"

I grinned and told her the truth. "It's great. I love it. I never take it for granted." I took a sip and offered her the glass.

She accepted it. "It's hard to imagine being so talented."

"What do you mean? You're talented. Besides all your fiber art, you're fast as hell. You run even faster than *me*."

"True." She handed the glass back, and I put it on the side table. "I've always been fast, but I'm not like you. I'm not in the Olympics. Did you always know you could sing?"

"Yeah, I knew. When I was a kid, my mom and I used to sing together. It was one of the few times she ever noticed me."

"What do you mean?"

"Just that. She was always focused on herself and basically ignored us, but when I sang with her, I could tell... she saw me. I wasn't just some nuisance." I remembered those days. The feel of it. Being noticed by someone whose attention I wanted so desperately, attention that should have been given freely. "Guess it's no surprise I became a singer, huh?"

She reached out to stroke my beard. "I'm sorry she was like that. You deserved a lot better. Both of you did."

I shrugged. "Water under the bridge."

"Can Jeremy sing too?"

"He can, actually. He's good. Not as good as—" I stopped myself. "Anyway, yeah, he can sing."

She studied me. "Not as good as you. Is that what you were going to say?"

I nodded and took a deep breath. "Just one more nail in the coffin of my guilt."

She sighed and put her head on my shoulder. "There's nothing I could say about this, is there? Nothing that would make you feel any different."

"No, honey, there isn't. Though I appreciate that you'd like to."

We both went quiet for a while then, and I thought about the time I'd spent here on her farm. Ironically, it felt like the first real vacation I'd had in years. Isolated from the rest of the world. No outside pressures. I couldn't remember the last time I experienced that.

I caressed Leah's hip and down to her smooth legs, enjoying myself.

And then there was this amazing woman. Pulling me in to the point of obsession. My chest felt tight just thinking about how much I'd grown to care about her.

She stirred against me, and then I heard her laugh softly.

"Something funny?" I asked.

"I just had a thought." She lifted her head and gave me a wry look. "How many women have you sung to over the years trying to get in their pants?"

"Who me?" I pretended to act innocent. "Are you suggesting that I'm trying to get in your pants?"

"Aren't you?"

"Hell yeah, I am."

She raised a brow. "So, am I being given the Josh treatment?"

"Maybe a little," I admitted. "Back in the day, when I was a horny teenager, I might have sung to a few girls."

"And did it work?"

I couldn't help my grin. "Every damn time."

———

EXCEPT I WASN'T GETTING into Leah's pants. Not now. Not at all. Instead I was lying on the couch in her living room, trying to sleep and having very little success.

All I could think about was her upstairs in her bed. Probably wearing that tiny camisole and a pair of lace panties again. So close and yet so far. More than anything, I wanted to go to her, to give her what I knew we both wanted.

But I shouldn't. I couldn't.

I ground my palms into my eyes.

Obviously I'd slipped up a couple of days ago. What I'd told her that night we fooled around was true, though. It wasn't just about the sex. I'd been lonely for a long time.

Tonight with her on the porch, I hadn't felt lonely. I felt great. Except I was horny too. And I knew damn well why. I shouldn't have had Leah on my lap like that, shouldn't have had my hands all over her. I couldn't seem to stop myself.

I felt different when I was with her. More relaxed. It was so easy. I hadn't realized how stressed I was all the time, how I'd let people's demands and expectations get in the way of simply enjoying my life. I'd laughed more with Leah than I had all year.

And it only made me want her more.

After tossing and turning, I doubled the pillow under my head and tried reading to distract myself. I started a John Rawls book a friend had recommended, then switched to Schopenhauer, figuring if that didn't put me to sleep, nothing would. Of course, it didn't work.

Finally, I put my Kindle down and lay in the dark, staring up at the ceiling, listening to the quiet of the house. Everyone was fast asleep.

When I started thinking about Leah's smooth legs again, the feel of her ass nestled in my lap, the way she'd kissed me with such heat, I decided enough was enough. Time for a cold shower. It wouldn't be the first one I'd taken here in the middle of the night.

Shoving the sheets back, I stood up, wearing nothing but a pair of tented boxer briefs. I'd rubbed one out in the bathroom earlier before going to bed, but it hadn't made a damn bit of difference. I was still in bad shape.

Prowling through the dark house, I passed the laundry room and stopped to grab a towel. I switched the light on. While I was in there, surrounded by the scent of detergent, I noticed something—a wicker basket filled with dirty clothes.

And what was lying right on top? Leah's panties. There was practically a spotlight on them. It was the same pair of lacy blue ones she had on the other night.

I couldn't believe my luck.

I paused and hovered next to the laundry basket like a shoplifter. *Am I really doing this?*

Apparently I was, because I saw my own hand reach down.

I switched the light off and left the room. It felt like I was carrying a bomb, and I could only imagine how I'd explain this to Leah if she caught me.

The house was quiet when I made my way into the bathroom. My hand stopped on the light switch. There was enough ambient light from the small window that I decided against it.

I locked the door behind me and found a spot on the wall to lean against. My heart pounded in my ears. The erection I'd been fighting all night felt uncomfortably stiff. I shoved my boxers down with my right hand, then grabbed hold of myself, stroking down the length. With the other hand, I brought the panties to my face and took a deep whiff.

Fuuuck. My head exploded. I nearly groaned out loud.

It was *her.* Definitely Leah. Tangy-sweet, pure feminine musk.

I closed my eyes. This was going to be perfect.

I imagined the way her pussy had been rubbing against this cloth and then imagined it rubbing against my face. Her legs spread open, grinding against me like the juiciest peach.

Hell yeah. My hand moved tighter on my cock with deliberate strokes. This was *good.* I pushed her panties into my face, inhaling her scent, letting it light me up like a firecracker.

The two of us were in the hayloft now. I pictured her on her back with her legs wrapped around my waist, heels digging into my ass. She was going crazy, moaning and scratching me up, begging for more while I fucked her like I was starved.

I could hear myself panting in the dark bathroom as I went at it, the deliberate rhythm while I tried not to make noise. Precum leaked from my dick, and I rubbed it over the head, stroking down the length again. I had the soft fabric with her scent still crushed against my face.

Now Leah was naked, wearing those black boots, and looking sexy as fuck. She lowered herself, sliding onto my cock as I reached out for her hips. Those pretty eyes were smiling at me as she played with her nipples just so I could watch. Then she leaned forward and fucked me, working me over good while I let myself drown in her.

My balls tightened. *Damn.* I licked my dry lips. My dick grew even harder as I stroked it faster, squeezing my fist. The base of my spine tingled.

Next, I had her bent over a bale of hay with her sweet ass in the air as I pounded her from behind. She was moaning my name, and when I thought of her orgasming all over my cock, it was too much. I lost it.

Biting down a groan, I smashed her panties into my face while a white-hot climax ripped through me. My whole body shuddered, riding it out.

Fuck me.

I sagged against the wall, trying to catch my breath. I felt like a man lost at sea who'd finally found a lifeline.

Coming down from my arousal, I glanced around the small space. *How the hell did I wind up in here? Jerking off in a dark bathroom with a pair of Leah's dirty underpants?*

Jesus.

I chuckled and closed my eyes.

Desperate times....

After cleaning up and washing my hands, I realized I had to wash my face and beard, too, since her scent was all over me. Smelling that all night would only get me worked up again.

Good thing I'd brought a clean towel.

Eventually I left the bathroom and headed back to the laundry room. I threw the towel in with the dirty clothes but hesitated about putting her underpants back. What if I needed them again?

I stood there for a long moment, deliberating. Finally, I forced myself to put them in the laundry basket.

When I lay back down on the couch, I felt kind of embarrassed that I'd been perving on Leah's panties.

On the other hand, I might finally get a decent night's sleep.

CHAPTER TWENTY-EIGHT

~Leah~

"There's only one insect on earth that creates a food eaten by people," Theo said to us as we walked down her long backyard toward her beehives. She glanced at Damian. "And you know what that is, right?"

He nodded. "But I don't understand. If bees need the honey for food, what happens if we take it from them?"

"That's a great question. Luckily, bees produce up to triple the amount of honey they need. So as long as we make sure they have enough, there's still plenty for us too."

"How do bees know how to get back to the hive?" Josh asked. "I've always wondered why they don't get lost."

Theo smiled. She was a little taller than Josh, her curly bright red hair pulled back into a short ponytail. Her green eyes sparkled as she talked about a subject she loved. "Well, it's a combination of things. They use the angle of the sun to guide their flight path, and they also create mental maps of an area so they know where they are."

Josh asked more questions, and I noticed that every time he spoke, Claire stared at him with abject terror. She told me she wanted to meet him, but now that she was here, she could barely squeak out two syllables. I could tell Josh was trying to be super gentle with her because she seemed so nervous.

As Theo led Damian and Josh over to put on some bee suits, Claire and I took a seat over at the nearby picnic table. We'd already seen Theo's hives plenty of times.

"I still can't believe I just met Joshua Trevant," Claire said, shaking her head with wonder. "I know I'm making a fool of myself, and I can barely talk, but I've never met an actual rock star."

"Honestly, you should just think of him as a regular guy." I brushed a few leaves off the table. "There's no reason to be nervous."

"*Regular* guy?" She laughed. "Are you blind? There's nothing regular about him. I mean, just look at him."

I turned my head and watched Josh zip the suit up, then adjust his hat with the veil. Theo was helping Damian to make sure there were no gaps in his suit. It was true what Claire said—there was something about Josh that caught your eye.

"He even looks hot wearing one of those silly beekeeping suits," she said. "Plus, he's so talented. I listened to their music on a loop when I was going through my divorce. I just don't know what to say to him."

Ironically, Claire was a bigger East Echo fan than I was.

"And what the heck is happening between the two of you?" she wanted to know. "You guys keep touching each other. I totally saw the way he brushed his hand against yours. There's no way I imagined that."

I took a deep breath and let out the truth. "All right, I admit it. Something romantic is developing between us."

Her eyes widened. "Really?"

I nodded.

She broke out in a huge grin. "My bestie is dating a rock star."

"I don't know if you'd call it dating." Frankly, I wasn't sure what to call what Josh and I were doing. "But we've grown close. You have to keep this to yourself, though, okay?"

"Don't worry, and I'll swear Philip to secrecy too. Are you guys sleeping together?"

I shook my head, though I couldn't help smiling.

"Your expression tells me something's happening. Come on, I need details. I'm a horny pregnant lady."

"Are you really horny from being pregnant?" I asked, curious. "It seems like it would be the opposite."

"You'd think, wouldn't you? It's bizarre. Philip's enjoying it, but I'm not sure if I like it. It's so distracting. I keep wondering if this is what it's like for guys all the time."

"I never would have thought."

She shook her head. "Anyway, don't change the subject. I need to know everything that's going on between you two, so spill it."

"All right." I slid my fingers over a rough spot on the table and then glanced up at her. "We've sort of fooled around, but we haven't actually had sex."

We both looked over at Josh as he examined one of the hives. "I'll bet he's good in bed."

I nodded. "He's intense and kind of dirty."

"Oh, wow." She gave a sly grin. "Philip's going to be very happy tonight."

I laughed out loud.

We talked some more about her pregnancy and how she still didn't want to know the sex of the baby. Philip's latest idea was that he'd find out alone but just not tell her so she could still be surprised.

"I'm not sure, though. I'm worried I'll be looking for clues every time he opens his mouth," she said. "How's he going to keep something that big a secret?"

She told me she'd already decided to paint their baby's room green so it wouldn't matter either way.

"How long do you think you'll keep working?" I asked. Claire still cleaned for some clients—most of them elderly—and shopped for some to. She also met with new clients regularly.

"I'm not sure yet. I think I'm just going to see how I feel, you know? Hopefully I can continue through most of it. Luckily, Taylor can step in once I'm on maternity leave."

"That sounds reasonable."

She asked me how things were going with my family since she knew how hard it'd been dealing with them. I told her about the pressure I was still getting from my mom and Lars to sell my farm, how they sent a real estate agent to my house, how no matter what I did, they wouldn't let up.

We talked for a while longer, and eventually Theo, Damian, and Josh came over to join us after finishing their tour of the hives.

"Did you know bees have five eyes?" Damian's face was flushed with excitement. "And that they can recognize human faces?"

"Wow, that's pretty cool," I said.

He began spouting off more bee trivia, and I listened with interest.

Theo asked us if we wanted to go back up to the house. "I can give you some honey," she told Josh. "Do you guys need more too?" she asked me and Claire.

We both said we'd love a jar.

Damian had his phone out and was looking through the photos he'd taken of the hives. "I have to show Eddie and some of my mates back home."

Once at the house, we all sat on Theo's back patio while she disappeared inside. When she returned she had four jars of honey for us.

"How's it going with your new neighbor?" I asked after thanking her. "Are they still hassling you about your hives?"

Her expression changed to anger. "I got another letter from his lawyer. I also found out who he is."

"What do you mean?"

"My new neighbor. His name's Gabriel Bardales. It turns out he's some idiot football player who everybody calls 'Beauty.'" She made air quotes. "It just figures. What kind of dumb egotistical name is that?"

I gawked at her and felt Claire and Josh do the same.

"Doesn't Beauty Bardales play for the Seattle Sentries?" Claire asked, glancing at us.

"He does," Josh said, nodding, still looking stunned. "He's their quarterback."

I shook my head. "I can't believe he's the one who bought all that land next to yours. That's amazing."

Theo rolled her eyes. "Please. There's nothing amazing about football. A bunch of overpaid jocks running around tackling each other and giving themselves silly nicknames. Who cares?"

Josh chuckled. "The guy is actually an incredibly talented athlete."

"Well, he must not be very bright if he thinks my beehives are interfering with his property. It's completely preposterous."

We listened to Theo rant. She was obviously upset. We all agreed it didn't seem right that he should try to force her to do anything with her hives.

Eventually I looked at my phone, and when I saw the time, I glanced over at Josh. "We should go. I told Salem we'd meet them at the house soon."

He nodded in agreement. We got up and thanked Theo for everything. I gave her a hug. Claire said she was going to stay and hang out a little longer.

Josh smiled at her. "It was very nice to meet you, Claire."

She turned bright red. "It was... um... nice to meet your acquaintance. I mean, get you acquaintance." She stopped talking. "Oh my God! I'm sorry. I'm so nervous."

He chuckled. "Don't worry. I'm used to it."

"You are?" Her expression turned hopeful. "It's just that your music has meant so much to me."

"Thank you. That's nice to hear."

"It really has been so special to meet with you, or just to meet you at all." She took a deep breath. "I wish I could stop being so flustered."

He shrugged. "You'll get past it eventually, and then you'll be like 'He's just some dude. No big deal.'"

Claire nodded and forced a laugh, though I could tell she didn't believe him.

I gave her a quick hug, too, and said I'd text them both later.

As we were leaving, I glanced back at my two best friends, who were still watching us. I waved, and they both waved back with big grins on their faces.

———

IT WASN'T long after we got back to the house that I got a text from Salem letting me know they were on their way over. It was late afternoon, and I'd invited them to stay for dinner. Shane told me Martha and Eddie were coming over, too, which made Damian happy. I planned to make a big pot of spaghetti so there'd be plenty of food.

Eventually they pulled up in a green SUV. "Oh wow, I love your place," Salem said. She had long auburn hair and bright hazel eyes. I'd forgotten she was so pretty.

Her husband's blue mohawk wasn't blue anymore but bleached blond. "Nice to see you again," he said. He was holding their daughter, Sasha, who smiled shyly at us, burying her face in her dad's shoulder.

Damian, Josh, and I gave the three of them a tour of Clarity Moon Farm. I brought some chopped apples so they could feed my girls. Sasha giggled with delight as Rhiannon took some apple from her palm. It was fun to watch Damian refer to all my animals by name and talk about them with such authority. You'd think he'd been living here for months. He introduced Phyllis and Alicia, explaining about guard llamas, then pointed out Rosalie, Martina, and Eva and described how they ran alongside us every morning.

I'd gotten so used to living alone and isolated that it surprised me how much I'd enjoyed socializing lately. Since I bought this farm, I hadn't really had a chance to share my joy in it.

"This place is magical," Salem gushed as she walked up next to me and slipped her arm in mine. "And I love the name. You've created something really special."

"Thank you. It's a dream come to life."

We were walking back from the second pasture when Shane came home from work. Introductions were made as we all headed back to the house. I got everyone something to drink, and then Salem and I headed into the living room. She'd brought along a bag with her knitting, and I got out my own supplies.

Sasha was nearby petting my cat Xena while Salem set up some toys for her to play with.

"That should keep her occupied for a little while, hopefully," Salem said with a smile.

We both sat on the couch, and she showed me the socks she was working on, except it looked more like a knotted mess.

"Hmm...." I examined what she'd knitted so far. It looked like she'd dropped a number of stitches and then had added some extras here and there, twisting them around. It was pretty much a disaster. "I'm so sorry, but I think it's best if you frog the whole thing and start fresh," I said, being honest.

"What does 'frog' it mean?"

"It's when you rip your knitting back. It comes from the expression rip it, rip it, like a frog."

"Oh!" Salem laughed. "That's cute."

I explained how I could show her the simplest way to knit socks for beginners. "First you'll need to knit a swatch so we can check your gauge."

"I did that!" She rummaged through her bag and pulled out a

small pink swatch. "I followed the instructions from a YouTuber. I even washed and blocked it."

"Perfect." It was a small swatch in stockinette stitch. A little rough but definitely usable. "This is great."

I looked over her pattern and explained how the sock measurement chart worked. When it was time to cast on, I pulled out some double-pointed needles and showed Salem how it was done. I could hear all the guys in the kitchen talking and laughing. Dean had arrived alone a short while ago to join us for dinner. Apparently Nalla decided she didn't want to come.

"Oh wow," Salem said with delight after she'd cast on and knitted a few rows of ribbing. "Look at me! I'm knitting socks!"

I grinned. I'd already pulled out the socks I was knitting as a Christmas gift for Lars and started working on them too.

I heard voices, and when I glanced up, Josh and the rest of the guys came trailing into the living room.

"Hey, we're going to go check out Shane's RV," Josh said. "Dax wants to see the inside. We might have to talk him into buying one."

Salem seemed amused. "He's been wanting a motorhome forever, but I have no idea where we'd park it. Those things are huge."

"Don't worry, babe," Dax said. "I'm just looking, not buying. Though these guys are ready to drive me to the nearest dealership."

When Josh saw the knitting in my lap, he peered over the couch. "That doesn't look like a sweater for me." He'd been telling me he wanted a sweater ever since he bought me that book on knitting with cat hair.

I held up what I was working on. "That's because it's socks for Lars."

"Where's my sweater?"

"Do you really want a sweater made from cat hair?"

He chuckled. "No, I want a sweater made from alpaca hair or wool."

"Hmm... if you're good, maybe you'll get one under the Christmas tree, Friedrich."

He wore a sly grin. "And what if I'm bad?"

"Then you'll get a lump of coal."

"Damn, honey, that's harsh. I'd better make sure I'm *real* good." His tone was flirty, except there was a sexual undertone that hopefully only I heard.

Eventually they all left, including Damian, taking enough male energy with them to light up a concert hall.

Salem and I continued with our knitting, though a few times I felt her watching me like she wanted to say something.

"All right, I just have to ask," she said. "Are you and Josh together?"

I put on my best poker face as I continued knitting. "What makes you say that?"

She smiled sheepishly. "Sorry, I hope I'm not being too nosy. It's none of my business, and you don't have to answer."

"We're good friends," I said carefully.

She nodded, and I suspected she knew I was stepping around the truth.

"It's just that Josh is a great guy."

"He's pretty wonderful," I agreed, barely keeping the smitten tone out of my voice.

"Dax and I think the world of him. He's been nothing but kind and generous with us, especially since Sasha was born. And he's always so fun to be around."

This time I couldn't stop my smile. "I know. Even his vanity is endearing."

She laughed. "It's true. It's kind of sweet, isn't it? I'm glad he's managed to stay positive despite everything he's had to go through with Charlotte."

I glanced up at her. "Have you met Charlotte?"

Salem nodded, working her needles. "I have. She joined us on the last European tour when I was there."

I hesitated. "What's she like?" I shouldn't have been asking, and it was obvious Josh didn't want to talk about her, but I couldn't resist. I was too curious.

"She's an odd bird." Salem put her knitting down. "In some ways she seemed obsessed with Josh, but in other ways, she ignored him."

"What do you mean?"

"Well, she never watched him onstage. When he talked to her, it always seemed like she was on her phone or just half listening. To be honest, I thought she was condescending." Salem shook her head. "I hate to say it, but I didn't like her very much. She seemed really self-absorbed."

My heart hurt for Josh hearing this. And then it occurred to me that Charlotte sounded an awful lot like the way he described his mother. "How was she obsessed with him?"

"She always wanted to know where he was! And if she didn't know, she went around asking everyone to find him. It's like she wanted him to tell her every time he went to the bathroom. It was crazy."

I put my knitting down and reflected on this. It was strange to hear about a part of Josh's life where I knew nothing.

"I don't know how he put up with her for as long as he did. Though I always figured he did it for Damian, who's obviously a great kid. I think she worried he was cheating on her."

"But why? He never cheated."

"I doubt he did either," Salem said in agreement. "Women were always coming on to him, and you know how he is, so flirtatious, but I never saw him with anyone else."

"Do you know anything about Jane Braxton?" I couldn't resist asking. Salem was obviously a gold mine of information.

She rolled her eyes. "I'd ignore all of those stories. From what Dax has told me she's a terrible manager."

"Josh told me the press made everything up about the two of them. That none of it's true."

Salem nodded and glanced over to check on her daughter, who was playing with building blocks. One of my cats sat nearby, watching Sasha build a tower. "There's no way those stories are true. I think part of them came from the fact that he's the one who convinced the guys to hire her."

"He did? I didn't know that."

"Apparently she worked for their old label. She approached Josh and convinced him she'd be right for the job."

"But she wasn't?"

"Dax says she's the worst. And then somehow she got involved with Rhys. It's super bizarre."

I didn't know what to say. It all sounded like such a different world from my own. And this was Josh's normal life?

Salem picked up her knitting again and laughed. "Gosh, we're really spilling the tea, aren't we?"

I picked up mine too. "Yeah, I guess we are."

"I don't know if you guys are involved or not," she said. "I hope you are because Josh deserves some real happiness."

I nodded in agreement but didn't comment.

"Don't let anything you read in the press or what people say get to you," she continued. "Just ignore it and stay focused on the two of you, because in this crazy business, that's what's real. If you guys are happy, that's all that matters."

CHAPTER TWENTY-NINE

~Leah~

After the guys came back from checking out Shane's RV, I cooked dinner, with Salem and Dean helping me in the kitchen. We made a big pot of spaghetti along with garlic bread and salad.

Dean regretted not having enough time to bake another pie before coming over, especially when he saw I was making brownies from a box. "Damn, I have a killer brownie recipe too—weed optional."

I chuckled. "You know we can't make pot brownies, right?"

"Of course, I only make those for adult consumption." He leaned against the counter. "By the way, I'm sorry Nalla couldn't make it tonight. I guess she just wasn't feeling up to it."

"Hopefully everything's okay with her," I said mostly out of politeness. Obviously I wasn't a fan of Nalla's.

He shrugged. "I guess. She's been real moody lately. I keep wondering if maybe it's female stuff. What do you think?"

"Could be. I've been known to get grouchy during that time of the month."

He nodded and stroked his dark beard. "It feels like anything I say sets her off."

"Have you tried talking to her about it?"

"I've tried, but she doesn't want to talk. I made her a bubble bath and poured her a glass of wine, thinking I'd do something nice, but she still seemed pissed at me."

It figured that Nalla didn't appreciate a guy like him.

There was a commotion outside, and when I went out there to check, I could see Martha had arrived with Eddie. He and Damian were "dude"-ing and high-fiving each other all over the place. It was cute to watch. They'd obviously become great friends.

Dean seemed in better spirits once we all sat down to dinner. Salem and her husband sat next to each other and took turns holding Sasha on their laps. They seemed like the coolest couple. Very much in love and super nice people. I sat next to Josh at the table and could feel Salem smiling at us with approval.

I was still keeping up the facade that we were just friends, though Josh didn't make it easy. He was constantly leaning into me, cracking jokes and catching my eye. "I can't wait to be alone with you later," he whispered in my ear at one point, running his hand down my leg and sending erotic shock waves through my whole body. "I've been thinking about you all day."

I'd been thinking about him too. I also couldn't help going over all the stuff Salem told me about Charlotte. It sounded like Josh had been trying to do his best by Damian, even if it meant putting up with mistreatment from her. I was sure all the guilt about his brother factored in with that.

After dinner, the guys took care of the cleanup. Except Dean. We forced him to come over and sit with Salem, Martha, and me.

"I get to hang out with all the hot women while those clowns have to do the dishes?" He grinned. "Sounds good to me. Let me grab a beer."

We'd set up some chairs on the grass. Salem was holding Sasha on her lap as the little girl fell asleep. Damian and Eddie were running around in the backyard playing with a beach ball that Shane had pulled out from the storage shed. Both of them yelled and laughed as they threw it at each other, pretending it was an attacking alien.

I smiled watching them, then leaned back in my chair and breathed in the summer-scented air. The familiar smell of hay and cut grass. It was early evening and not quite dark yet.

"I should probably go help the guys in the kitchen." Martha glanced toward the house. "It's not like I helped make dinner."

"What are you talking about?" I said. "You brought those cookies."

"I know, but I bought them at the store."

I waved my hand. "That's good enough for me."

Salem nodded in agreement. "Let the testosterone deal with the dishes. It'll do them some good."

"It does feel nice to relax," Martha said, putting her head back against the chair. "It was super busy at the library all day."

We talked some more about her job. It turned out she wasn't a librarian yet but was working on her master's in library science. I wanted to ask how things were going with her and Shane, but I wasn't sure how to phrase it. Luckily, Salem did it for me.

"So, is Shane your boyfriend?"

Martha shook her head. "I like Shane a lot, but I wouldn't call him my boyfriend. We're just taking it slow for now."

Salem nodded. "Nothing wrong with that. Although he sure seems enamored with you."

"He's just so different from any guy I've ever dated."

"What do you mean?" I asked.

"I don't know. There are always girls around him. Whenever I see him outside the library, he's always with someone."

"Have you asked him about it?" I wanted to defend my brother, but I also knew what Martha was talking about.

"He says they're just friends."

As we were discussing this, Dean came back over with his beer and took a seat. "All right, what are we talking about?" He settled in his chair and popped the cap off his bottle. "I'm ready to give you the guy's perspective on whatever it is, so lay it on me."

"Martha's not sure if she should start dating Shane," Salem told him. She glanced down at her sleeping daughter. The little girl looked so sweet.

"I like Shane, but he seems to have a lot of girlfriends," Martha said. "I'm not sure if I should get involved with someone like that."

Dean stroked his beard and listened thoughtfully. "First, I have to ask you something. When you say you like Shane, are you *into* him?"

Martha shrugged but then nodded. "I'm into him, but that's what worries me. I don't want to be one of many."

He studied her. "I'm going to give it to you straight. Are you ready?"

Martha nodded.

"If you're into him, then I say go for it. Because that guy is completely crazy about you."

"He is?" Her eyes widened, and she glanced toward the house. There was a growing smile on her face.

"Hell yes," Dean said. "I barely even know him, and the dude's already told me all about you. You work at the library—which is pretty cool, by the way—you used to be a ballet dancer, you play the piano, and you have a dog named Snuffles or Muffles?"

"Ruffles," Martha said, laughing.

Dean grinned. "I rest my case."

I smiled at Dean. It was a pretty nice thing he just did for my brother.

He took a swig of beer and began stroking his beard again. "All right, whose love life are we working on next?" He turned in my direction.

In fact, *everybody* turned in my direction.

My brows shot up. "What? Why are you all looking at me?"

"You know why," Dean said.

"I don't."

"Josh is my best friend. I can see what's going on there."

"Nothing's going on there. We're just friends."

He snorted. "Friends who play grab-ass under the table."

My cheeks grew warm. "I'm sure I don't know what you mean."

"Yeah, it's a big mystery." He eyed me in a considering way. "For what it's worth, I think you two are damn good together."

"You do?"

"I haven't seen him this happy and relaxed since... shit, I don't even know when. You guys fit."

EVENTUALLY THE PARTY came to a close. After everyone left, Josh told Damian it was time for bed.

"But I'm not tired," he insisted, yawning for the second time.

"Skip the shower tonight, Little D. Just get your pajamas on and hit the hay—so to speak." He glanced at me. "Staying on a farm is changing the way I talk."

While he made sure Damian brushed his teeth and was set up with his red night-light and a glass of water on his nightstand, I slipped my boots on to go check on my animals. By the time I got back, Damian was in bed, and Josh was sitting on the living room couch. He had his computer on his lap but closed it when he saw me.

"Come here, honey. I need to talk to you about something."

I slipped out of my boots by the front door. "Is everything okay?"

He placed his laptop on the coffee table, and when I sat next to him, he wore a thoughtful expression.

"What is it?" I asked.

"Dean told me the vultures have left my house. Damian and I can finally go home."

My stomach dropped. I should have been expecting this. There hadn't been any helicopters for days. "That's great news," I said, though it didn't feel like great news. It felt like a shock. "When will you be going back?"

"Tomorrow." He was watching me closely. "I already told Damian that we'd head home in the morning."

"Good for you. I wonder if this is Delores's doing." I shared what Claire had told me, how Delores had been encouraging innkeepers to stop renting rooms to all the reporters.

His brows went up. "Damn. If that's true, I'll need to thank her and everyone else."

I nodded and tried to smile, tried to act enthusiastic for him. "You must be so excited to get back to your house. I'm sure you're sick of sleeping on my couch."

He nodded, his eyes still on my face.

Obviously he and Damian couldn't stay here forever, and I should have been happy to get my privacy back. *I mean, there's nothing worse than houseguests who won't leave, right?*

Except I felt sick to my stomach.

But then something else occurred to me. "Why didn't you guys just leave with Dean tonight?"

He reached for my hand. "Because I wanted to spend one more night here with you."

One more night. So this was it. Josh was going back to his glamorous life, and I was just some kind of pit stop.

I had told myself that I'd enjoy whatever time we had together, that I didn't care if it was temporary or if it broke my heart, that some rides were worth taking no matter the cost.

Well, it turned out that was all bullshit, because I sure as hell did care.

"Thank you for taking us in, Leah," he went on. "Meeting you has been something I never expected."

"Sure. Whatever." I looked out toward the window. I could see a sliver of the moon and tried to let that comfort me.

He tugged on my hand. "Hey, what's wrong?"

"Why should anything be wrong? I'm happy you guys can get back to your lives."

"You've been incredibly generous. Most people wouldn't have allowed two strangers to invade their home like you did."

I pulled my hand from his. "You're very welcome. I'm glad I could be so helpful. Guess I'll see you around." I pretended to yawn. "I should get some sleep."

His brows came together.

I started to get up from the couch, but he grabbed my hand. "Where the hell are you going?"

"I just told you. I'm going to bed."

"Sit down."

I gave him a look and let him pull me back down. I stared over at the coatrack by the door with annoyance. I wished I was handling this better, but I just wanted to be left alone to lick my wounds.

"There's one more thing." He paused. "I told Damian tonight that something romantic was developing between you and me."

"You *did?*"

"Was I wrong about that?"

I blinked at him but couldn't speak.

"Why are you acting so weird?" His intelligent eyes studied me. "Jesus, did you really think when I left here that what's been happening between us would end? Is that what you want?"

"No, it's not what I want. It's just that I'm a normal person, and you're a rock star."

He snorted and rolled his eyes. "Since when have you ever treated me like a rock star? You've got me out there shoveling alpaca and llama shit, weeding your garden, cleaning your hen house, and then being chased by a crazy rooster."

I smiled. "When you put it like that, I guess I do mostly think of you as a regular guy. But the reality is you're famous, and I'm just a farmer."

"Come here, honey." He reached out and pulled me onto his lap so our faces were close. "Have you been paying attention at all?"

"I pay attention."

He appeared skeptical, but then his expression softened. "I like being with you, Leah. I know my situation is messed up right now, but I was hoping you'd stick around. Eventually all this adoption business will be resolved."

I nodded and played with his ponytail. "Okay, I'll stick around."

"Good. In the meantime, I'll be thinking about you." His voice was low and inviting. "Imagining all the things we're going to do together."

My stomach fluttered with anticipation. "Me too."

He kissed me, and his lips were tender. I opened my mouth so our tongues could share the intimacy that we weren't sharing otherwise. When the kiss ended, we hugged. I closed my eyes, dizzy with relief that I'd been wrong. But then something else occurred to me.

"Do you think it was wise to tell Damian that we're romantically involved? Couldn't that mess things up if Charlotte gets wind of it?"

Josh sighed. "Yeah, I considered that, and it's a concern." He chewed his lower lip. "The thing is I don't want Damian to be blindsided by any of this, you know? So I decided to tell him."

"What did he say?" Damian and I had a good relationship, and I hoped he didn't suddenly see me as the enemy.

"He was quiet at first, but we talked it out. He knows Charlotte and I will never be together again. It turns out he's mostly worried about the adoption. He doesn't want anything to interfere with that." Josh shook his head and frowned. "That's what Charlotte doesn't seem to understand. Dragging all this shit out is hurting him too."

I nodded, feeling awful about everything they were going through. "I just hope our relationship doesn't become a problem."

His jaw flexed. "I won't let it." He pulled me in close and kissed me again. "Let's lie down a little. I'm beat. I haven't been getting enough sleep lately."

He spread his long, muscular body down on the couch, and I

snuggled in, half draped over him. "Why aren't you sleeping enough? Is it because it's so quiet?"

Josh nodded. "Partly."

I waited for him to elaborate, but he didn't seem inclined to, so I rested my head on my hand and watched his handsome face, enjoying the feel of his body pressed next to me. His eyes were closed. "I hope my couch hasn't been uncomfortable."

He smirked. "It's more knowing that you're upstairs in your bed that's been uncomfortable."

I nodded with understanding. "That's kept me awake too."

His eyes opened. "It has? I didn't know that."

"Well, how would you?"

He paused and thought this over, then got a sly grin. "I never heard any buzzing noises. Guess you weren't using a vibrator, huh?"

"Oh, it's a quiet one."

"Damn, really?" A smile grew on his face. "It's probably a good thing I didn't know about that. I might not have been able to stop myself from joining you."

I played with his beard. "I had no idea you were suffering in silence down here. You poor thing."

"I'm surprised you didn't hear all the cold showers I've been taking."

I tilted my head. "I think I did hear some of those. I just figured you liked to shower a lot."

He laughed. "I don't like showering *that* much."

CHAPTER THIRTY

~Josh~

Instead of that crazy rooster crowing, it was a doorbell that woke us up the next morning. Leah was still beside me on the couch, where we'd slept close all night. We'd shifted position a few times and were now facing each other.

"Who could that be?" she grumbled. Two cats slept on us, and she reached out to pet the nearest one.

Sunlight shone through the windows, but I could tell it was still early morning.

"That's weird," I muttered. "I never heard Cary Grant."

Leah sat up, yawning. We both still had our clothes on from yesterday. "I heard him," she said, climbing over me and the cats. "I skipped my morning run since you were sleeping so hard." I reached for her hand and tried to pull her back onto the couch, but the doorbell rang again. She rolled her eyes. "God, I hope it's not Lars with some problem."

She left to go answer it, so I sat up, too, and scrubbed my face with both hands. My back was stiff, not that I was complaining. Far from it. I grinned to myself, feeling pretty damn good.

Then the front door opened, and everything turned to shit.

"So *you* must be his whore!" an all-too-familiar voice seethed. It woke me up faster than a bucket of ice water. Those razor-sharp vowels.

I leapt over the back of the couch.

"Who are you?" Leah asked. She sounded bewildered. "I think you have the wrong house."

My stomach churned when I saw her standing in the doorway. Black hair streaked purple. Dark leggings, hip boots, and a flowing sapphire top.

"What are you doing here, Charlotte?" I tried to keep my voice level, though my insides were tight, bracing myself for the coming disaster.

Her dark eyes stared into mine like lasers. "What the fuck do you *think* I'm doing here? I've come to collect my son."

I put my hand against the wall. "What is this? Damian's asleep."

"I don't care. Wake him up!"

She pushed her way into the house. That was when I noticed there was someone else with her. It was Malcom standing behind her in torn jeans and a leather jacket. He followed her inside. A black town car with a driver sat waiting out front.

"Where is my son? *Damian!*" Charlotte yelled.

"Stop it," I said, already exhausted from her drama. I'd dealt with enough drama from this woman to last me two lifetimes. "What the hell is wrong with you?"

She whipped around. "What the hell is wrong with *me*? Oh, you've got some nerve. Shacking up, and with my son under the same roof!" She sneered at Leah.

"We're not shacking up," Leah said angrily.

Charlotte scoffed. "You must think I'm a complete fucking idiot."

I tried to rein in my temper. "Knock this shit off, Charlotte. You're making a fool out of yourself."

"Don't you dare call me a fool."

"Leah's done nothing but help me and Damian. You should be thanking her."

Charlotte laughed. "I should be *thanking* the whore who you're fucking? Are you insane?"

"That's *enough*." My voice hardened. "Don't speak about her like that."

"I'll speak about your *whore* in whatever manner I choose!"

"Jesus, are you hearing yourself? This is pathetic. It's been a year and a half since we broke up." I gestured to Malcom, who stood there like a mannequin. "You even brought your boyfriend. Yet you still want to sink your claws into me. I'm done with this shit. I've jumped through every hoop you've demanded, and I'm finished."

"*Damian!*" she shrieked.

"Mum? I'm right here." Damian had come out from the bedroom and was rubbing sleep from his eyes.

She smiled and went over to hug him. "Hello, darling. Grab your things. We're going home."

He blinked at her with confusion and then looked at me. "Home? Are we going back to Dad's house?"

"We're flying back to London."

He went still, the sleep clearing from his face as he grasped what was happening. "But... I'm staying with Dad until the end of August."

"Not anymore you're not. I have flight reservations for this afternoon."

"I don't want to leave!" Damian's voice shook. "You promised I could stay the summer. The summer isn't over!"

Charlotte snorted. "It's over when I say it is. I'm taking you from this... this...." She looked around. "*Horrid* place."

I felt Leah grow tense, ready to give Charlotte a piece of her mind, but I glanced at her and shook my head. It would only make things worse.

"This place isn't horrid. I love it here," Damian told her. "I've gotten to know all of Leah's animals."

"It doesn't matter. We're leaving. Grab your things."

"But I'm staying with Dad! What about the adoption?"

Her expression hardened. "That's over too."

Damian's face crumbled. "You can't do this!"

"I'm your mum, and I'll do as I please!"

"Charlotte, stop it," I said. "Just stop. Let's talk this out." I had to try and reason with her. There was a heavy sense of dread in my gut. "Think about what you're doing. You're not just hurting me. You're hurting him too."

Before I knew it, Damian ran to me and threw his arms around my waist. I hugged him back. This was insane.

I stared at her. "After all these years, are you really going to tell me I'm not his dad?"

"Legally, you're nothing." She gave me a spiteful smile. "This was your decision, remember? You're the one who left."

So that was what it came down to. She wanted me to suffer because I couldn't stand living with her anymore. It was hard to believe I ever cared for her, ever saw the good in her.

Damian looked up at me. "You're still going to fight for the adoption, right? You're not giving up, are you?" His bottom lip quivered. I could tell he was trying to be tough, trying not to cry, but he was just a kid caught in the middle.

"I'll never give up." I put my hand on his shoulder to steady him. "You're my son, and you always will be."

He nodded, wiping his nose with the back of his hand. "Thanks, Dad."

Charlotte wasn't enjoying this little exchange one bit. "We're leaving," she snapped. "*Now.*"

"I don't *want* to." Damian shook his head defiantly.

I turned to Charlotte. "Just let him stay until the end of August. It's only a couple of more weeks."

"Get your things," she told Damian. "We're flying back this afternoon, and I won't hear another word about it." She glared at me. "You can make this difficult, but it won't change anything. He's leaving."

"I won't go." He stared at her, then turned to me. "I want to *stay*."

I sighed to myself. *What a fucking mess.* "I know you do, Little D." I did my best to sound calm, to not let this get any uglier. "I'm going to do everything in my power to fight for the adoption, but you're going to have to go with her. She's your mom." I looked at Charlotte. "He has to get his stuff. Some of it's back at my house."

"You can send it."

"*No*," Damian said, turning to her. "I have to get it. It's gifts for Granny and you and Uncle Will. My friends too." His voice took on an edge of hysteria. "I *have* to get it!"

"All right, *fine*." She frowned with impatience. "Get changed into some clothes. Malcom and I will wait in the car."

Damian trudged off, leaving the room with slumped shoulders.

"I'm coming too," I told her.

Her eyes met mine, and for one instant I saw the old Charlotte, the one who used to be my partner in crime, the one I'd once cared for deeply. I softened my voice, hoping that somehow I could reach her. "Let's talk about this, Char. It doesn't have to be so ugly between us."

Her mouth opened, but then she glanced at Leah, and the old Charlotte vanished, replaced with this jealous, spiteful creature. "You've made your choice," she snapped. "Guess you'll have to bloody well live with it."

"Is this because of the video?" Leah asked her. "Because Josh was just helping me, that's all."

Charlotte's brows went up. "Video? What video? My *God*. Please don't tell me you two made some sort of pornographic video."

"Don't be ridiculous," I said.

"It doesn't matter now," Charlotte told me. "I hope you and your whore are happy together."

"That's *enough*." I took a step toward her, my voice menacing. "I don't *ever* want to hear that word again."

Our eyes locked on each other. She knew me well enough to know when I wasn't fucking around.

My eyes narrowed. "If I hear one more insult toward Leah, I'll make sure there's a sizable dent in your social calendar."

If I wanted to, I could wreck her life. There were a number of people—friends and club owners in London, New York, and LA—who'd slam their doors in her face if I asked them to.

Her eyes were still on mine, but I could see the wheels turning, could see her weighing her options. She didn't want to lose her social standing—even as my ex.

"We're not sleeping together," Leah said. "You've got it wrong."

Charlotte was still watching me. "Is that true, Josh?"

It was a strange moment. I could probably make this whole thing go away. I wouldn't even have to lie. But I was done playing Charlotte's games. Finished with her bullshit. It was obvious that it would never end, so I was ending it here and now.

"It's true," I said. "We haven't slept together. But I'll tell you what else is true." I gazed over at Leah. "I've fallen in love."

CHARLOTTE LOOKED SHOCKED.

I hadn't meant it to be cruel.

I knew what it was like to be in love. How much I wanted to be with Leah. How I couldn't stop thinking about her. How happy I felt whenever I was with her. I trusted her more than I'd trusted any woman in a long time.

When Dean told me the vultures were gone, I'd actually been disappointed.

I couldn't say I wanted to feel this way. Being in love seriously screwed me up in the past, but there was no point in lying to myself about it.

Leah's eyes were on me, but I couldn't tell from her face how she was taking this.

Obviously the timing was pure shit. Not exactly the best way to tell someone you'd fallen for them. I hoped she wasn't regretting the day I walked through her door with all the drama this had brought into her life.

Damian emerged from the guest bedroom carrying his backpack. He still looked miserable, and my heart ached seeing it. I was never giving up on this kid. Never. I'd die first. Charlotte had to know that, but then that wasn't what this was about.

She still hadn't said a word since my revelation. Apparently I'd finally shut her up.

I grabbed my backpack and quickly shoved what I could into it, and then the four of us were ready to leave Leah's.

"Bye, Damian," Leah said to him. "I've really enjoyed meeting you."

To my surprise, he hugged her. My throat tightened as I watched the two of them.

I was the last one out the door and reached for Leah's hand. Our eyes swallowed each other. When she squeezed my fingers back, I felt it through my whole body.

I sat up front with the driver of the town car and gave him directions to my house. Malcom still hadn't said anything, and I didn't know why Charlotte had bothered to bring him at all. He spent most of the time on his phone.

Dean and Nalla were still asleep, but our arrival woke them up. I could see the shock on Dean's face at the sight of Charlotte as he quickly surmised the situation.

"Don't bother saying anything," she said to him in an icy tone. "We're not staying long."

She gazed appraisingly at Nalla still wearing a nightgown.

Dean's eyes cut to mine, and I saw the anger in them over what was happening.

"I'm going to go help Damian pack," I gritted out. I strode past everyone and followed him as he headed toward his bedroom.

Charlotte and Malcom came after me, and I could feel her taking in the house, though she didn't comment.

While Damian went through his closet and drawers, sniffing and trying not to cry, I helped him pack his suitcase. "What if I've forgotten something?" he asked morosely. "What will I do?"

"Don't worry. I'll send you anything you missed."

Charlotte huffed and seemed impatient again as she stood in the doorway. "Let's get moving. We have a plane to catch."

Part of me wanted to roar at her, to show my rage at what she was doing, but I tamped that shit down. I didn't want to waste these last precious moments with Damian, so I ignored her.

"It's going to be okay, Little D. I'm going to fix this." I put my hand on his back and could feel him sweating through his T-shirt. "I'm going to fight this with everything I've got. I promise. Just remember, no matter what happens or what anybody says, you'll always be my son. No one can take that away from you."

His face was solemn, but I could tell he saw the truth of it. He nodded. "I know."

Charlotte made a strangled noise in her throat. "Malcom, get his suitcase. We're leaving." She turned and left, her boot heels clicking down the hall.

Damian and I watched as Malcom lugged the suitcase off the bed, but then he stopped and faced me. He wore a peculiar grin. "Sorry about all this, mate. I hope you don't take it personally. I'm actually a big fan of the band."

I scowled.

Malcom continued his strange grin. "If it's not asking too much, do you think I could get an autograph before I go?"

It took everything I had not to punch him in the face.

Malcom stopped grinning when he saw my dark expression.

In fact, he shut up entirely, which was the smartest thing I'd seen him do so far.

When we got to the front door, I hugged Damian one last time. His familiar boyish scent filled my nose.

And then he was gone.

Dean and Nalla were there, but I strode past them. I didn't want to talk right now.

When I was back upstairs in my bedroom, I called my lawyer in England. It was early evening there, and he was probably having dinner, but I didn't give a shit. I paid his firm enough money that I expected attention whenever I needed it.

I paced around the room with my hand on my head, the phone pressed to my ear, trying not to rant and rave, though that was mostly what I did. Next, I called my lawyer in the States and did the same thing all over again.

Lastly, I called Philomena. She didn't answer, but I left a detailed message, explaining everything that just happened. I kept my voice as calm as possible, and I asked her if she could please check to make sure Damian was okay.

I was out of breath when I finally hung up.

My gut churned. I hadn't felt this helpless since my brother was arrested.

As I sat on the end of the bed, trying to gather my thoughts and decide what to do next, I heard someone coming up the stairs. I expected to see Dean, but it was Nalla.

"I prefer to be alone," I said in a clipped tone. "I still have more phone calls to make."

She wore a look of compassion. "Of course you do. I'm so sorry this happened. I guess it was inevitable."

To my annoyance, she came into the room and sat next to me on the bed. She placed her hand on my shoulder. I was beyond irritated with her unwanted advances and shrugged it off.

"You need to leave," I said, full of impatience. "Go back to Dean."

"How can I leave when it's obvious you're suffering? I wish you'd just come home with us that night I asked you to. None of this would have happened."

There was something odd about what she was saying, but the phone buzzed in my hand. I was too distraught to pay attention to Nalla. I looked down at the message from my lawyer in London. He'd booked me on a private flight into Heathrow tomorrow, and then a car would meet me once I landed. I didn't know what I'd do when I got to England, but I sure as hell couldn't stay here and do nothing.

"Let me be here for you," Nalla said, softening her tone. "I want to comfort you."

My jaw muscles flexed. The last thing I needed was to deal with her shit right now. "I don't want your comfort. I want you to leave me the fuck alone."

She seemed taken aback. "You don't know what you're saying."

"I do know what I'm saying. Fucking *go*."

"You're upset, so I won't take that personally." She stood up. "But you should remember that we all love Damian. You're not the only one who'll miss him."

She left. I felt bad for being harsh on her, but I was relieved she was gone. I knew Dean cared about her, so I tried to like her, but at this point I was barely tolerating her.

Once I was alone again, I sat there staring at the blank wall. My throat felt like it was closing up, like I was being strangled. I was famous for the way I could sustain long notes at an earsplitting level, but right now I couldn't sing if someone held a gun to my head.

Eventually I got up and stumbled into the bathroom, stripped my clothes off, and stood under the hot shower, letting it rain down on me.

I didn't know how long I stood there. At some point, I heard a sound behind me, and when I turned, I discovered I wasn't alone anymore.

Leah.

I blinked with amazement. It was like seeing a mirage, something wondrous in the middle of a terrible landscape.

She didn't say a word, just stepped close to me. I glanced down at her naked body. She felt like home, felt natural and right, and when she wrapped her arms around me, all I could do was fall into them. The strangled sensation in my throat loosened, and the first rough sound escaped.

Leah held me while I broke down sobbing. Tortured. A wounded animal whose young had been taken. Her hands stroked my back. She held me up as if I were made of sand instead of muscle and bone. My shoulders shook with hurt, unable to lock it down. We stood in that warm shower for a long time as she offered me solace.

Finally, I opened my eyes and gazed into hers. Beautiful and feminine. I should have seen it from the start, should have seen the rightness of her.

"Look at me, crying like a baby," I croaked. "Guess I'm all out of masculine pride." I tried to make a joke, but it came out wrong. Ragged. A spool of rusty barbed wire. My million-dollar voice wasn't worth two cents.

"It's going to be okay," she said, caressing my jaw.

I shook my head. "I failed him, just like I failed Jeremy."

"That's not true."

"It *is*."

She held my face with both hands. "Listen to me. You didn't fail Damian. You're a good father. None of this is on you."

I wanted to believe her. I wished I could.

CHAPTER THIRTY-ONE

~Leah~

After the shower, we lay in Josh's bed together just to be close to each other. Surrounded by cool sheets, I held him while he slept.

His room was airy with big pieces of Scandinavian furniture. The walls were mostly bare, and judging by the moving boxes stacked in the corner, I suspected he was still unpacking. I smiled when I saw his nightstand. He'd placed the Sasquatch doll I'd given him right next to a framed photo of him and Damian on a ski slope together. There were a few books and a Kindle in a black leather case. On closer inspection, the titles were mostly on parenting. Seeing them, my heart hurt all over again.

It had been a terrible day.

After everyone left with Charlotte, I did my chores in a rush. An instinct told me to come here, that Josh needed me, so I threw on clean shorts and a tank top, then headed over as fast as I could.

I drove here not sure what I'd find, and to my surprise, the place appeared empty. Deserted. All the reporters were gone, the black gates were wide open, and the only vehicle in the driveway was Josh's truck.

When I knocked on the front door and rang the bell, no one answered. I tried the knob and discovered the door was unlocked.

It felt strange walking through the empty house, considering the last time I was here, it was their birthday party.

That was when I discovered the house wasn't empty.

Nalla was in the kitchen. When she saw me her mouth dropped open. "How the hell did *you* get in here?"

"Sorry if I startled you," I said. "I rang the bell and knocked, but nobody answered."

She strode toward me, waving her hands in the air. "Get the fuck out of here! Go!"

I was taken aback. "I'm here to see Josh."

"Josh doesn't want to see you!"

"Of course he does. What are you talking about?"

"He wants to be left alone!"

"What the hell is your problem?" I was fed up with her nonsense. She was standing right in front of me now, blocking my way.

"I won't let you go to him." She held her skinny arms out on both sides as if she could stop me.

I stared at her with comic disbelief. *Is she nuts?* "Look, I don't know what's wrong with you, but I'm going to see him." I pushed past her, but she grabbed my forearm. I felt her nails digging into my skin, trying to hold me back.

"Let go!" I yanked my arm away.

She got a crazed look on her face and grabbed my arm again with both hands this time. Did she really think she could fight me and win? Not only was I bigger, but I was stronger. I carried bales of hay and bags of animal feed around regularly. The heaviest thing I suspected she ever lifted was a tube of lip gloss.

"Get your hands off me," I demanded.

"Why can't you just leave?" She sounded desperate. "You're ruining everything!"

"What the *hell* is going on here?" It was Dean's booming voice. He'd just come around the corner.

Thank God.

"Nalla, let go of her!" he said, taking her by the shoulders.

"She can't go to Josh. I won't allow it. I should be the one comforting him. Not this bitch!"

Dean pulled her away from me. "What are you talking about?"

Nalla was breathing hard and seemed on the verge of hysteria. "Josh said he wanted to be left alone, that he didn't want anyone bothering him."

"Leah is Josh's girlfriend," Dean said, trying to be patient with her. "Trust me, he wants to see her."

"No, he doesn't!" She began to cry. "She can't be his girlfriend. It wasn't supposed to be like this. Josh is supposed to fall in love with *me!*"

My mouth dropped open, stunned at her words. Dean stiffened, obviously stunned too.

By that point Nalla had turned away from us both, still ranting and crying. "I didn't know she'd take Damian away from him. How was I supposed to know that? I just wanted him to come home!"

Dean and I glanced at each other with surprise.

"Nalla, what did you do?" His voice was worried. "Did you contact Charlotte?"

She stopped sniffing and glared at me. "It's *your* fault! If he'd just left your house when I told him to, none of this would have happened. He would have fallen in love with *me* if it weren't for *you!*"

I didn't know what to say. Obviously I'd suspected she had a thing for Josh, but I had no idea it was this bad, or that she'd go to such terrible lengths.

Understandably, Dean seemed shell-shocked. "Go on, Leah," he said to me in a quiet tone. "I'll handle this. Do you know where Josh's room is? It's down the hall and up the staircase."

I nodded and felt bad leaving him, but there was nothing I could do.

As I walked away, I could hear Nalla crying again. I heard Dean's deep voice. "What the fuck, Nalla? Are you in love with Josh?"

I ran down the hall, glad when I saw the spiral staircase.

Once I climbed it, I didn't see Josh anywhere. His bedroom was big, bigger than my first apartment, with high ceilings, slanted wood beams, and multiple skylights overhead. I heard water running and followed the sound.

I found him standing in the shower of a luxurious bathroom. Steam filled the space, and I could just make out his form through the glass. His arms were in front of him with his head bent down. He hadn't noticed me, and I wondered how long he'd been standing like that.

Immediately I stripped my clothes off, and when I opened the shower door, he turned around. In that moment, I was so glad I came, so glad I'd followed my instincts. All of Josh's bright energy was drained away.

His eyes on mine were sad. A wounded lion.

It hurt to see him like this. I stepped into the shower, and without a word, I walked over and put my arms around him.

———

I MUST HAVE FALLEN ASLEEP, too, because when I woke up, I was still in Josh's bed. He was awake, lying there watching me.

"You're pretty when you sleep."

I blinked at him, dazed from napping in the afternoon.

He slipped his arm around my waist. "Thank you, Leah."

"For what?"

"Taking care of me."

I reached out to stroke his face, and then I wrapped my arm around his neck, moving closer. "How are you?"

He shrugged. "I've been better."

We were both quiet. It was cloudy outside, and I could hear rain tapping lightly on the skylights above us.

"I meant what I said earlier." His deep voice broke the quiet. "I love you."

My breath hitched. I'd been thinking about it all day. "What happened? I thought you were never going to fall in love again."

He snorted. "Believe me, I wasn't planning on it." He brushed his fingers against my cheek. "It's you. You've slipped past all my defenses. I don't know how you did it."

"You've slipped past mine too," I whispered, then smiled. "If it's any consolation."

"You're the one good thing in the middle of all this," he said. "The one thing that's been amazing. I just wish the timing was better."

"I know."

He sighed. "I want to explore this with you, but I can't right now. I have to fly to London tomorrow."

I nodded, not really surprised.

"I'll go crazy if I stay here," he continued. "I figure I'll go by the flat in Kensington. Charlotte will freak out, but I need to make sure Damian's okay."

"I understand. That makes sense." Suddenly I remembered the whole mess that happened with Nalla. "I have to tell you something bizarre that happened when I got here earlier."

His brows came together with concern. "What do you mean?"

I relayed the story to him.

Josh's expression grew thunderous. "What the fuck!" He sat up in bed. "Are you kidding me? *She* did that? Created this mess?"

I sat up with the duvet tucked over my breasts. "That's what it sounded like. I don't know what happened next. Dean told me to go to you, and that's what I did."

"She actually attacked you?"

"Well, she tried." It had felt more like I was swatting a fly away. "Dean put a stop to it."

He shook his head, then threw the bedding aside and stood up. I watched him stride across the room. Normally I'd be enjoying this, the magnificence of Josh in the buff, but obviously the circumstances sucked. He opened some dresser drawers and pulled out clothes.

I reached for the white towel at the end of the bed and stood up, too, wrapping it around myself.

I felt his eyes as he walked toward me wearing loose black athletic shorts and a white T-shirt. "You don't have to be shy around me, honey."

I smiled. It was one thing to be naked while comforting him, but it was another to walk around without a stitch of clothing on. This was all still very new. "I'm not being shy. I'm just being... mysterious."

"Don't hide your light under a bushel," he murmured. "Isn't that what they say?" He put his hand on my hip over the towel, smiling, and I was happy to see it. He looked a little more like his normal self. But then his expression changed. "I need to talk to Dean. Obviously Nalla has to get the fuck out of my house. I can't have her staying here anymore." He stroked his short beard as he considered what he was saying. "And you're sure she's the one who told Charlotte about you and me?"

"That's what it sounded like."

"Fuck. I should have seen this coming."

"How could you?"

"Just a weird sense I had about her. She was always trying to put her hands on me. Always telling me I was a genius."

I touched his arm. "Give me a second to get dressed, okay? I want to come downstairs with you."

I went into the bathroom and quickly threw on my clothes that were still in a pile on the counter. I glanced around. His bathroom was mostly gray-and-white marble. There was another skylight above the huge bathtub.

When I came back out to the bedroom, Josh was sitting on the bed, studying his phone. "I texted Damian earlier. I was hoping to hear something back by now."

I sat down next to him. "You know, you could have lied to Charlotte, told her there was nothing between us. I would have understood."

He tossed the phone on the bed. "I'm done playing her games. I never should have played them to begin with, but at the time, I thought I didn't have a choice." He reached for my hand and slipped his fingers through mine. "I've put up with people like her my whole life. I'm finished with that."

"I'm pretty sure she's still in love with you. Just look at her boyfriend. The guy's like a watered down version of you."

"That motherfucker had the nerve to ask me for an autograph."

My brows went up. "Seriously? What did you say?"

"Nothing. It took all my willpower not to punch him."

We both got up and headed downstairs. Josh wore a stern expression, and I sensed he was bracing himself to deal with Nalla. I could tell it wasn't in his nature to be harsh to a woman, even if it was deserved.

I braced myself too. I'd rather not deal with any more of her theatrics.

We didn't see Nalla anywhere but finally found Dean lying on the black leather couch in the music room. There was a pair of drumsticks on the table next to him, and he was drinking a beer and eating from a large bag of potato chips.

His sapphire gaze took us both in. "What's up, brother?" he said to Josh, then smiled at me, or tried to smile. He looked miserable. "Hey, Leah."

"Hi, Dean." I looked around the room for Nalla.

"I guess Leah told you what happened," Dean said to Josh. He stuffed a couple of chips in his mouth and then washed it down with a swig of beer.

"She told me." Josh's voice was quiet, but I heard the resolve in it. "I'm sorry, Dean, but Nalla has to go. I can't have her staying here anymore."

"Already gone."

"She left?" Josh asked.

Dean took another swig of beer. "We broke up. I called her a cab, and she packed her shit and took off."

"Damn, dude." Josh blew his breath out. "I don't know what to say. I'm fucking sorry as hell."

Dean shook his head. "No, brother, don't apologize. I'm the one who's sorry. I had no idea what she was about. If I'd known, I would have kicked her ass out ages ago. It turns out she called Charlotte and created this whole mess for you, and now you've lost your son."

Josh's jaw muscle flexed, and he nodded. "Don't worry. I'm not giving up."

"I know you're not, but still. She fucked things up."

"Are you okay, Dean?" I asked, since it was obvious he was really hurting. "Can we do anything for you?"

"Don't worry about me, Leah. I'm good. I'm going to drink a few more beers and play some drums. That's all I need. You two go on. I don't need a babysitter."

He kept insisting, so reluctantly we both left. When we got to the kitchen, Josh opened the fridge and asked me if I wanted anything.

"I feel bad leaving Dean alone," I said, sitting in one of the tall chairs next to the island. "Shouldn't we stay with him?"

He pulled out a couple of beers and offered me one, though I declined. "I've known Dean a long time. It's best to let him be right now, give him his space." He popped the cap off and took a swallow, then shook his head. "What a fucking shit show today has been."

I nodded, noticing the clock on the stove. It was later than I thought.

"What is it?" Josh asked, noticing my expression.

"I'm sorry, but I have to leave and do my evening chores."

He nodded. "I understand. Can you... come back after? Maybe stay the night?"

His eyes lingered on mine, and I saw he was still struggling. I got up and went to him, resting my head against his shoulder as we hugged each other.

"I'll ask Shane if he can stick around tonight and keep an eye on things." I gazed up at him. "If that doesn't work out, you could always come and stay with me."

"I'd like that, except I'm not sure if I should leave Dean completely alone right now."

I nodded. "I'll try to come back, then, even if it's just for a little while."

When I got back to my farm, I was hoping Shane might already be there, but there was no sign of his truck. I texted and explained the situation to him the best I could. Everything that happened this morning with Charlotte. It was hard to believe it was still the same day. It felt like it had gone on forever.

I took care of the chickens and then went over to gather feed for my girls. I wondered if they were going to miss Damian. He was out here a lot. I knew for sure I'd miss him. In a short time, he and Josh had become a part of my life.

It was just after I finished filling up all the troughs with fresh water that my phone rang with a call from Shane.

"Damn, the little dude has really gone back to England? I can't believe I slept through all that."

"It was awful."

"How's Josh doing?"

"About how you'd expect. He's pretty messed up." I asked Shane if he could stay here and keep an eye on things for me tonight. I didn't like to leave my farm all night without anyone around.

"Sure, that's not a problem." He grew quiet. "So you and Josh, huh?"

I gazed out across the pasture to the copse of trees. The one I first followed Damian through. "We're sort of involved." I wasn't quite sure how else to describe it.

"I had a feeling there was something up with you two. He's cool. I like him." Then he chuckled. "Wow, if you marry him, I'll have a brother-in-law who's a rock star."

"I'm not going to marry him." I laughed.

"Didn't you marry some rocker dude before?" Shane was just a kid when I married Derek.

"Yes," I admitted. "But that was different."

"Doesn't seem all that different to me, but then only you would know."

I heard someone else talking in the background.

"Is that Martha?" I asked.

"She said Eddie is going to be upset when he finds out Damian's already left." There was more talking. "Do you mind if she comes over too?" I heard the smile in his voice. "She can keep me company."

"Not at all. I appreciate you guys doing this for me."

CHAPTER THIRTY-TWO

~Leah~

"So Dean's staying with you now?" Josh chuckled as I told him the news when he called me from London a few days later. "I guess in a strange way that makes sense. Where's he sleeping?"

"In the guest bedroom."

"It's like you're running a bed-and-breakfast for displaced musicians," he said, still chuckling.

Lars had said something similar when he'd come by to check on me. "That drummer is staying here now too?" he asked with amazement. "How long's that been going on?"

"Not long."

He scratched his forehead. "What is this? A halfway house for homeless rock stars?"

"I couldn't just leave him alone, not after everything that happened."

"He's not a puppy, Leah."

"I know, but he just lost his girlfriend—who turned out to be a nutjob, I might add. He's upset and hurting."

"Doesn't he have someplace else he could go? Like a house of his own? The guy's got to be worth millions."

"He sold his house in LA. That's why he was staying here with Josh." Dean told me this a couple of days ago, how he and Nalla had been planning to get a place together in Seattle.

I'd taken Josh to the airport for his flight to London, and then I'd come back and checked in on Dean. He looked so miserable that I invited him over for dinner. At first he didn't want to come, but it wasn't good for him to sit and stew in that big house alone. After dinner, we hung out and played cards with Shane and Martha, and that was when I suggested he sleep in the guest bedroom. The next day, I told him he could stay as long as he wanted.

"Maybe for a little while," he'd said in a gruff voice.

So far he'd been here a week. He had a very different style than Josh. Dean never joined me on my morning runs or did any chores. He usually got up late and took off on his motorcycle. He'd be gone all afternoon and then show up around four o'clock with a big bag of groceries. Then he'd go into the kitchen and cook us all a magnificent dinner.

"Wow, delicious." I leaned back in the chair, discreetly popping open the top button of my jeans, after indulging in two helpings of lasagna. "I'm stuffed. I hope you aren't feeling obligated to cook every night."

Dean shook his head. His black beard was braided with colorful beads on the end. "Cooking is good for me. It's like therapy."

Shane grabbed the spatula and helped himself to what I was pretty sure was his fourth helping. "Well, this is the best damn therapy I've ever tasted."

Dean chuckled. I could tell he was a people pleaser and enjoyed feeding us. I could also tell he was in emotional pain over what happened with Nalla.

Some evenings, he stuck around, and we played cards. Other

evenings, he left on his bike again and didn't come back until the next day. Shane said he'd come into Walk the Plank a couple of times while he was there working. He kept it low-key, just sitting at the bar sipping a beer. Women approached him, but Shane said he never saw him conversing with anyone for long.

"Where do you go all day?" I asked him one night after a delicious dinner of smoked ribs, collard greens, black-eyed peas, and apple cobbler. I didn't even like black-eyed peas, but his were tasty.

He shrugged. "I just ride my bike all over. Take in the scenery. Spend a lot of time thinking."

I talked or texted with Josh most days and gave him updates on Dean while he gave me updates on the situation with Damian and Charlotte. Apparently he'd gone by their flat in London a few times, but the place was empty. He'd been calling and texting both of them to no avail and was really worried. None of his friends had heard anything. Yesterday he told me he was traveling to Bath to see Damian's grandmother since she hadn't been returning his messages either.

"Good news," Josh said when he called me that afternoon. He sounded relieved. "I found Damian. He's staying here at Philomena's. I guess Charlotte and Malcom dropped him off last night."

"Thank God. How's he doing?"

"He's fine." Josh sounded the most upbeat since I'd talked to him all week. "I guess Charlotte took his phone away, so that's why he never texted or called me back. They were staying at Malcom's place —which sounds like a real shithole. Charlotte decided she wanted to go to France, so they dropped him off here."

"Why didn't his grandmother return any of your messages?"

"I'm not sure," he said. "I asked her about it, but she didn't reply. She's been real friendly since I arrived. I can't complain. In fact, I'm staying in one of her guest rooms right now."

"One of them? How big is her house?"

He chuckled. "It's more like an estate than a house. She raises horses. Of course, Damian's been trying to convince her to get some alpacas."

I smiled hearing this. "Is she going to do it?"

"I don't know. She hasn't said no, so she might."

I sat down on my bed, holding a towel to my wet hair after just taking a shower. "I'm so relieved to hear he's okay. Was he glad to see you?"

"He was. And I told him I wasn't giving up on the adoption. Philomena overheard me, but she didn't seem to have a problem with it."

"Really? Does she have any sway over Charlotte?"

He snorted. "Let's just say Philomena holds the purse strings."

"I didn't know that."

"Yeah, so I'm hopeful." He took a deep breath. "I have some other news too. Have you talked to Dean at all today?"

"No, we had dinner last night, but then he left again. Why?"

"Terence is flying out from Nepal in a couple days. We're going to rent a house here in England together. A friend of his is setting it up. He's already spoken to Rhys, who should be flying out Monday. Dean's going to fly out the day after tomorrow."

"Wow. Does this mean you guys aren't breaking up the band?"

"I sure as hell hope that's the case. We'll see."

"More great news then."

"Yeah, it is." He paused. "Except this means I won't be seeing you as soon as I'd like. I can't say how long exactly."

"That part sucks," I agreed.

"I miss you, my little spinster. I love you, honey."

My heart fluttered. "I love you too."

"You've helped get me through this crazy week. I don't know what I would have done without you." He sighed. "Dammit, I just realized we should have done a video call so you could show me a little something to keep my spirits up."

I smiled. We'd done a few video calls where I'd "kept his spirits up." Mostly this entailed me wearing a pretty bra and panties and giving him a show-and-tell.

His voice lowered to a rumble. "I've been thinking about all the things we're going to do when I see you again."

After that terrible day with Charlotte, we just held each other all night, so we still hadn't had sex. The next morning, he flew to London.

"All this waiting has got my blood running hot," he continued. "I should warn you, it's going to be intense."

"What can I do to help?" I asked suggestively.

He blew his breath out in what sounded like frustration. "Right now, nothing. Staying here, it occurs to me that the walls might have ears."

"I guess we'll be waiting for a while, Friedrich."

THE NEXT FEW weeks went by slower than I would have liked. Dean left for England to join the guys at the house. Josh and I still spoke on the phone and texted each other, though not as often, since he was so busy. He told me things were great with the band and that not only had they put aside their differences, but the four of them were writing a bunch of new music.

"We're really in the zone," he said on the phone one evening. I could hear the rest of the guys in the background. It sounded lively. "It's crazy, but it almost feels like the early days. We've already written three new songs. You're going to love them."

Most nights I moonbathed on the porch or walked my property. One night I noticed Martha's car parked in front of Shane's RV, and it was still there the next morning when I went for my run.

My mom and Lars seemed to have backed off from convincing me to sell my farm. Now they had a new agenda—convincing me not to get involved with a rock star.

"He's just a different kind of person and leads a different kind of life than you," Lars said upon stopping by one afternoon for a visit. "You've got to admit that's true."

"I'm not worried about it," I said. "We'll figure it out."

My mom's approach was less nuanced when I had dinner with her in town. "Getting involved with this Josh person is a mistake," she stated. "In the same way your marriage to Derek was a mistake."

My brows went up. It surprised me that she knew my ex-husband's name. In the past she'd always referred to him as "that idiot musician"—an appropriate moniker in his case.

I did my best to tune them both out. They may think Josh was a mistake, but I knew better.

A few nights after that dinner with my mom, I sat on the front porch moonbathing with two of my cats, Basil and Xena. I hadn't spoken much to Josh in the past week. The time difference made things difficult, and it also sounded like there might be some movement on Damian's adoption. I had my fingers crossed for the two of them.

As I sipped my ice water, I heard what sounded like an engine. I put my glass down and opened my mouth, listening. It was a motorcycle, and it was getting louder.

My pulse shot up as a bike swept around the corner, illuminating the dirt driveway in front of my house. Both cats jetted off the porch while I jumped to my feet, squinting into the headlight. My heart twanged like a guitar string.

The night went quiet as the owner of the bike turned it off. And when I saw that graceful body, those muscular thighs encased in soft denim swinging around to stand up, I knew.

Josh pulled his helmet off as he walked toward me, his hair falling in a mess of blond waves.

He didn't say a word as he strode up the porch steps, dropped his helmet in the chair, and took me in his arms.

I was too stunned to say or do anything. It was like something from a fever dream.

Josh's warm and musky scent surrounded me. His mouth came down on mine in a searing kiss as his arms lifted me off the ground.

We were still kissing as he opened the front door and walked us into the house. I laughed against his mouth as he carried me up the stairs. "What are you doing? I can't believe you're back."

"I'm going to show you how much I've missed you, honey."

My emotions were all over the map—excitement, joy, and love—all of them tumbling around inside me like a carnival ride.

Once we were in my bedroom, he laid me on the bed and stripped off his motorcycle jacket. I was mesmerized watching him. He was crazy gorgeous. Had I forgotten he was this good-looking?

God, help me.

"Don't stop there," I said, and he grinned, pulling off his T-shirt next. I was grateful I'd left my bedside lamp on because I could see everything. That chiseled broad chest and those beautiful abs.

"Your turn."

I lifted my arms to help him remove my top, then wriggled my hips as he pulled my jeans and panties off.

The whole time, we kept finding each other, our gazes colliding in the small space. I had so many questions, but I didn't want to ruin the moment. Part of me couldn't believe he was here.

When I was naked, his eyes roamed over me as I lay on the duvet. "You're beautiful, Leah. So damn beautiful."

He leaned in and kissed my stomach before moving up to my breasts, lavishing them with attention, first one and then the other while I moaned and grabbed him, his long hair brushing over me. My whole body was caught up with desire.

His thigh pressed between my legs, and I couldn't stop myself from moving against him. I reached down for his belt buckle, but he pushed my hand away.

"Take your jeans off," I breathed. "I'm the only one naked here."

"All in good time," he murmured.

He sat on his knees and slipped his hand between my legs, caressing me gently. My eyes fell shut, my breath thready.

When I finally looked at him, he was watching me, his cheeks flushed.

"Is that nice?" he asked softly.

I nodded, moving mindlessly.

"Do you want more?"

"You know I do."

"I've been thinking about you like this," he said, his voice ragged. He reached up for a pillow and tucked it under my hips. "Let me see you, honey. Show me that sweet pussy."

I'd do anything he wanted. Josh had that kind of effect on me. He was still wearing jeans, and I could see the column of his erection pressing against the fabric. I swallowed. I wanted him, wanted everything.

He moved down between my legs, kissing my thighs and lightly stroking my center while I squirmed beneath his touch. "Look at you," he whispered. "So hot and wet. So ready for me."

When he finally put his mouth to my center, I moaned and nearly climaxed. Thank God I didn't because it turned out Josh was a rock star in more ways than one. There was no confused tongue poking at me. No question of where to go or what to do. It was all lips and a swirling tongue, and he knew exactly what I needed.

I gasped with pleasure and tried not to think about how much pussy he must have eaten to get this good at it.

Instead I closed my eyes and gave in to the sensation, the way he took it slow, savored me. Time seemed suspended as I slipped through layers of silken pleasure.

When my climax grew near, I gazed down at him. His eyes were closed as he moved his head back and forth. I slid my fingers into his soft hair. Josh's eyes opened, the color so dark, I couldn't see any blue at all. Watching me, he purposefully brought me to the edge, then pulled back. And then he did it again, and again. Our eyes locked on each other. It was intensely intimate.

Eventually I grew frantic and didn't know how much more I could take, which was when Josh did this tongue-vibrating thing that pushed me right over. My whole body shuddered as I gave in to a long powerful climax that had me making sounds I didn't even know I was capable of.

When I came back to Earth, I was wrung out. "Dear God... that was...."

"Good?"

I stared up at him. He was kneeling on the bed and wore a little smile. His eyes were hot on mine. Filled with need. And I could see it wasn't just sexual. It was emotional.

"Crazy good," I whispered.

"Come here. You don't know how much I've been thinking about you." He motioned toward the very obvious bulge in his pants, breathing hard. "Undress me, honey."

I smiled and sat up. "With pleasure." I cupped his erection a bit before unfastening the button and then pulling his zipper down. He wore black boxer briefs, and I tugged them low enough so finally his cock sprang free.

Well... it turned out he'd been telling the truth. Josh had a big dick. Not scary big but long and thick—and currently harder than a shotgun.

I ran my hand down his length and decided to give him the same pleasure he showed me. "You're gorgeous everywhere too," I said. And I leaned in and took him in my mouth.

CHAPTER THIRTY-THREE

~Josh~

"*Daaamn.*" My head fell back, and I nearly lost it as Leah swallowed my cock. This wasn't what I intended when I asked her to undress me, but now that she was doing it, I couldn't force myself to stop. It was too good. I slipped my hands into her silky hair and massaged her neck. I gasped as she worked me over. "Jesus," I breathed. "Slow down, honey."

I gazed down at the top of her dark hair and could barely believe I was here. I'd spent so much time dreaming about her that it didn't seem real. Except it was, and now I was about to embarrass myself.

I had this complete fantasy worked out where I'd come here and sweep Leah off her feet, where I'd blow her mind, except that was going to end in about two seconds.

"I don't care if you come," she said, her voice breathy, glancing up at me as she squeezed me. "I want you to."

I tried to speak but couldn't as she took me deep in her mouth again. I swallowed, still trying to pace myself. Except this was too much. *Fuck.* I was only human, and it'd been a damn long time. Her scent was still all over me from going down on her. I thought about the way she'd looked only moments ago, spread before me, and my blood grew thick.

"Can I come on you?" I rasped as she continued to suck me off. I was so close my hands were shaking.

"Where?"

"Your tits," I panted.

It felt like a million years since I'd had this kind of intimacy with a woman. This closeness. And my mind wanted to slow down and savor it, wanted to relish it, examine it with gratitude, but my body didn't give a shit.

"Oh, *damn*," I groaned, and then I pulled out from Leah's mouth. She moved up close to me, and I climaxed all over her pretty breasts.

"Jesus, I keep embarrassing myself with you," I said after collapsing on the bed to recover. Meanwhile, Leah grabbed a shirt off the floor and wiped herself. I reached over to stroke her leg. "I hope it was all right to come on you like that."

There was a strange tightness in my chest and throat as I gazed at her, so pretty in the glow of her bedside lamp. I swallowed a few times, trying to make the feeling go away, but it persisted.

She shrugged. "Of course it was all right. I didn't mind."

"I had something much bigger planned for the two us. Something hot and romantic. Not that."

"What do you mean?" she asked.

I snorted. "Let's just say I wanted to blow your mind, but instead you blew mine."

She tossed the shirt aside and then slid up close to me. I reached down for the duvet and pulled it over us, remembering all over again why I'd fallen so hard. Why she was special, how it was so easy between us.

"You *did* blow my mind," she said. "From the moment I saw you.

I couldn't believe it." She brought her fingers up to her face and then pulled them back, making an exploding sound.

I chuckled. "My grand entrance. Did you like that? You have to admit I know how to make an entrance."

"You sure do. That was wild. I loved it."

I grinned, pleased at the compliment. "Just like I love *you*." The words slipped out. I had meant to choose my moment to say them to her again in person, but apparently the moment chose me. "I know the timing has been terrible for us, but that's all in the past now."

Her eyes held mine. "I love you too."

I drew her closer. "I haven't said those words to many people."

"Neither have I."

We contemplated each other. Birds of a feather. At least the strange tightness in my throat and chest had eased.

"How has the timing improved?" she asked. "Did something happen?"

I grinned. "I adopted Damian."

"You *did*?" She pushed up from me with excitement. "That's amazing! How did it happen?"

I laughed, enjoying how thrilled she was. "It's a long story, but Philomena finally intervened. Charlotte's partying has been getting out of control, and her mom insisted she go spend time at a mental health spa. Before she left, Charlotte finally agreed to sign all the adoption papers."

"That's wonderful."

I was still grinning. "It's pretty great."

"You and Damian must be so happy."

I could feel myself getting choked up. "It's hard to even put into words. It's an incredible relief for us both. Damian and I had a small celebration afterward since he had to leave for school, but we're going to have a bigger one at his next break."

"I'm so thrilled for you guys."

I took a deep breath. "In a way, nothing's changed, but then in another way, everything's changed, you know?"

"Of course. And what about Charlotte? I've never heard of a mental health spa. Is that a euphemism for rehab?"

"Not quite. She's trying to pull herself together emotionally. I guess she's been having a rough time. It sounds like she had some kind of breakdown while she was in Paris with Malcom."

She frowned. "I'm sorry to hear that. I can't say I liked her because she was horrible to me, but I wouldn't wish that on anyone."

"Me either. The good news is she's agreed to get help."

She squeezed my fingers. "This has obviously been momentous."

"It has. I couldn't wait to tell you about it." I thought about my time staying on the estate with Damian and his grandmother, and how she apologized to me. For so long, Philomena treated me like I was the enemy, like I was the one who brought out the wildness in her daughter. She said she'd finally come to realize that I'd been a stabilizing influence on Charlotte all along.

I studied Leah in the soft light. Her long dark hair and those lively eyes. There was a pink color to her cheeks.

"And what about you, honey?" I reached over to pull her down on top of me. "How have things been for you?"

She came willingly, her soft body pressed into mine. I slid my hands over the dip in her back, then down to her to ass, her skin like silk.

"Oh, you know." Leah played with my hair. "Just the usual farm stuff."

I continued to stroke her body and felt myself getting aroused again. My voice grew husky. "Tell me. I want to hear."

She told me about all the latest social dynamics with her alpacas, how there were two matriarchs now, and how she had a big hay delivery that Shane and Martha helped her with. "Oh, and by the way, those two are together now."

"They are?"

She nodded. "Totally in love, it appears."

"Damn, really? Good for Shane."

"Yeah," she whispered.

We gazed at each other. The whole time she'd been talking we'd been slowly moving our bodies.

She started telling me about her chickens, but I was drowning at that point, lost in these feelings of lust and love.

"Are you hearing a word I'm saying?" she asked, though I noticed her voice had a breathy sound and she was pushing against me.

My cock was between her legs, and I reached down and centered myself so it slowly slid into her.

"Oh my *God*," she gasped.

She was perfect. So damn perfect. Hot, slick, and tight. I swallowed, trying to steady myself, determined to make this first time last for us both.

Leah's hair fell around me like a dark curtain. Everything about her was a kaleidoscope of silk and satin. We went at it for a while, enjoying ourselves, getting hotter by the minute.

Her breasts pressed into me while my hands kneaded and stroked her ass. I'd had a million fantasies about Leah, and this already beat them all.

"Aw, damn, honey," I said when she lifted up and rode me in earnest, absorbing the experience. Not just the sex but Leah. Her essence. I let it permeate my senses, let it consume me. I'd been alone so long. An intense joy filled me, the joy of knowing those days were over.

I gripped her hips, and for a while, she swept me along, both of us burning hot as a flame.

"Hold on tight," I told her, sitting up. When she did, I flipped us both over.

I loved her then. Loved her all the way.

CHAPTER THIRTY-FOUR

~Leah~

"You annihilate me," Josh whispered as we lay together in a tangle of sheets. It was still dark out, but I could sense the dawn coming.

"That sounds serious," I whispered back.

"It is."

We were both basking in the newness of us.

My mouth felt swollen, and my body ached, especially between my thighs, but it was a good ache. There was a delicious energy moving all through my limbs.

Josh wasn't unscathed either. I'd left my mark on him. I hadn't meant to, but I couldn't stop myself. All that acute lust mixed with love was a powerful combination.

I thought about how I once told myself that the price of being with Josh was worth it. No matter what. Even if it all blew up, it was worth it. I sure hoped that was true, because I sensed this could destroy me.

I slid my hand across his shoulders and down his arm. "What is this, anyway?" I asked, tracing my fingers over the swirling black FTMF on his forearm. "Dean has the same tattoo."

Josh glanced down. "All of us in the band have it. We got them back when we were still playing bars."

"What does it mean?"

"Fuck those motherfuckers."

"What? Who are you talking about?"

He chuckled a little. "That's what FTMF stands for. It's a reminder against all the haters and anyone who tries to tear us down."

"But everyone loves East Echo. You guys are so popular."

"Trust me, there's always someone trying to tear you down. Haters are everywhere. That ink reminds us to do what we love, and to hell with anyone who tries to stop us."

I nodded in understanding. "Fuck *those* motherfuckers."

"Exactly."

My eyes wandered over the rest of him as I trailed my fingers across his shoulders and down his chest. There was the sun on his pectoral, but most everything else was script. "What kind of rocker has this many tattoos that are words? Where are the skulls and daggers? The naked ladies with snakes?"

"You're thinking of Dean. He's got tats like that."

"I need to read you," I murmured. "Just like a book."

Josh grinned and spread his arms wide on the bed. "I'm all yours, honey. Read me at your leisure."

I smiled and slid my hand down the hard wall of his chest just as Cary Grant crowed at the dawn outside.

"Aw, shit. There goes that damn rooster." Josh's eyes were closed when he spoke, and I noticed the dark circles beneath them.

"When's the last time you slept?"

"I can't remember."

"You should get some sleep. I need to get up anyway."

His eyes opened. "I'll join you."

I shook my head. "Just rest. I'm going for a run." Even though I'd been up all night, I wasn't in the least bit tired. I felt light as air.

"Wake me up when you get back, and I'll help with the chickens," he murmured, his eyes already closing again. Between the jet lag and everything else, he probably hadn't slept in days.

I slipped out of bed and threw on my running shorts, grinning in the bathroom mirror as I brushed my teeth. Last night flashed through my mind like images from an erotic film reel.

I spent the rest of the morning on a cloud of happiness, floating through my run and all my chores. I peeked in on Josh at one point, but he was sleeping so hard there was no way I was going to wake him.

At noon, I was sitting on my front porch eating an egg salad sandwich when Lars pulled up in his police SUV. It was a warm September day, though I could smell fall in the air.

He stared at Josh's bike before walking up to join me on the porch, his mirrored aviators reflecting the summer's green.

I wondered what the fresh problem was going to be today.

It was sad. I used to love spending time with my twin. We were close growing up and always had a special bond, but things had changed between us this past year. I'd been patient, but I was beyond tired of all his criticisms.

"I take it he's back," Lars said, motioning at the motorcycle.

I swallowed a bite of my sandwich. "He is."

Lars took his sunglasses off and tucked them in the front pocket of his uniform before sitting down in the chair next to me. "So where is he?"

"Asleep."

He nodded.

"So what's up?" I asked. "Can I get you something to eat or drink?"

"I recently received some information that I thought I should share with you. It's about your guest snoring upstairs." His expression grew serious as he leaned forward and laced his fingers. "It turns out he has a brother in prison for armed robbery."

I picked up my glass of ice water. "Yeah, I know. He told me a while ago."

"Jesus Christ, Leah. You knew? And you're okay with it?"

"I think it sucks, but it's not like Josh is in prison for armed robbery."

Lars studied me and then turned to gaze out at the pasture. I sensed his frustration. Both he and my mom weren't the kind of people who colored outside the lines, and yet here I was doing so with the brightest paint possible.

"I'm happy," I said. "Does that count for anything?"

His expression softened. "Of course it does."

"How do you even know about his brother? From what Josh told me no one knows."

Lars snorted. "Give me a little credit. From what I understand, the rock star's set up some kind of special visitation at the prison recently."

I nodded, not surprised that Josh wanted to see Jeremy. "Is that the only reason you came by?"

"I figured it was reason enough."

I thought Lars might leave now that he'd unsuccessfully tried to rain on my happiness. Instead he leaned back in his chair while I finished the last of my sandwich.

"Something else on your mind?" I asked.

"I'm thinking about running for sheriff next election."

My brows shot up. "I didn't realize you had aspirations in that department."

He shrugged. "Charlie is stepping down, and I've decided to throw my hat in the ring."

"I think you'd make a great sheriff."

"I'm not much for the politics, but beyond that, I think I'd do a decent job."

Lars continued to study me.

"What is it?" I asked, but then I understood. I knew him too well. "You're worried who I date might affect your chances of winning?"

His lips pursed together. "Truth Harbor is a small town. People pay attention."

"It's never occurred to you that my dating Josh might be a good thing?"

"How? The guy's got a brother in prison."

"Nobody knows about that."

"I doubt it'll stay a secret." He shook his head. "There's always some kind of drama surrounding him. Have you ever noticed that?"

"That's only because he's famous. I know you're not an East Echo fan, but a lot of people love them. They're huge." My brother's musical tastes ran mostly to country, though he also liked some older rock bands like Led Zeppelin and the Beatles.

He shrugged. "East Echo is all right. I've got nothing against them as a band. I'm more worried about all the attention that follows this guy and how it's going to rub off on you."

"Really?" I scoffed. "Well, I have a great idea. How about you live your life and I'll live mine."

———

IT WAS EARLY EVENING, and I was in the kitchen making rigatoni casserole for dinner, trying not to be irritated at Lars and his control-freak ways. Two of my cats, Nutmeg and Storm, sat on kitchen chairs nearby, watching me slather garlic butter on slices of crusty bread. I suspected my cats all missed Damian and the extra affection he lavished on them.

The floor squeaked overhead, and I heard the water upstairs turn off. I finished with the garlic bread and had just put it in the oven with the pasta when I heard a voice behind me.

"Hey, my little spinster."

I turned around, thrilled to find Josh standing in the doorway. He wore the same jeans and fitted T-shirt he had on yesterday, and his blond curls were long and damp.

"Hi," I managed to say.

Barefoot, he strolled toward me until his clean scent surrounded me. I practically melted into his arms.

"You're still wearing your running clothes."

I stuck my nose in his warm neck. He smelled like the coconut shampoo from my shower. "I didn't want to wake you up to change."

"You didn't have to let me sleep all day. You could have woken me."

"I know, but it seemed like you needed it."

He squeezed my ass and gave me a wicked grin. "And now my battery is fully charged."

We kissed, and the heat between us grew. I shivered when he bit my ear. Erotic sparks raced down my spine as he backed me away from the counter.

"I'm so sweaty," I protested weakly. "I've been working all day."

"I don't care."

Pretty soon my cats had scattered, and Josh and I were going at it on the kitchen table of all places. Anyone could have walked in. It was madness. He whipped my shorts off, and I helped him with his zipper. *I shouldn't want him so much*, I thought, my inner voice seeking self-preservation. *I should hold back*. Except I couldn't. It was too perfect. Hot and dirty. Stars burst through me again and again.

"Damn, that's so good, honey," he groaned. He held me tight, and I didn't want to let go, even when it was over. Even when his weight pressed my shoulder blades into the table.

But then I heard a truck outside.

"Shit! That's Shane!" I frantically shoved Josh away.

We both jumped up and quickly pulled our clothes back in place.

"I warned you my blood was running hot," he teased as I swatted his hand away from my ass.

We were standing only inches apart when I heard the front door open. Moments later, Shane walked into the kitchen.

"Uh-oh, am I interrupting something?" he asked with a grin.

"Not at all." I tried to look innocent as I patted my messy bun, which was, of course, in shambles.

"Shane, it's good to see you," Josh said, going over and giving my baby brother a hug. "How have you been?"

"Good. Really good. How about you? How's Damian?"

Josh told Shane about the adoption, and I excused myself to go upstairs and take a quick shower. The rigatoni and garlic bread were in the oven on warm, so they'd keep.

After my shower, I pulled on jean shorts and a camisole, then took a little time putting on some makeup along with a spritz of perfume.

When I got back downstairs, Josh and Shane were in the living room having a beer and filling each other in on their lives, so I went into the kitchen to make salad. I could hear the two of them laughing it up. I sure wished Josh and Lars got along as well.

We ate dinner outside on the back deck, and I told them about Lars's lunch visit and how he was planning to run for sheriff. I didn't mention anything about Jeremy.

Shane told us how Wendy, one of Walk the Plank's owners, was selling her share in the bar and that he was thinking of buying her out.

I gaped in surprise. "You never told me that."

"I didn't know if I wanted to or not, but I've been talking it over with Chris, the other owner, and he agrees the bar needs a makeover. There's a lot of potential there." I could hear the enthusiasm in Shane's voice. "We could start having regular live shows. The space is big enough if we widen the stage and get rid of the pool tables. Truth Harbor could use a venue like that."

I nodded. It was true. Our little town had a number of bars but no place that really offered much in the way of good live music.

"That sounds awesome." Josh swallowed a bite of garlic bread. "Let me know if there's any way I can help."

"Actually," Shane said, "do you think you'd be willing to come by and hang out after we remodel? Maybe go onstage and sing a song or two? It could go a long way toward drawing attention to us."

"Hell yeah. I'd be happy to do that."

"Really?" He grinned. "Thanks, dude. I know it's a lot to ask."

"Don't worry about it."

After dinner, Shane went back to his RV, which left Josh and me alone in the kitchen cleaning up.

"I didn't want to say anything in front of Shane, but Lars knows about Jeremy," I said.

"What do you mean?"

"He knows you're going to see him soon with some kind of special visitation."

He stopped what he was doing. "Jesus, are you kidding me? How would he know that?"

"I don't know. He's got connections, I guess."

"That nosy motherfucker." He threw the dish towel down. "Who else has he told?"

"I doubt anyone." It wasn't Lars's style to gossip. If anything, he could be too tight-lipped. "If you start visiting Jeremy in prison, it seems like more people are going to find out."

Josh was leaning against the counter with his arms crossed, shaking his head. "I don't want anyone messing with my brother. So far we've managed to keep our relationship quiet."

I nodded. "Anyway, I thought you should know."

"Shit." He rubbed his forehead with his palm. "It's just one thing after another."

I closed the dishwasher and went over and wrapped my arms around him. "It'll be okay." I tilted my head up and kissed him. "That was nice of you to offer to help Shane."

"I don't mind. He's helped me."

"This is a lot more than him loaning you a safety vest."

He smiled a little. "Don't forget about the hard hat. He loaned me that too."

"You never even wore the hard hat."

"So?" He drew me in closer, his voice rumbling low. "Speaking of hard...."

"Wow, you're like an insatiable beast, aren't you?"

"I have a gift for you," he whispered in my ear. "And I think you're going to love it."

I slid one hand down his muscular arm. "If it's what I think it is, I already know I'll love it."

He laughed out loud. "It's in my jacket upstairs. Let me get it."

"Wait, what?" I pulled back. "You're talking about an actual gift?"

He nodded. "Yes, the insatiable beast bought you a present."

I tried not to smile. "What is it?"

"You'll see." He wore such a playful expression that for a moment, I could imagine what he must have been like as a kid. Full of energy and mischief.

While he went upstairs, I grabbed a beer for us to share and went out to the front porch. It was near dusk, and I could already see the moon shining pale and luminous.

I wondered what he got me and hoped it was something I could accept. Josh was generous, but it was easy to imagine him going overboard too. I didn't want a diamond tiara that was worth more than my house.

When he returned, he took a seat in the other chair and handed me a black velvet box.

I hesitated. It was too large for a ring but was clearly some kind of jewelry. I opened it slowly, and my jaw dropped.

On a dark satin pillow lay a small gold spinning wheel attached to a delicate chain. There was some kind of pearly stone set in the center of the wheel.

"That's a moonstone," he said, leaning closer. "Figured it was appropriate."

"Oh my God." I gawked at the necklace. "Where did you find this? It's incredible."

"I had it made."

I turned to him. "You did?"

"A jeweler in London. He's done some custom work for me in the past. Actually, he did my tiger's eye ring."

I ran my finger over the moonstone. "I love it."

Josh grinned. "Yeah?"

I nodded, and tears stung my eyes.

"Hey, are you okay?" He tugged on my arm. "Come over here."

I got up, and he pulled me onto his lap as I tried to get my bearings. "It's so thoughtful. I don't think anyone has ever given me a gift like this."

He stroked my hair as I continued admiring the necklace. "Well, we both know I'm not just anyone. I also happen to be extraordinarily thoughtful."

"Extraordinarily modest too."

He wiped the tear from my cheek. "I'm pleased that you get me so well."

We smiled at each other.

"Would you like me to put it on you?" he asked.

I nodded and handed him the box. "I'd love that."

He pulled the necklace out, and I turned around and lifted my hair for him. I felt Josh's gentle hands against the back of my neck, and then his soft lips when he kissed me.

I turned back and brought my mouth to his. "Thank you," I whispered. "I love my gift, and I love you."

"I love you, too, honey. Now let me see how this looks." He drew back and studied me. "I knew it. Just beautiful."

I fingered the gold spinning wheel. I'd never been with a man who took my spinning and knitting seriously. They seldom acknowledged it and always acted like it was some kind of "woman's" hobby.

"I have a gift for you too," I said.

"And what might that be? Because you know I have one more *package* for you to open." He glanced downward and playfully waggled his brows.

"I haven't wrapped it yet, but I'm going to give it to you early."

I got up from his lap and left the porch, heading for the dining room cabinet where I kept all my finished knitting projects.

"What do you have there?" Josh asked when I returned holding a dark bundle. He took a sip of beer.

"I was planning to wait and give it to you for Christmas, but it looks like Christmas came early this year." I held out over a month's worth of hard work. "I made you a sweater."

His eyes widened, and he quickly placed the bottle on the table. "No shit? You really knit me one?"

"I did."

He accepted the bundle, and I watched as he unfolded the sweater and held it up. "Holy shit. This is amazing."

"Thank you." I was proud of how it turned out.

He stood and held the mesh sweater against himself. I'd created a sunburst pattern where it started out black at the shoulder and then turned into fiery strands of purple, orange, and yellow as it moved toward the lower hem, which had a jagged line.

Josh whipped his T-shirt off and slipped the sweater over his bare torso. "How did you get the size right?" he asked, running his hand down the front, which came to just below his waist.

"I measured Shane and then mostly guessed from there."

"Damn, I need a mirror." He strode into the house, and I followed him to the downstairs bathroom, which had a full-length mirror behind the door.

"It looks great," I said, coming up behind him as he checked himself out. I reached up and adjusted the shoulders a little.

"Damn, Leah, this is a work of art. Seriously." He admired his reflection.

"I'm glad you like it. Though I should tell you it comes with a warning."

"What do you mean?"

I sighed to myself and wondered if I should even mention this. "The boyfriend sweater curse."

"What the hell is that?"

I leaned against the wall. "People say if you knit a sweater for your boyfriend, the curse will cause you to break up."

He seemed taken aback but then glanced over his shoulder at me. "That's weird. Have you ever knit a guy a sweater before?"

I hesitated. "My ex-husband."

"That talentless idiot?" He snorted and turned back. "Trust me, it wasn't any curse that broke you up."

For an instant, I thought of my darkest secret. The one where I'd betrayed Josh's trust. But I quickly pushed that aside. I rolled my eyes. "It's just this silly thing people say. I don't believe in curses."

"Neither do I." He turned around and stepped close to me. "There's no way a curse could keep me from you. Ever."

"I know."

"We fit. We belong together."

My heart swelled. It was the truth.

He glanced down at himself. "And this sweater is kick-ass. I fucking love it."

It really looked amazing on him, and the mesh was just right, just enough that you could see some skin through it so it had a total rock-and-roll vibe. I was pleased he liked it so much.

"It took a lot of cat hair, I can tell you that," I said. "Mountains of the stuff. It's not easy to spin either."

His mouth twitched. "All those little pussy cats. I appreciate the effort."

"I had to chase them down. They can be persnickety."

"Don't I know it." He turned to look at himself in the mirror again, smoothing his hand over the sunburst. "What's it made of for real? Alpaca?"

"Partly. It's a combination of a few types of fiber. The bamboo gives it that shimmer."

"I'm going to wear it onstage. It's perfect." His eyes found mine. "You're going to have to be there for that."

"Sure. Though you're not going onstage anytime soon, are you?"

"Yeah, we're playing Emerald Rockfest on the twenty-third."

"You *are*?" My eyes bugged out of my head. "That's less than three weeks away." I'd been hearing ads for it on the radio and was stunned. Emerald Rockfest was an all-day concert held in an outdoor amphitheater. It was about an hour drive from here after the ferry.

"I know. Kat set it up. We're one of the headliners."

Kat was their new manager. Apparently Jane quit right before they all met up in England, which went a long way toward easing tension in the band. Kat, short for Katerina, was German and used to manage a couple of other big-name acts.

"We're also doing *Saturday Night Live* the week after that."

"*Saturday Night Live?*" I swallowed and tried not to show my shock. "Wow." I didn't know what else to say. My head spun.

Josh was still admiring himself in the mirror. He sneered and then put a hand on his hip, pouted, and gave himself an intense eye smolder. I watched his theatrics with amusement, though my head was still spinning.

"What?" he asked, noticing my expression. "You look kind of pale."

"I'm just trying to adjust, that's all."

"Adjust to what?"

"That you guys are headlining Emerald Rockfest, and that you're going to be on *Saturday Night Live*."

"It's all good. Kat's doing her job."

"I know, but this is a lot. I'm out of my depth." My ex-husband's band had gigs, but they were mostly bars in New York. Nothing on this level.

Josh turned around, pulled me into his arms, and eye-smoldered *me*. "Better get used to it, my little spinster. Because from now on you're flying first class."

CHAPTER THIRTY-FIVE

~Leah~

O ver the next couple of weeks, Josh mostly stayed with me. He went home for a change of clothes but was usually back right afterward. He FaceTimed with Damian, who wanted to say hello to all my cats, alpacas, and both llamas, so we chased them around with the phone as we cracked up with laughter.

Some evenings, Shane and Martha would hang out with us, and we played board games or watched a movie together. Mostly Josh and I were alone. During the day, he helped me with chores, or when I was off spinning, he worked on his music. And at night... well, at night we were all over each other. I'd never felt so in love, so in sync with a guy, so pulled into the cyclone of this relationship.

"It's weird how your right palm is more calloused than your left one," I said, playing with his fingers and comparing his two hands. We were naked in bed, as usual, except we were at his house for a change. His bed was big and comfortable, and we could see stars through the skylights above us.

"It's from all the jerking off I do."

I snorted with laughter. "I don't know why I think all your dumb jokes are so funny."

"Because you think I'm kidding."

I continued to caress him. "Your fingers are calloused too."

"It's from holding a microphone."

I glanced up at him. "Really?"

He nodded, watching me with a relaxed expression. A big cat, letting me stroke the toughened skin on his paw. "When we're touring, I'm onstage for hours every night. I try to switch hands, but I prefer my right. I've gotten blisters from holding a microphone."

"That sounds exhausting."

He shrugged. "It's intense. I like touring, except by the end of it, I'm wiped."

"It's hard to imagine doing what you do." I played with his fingers some more. He wore a couple of rings—the tiger's eye and a silver puzzle ring. "I'd be nervous in front of all those people. Do you ever get nervous?"

"Sometimes. I think it's why so many musicians drink or get high. There's a lot of pressure."

"How do you handle it? Do you drink? My ex used to drink onstage all the time."

Josh shifted position and tucked his left arm behind his head. I couldn't help but admire his beauty. The dips and shadows of his well-formed body. "Nah, I never drink before going onstage. I enjoy it too much. I guess it's the Leo in me."

"All that adulation," I teased. "People worshiping you."

He grinned. "I love the music, but I enjoy performing too. Taking people on a ride. It's satisfying somehow."

I tried to picture it. I'd watched videos of Josh performing live, and he was so good at it, and at getting the crowd excited. "What's it like being famous?"

He considered my question and took his time answering. "It has its good and bad points. Obviously losing your privacy sucks—you've seen that. People try to use you, and it's not easy knowing who you can trust. But being famous can come in handy too. If you need something or are trying to help someone, people will usually bend over backwards for you. Mostly it's like being a member of an exclusive club."

I pondered his words. "And the other people in the club are famous too?"

"Exactly. It's weird, but if I wanted to, I could contact practically anyone in the world."

"Have you ever used it like that?"

"I've gotten to meet some of my favorite musicians, which has been mind-blowing. I've also met some famous athletes at football and baseball games. In fact, I've met your friend Theo's new neighbor."

This got my attention. "Beauty Bardales?"

"I met him after a game when they were playing in LA a couple years ago."

"What's he like? He sounds like a privileged asshole. I hope Theo isn't going to have a big problem with him."

"Actually, he seemed all right. He's a fan of the band, which is always nice. I didn't get an asshole vibe, despite his reputation."

"He has a reputation?"

Josh nodded. "As an ill-tempered prick."

"That figures. And of course he was nice to *you*. You're in the club."

"True."

He brought his hand down and ran his thumb across my temple. "I've been meaning to ask. What's with the gray in your hair right here?"

I rolled my eyes and groaned. "I need to color it, but I haven't had a chance lately. This white streak has been in my hair forever."

"Really? You should grow it out."

"I don't think so. It looks weird and witchy."

He grinned. "I like weird and witchy. I want to see what it looks like. The real you."

I put my head down on the pillow, facing him. "I'll think about it."

"I cut my Sasquatch beard for you, remember?"

I reached over to touch his chin. "That's true, you did." I ran my hand along the bristle on his jaw. "How are you feeling about tomorrow?" He was going to see Jeremy tomorrow, which was the reason we were staying at his house tonight. He was leaving early and had a box of stuff he was taking to his brother—mostly books and snacks, though he wasn't sure if Jeremy would be allowed to accept it. The lawyers said it would have to go through an approval process.

"On edge." He rolled onto his back and took a deep breath. "I'm looking forward to seeing him, but at the same time, I'm trying to brace myself."

"You talk on the phone regularly, so hopefully it'll be okay. How was it the last time you saw him?" It had been a couple of years since they saw each other in person.

"Hard. It was really hard seeing him in a place like that."

"Does your mom ever visit him?"

He scoffed and rolled his eyes. "What do *you* think?"

"Never?"

"Nope. Not even once."

I went quiet. I may have had a difficult relationship with my mom, but if I were in prison, I had no doubt she'd visit me. Lars too. "I'm sorry."

He shrugged. "It's never surprised me. I don't think it surprised Jeremy either. We both know what she's like."

"He'll be glad to see you. Just remember that. It's why you moved here, right? And you've done everything you can for him." Josh told me how he'd hired the best lawyers money could buy, how they'd done a lot, including getting Jeremy moved to the prison up north, which was apparently much nicer than the one he'd been in initially.

He turned his head to look at me. It was dark, but there was enough light from the skylight overhead that we could see each other.

"Let's talk about something else," he said quietly. His gaze roamed down my body, and he gave me a lazy grin. "In fact, let's not talk at all."

"Hmm... what do you want to do instead?"

That lazy grin grew into a sexy one as he reached for me. "How about you bring those candy tits and that luscious ass over here, and I'll show you."

I scooted close so I was over him and let him lick and suck my nipples, molding my breasts with his hands until I was so aroused I could barely see straight.

"I shouldn't let you objectify me like this," I said, breathless. "I'll have you know I'm more than my body parts."

A hand slid down to my ass and squeezed, but then he paused and seemed to grow serious as he met my eyes in the dark. "We're the only ones in this bed, honey. And we both know what we're about."

It was true. We did. Josh liked it dirty sometimes, and God, if it wasn't arousing, but he never made me feel like I was less or just a body. We were always equals.

He snorted. "Besides, if anyone's getting objectified here, it's *me*. I haven't named your pussy, have I?"

Uh-oh. I kissed his mouth to try to distract him.

"Beast banana," he muttered. "I still can't get over it. What the hell kind of nickname is that for my dick?"

"It was a compliment," I said. "Because it's so big and hard and—"

"Like a *banana*?"

"Delicious like a banana."

"Give me a break." He chuckled. "I'd give up trying to justify this if I were you."

"How about beast hammer? Would that be more to your liking?"

He seemed skeptical. "It's better than beast banana, but I'm not writing any songs about it, I can tell you that."

"Oh, come on. I think you should write a song about a beast swinging his mighty hammer and hitting every nail."

"Maybe *you* should write it." He stroked his fingers down my stomach and then slid them between my thighs. "Who knows? Might be a big hit."

"Maybe I should." I closed my eyes and gave in to the sensations he was creating. "I'll probably need more inspiration."

"Yeah, you will." His breath hitched as he guided his beast banana into me. "And I'll be the one to give it to you."

IT WAS LATE AFTERNOON, and I was working in my garden harvesting tomatoes, lettuce, and corn for the local farmers market. My neighbors, Naomi and Tim, had agreed to sell some of my produce along with their apples this year. It was nice of them, and as always, I could use the extra cash. Luckily, my yarn and fleece were still selling well since that spinning video with Josh went viral. In fact, I was almost in the black this month.

It was the warmest part of the day, and I should have done this earlier, but I'd been too busy. Neil, the large animal vet I used to date, had come by to help me vaccinate my herd. It took us about two hours, but then we sat and chatted for a bit. He appeared to be doing well. He also seemed to know all about Josh and me. Apparently the whole town knew. I shouldn't have been surprised, since that was how small towns were.

I was stretching my back after harvesting five boxes of lettuce when I saw Josh's black truck pull up. I finished the last row and, after stacking the boxes, headed over to the house.

He wasn't on the porch or inside, and I finally found him sitting on the steps of the back deck, looking out over the yard while wearing a solemn expression.

"Didn't you once tell me there's a creek back there?" he asked when I came and sat next to him.

"There is."

"I think I hear it."

I listened closely. "I hear it too." It was a soft swishing sound.

He reached for my hand, and I scooted closer and draped my arm over his leg. We sat in silence for a while. I figured he'd talk about how it went at the prison when he was ready, and if he wasn't ready, that was okay too.

"How was your day?" he asked.

I told him about harvesting vegetables for the farmers market and how Neil came by earlier to help with vaccinating the herd.

"Neil? Why does that name sound familiar?"

"Because I dated him for a while."

Josh's brows came together. "*That* guy was here *today*?"

I nodded. "He helped me with the herd. He's a great vet."

"On the one day I'm gone, you invite your ex-boyfriend over?"

I looked at him with surprise. "It's not like that. You're mischaracterizing it."

He went silent. A gloomy silence. "How long was he here?"

"You're not seriously jealous of Neil, are you?"

Josh turned to me, and when I saw the pain in his eyes, I realized this had nothing to do with Neil or any ex-boyfriend of mine.

I sucked in my breath. "*My God*, what is it? What's wrong?"

All he could do was shake his head. He pulled his hand from mine, leaned forward, and covered his face.

"Talk to me, Josh. Are you okay?"

"No."

I ran my hand down his back. I could only imagine what it must have been like today. Terrible. "Are you sure you don't want to talk about it?"

"I can't."

"How about a beer?"

He scrubbed his face with both hands and stared up at the sky before finally turning to me, his eyes filled with suffering. "Do you have anything stronger?"

"Whiskey."

"I'll take some of that."

I got up to get it for him. From what I'd seen, Josh rarely drank anything stronger than beer.

I found the bottle in the cabinet and poured a couple fingers of whiskey into two glasses, then brought them outside.

"Here you go." I handed him a glass and sat down.

"Thanks, honey."

"Sure."

He reached for my hand and pulled me close again. "I'm sorry for acting jealous. My head's messed up right now."

"It's all right."

"I trust you, Leah. Believe me. I trust you all the way, and that's saying something for me."

"I trust you too."

He laced his fingers with mine, and we sipped our whiskey.

"Is this Jack Daniel's?" he asked, licking his lips.

"It is. Claire and I used to drink it with Coke sometimes."

"It's good. Been a while since I've had it."

I rested my head against his shoulder. The liquor was already going to my head. I closed my eyes. The smell of grass and hay wafted by on a breeze. I could feel Josh, warm and solid beside me, could smell his lemongrass soap.

"Jeremy doesn't belong in that place," he said, his voice low. "He just *doesn't*."

I lifted my head to look at him.

He finished the last of his whiskey and set the glass down. "My brother would never hurt a fly. He was always the soft one. And now he's turning into someone I barely recognize. Someone he was never meant to be."

I gripped his hand tighter and watched his profile. Handsome but anguished. "I'm so sorry, Josh."

"I feel so fucking helpless! I've got all this money, and there isn't a damn thing I can do."

"He won't be in prison forever." Though Jeremy still had years on his sentence.

"And who will he be then?" He turned to me, his expression stricken. "You should have seen him, Leah. Almost unrecognizable. If I saw him in the street, I wouldn't have known who he was. That's not my baby brother."

"How was it talking to him?"

"Weird. His lawyer was there, since it was the only way I could see him in private. The place is cold. Institutional. I didn't know what to say to him."

"What do you guys usually talk about on the phone?"

"I don't know. It's different. We shoot the shit. I tell him about the band, and about you and Damian, but now that I've seen how he's living? *Jesus.*" He was getting choked up, and he shook his head. "Our lives are the exact opposite. I've gotten everything I've ever wanted, ever dreamed of, and he's got *nothing.*" He pinched the bridge of his nose. "How the hell did we get into this mess? I should have kept him closer, should have brought him with me when I left home."

"Stop it. Stop blaming yourself." This was tearing him up and obviously had been for years. "You would have done it differently if you'd known."

He went silent, and I sensed he was trying to pull himself together. "You're right. I would have done it differently. *Fuck.*" He wiped tears from his cheek with his palm. He smiled a little. "You must think I'm a real crybaby. This is the second time I've cried in front of you."

"I think you're a man who feels things deeply."

He nodded. "Thank you, Leah."

"For what?"

"For being here. For being someone I know I can count on even though I don't deserve it."

"That's not true. You deserve it. And you don't have to thank me for being here."

"I do, honey." He leaned in and brought his mouth to mine. His lips were soft. "You're my heart."

CHAPTER THIRTY-SIX

~Leah~

"What's happening with your hair?" my mom asked.

We were having lunch in town at Bijou's, just the two of us. Isabel came out and chatted briefly, but she had to go back to the kitchen. "I'm growing out my white streak."

"Why would you do that?" She took a sip of her water. "I thought you disliked it."

I shrugged. "Josh asked me to, and I decided to see what it looks like."

She pursed her lips, and I waited for some rude comment, except surprisingly, there wasn't one.

Also surprising was Lars clearly hadn't told her about Jeremy. There was a fifty-fifty chance he would, and I was glad he didn't. Relieved. She'd find out eventually, but it was one less problem right now.

"Delores told me he was signing autographs at Scallywag Sweets a couple of days ago."

"That's true." I kept my tone light. Delores was one of my mom's oldest friends, and Josh said the signing had gone great. Lots of people came in, and he met a lot of the local business owners.

"She seems to think highly of him. Apparently he's given out a bunch of free tickets to some concert his band is performing at next week."

I nodded with what I hoped was a neutral expression. "He thought it would be a nice gesture to all the people who tried to help him when he was dealing with the press nightmare at his house."

She studied me, and I waited with bated breath. Was there going to be an ice storm in hell? Was my mom going to admit she was wrong?

She frowned and leaned forward. "So what do you know about this business that Shane bought into?"

Sorry, folks. No ice skating in hell today.

"It's a bar that he's turning into a live music venue."

"I know, but is it a mistake?"

I considered this. "I don't think so. I can't say for sure, but it could be great."

"I went by this bar, and I wasn't impressed."

"They're remodeling it. Also, they want to keep it kind of grungy and dark. It *is* called Walk the Plank."

She sighed. "I was really hoping your brother would go to school with that lottery money."

"I don't think Shane is the college type."

My mom leaned back in her chair and glanced around the restaurant. "I suppose not. As long as he's happy."

"I think he's very happy."

She focused on me again. "His girlfriend, Martha, certainly seems like a nice young woman."

The server came by with our food. I had a burger and fries while my mom had a Caesar salad. We both had iced tea.

"Martha is great," I said, pouring some ketchup on my fries. "I really like her. We've hung out with the two of them quite a bit."

"You have?"

"She's been nice enough to help me with the harvest recently." I glanced at my mom, waiting for some rude comment about my farm.

"She seems good for Shane."

I nodded. It was weird to be agreeing with her on something. It happened so infrequently that I'd forgotten what it felt like.

"And how are you doing?" she asked, squeezing more lemon into her iced tea. She added sugar next and stirred.

"I'm happy."

"Are you?"

I couldn't contain my smile. "To be honest, I'm the happiest I've ever been in my life." It was the truth. I had everything I'd ever wanted. Life didn't get any better than this, and I was grateful for it every day.

"So it's serious between you and this rock star?"

"Josh," I corrected her. "His name is Josh. And yes, it's serious."

"I guess I should get to know him better."

"You should." That was when I did something impulsive, something stupid that I should have thought through first, but unfortunately I'd gotten lulled by our pleasant conversation. "Would you like to come over for dinner this Friday?"

She considered me. I hadn't invited her over for dinner in ages. I didn't see the point since all we did was argue. These restaurant meals were at least on neutral ground.

"All right," she said, wiping her mouth with a napkin. "I'd like that."

I changed the subject and asked how work was going. She began to tell me about some new school initiative and the problems it was creating.

My mind spiraled down a black hole as she spoke.

What have I done?

I tried to calm myself. *How bad could it be having her over for dinner? She is my mother after all.*

But then I remembered having boys over as a teenager and how, as soon as they saw her—or worse, spoke to her—they ran so fast you'd think I'd lit their clothes on fire. I never had a boyfriend in high school. They were all too terrified of her.

"PLEASE," I begged my little brother. "You *have* to come for dinner on Friday. I'll do anything." I held up the frozen bag of chocolate chips I was comfort eating from my fetal position on the couch. "I promise I'll make you chocolate chip cookies every single day for the rest of your life."

Shane scratched his chest. "That's a tempting offer. I wish I could, but we're still in the middle of the bar's remodel. I'm doing a lot of the work myself."

"Can't you leave early or just come by for an hour?" I pleaded. "I'm throwing myself on your mercy."

He chuckled. "Come on, Leah. It won't be *that* bad having dinner with Mom."

"Are you kidding? I *need* you as a buffer." Because now that reality had sunk in that I'd invited my mother here to spend *hours* berating Josh and me at her leisure, I could only assume that I'd gone temporarily insane during that lunch.

"A buffer for what?" Josh asked, strolling into the living room with his phone. He'd been on it half the day talking to Kat, Margo, the guys in the band, and the guitar player from the Beaver Kings, who were also appearing at Emerald Rockfest.

"I sort of invited my mom over for dinner," I said, shoveling another fistful of chocolate into my mouth.

His brows went up, but then he nodded. "Okay... it's probably a good thing I get to know her, right?"

"I'm so sorry," I said through a mouthful of chocolate. "It was a dumb impulse. I'm sometimes prone to those."

He glanced over at Shane, who was studying him with sympathy. "What?"

"Don't worry, dude. It'll be all right."

"I'm not worried," Josh said, though he seemed uncertain. He looked at me. "Should I be worried?"

I held out my bag of frozen chocolate to him.

"She's tough but fair," Shane said. "You'll be fine."

I rolled my eyes. "'Tough but fair'? Only in the Shane universe. Come on, you *have* to save us."

Josh came over and sat next to me on the couch, placing his phone on the coffee table. "It's not like I haven't met her," he said, digging into the bag of chocolate. "I've met her. I have to admit, she was tough. Quite the interrogator."

I snorted. "Imagine hours of that with lots of criticism and suggestions for how to improve your life thrown in for good measure."

He tossed some chips in his mouth. "Sounds like fun."

"You have no idea."

"Maybe I *could* stop by for a little while," Shane said, rubbing his chin. "Just to keep things healthy for everyone."

My eyes lit up. "Oh, thank you! You're the best! And you won't regret it. I promise you'll be showered in cookies."

Shane laughed. "You're crazy." His phone pinged, and he pulled it out of his pocket.

"When is this dinner taking place?" Josh asked, reaching into the bag again.

"This Friday."

He turned to me. "That's not going to work. The guys in the band are all coming over that night."

"What do you mean? I thought that was happening on the weekend." Josh had already told me how all the guys were flying up and were planning to stay at his place the week before the show so they could rehearse.

Josh shook his head as he crunched on some chocolate. "I said the weekend *or* Friday. Terence has family coming up Saturday, so I know for a fact he won't be around. And I think Rhys is going to Vancouver."

"Shit." I remembered now that he had mentioned Friday. But then I perked up. "I'll just cancel dinner with my mom."

Shane was typing on his phone, but he glanced over at me. "Mom's not going to let you cancel dinner. You know that."

I chewed my lip. He was right. My mom hated changing plans. It came from years of dealing with flaky teenagers. Even if I told her an entire rock band was going to be here—which was exactly the case— she'd still insist that I follow through with dinner.

"Dammit." I reached into the bag for more chocolate, except there wasn't enough chocolate in the world for this fiasco. "I think we're stuck."

Josh rested his hand on my leg and grinned. "Sounds like it's going to be an interesting evening."

CHAPTER THIRTY-SEVEN

~Josh~

"Do you take drugs?"

"No, ma'am."

"Are you on drugs right now?"

"No, I'm not—wait, does alcohol count?"

The steel mama glared at me. "Don't get smart. Have you ever shot up heroin?"

"Hell no."

"I can check your arms and toes for needle marks."

"I've never taken heroin."

She stared at me so hard that I almost glanced down at my arms, though I'd never done heroin in my life.

"What about smoking marijuana or snorting cocaine?"

I licked my lips nervously. "Which one are you asking about?"

"Both."

I glanced around Leah's house for an escape. Her mother had me trapped in a corner of the living room and was probably going to pull out a rubber glove, bend me over, and perform a cavity search next.

"You're not answering my question," she said.

"Uh... which question was that?"

"Have you ever smoked marijuana or snorted cocaine?"

"I think I need a lawyer."

She smirked. "Lawyers are for guilty people."

I rubbed my palm against the side of my leg and tried not to show fear.

"Don't worry." She smiled and patted my arm. "I'm just kidding with you, Josh."

"Ha ha." I tried to smile as I inched my way along the wall away from her.

"Where do you think you're going? We're not finished here."

"Nowhere, ma'am."

In that moment, I saw Shane across the room. He must have just arrived. I waved at him and hoped he saw the SOS in my eyes. I now understood completely why Leah wanted him here so badly.

Thankfully, he came right over and broke up the interrogation.

"Hey, Mom. It's good to see you."

The steel mama turned and smiled at him with surprise. "Sweetheart, I didn't know you were coming tonight."

"I just wanted to drop by and say hello." He kissed her cheek.

"That's nice of you. But shouldn't you be working at your bar? You guys are opening soon, aren't you?"

"I'll get back to it shortly."

The two of them continued to talk, so I eased my way out of there, searching for Leah.

I needed a hug.

The evening had turned into a small party. The guys were all here, along with the friends they brought. Rhys and Jane broke up. Instead he came with Ranger, one of our sound engineers, who also brought his wife and two sons. Terence brought a woman he'd met in Nepal and another friend. Dean came alone on his bike. Dax was here with Salem and their daughter. He was managing both our stage crew and security for the show next weekend. Also Leah's friend Claire and her husband, Philip, came for a little while, though they had to leave early. Leah's neighbors Naomi and Tim were here too.

Some people brought food, and Leah had cooked as well, so the table in the kitchen was laid out with everything buffet style. It wasn't raining, so most people were outside in the backyard.

I grabbed a cold beer from the fridge and headed outside to find Leah, but Rhys stopped me.

"Who the hell is that *woman*?" he asked with a squeak in his voice I'd never heard before.

"Who do you mean?"

He motioned over to the steel mama, who unfortunately had Terence in her clutches now.

Rhys's eyes were wide. "I said a simple hello to her by the food table, and she asked me if I've ever smuggled anything illegal across the border and if I know the statute of limitations."

I nodded in sympathy. "That's Leah's mom."

"She totally freaked me out."

"She's a high school principal."

His mouth dropped open. "*Fuuuck.*"

I chuckled. "That's the same reaction I had."

He shook his head, still watching the steel mama cross-examine our bass player. "We should rescue Terence, but I'm afraid to go near her again."

"Let's go together. There's no way she can intimidate us both."

Rhys nodded, except he still looked nervous.

I searched around for Shane and hoped he hadn't left yet. Thankfully, I saw him outside talking to Dean. "Look, her son's out there with Dean. He handles her the best."

Luckily, we didn't have to pull Terence from her clutches after all because his girlfriend came over and dragged him away.

Leah's mom didn't look happy, and I saw her eyes roam the room, searching for her next victim.

"I'm going in the backyard to find Leah," I said quickly to Rhys. "You want to join me?"

"Hell yes!"

We both sprinted outside.

I found Leah talking with Salem and Dax. Martha had arrived, too, and I nodded my hello to her.

"Everything okay?" Leah asked worriedly. She'd been trying to protect me from her mom all night. I finally told her to stop. I was a grown man and could handle myself.

That was, of course, before the steel mama cornered me in the living room with her rubber glove and bottle of hand sanitizer.

"Everything's fine," I said to Leah, then leaned down to kiss her. She smiled up at me. There was a pretty pink flush to her cheeks, and I felt a rush of emotion gazing at her.

God help me. I'm so crazy in love with this woman.

I brushed my hand against hers, and we smiled our little secret smile.

I hung out and listened to a funny story Rhys told us about his pet tarantula, and as I was standing there, I noticed the steel mama had come out to the backyard. I watched her from the corner of my eye, waiting for any sudden movements.

She stood off to the side with a near-empty wineglass, and it struck me that she might feel awkward. Clearly nothing intimidated this woman, but this wasn't exactly her kind of party.

Finally, I made a decision. Squeezing Leah's hand, I left the group and strolled over to her mom. This was probably a suicide mission, but no one had ever accused me of being a coward.

"How are you doing, Camilla? Can I get you a refill on your wine?" I asked.

She slammed her brows together, obviously searching for a trick.

I continued to smile politely and held my hand out for her glass.

She hesitated but then finally agreed. "It's white wine," she said. "Chardonnay. Thank you."

I accepted the glass and glanced back at Leah, her eyes following me.

Once inside the house, I discovered the bottle of chardonnay was empty and nearly panicked. Luckily, I found an unopened bottle in the fridge. I uncorked it and filled her glass with a nice, healthy pour.

On the way back, Ranger waylaid me, asking how many monitors I wanted onstage next week. We talked, and I did my best to keep it brief.

When I finally got back to Camilla, I was pleased to see she wasn't alone anymore. Leah, Salem, Dax, and Martha had all joined her. Rhys was nowhere in sight, not that I blamed him. When I glanced around, I saw he was talking to Shane.

I handed her the glass of wine.

"Thank you... Josh."

I stood next to Leah, who gave me a little grin. Camilla was telling us about a trip she took with her friend Darlene to Scotland a few years ago.

As she spoke, my eyes wandered the backyard, taking in the fairy lights Leah had strung around the deck and the lanterns that cast a warm glow. Kids ran around playing, and my heart stuttered, wishing Damian was here.

Music drifted over. Rhys must have found my guitar in the house.

I took a deep breath and let it out. All my life I'd wanted to belong somewhere. To someone. To have a real home.

The conversation changed to Camilla's job, and she started telling us about a student of hers and how proud she was of them for getting into Stanford University, despite dealing with a learning disability.

"That's wonderful," Salem said. She motioned at her husband. "Dax has a learning disability too—ADHD. Unfortunately, he got very little help for it when he was growing up."

I turned to Dax in surprise. "No shit? You have ADHD? So do I."

"Really? It was a bitch dealing with it when I was in high school." He glanced nervously at Camilla. "Excuse my French."

I snorted. "I barely even graduated high school."

He nodded. "Same here."

Camilla watched us intensely and seemed outraged. "This is disturbing to hear. Neither of you had any accommodations?"

"What kind of accommodations?" I asked.

She explained how there should have been a learning plan drawn up for us both to help manage our ADHD.

"I've never heard of that," I said.

"Me either," Dax agreed.

We were still talking about this when Dean came over to join our group. One look at his face, and I could tell he was high as a kite.

Shit.

I glanced around at the others. No one seemed to notice, and I hoped Camilla didn't either. Dean was usually good at hiding it, but I'd known him too long. He'd moved back to LA after our month in England and was still in bad shape over what happened with Nalla. Last we heard, she'd gone back to the East Coast. She tried to text me, but I deleted and blocked her number.

"I really like all these lights," Dean said, waving his hand around. "This farm is fucking awesome."

Camilla eyed him with disapproval, but then everyone else chimed in.

"I agree," Martha gushed. "I love it here so much. It's amazing what Leah's created."

"Thank you," Leah murmured. "That's nice of you."

"It's such a magical place. It truly is." Salem turned to Camilla. "You must be proud to have a daughter who's so talented and industrious."

The steel mama's brows went up as she stared at Salem. She seemed speechless. But then she turned to Leah and smiled. "Of course I'm proud of her. I'm always proud of my daughter."

"CAN YOU BELIEVE SHE SAID THAT?" Leah asked me later that night when we were in her bedroom. The guys were all back at my house, but I was staying with Leah one more night since we'd be rehearsing all next week before the show on Saturday. "She was *proud* of me?"

"Well, she sure as hell should be proud." It bothered me hearing how Leah's mom criticized her. I'd have cut someone like that out of my life in two seconds, but Leah wasn't made that way.

"That party went a lot better than I thought it would." She was sitting on the edge of the bed, putting lotion on her legs after taking a shower. "It was good of you to be so nice to her."

"I did it mostly for you."

She smiled. "I know, but it was still nice. I think she might have even enjoyed herself."

"Speaking of enjoyment. Come here." I patted the bed. "The beast is getting lonely."

She laughed and put the cap back on the bottle. When she was settled next to me, I folded her in my arms. "I won't be staying over at all next week," I said, sticking my nose in her damp hair. "We're going to the mattresses." It was a term we used in the band whenever we closed ourselves off to work.

"I'll miss you."

"Same here. Also, I have something for you." I reached around to what had become my nightstand at her place. I opened the drawer, pulled out the All Access Backstage Pass I'd asked Dax to bring, and handed it to her.

"What's this?"

"A golden ticket. It'll get you backstage anywhere we're performing. Security will just scan the barcode and you're in."

"Anywhere? Not just Emerald Rockfest?"

"Anywhere in the world. You've been added to the list."

Her brows went up. "I guess I'd better keep it safe."

"Definitely. Though if you lose it, just tell me. They'll cancel the code, and I'll get you another one."

She smiled at the pass and then placed it around her neck. "I guess this means I'm all yours." Her eyes went dark and seductive. "To do with as you will."

"Mmm...." My voice turned husky. "I like the sound of that."

"Any requests?"

I leaned back on the pillow and licked my lower lip. "How about you show me a little something, honey?"

Leah raised a brow. "Are you sure that's what you want?"

"Oh hell yeah." She knew exactly what I liked.

She grinned playfully, and I watched as she pushed the covers back and sat up, kneeling in front of me. She began to strip off her tank top.

"Slow," I murmured in a low rumble. "Yeah... just like that."

She swung her dark hair around, and I watched as she removed her top but left the golden ticket around her neck. Her nipples were pert and stiff, the color like pink bubble gum. More than anything I wanted to taste them, but all in good time. She inched her lace panties down next, and I watched as that little purple bow moved lower, revealing smooth skin and the top of her trimmed pussy.

"Damn, honey," I breathed, getting more aroused. "You're sexy as *fuck*."

She smiled and then turned all the way around so I got a perfect view of her hips and ass. Her hair hung long and silky down her back.

The panties slid lower but were still half on and off. By that point my cock was harder than quantum mechanics, and I knew exactly what I wanted to do with it.

Leah knew too. She glanced coyly over her shoulder, and then she straddled me, still facing in the opposite direction. I slid my hands down her hips, then over her gorgeous ass, her skin like satin.

It felt like I was going to explode. I could hear someone breathing hard, and it was me. I sat up and kissed her back, working my way down to her ass, and then I yanked her panties aside and kissed and licked her everywhere, playing with her pussy as she moaned and squirmed against my mouth.

I couldn't take it anymore. "Goddammit, I have to have you." With a groan, I positioned myself and took her slowly from behind. She gasped when I entered her fully. We went at it for a while, slow and deep and tortuously good. When she began to moan and push against me, begging me to touch her, I stroked her clit.

It didn't take long for the fireworks to start, and it was too much for me. Leah's climax put me right over the edge. I saw stars and galaxies, but I also saw my place in this vast universe, and it was right beside her.

AFTER A LONG WEEK OF REHEARSALS, the band felt pretty damn good when we arrived backstage at the amphitheater for Emerald Rockfest.

I could hear the thump of the bass from the current group onstage vibrating through the walls as we hung out in one of the large dressing rooms.

We'd played rock festivals in the past and rarely rehearsed so much beforehand, but this time was different, and we all knew it.

We'd broken up and were back together. There were a lot of eyes on us, as witnessed by the amount of press surrounding our limo when we arrived. It felt like the whole damn world was watching, and that meant we had to blow their minds.

Luckily, things were better than ever. Rhys and I were getting along great, and I was trying to be more flexible and less stubborn. I had Leah to thank for that. I was on top of my game creatively, and it was all because of her. She brought out the best in me.

"You guys want some of this?" Dean asked, holding his breath as he held out a joint to everyone.

I shook my head. I rarely smoked weed—it wasn't good for my voice—and I never smoked it before going onstage because it sometimes made me sleepy.

He passed it along to one of the women at the poker table. The game had obviously been going for hours. The guys from the Beaver Kings were already here, waiting for their set. There was a large flatscreen television on a stand nearby with the sound muted that appeared to be showing some kind of ESPN poker tournament.

I didn't join the card game but went over and sat with Rhys, who was working on the bridge for one of the songs we wrote together in England.

"What do you think?" he asked, fiddling with the melody. "Something moodier, right?"

I listened and nodded. "Yeah, definitely." I reached for my mug of warm water with honey. I'd done some of my vocal warm-ups earlier and would do a few more before we went out there in a little while.

I glanced around the room, noting we were all doing our pre-stage rituals.

Terence was playing cards, his colorful dreads pulled back into a high ponytail. He'd be off listening to music or meditating soon. He liked to go quiet for a while before we performed.

Dean was playing poker, getting high, drinking, and eating the food that craft services had put out. To be honest, I was worried about him. He was prone to excess and seemed to be taking that shit with Nalla hard. I tried to talk to him about it at the house, but he kept blowing me off and telling me he was fine. There was a pretty redhead sitting on his lap, giggling and whispering in his ear.

As usual, there were a lot of women around. Some were fans, some were girlfriends, a few were musicians, and a lot of them were groupies. People assumed groupies were only interested in band members, but trust me, they were interested in anyone even associated with the band.

I hoped Leah didn't get upset when she came backstage and saw all these women. I felt edgy about it at first, then realized Leah wasn't Charlotte. There wouldn't be any temper tantrums. No screaming fits or objects thrown. Leah trusted me.

What a relief.

She'd texted earlier that she'd gotten here around noon. I told her

I'd send Dax to bring her backstage once we arrived, and he was out getting her now.

As I looked around, I noticed that some of the women looked familiar, and that I recognized them from the birthday party at my house. It occurred to me that one of these women, or whoever they were with, might have been the person who gave my address to the vultures.

"What is it?" Rhys asked. "You look pissed."

I sighed and rubbed my brow. I told him how I still hadn't figured out who destroyed my privacy. "I get pissed off every time I think about it. All the shit they put me and Damian through."

He snorted. "I'm glad you finally realized it wasn't me."

"I know, man. Sorry I accused you. I was so angry I wasn't thinking straight."

"So you still have no idea who did it?"

I shook my head. "I'd love to find the motherfucker who stabbed me in the back."

He seemed to be thinking about something. "You should talk to Margo. I'll bet she knows someone who could probably help you track down the source."

My brows went up. It was a damn good idea. Margo was our publicist, and she had a lot of connections with the media. "You know, you're right. I'm going to call her."

He nodded and went back to playing guitar.

"Holy shit, Josh," I heard Terence from the poker table. "Isn't that your ex-wife on TV?"

"What?" I asked, turning toward him.

"That's *Lindsay*," Dean said, waving me over. "Josh, you've got to come see this."

I got up and went over there. Everyone was staring at the large flatscreen that still showed some kind of poker tournament. I stood and watched as the camera panned over the group of players and focused on one female player in particular. A beautiful brunette.

It *was* Lindsay.

I was stunned.

"That's her, isn't it?" Terence asked.

"Yeah, it is." I couldn't take my eyes off the screen. I hadn't seen Lindsay in years, and there she was in living color. The woman who once broke my heart.

"Damn, how long has it been since you guys split up?" Rhys asked. He'd come over, too, and was standing next to me, still holding his guitar. "Ten years?"

"Longer than that," I murmured.

"I didn't know she played professional poker," Dean said. "I thought she was an artist."

"Actually, her dad was a famous poker player," I said. "He won the Main Event at the World Series one year."

Dean's eyes widened. "No shit?"

I nodded. "She might still be an artist." My eyes went back to the screen. As I watched Lindsay, I searched myself for any remnants of feeling for her, any of the love or heartache that had once consumed me.

And there was nothing.

I felt a bit of nostalgia, but that was all. Lindsay was in the past.

"I hope she's doing well," I said and meant it. I hoped she'd finally found what she was looking for in life.

CHAPTER THIRTY-EIGHT

~Leah~

It was a sunny day, and there were a lot of people milling around when we arrived at the amphitheater for Emerald Rockfest. We all took one car, with Philip driving. There was me, Claire, Theo, her boyfriend Clement, Philip's sister Eliza, and her friend Jan. After parking, we made our way to our seats. Josh had bought out a whole center section near the front of the stage for Truth Harbor.

Our group took over a partial row, and I wound up between Claire and Theo. The first band was already onstage, and I texted Josh to let him know we'd arrived. He was coming by limo with the rest of the guys.

For the next few hours, we danced and sang and had a lot of fun as each new band came onstage. At one point, Philip, Claire, and I hit the refreshment stand and brought back food and drinks for everyone.

When I felt my phone buzzing in my pocket, I pulled it out. It was a message from Josh. Apparently he and the band had just arrived.

Do you want to come backstage?

I felt a jolt of excitement. *Definitely!*

I'm going to send Dax for you. Where are you?

I glanced around. The place was jam-packed. *Tell him I'll meet him at the west exit door.*

I told Claire and Theo I was going backstage to hang out with Josh.

"Have fun!" Claire took my hand and squeezed it. "Tell everyone we said hi."

I got up and made my way to the west exit. I could still see the stage, so I watched the current band as I waited.

"Leah?"

I turned to find Dax and his ever-changing spiked hair, which was currently turquoise.

He grinned, and I noticed he wore a Bluetooth device that attached to his ear. "I've come to escort you backstage. Are you ready?"

I followed him as he led me through the amphitheater. The security was tight. There were multiple doors, and I had my golden ticket scanned three times before I was even allowed into the main backstage area.

Eventually there was one more door, which opened to a large room. I held my pass out for one final scan by some dude with an iPad.

Since my ex-husband's band had only played bars, I'd never been backstage at a rock concert before. The room was more crowded than I expected. A bunch of people were gathered around a table playing cards while others were sitting off to the side. There were guitars and clothes draped on some of the furniture. The smell of perfume and weed hung in the air.

"My little spinster," Josh said, appearing in front me with a grin and looking as hot as ever. He turned to Dax. "Thanks for bringing her back, man. I appreciate it."

"No problem."

I thanked Dax as well, and then the next thing I knew, I was being guided around the room.

"Do you want anything to eat or drink?" Josh asked me.

I shook my head, still glancing around in a daze. *So this is the inner sanctum.* I waved at Dean, who winked at me from across the poker table. There was a pretty woman with red hair sitting on his lap.

I said hello to Terence and Rhys as well, and then Josh introduced me to the guys from the Beaver Kings. "This is my girlfriend, Leah."

"Hey."

"Nice to meet you."

"How's it hanging?"

"Do you want a hit?" This came from some pink-haired guy, who was apparently the Beaver Kings' lead singer. He'd just taken a bong toke and had "bad boy" and "probable asshole" written all over him.

I shook my head. "No, thanks."

Eventually Josh and I went over and sat on one of the couches. He reached for my hand, and we played with each other's fingers as we talked. I kept glancing around. A few of the women were staring at me. "I think I recognize some people here from your birthday."

He nodded and then frowned.

"What is it?"

He shook his head. "Nothing. So how's the show been so far?"

"Really good." I told him about the bands we'd seen and which ones I liked best. "How are you doing? Are you nervous?"

"Mostly excited." He seemed to think it over. "Maybe a little nervous. Being the band's front man has its unique pressures."

"Don't worry, Friedrich. You guys are going to kill it."

He grinned. "Yeah, we are."

"I can't believe I'm finally going to watch you perform live for the first time."

He leaned in close and whispered in my ear, "I'm going to make it extra special for you, honey."

My breath caught. And when I looked at him, he eye-smoldered me. "How do you do that?"

"Natural talent," he murmured and then brought his mouth to mine.

His lips were soft, and his tongue tasted sweet. Our mouths lingered, and as the kiss grew deeper, I couldn't believe how arousing it was. I had a hard time catching my breath.

Finally, I pulled away. We gazed at each other, and I could tell it had turned him on too.

It was while we were contemplating all this heat between us that some woman came over.

"Hi, Josh," she said. "I'm sorry to interrupt. I don't know if you remember me. I'm Miranda, Tyler's girlfriend?"

He turned and took a moment. "I remember."

"I just wanted to wish you good luck today. I'm a huge fan of the band, and I'm so glad you guys are back together. Your set is going to be amazing."

"Thank you," he said.

She smiled nervously and then glanced at me. "Anyway, I just wanted to tell you that."

He nodded. "That's real nice of you."

After she walked away, I studied her back. "She looks familiar. Was she at your house?"

"Yeah, she was." Then he glanced to the side with another annoyed expression.

"What's wrong?"

He drew in a sharp breath and pursed his lips. "I'm pissed that someone from that birthday party stabbed me in the back, and I still haven't figured out who it is yet."

I blinked in shock. It was like being dipped in ice water. I couldn't even speak.

He started telling me how he might have a way to figure it out. He was going to see if their publicist, Margo, could use her press connections to find the person who gave out his address.

"I can't believe it means that much to you," I said, trying to control the tremble in my voice. My heart raced like a trapped bird. "Does it really matter anymore?"

"Hell yes, it matters." There was a determined set to his jaw that I recognized. I'd discovered he could be surprisingly stubborn. "That person betrayed me after I invited them into my *home*. For God's sake, Damian was there. I hate that he had to deal with that shit. You have no idea what it's like to have your privacy ripped away like that."

I nodded. I could barely feel my body anymore. "I'm sure I don't."

Josh talked about it some more, but I hardly even heard the words. All I could think about was that I wished I'd told him when I had the chance. Telling him the truth after all this time was going to be terrible. Would he even forgive me?

I needed to find the right moment. Certainly not now.

Maybe after we're both dead and reincarnated.

Eventually he changed the subject, and we spent the rest of our time hanging out, chatting with everyone. When the Beaver Kings went on for their set, Josh took me up front to watch. We were off to the side of the stage, both watching the band live and on the television screens nearby.

He kept grinning at me. Everything was so good between us.

"What do you think of them?" Josh asked, nodding to the beat, studying one of the screens. "They're great, aren't they?"

"They are," I said in agreement. And it was true. Despite my asshole impression of the lead singer, the Beaver Kings were excellent.

After watching most of their performance, we went back to the large dressing room. I did my best to hide my worry about *the problem.*

In fact, I even convinced myself that there wasn't a problem. That everything was fine. We loved each other. Nothing could ever change that.

WHEN IT WAS close to the time for East Echo to perform, I left the dressing room and made my way back out to my seat. Josh told me I could watch from backstage, but I wanted to experience them as a member of the audience. It felt more authentic.

Claire and Theo were excited to see me again. When the MC came out and announced the next band performing was East Echo, there was a lot of clapping and whistling with all of us joining in.

We waited with bated breath, and then finally the four guys walked out. I was thrilled. I couldn't take my eyes off of Josh.

He'd changed from what he had on earlier and now wore a pair of tight black pants along with *my* sweater. Even though he said he was going to wear it, I still couldn't believe it.

"That's my sweater!" I told Theo and Claire. "The one I *made* him!"

"Oh my God, it's fantastic!" Claire said. "It looks amazing on him."

Theo nodded. "Very nice. I love that sunburst."

"Thank you," I told them both with a grin.

Josh was talking to the audience. "Hellooo, Seattle. How are you this evening? Everybody enjoying the show?"

People clapped and hooted.

"We're so happy to be here." He spoke in a seductive voice, his eyes scanning the crowd. "As you know, the four of us are nothing but a group of Seattle boys, and I speak for the entire band when I say it sure is good... *so good...* to be *home!*"

The opening riff for "Blonde Bomb" started, and everyone went wild. It was a great song. One of their hits, and the perfect high-energy opener.

We spent the next hour watching them perform a bunch of their best songs, along with a couple of new ones they must have written in England. Everything sounded fantastic. As a band, they were super tight. And Josh... oh my God, *Josh* was the hottest thing ever. He strode and strutted across that stage, seducing and teasing the crowd with his beautiful voice and body. It was intoxicating to watch. Talk about an aphrodisiac.

"I can't believe he's your *boyfriend*," Claire said to me at one point.

In a way, I couldn't believe it either. Joshua Trevant—beguiling, sexy, and ridiculously talented—was all mine.

It was obvious the band was glad to be back together. At one point between songs, Josh went over to Rhys holding his guitar, hugged him from the back, then leaned in and kissed his cheek.

Rhys burst out laughing, and the audience went crazy. The chords for "Truth in Madness" started, and everybody went even crazier. I was screaming right along with them. During the "La la la dee da dum," Josh clapped his hands overhead and had everyone in the amphitheater singing.

There were so many astonishing moments. During the guitar solo for "Muddy Riches," Josh stripped off my sweater and did a handstand, then literally walked around on his hands in the center of the stage.

People went nuts, especially after he gracefully landed on his feet and grabbed the microphone just in time to sing the next verse.

The most memorable moment for me was when they were between songs, and Josh had changed clothes again. Instead of my sweater, he'd put on a suit jacket with a white shirt. He took a seat at the piano.

The other guys in the band were fiddling with their instruments. Rhys changed from an electric to an acoustic guitar.

Josh waited until the guys were ready and then leaned into his microphone. "This one's for you, Leah."

I *died*.

Claire and Theo were losing their minds next to me. It felt like I was having an out-of-body experience.

I could barely breathe when he played the familiar opening to "Silver Days" on the piano.

I closed my eyes and let the notes wash over me.

It was beautiful in every way.

When he began to sing, it seemed otherworldly. Listening to Josh, my heart filled with joy, with all the love I felt for him.

CHAPTER THIRTY-NINE

~Leah~

After the concert, we stayed at a swanky hotel in downtown Seattle. Shane had agreed to keep an eye on my farm.

Josh was lying on the couch with his eyes closed, balancing a cold beer on his chest. He was wearing the clothes he'd worn onstage, except he'd taken off the jacket. He still wore the white button-down shirt with the sleeves rolled up.

"What's it like knowing that every single woman in that audience wanted you?" I asked, cracking open a bottle of water from the minibar.

His mouth twitched. "It feels about how you'd expect it to."

"And how's that?"

"Pretty damn good."

We'd just come from a party in Dean's room. Lots of people. Lots of cocktails. Loud music. Not really my scene, and I was glad when Josh said he wanted to leave.

I'd gone backstage before the band's encore—just as Josh had instructed me to—and waited for him in the dressing room. It surprised me how quickly we all left after their set. The whole band raced out to a few black SUVs in back of the amphitheater. He told me they did it after every big concert. Otherwise, leaving became a logistics nightmare.

"If I had to guess, even some of the straight men in that audience wanted you," I teased. "I'll bet you had more than a few questioning their sexuality."

"What can I say?" He shrugged lightly. "I'm hard to resist."

"The ego on you knows no bounds, does it?"

"Not really."

I wanted him just as much as all those strangers did. More even. Much more. The ride down here in the SUV was wild. Terence and his girlfriend took a separate vehicle, as did Rhys, but if we hadn't had Dean and the redhead sitting behind us, I would have been all over Josh. I doubted he'd be able to walk when I was done with him.

"And what about you, Leah?" His gaze drifted down my body before returning to meet my eyes. He wore a sexy smirk. "Are you one of those women? Do you want me?"

I put my water down and moved toward him on the couch. It must have shown on my face because his expression changed to alarm.

"What?" I asked.

"*Damn*, honey. Please be gentle."

It was my turn to smirk. "Better buckle your seat belt, Friedrich. It's going to be a long, *hot* night."

I STRETCHED out naked on sheets so smooth it felt like angels wove them. "Wow, this is luxurious."

It was morning, and sunlight streamed through the hotel room curtains. Josh had just come in from the living room part of our suite.

He wore a white hotel bathrobe, and when he sat down, the bed's wood frame made a loud, protesting creak.

"Jesus," he said. "I think we broke the bed."

"The chair too." I motioned at the desk chair we'd gotten quite creative in and that now looked lopsided.

He gazed at me, his eyes clear and blue. Despite the tattoos, mess of long hair, and bad boy persona, he seemed quite comfortable in this luxurious hotel suite. "That was a wild night, honey. And this is coming from someone who's had their share of wild nights."

I smiled coyly and arched my back a little. "It certainly was."

When he scooted up on the bed, there were more loud creaks, and we both laughed. "Shit, they're probably going to charge me an arm and a leg for this damn thing."

I put my nose in the air and sniffed. "Am I hallucinating, or do I smell coffee?"

"They delivered room service while you were in the bathroom."

"They did?" I was delighted. I hadn't had room service in ages.

I got up and walked out to the living room, noticing all the places my body ached. I didn't care. It was worth every sexy moment.

"Look at you," he said, coming up behind me and lightly slapping my ass. "We might have to break some more furniture before we leave."

We got scrambled eggs, bacon, potatoes, and fruit along with my coffee and Josh's warm honey water. We took it all back to bed and sat close as we ate.

"I've been wanting to ask you something," he said after we finished breakfast and put our plates on the nightstand.

"What's that?" I held my coffee mug with both hands.

He shifted position to face me, then hesitated. "I hope this is okay, and if it's not, just tell me."

I wondered what was going on. He seemed serious.

"How would you feel about talking to Jeremy sometime?"

My brows shot up.

"If you don't want to, that's cool," he said quickly, putting his hand up. "Don't feel pressured. I've told him how important you are to me, and he wants to meet you."

"In person?"

He shook his head. "Just on the phone. Not in person."

I took a deep breath and considered it. "Sure, I wouldn't mind that. In fact, I'd like to get to know him."

"You're sure? You can say no. I wouldn't hold it against you."

I put my mug down on the nightstand. "I know you wouldn't."

"Okay." He grinned a little. "I've been wanting to ask, but I wasn't sure how you'd take it. I know it's a weird request."

"I'm happy to meet him." My gaze lingered on Josh's broad shoulders. I scooted closer and then slid myself onto his lap, ignoring the bed's loud creak. "Do you have any more weird requests?"

"Yeah, I do," he rumbled as he slid his hands down to cup my ass. He put his mouth to my ear. "Let's go break the shower."

———

ALL GOOD THINGS MUST END, and unfortunately we could only stay one night at the hotel. I needed to get back to my farm. Not that Josh minded. I got the impression he'd seen the inside of a lot of hotels and wasn't impressed by any of them anymore.

I was surprised to discover that all the guys in the band were still staying at Josh's house, and even more surprised when I found out the reason.

Besides flying out to perform as the musical guest on *Saturday Night Live* this week, they were all coming back to Truth Harbor afterward to do an acoustic set at Walk the Plank's grand reopening.

"Everyone thought Shane was cool, and they wanted to help him," Josh explained a couple of days later. "We all agreed it'd be fun to play a small venue. It would give us a chance to work out the kinks in some of our new material."

He was outside helping me with the chickens. There wasn't

much for him to do, so he was mostly standing around keeping me company. Cary Grant was staring at him with his usual animosity.

Heading into the coop to fetch eggs, I could hear Josh talking to my rooster. "I *know* why you don't like me," he called over to him. "I finally figured it out. You want to be the only *cock* around here, don't you?"

I laughed to myself listening to this.

"Well, better get used to it, buddy," Josh continued. "Because I plan to stick around for a long time."

Since the band was flying to New York tomorrow, we decided I'd talk to Jeremy on the phone today. I was a little nervous but also curious to see what he was like. We were on the front porch just after lunch when Josh's phone rang, and he accepted the call from prison. He spoke to Jeremy a few minutes and then told him I was here if he'd like to say hello.

I accepted the phone. "Hi, Jeremy."

"Hi, Leah. It's nice to meet you."

Right away the biggest surprise was his voice. He sounded a lot like Josh. "It's nice to meet you too."

"Thanks for talking with me. You probably don't know too many guys in prison."

I smiled a little. "I can't say I know any."

"I appreciate you taking the time. Josh tells me you have a farm and that you're a fiber artist."

"That's right." I began describing my farm and animals to him. I told him about my knitting and the various fibers I sold and worked with. He listened and sounded interested.

"Where are you right now?"

"I'm standing on the front porch."

"And what do you see from there?"

It felt weird describing my beautiful view when all he had was the gray interior of a prison. I glanced at Josh, who had taken a seat in one of the porch chairs, watching me.

"That sounds wonderful," Jeremy said. "I can almost smell the hay."

I asked him what he was interested in and then remembered the books Josh had taken him. "Do you like to read? Are you into philosophy like Josh?"

"I do like to read." He told me how he wasn't so much into philosophy, though he'd read a few books his brother had recommended. Mostly he enjoyed reading fiction, but he also liked reading about travel, and he hoped to do some traveling someday.

"I'm sure you will."

"You sound like a really nice woman, Leah. Josh has told me a lot about you."

"Thanks. I've heard a lot about you too."

He chuckled. "Not all bad, I hope."

"Mostly good stuff."

"I'm glad to hear that. Please take good care of my brother. He's important to me."

"I'll do my best. He's important to me too."

We said our goodbyes, and I handed the phone back to Josh, feeling like the conversation had gone well.

He spoke to Jeremy briefly again before hanging up.

"Come here, my little spinster." Josh put his hand out to me and pulled me onto his lap. I slipped my arms around his neck, and we held each other. Neither of us spoke for a little while. "Thanks for doing that."

"I didn't mind. I liked talking to him."

"Still, I appreciate it."

I pulled back to look at him. "His voice sounds like yours."

He nodded. "I know."

"Jeremy seemed nice. I hope he gets to do all that traveling someday."

Josh was gazing at me with tenderness. "I'm so damn in love with you. Do you know that?"

I caressed his bearded jaw. "I love you too."

"I trust you like I've never trusted anyone."

"Me too." Except his words sent a shot of adrenaline through me and brought back *the problem*. I licked my lips. "Listen, there's something I need to talk to you about."

"What's that?"

I took a deep breath. *Am I really doing this? Finally confessing my idiocy?* I could only hope and pray it didn't hurt Josh and that he'd forgive me. I shifted position on his lap so I was a sitting up straighter. "I'm not even sure how to begin. It's weird how sometimes things can snowball and get away from you."

His phone buzzed, and he glanced down to where he was still holding it. "Oh shit, it's Margo. I've got to take this. Hang on a second."

"Wait, don't. I need—"

"Hey, Margo." Josh put the phone to his ear. My heart pounded so hard I was seeing spots in front of my eyes. I nearly ripped the phone from his hand. Instead I sat there watching him, barely able to breathe.

"Is that right?" Josh said and glanced at me. His brows wrinkled. "A Seattle station?"

I waited for the guillotine. For our happiness to be destroyed.

He listened some more. "All right, thanks for everything. I appreciate it." He hung up.

I stared at him, and he stared at me.

"What did she say?" I asked, my voice sounding unnaturally high.

He took a deep breath. "She can't find the source. All she knows is a local news station in Seattle got a hold of my address, but she's not sure which station, and no one's talking."

I blinked. "Oh."

"Fuck." He set his phone on the small table nearby in frustration. "I guess that's the end of that."

"I guess so." My heart was still racing like a rabbit. But I had to admit relief was flooding through me.

He rubbed his brow. "What was it you wanted to talk to me about?"

"Oh." I paused. My head swam as I sifted through my options. *Should I be honest and hurt Josh, or should I put this whole mess behind us?* "I wanted to thank you again for getting the band to play at Walk the Plank's grand opening."

CHAPTER FORTY

~Leah~

It was surreal watching East Echo perform "Truth in Madness" on *Saturday Night Live*. Even more surreal was that he wore my sweater again.

After they finished their song and the applause died down, the celebrity guest host—a famous actress—came over and complimented the band. "That sounded great. You guys are so amazing. I'm a big fan."

"Thank you," Josh said. "It's an honor to be here tonight."

She glanced down at his body. "I just love your sweater. It's gorgeous."

He grinned. "Thanks. My girlfriend made it."

"Really?"

"Yeah, she's a fiber artist. If you're interested, check out Clarity Moon Farm."

She laughed. "Okay, I'll do that." Then she grabbed Josh's hand

and raised it above their heads, turning back to the audience. "East Echo, everybody!"

There was more applause, and the television cut away to a commercial.

My jaw hung open in disbelief. I was now a puddle of goo in the middle of the floor. Someone could have wiped me up with a sponge.

"Oh my *God!*" Claire was shrieking and jumping up and down.

Even Theo was shrieking, and she wasn't the shrieking type.

They'd both come over to have a girls' night and watch the show with me. The coffee table was littered with snacks—chips, salsa, and a plate of tacos. Claire brought cookies, and Theo brought honey cakes.

Claire continued yelling and bouncing on the couch. "He just said the name of your farm on *TV!* You're famous!"

"This is huge," Theo said to me, her voice excited. "Get ready for an avalanche."

"What do you mean?"

"He's wearing your sweater, and he just told millions of people the name of your business. That's major."

I pulled myself up from being a puddle of goo and sat back on the couch. "Wow."

"Yeah, wow," Claire said. "That's the best kind of advertising there is. Authenticity. Trust me, I've learned everything I know from Philip."

As I was absorbing all this, my phone started pinging and buzzing. I picked it up. There were messages from Isabel, Naomi, and Salem. As I was reading them, a new message came in from Shane, and there was a phone call from my mom that went to voice mail. They were all saying how excited they were for me. Even Lars texted and said, *That was something else.*

The irony was that my sales were already up by a lot. After their performance at Emerald Rockfest, Josh told me people were asking about his sweater on social media. He instructed Margo to make sure my website was mentioned to everyone.

As I was sitting there with Claire and Theo, I sent Josh a text thanking him for what he just did on *SNL*.

Amazingly, he responded right away.

I love you, honey. Get ready for the whole world to see how talented you are.

My heart ached with happiness. I'd never been with a man who supported me so much. *Thank you. I love you and miss you. And you guys were great on SNL!!!*

Thanks! BTW, your mom texted me three times today.

Uh-oh. She'd asked for his number a couple of days ago, so I'd asked Josh, and he'd said to give it to her.

"Are you sure?" I had asked. "It's okay to say no."

"I don't think it's a good idea to show fear with that woman."

I laughed. He wasn't wrong.

I texted him back. *Is she sending you more stuff about ADHD?*

Yeah. Websites and books to read.

He'd asked me yesterday why she was sending him all this stuff, and I told him it was because she was an educator. I'd explained how, before she was a high school principal, my mom used to be a teacher. "I think she honestly wants to help you."

I texted him again. *You should read through them when you have a chance. You might find them useful.*

Okay, I'll take a look later. We're all headed over to a club in the East Village.

Who's with you?

He said the guys, of course, and then told me the actress who'd hosted *SNL* was there, along with some of the show's crew and cast members.

I stared at the phone, digesting this. My boyfriend was out partying with movie and television stars.

Have fun!

What else was there to say?

BY THURSDAY, Josh was back and joining me on my morning runs again.

"My sales have been skyrocketing," I told him. "I'm going to have to start buying fleece wholesale from another supplier because I'm nearly out of stock. This whole thing is wild. I've been spinning like crazy."

He grinned. "I'm glad to hear it."

Rosalie, Martina, and Eva galloped over, and Josh filmed them to send Damian later. It had rained last night, and the days were definitely cooler now that we'd moved into fall. I told him I was stopping by Walk the Plank that afternoon to bring Shane the cookies I'd baked for him last night. Their grand reopening was tomorrow, and I was curious to see how things were progressing.

"I'll come with you," he said. "I'd like to see how the stage is set up."

He told me Rhys and Terence were arriving tomorrow, along with the sound crew, and that Dean should be here later today.

After our run, we took a shower together and made love.

"Have you ever been this happy?" he whispered. Our hearts pounded against each other, the two of us encapsulated in a bubble of warm water and ecstasy.

"No." I gazed into his blue eyes. "Have you?"

"Never."

Later, we took my truck into town with Josh in the passenger seat holding the container of cookies.

"You have to stop eating those," I said. "At this rate there won't be any left for Shane."

"What? I'm not eating them," he said, trying to hide that he was chewing. "You're imagining things."

"Okay then, I demand you serenade me."

There was silence in the car, and I glanced over to where he was obviously trying to swallow a bite of cookie.

"Cat got your tongue?"

He laughed and wiped his mouth. "All right, fine. What would you like to hear?"

"Hmmm... I've never had my own living jukebox." I drummed my fingers on the steering wheel. "How about I let the jukebox decide?"

He nodded, paused for a second, and then began singing "Fly Me to the Moon."

It wasn't the kind of music I'd ever heard from him before, but it sounded great. He took my hand as he sang, and it became the most romantic thing ever. There were a few eye smolders thrown in, but mostly it was sweet.

"That was incredible," I said after I pulled into a parking spot in town. "I've never heard you sing anything like that."

"It made me think of you." He turned toward me in his seat. "All the places you take me, Leah."

We gazed at each other, and I felt myself sinking into him like quicksand.

Eventually we got out of the car and walked down the sidewalk together holding hands. As we approached Walk the Plank, there were a couple of news vans parked in front. I felt Josh stiffen beside me.

"Should we go around back?" I asked.

He shook his head. "It's fine. This is good promo for Shane."

We walked past the news vans. There were a few reporters standing off to the side, talking to each other and messing with their equipment.

Just when I thought we'd gotten away, some woman with short dark hair and glasses materialized in front of us.

"Oh wow, it *is* you!" she said. "I was hoping to see you here." Except she wasn't talking to Josh but to *me*.

I stared at her with uncertainty. She looked familiar.

"It's Leah, right?" She smirked and then glanced down to where Josh and I were still holding hands. "And I understand the two of you are a lot more than just neighbors."

My pulse shot up in horror. I recognized her now. She was one of the reporters I'd given Josh's address to.

"Do you think we could do an interview with both of you?" she asked. "Everyone would love to hear about your relationship. I understand your brother owns the bar that East Echo is playing at tomorrow."

I felt Josh studying her with confusion.

I was disturbed that she knew so much about me. I'd never told her my name or about Shane. How could she know that? I remembered what Lars had said, how all the attention on Josh would rub off on me. "I don't think so," I said stiffly, moving past her. "We're in a hurry." My hand was sweating in Josh's as I pulled him along.

"C'mon, just five minutes," she said, chasing after us. "It could help promote your farm. People are interested in your story."

Luckily, we were at the entrance to Walk the Plank, and I jerked the door open, dragging Josh inside.

"Who was that?" he asked, bewildered. "You never told me you knew any reporters."

"Nobody," I said, my heart pounding. The bar was a hive of activity. "I don't know her."

"She seems to know you. How does she know we're neighbors?"

The whole episode had upset me to my core. I remembered that quote from the Buddha: "Three things cannot be long hidden: the sun, the moon, and the truth."

Josh was still studying me, trying to puzzle it out.

I took a deep breath and realized I couldn't keep running from this.

My mouth went dry. Was this really the right time and place? But then I realized there would never be a right time and place.

The sun. The moon. And now the truth.

"It was me," I said, trying to stay calm.

"What? I can't hear you."

"It was *me*," I repeated louder over the noise of someone hammering. I was still holding Shane's cookies and tightened my grip. "I'm the one who gave your address to the press. That's how she knows me."

Josh still seemed confused. "You gave my address to that woman?" He glanced toward the door behind me.

I nodded. There was a roaring in my ears. Everything seemed to come into sharper focus.

"When was this?"

"Right after the birthday party."

Josh stared at me, and I saw the truth work its way through him. I saw the exact moment he understood because all the color drained from his face. His eyes widened. "It was... *you?*" He seemed to be struggling to find the words. "You did that to *me?* To *Damian?*"

"I'm sorry, Josh. I didn't know it would be such a big thing. It was a mistake." My voice shook. "A dumb impulse. I never meant any harm. In fact, I didn't even know she was with the press. I thought she was a fan."

"Why would you give my private address to *anyone?*"

"Because I was angry with you. I was angry at the way you lied to me about who you are."

His face contorted into an expression between pain and outrage. "So it was some kind of sick revenge?"

"I was just mad, that's all, and I did something stupid. I'm so sorry. I've wished a million times I could do it over. I should have told you sooner." I stepped toward him and tried to put my hand on his arm, except he jerked away.

"Why didn't you?" The color came rushing back into his face, and his cheeks flushed. "I don't fucking believe this." He was blinking at me in shock. Like I was a stranger. "I trusted you, Leah. Jesus, I trusted you, but you're just like all the rest of them. You've been *using* me."

"That's not true!" I went into a panic and tried to breathe, tried to think of some way I could fix this. "Come on, you've never made a mistake before? You weren't honest with me when me first met. Wasn't that a mistake?"

"It's not the same thing. Not even close. You nearly wrecked my adoption."

I opened my mouth, but I didn't know what to say.

"You *betrayed* me. Right from the start."

In that moment, Shane walked over. Apparently he didn't notice we were in the middle of a heated argument. "Hey, are those cookies for me?"

Josh and I were staring at each other, and I could see all the hurt and anger in his eyes. My stomach twisted into knots. I glanced at Shane and handed him the container. "Here you go."

He took the cookies, and our expressions must have tipped him off. He glanced between us. "Is everything okay?"

Josh was breathing hard. "*Fuck* this shit," he spat out. Then he strode toward the door and left.

"What's going on?" Shane asked with wide eyes. He turned to me. "Are you guys having a fight?"

"I'll tell you about it later," I mumbled. "I have to go." Then I chased after Josh.

He was already halfway down the sidewalk in the opposite direction of the press vans. Luckily, they hadn't noticed us.

I ran down until I was beside him. "I know I screwed up. I never meant to hurt you. You have to know that."

"I don't believe you. I don't believe a fucking word you say to me. How can I ever trust you again?"

I was stunned. "Are you serious?"

"Just leave me alone, Leah. I don't want to talk to you. We're finished. It's over."

"*What?*" My stomach dropped. He sounded so different. So cold. I'd never seen him like this. "How can you say that? I *love* you, Josh."

"Just get away from me." And with that, he crossed the street.

I stayed on the sidewalk and watched him go. He was obviously furious, and I thought maybe he needed to cool down. I knew he'd be hurt and angry, but we'd been through so much together.

I glanced toward Walk the Plank. I didn't feel like going back inside and wasn't sure what to do with myself, so I headed toward my truck, crossing the street to avoid the reporters.

When I got home, I began my afternoon chores, but it felt like I was coming out of my skin. *Did he really mean it when he said we're finished? That it's over?* Loyalty meant a lot to Josh. It was everything. Despite having a lot of friends, there were only a few people he really trusted.

I tried texting him, but he didn't respond. After a couple of hours, I couldn't take it anymore. I drove to his house. Except when I got there, the black metal gates were closed. It looked deserted. I pulled up to the intercom and pushed the call button.

After a few seconds, a voice came through the speaker. "Oh hey, Leah." It was Dean. "Let me buzz you in."

The gates began to open, and I drove my truck inside and parked in the driveway. Dean met me at the front door. "Josh isn't here. It's just me."

I followed Dean into the kitchen, where I could smell something delicious cooking. It turned out to be fried chicken.

"Have Rhys and Terence arrived yet?" I asked.

"Not until tomorrow," he said, turning the chicken in the pan with a pair of black tongs. "Can I get you anything? Do you want a beer? This chicken's almost done."

"No, thanks. Have you spoken to Josh today?"

He glanced at me and seemed to notice how upset I was. "Is everything okay?"

I shook my head. "We had a fight. A bad one."

"Damn, I'm sorry to hear that. I'm sure whatever it is, you guys will work it out."

I chewed my bottom lip, debating what to do, and then I decided to hell with it. I told Dean everything.

His brows shot up to his hairline "Jesus, that was *you*? You gave Josh's address to the press? What the hell were you thinking?"

"I wasn't thinking. That's the problem. I was angry and acted impulsively. I screwed up."

TRUTH ABOUT CATS & SPINSTERS 379

"You put us in a bad situation while Damian was here. That's how Josh is going to see it."

I rubbed my arms, hugging myself. "I didn't even know they were the press. I thought they were fans—not that it makes it any better."

"This is not good." He turned down the heat on the chicken, shaking his head. "*Fuck.*"

"What can I do? I've told him I'm sorry. I love him, Dean."

He nodded. "I know you do. He loves you too. I'll try talking to him when he gets back."

"You will?"

He leaned against the counter and crossed his heavily inked arms. His biceps were nearly the size of my thighs. "I will. But I can't guarantee he'll listen. He can be a stubborn sonofabitch."

"I understand. I appreciate it."

Dean was still shaking his head. "He's been really bugged trying to find out who gave his address to the vultures, and this whole time it was you. I can't believe it."

I swallowed. "Do you think he'll forgive me?"

"I honestly don't know."

———

I DIDN'T HEAR from Josh all night. I couldn't sleep and was already awake when Cary Grant crowed in the early morning. After my run, I started on my chores, grateful for the hard work. I needed something to stop me from freaking out.

I tried texting Josh again during lunch.

Can we please talk?

No response. Nothing. I wondered if they were even still performing at Walk the Plank tonight. I assumed things were still a go because I would have heard from Shane.

After spinning for a couple of hours, I decided to go to the show like I had already planned. All my friends were going to be there. Even Lars and my mom were going to the grand reopening.

I took a shower and slipped on a new black top along with my most flattering jeans. My stomach felt queasy, but I choked down some leftover soup I had in the fridge.

When I arrived downtown, I couldn't believe the crowd. It was a mob scene. There were reporters and people lined up on the sidewalk outside the bar. Shane said tickets had sold out within hours.

Despite my worries over what was going on between Josh and me, I was proud of what Shane was accomplishing here and grateful to Josh and the band for helping him like this.

I cut through the alley and went into the back of the bar to avoid the crowds. There was a beefy security guy blocking the back door.

"My brother owns this bar," I said. "Plus, I'm Joshua Trevant's girlfriend."

He rolled his eyes. "Sure you are."

"I *am*."

Thankfully, Shane walked past. "Oh yeah, dude, let her in. That's my sister."

Once inside, I could feel the preshow energy in the air. The place was packed. Shane said they'd already let people with tickets inside. Apparently that mob out front were people who couldn't get tickets.

"I'm surprised you didn't come with the band," Shane said, puzzled. But then his eyes widened. "Are you and Josh still having a fight?"

"Where are they?" I asked, avoiding his question.

"In the dressing room behind the stage. C'mon, I'll take you there."

But as we headed in that direction, some woman came up to Shane. "We've got a problem," she said and started talking about an issue with the cash register.

He glanced at me. "I need to take care of this. Just keep going down the hall." He pointed. "It's the last door on the right."

I headed in that direction, moving past all the people standing around, everyone styled in the latest fashion.

When I got to the dressing room door, there was another beefy security guy holding an iPad. "I'll need to see your pass," he said.

I put my hand over my chest in frustration. I'd been in such a crazed state of mind that I completely forgot my golden ticket. "I don't have my pass," I said. "I left it at home. I'm Josh's girlfriend."

He eyed me skeptically.

"Seriously. Just open the door and ask him."

He touched his iPad screen, opening some app on it. "What's your name?"

"Leah Kelly."

The guy scrolled a thick index finger down some list. "I don't see it."

Just then the dressing room door opened, and a young woman slipped out.

"He's right there!" I pointed inside to where I could see Josh sitting at a table with the guys from the band and a few other people. I tried to walk into the room, but the guard stopped me. "Josh!" I called over in frustration.

He turned his blond head and met my eyes.

The guard was looking at him as well. "Do you know this woman?"

"Of course he knows me."

But to my surprise, Josh wasn't responding. His eyes were still on mine, and for a moment, I saw the pain, but then it changed to ice.

He shook his head. "Nah, I don't know her." He turned away.

I stared at him in shock. "*Josh?*"

The guard shrugged his beefy shoulders and reached down to close the door. "Sorry," he said. "I can't let you in."

I was reeling. It felt like I'd been slapped. I could barely believe what had just happened.

Was that really the same guy who told me yesterday morning, after making love to me in the shower, that he'd never been so happy in his life?

CHAPTER FORTY-ONE

~Josh~

Waves of acid tore through my gut, ripping at my insides. All the guys were staring at me as I took a deep breath and tried not to throw up.

Dean was blinking at me in shock. "You *didn't* just do that to Leah."

"What the hell?" Rhys seemed incredulous. "Did you just throw your girlfriend out of here?"

"Damn, that was cold," Terence said. "Why would you do that?"

I gulped air and tried to get through this avalanche of pain. "We broke up," I managed to say.

Dean's eyes were on me. He already knew what happened. Apparently Leah had come to the house yesterday and tried to enlist his aid.

"I agree this is bad, but come on," Dean said last night. "You're acting like she cheated on you."

"It the same thing. A *betrayal*."

"It's hardly the same thing and you know it."

I clenched my jaw. "I'll be the judge of what I know."

The guys were still staring at me when I reached across the table for the bottle of whiskey. I brought it to my lips and took a large swallow.

I *never* drank before going onstage.

Rhys was studying me with alarm. "Are you okay?"

"I'm fine." I tried to smile but couldn't manage it.

Just then, the dressing room door opened, and Shane came inside. "This is your five-minute warning." He grinned. "We've got a packed house tonight. I can't thank you guys enough for this."

Everyone nodded and murmured how they were glad to help.

I didn't say anything. Obviously Shane had no idea what had just happened with his sister or he wouldn't be so friendly.

I turned my head away. I couldn't even look at him without thinking of Leah. I took another swig from the bottle, wiping my mouth.

By the time the four of us went onstage, I was half drunk. It was the only way I was getting through this. I tried not to search the audience for the woman destroying me but did it anyway.

She wasn't there.

I saw her friends Claire and Theo. Shane's girlfriend, Martha. Lars and Camilla were also there, but no sign of Leah.

Our acoustic set began, and it was a disjointed blur. I'd never dialed in a performance before, never gave less than 100 percent, but tonight I was running on autopilot. I tried to bring up the flirtatious character of Joshua Trevant, tried to seduce the audience, but it felt hollow.

It had been years since we'd performed in a small club, and if my life hadn't become a train wreck, I'd be enjoying it. I'd be enjoying having Leah watch me onstage. It had given me great pleasure to know she was in the audience at Emerald Rockfest.

When our set was over, I didn't speak to anyone, just pushed my way through the crowd to the back door, where a couple of black SUVs waited to take us out of there. I left alone.

The driver took me to my house, and once inside, I searched for another bottle. I never drank like this. But I'd given Leah my heart. My soul. Everything. I'd have been loyal to her until we breathed our last breath, and this whole time she was hiding something. Her *betrayal.*

I could barely wrap my head around it.

It was a couple of hours later, while I was sitting in the living room, sipping a bottle of gin, that Dean showed up.

He glanced at it and made a face. "Never knew you were a gin drinker."

"It's all I could find." I brought it to my lips and took another swallow, grimacing. It tasted like kerosene.

"What about the vodka?"

"I didn't see any... vodka." My words came out slurred.

"I probably shouldn't tell you where it is. You're already wasted."

"What are you, my mother?" But then I snorted with laughter because my mother wouldn't give two shits if I was wasted.

He shook his head. "Maybe you should go to bed."

"I'm watching TV," I insisted, though I didn't even know what I was watching. I only had it on so I didn't feel alone.

He didn't say anything.

"What happened after I left the show?" I asked. "Did—" I couldn't say her name. "Did anyone show up?"

He studied me. "No, she wasn't there."

I acknowledged this by taking another swallow of kerosene.

"You shouldn't have treated her like that," he said. "That was seriously fucked-up."

I stared at the television. I knew what I did was fucked-up. "I don't want to talk about it. Where have you been so long?"

Dean ran a hand down his beard. "We hung out and signed autographs and spoke with everyone. It was pretty cool. You should have stayed. I think a lot of people were disappointed you left."

I didn't respond to that either and continued to stare at the TV. I hated that I'd disappointed fans. Except there was no way I could have stayed.

He sat on the couch and put his hand out. "Give me a drink of that."

I handed him the bottle, and he took a sip. "Damn." He made a face. "That shit is nasty."

I shrugged and leaned back, closing my eyes. The room spun.

"Terence and Rhys nearly came back with me," he said. "They're both worried about you. I talked them out of it and told them you just needed some space."

I was glad Dean had talked them out of coming here. I hadn't exactly given my best performance, and they were probably pissed. Not to mention the way I'd split afterward.

He handed the bottle back and stood up. "I'm going to hit the sack. I'm flying back to LA tomorrow morning."

"You are?" I imagined myself in this big house alone, knowing Leah was only a walk in the woods away. It sounded like torture. "Do you mind if I join you?"

"You want to come to LA?" He seemed surprised.

"I need to get out of here."

He considered me for a long moment. "Sure, brother. Of course you can come. Stay with me as long as you like."

———

I TRIED to sleep on the flight to Los Angeles since I was hungover as shit. Thankfully, it was a private plane, so I didn't have to deal with anyone talking to me.

Dean left me alone and was mostly on his phone. He didn't mention Leah to me again, so that was a relief.

After we landed, a driver took us to the house he'd rented in Laurel Canyon. It was a furnished Spanish Colonial with views of the Hollywood hills. There were cars in the driveway when we arrived, and it turned out the house wasn't empty. Dean's new girl-friend, Christie, an aspiring actress he'd met at some party, was hanging out by the pool with a few people.

I wasn't sure if I wanted to deal with them, but then somebody handed me a joint, and I figured, *What the hell?* Maybe it would help my hangover. I leaned back in the lounge chair and sent text messages to a couple of friends I had in the area. October was one of the best months for surfing, and I planned to do a lot.

Except that wasn't what happened.

Every day I told myself I was going surfing, and every day I woke up and within hours was too drunk or high to go anywhere. Dean being prone to excess didn't help matters. He was usually in the kitchen blending cocktails or cooking for all his guests or hanging out by the pool getting stoned. It was one endless party. I didn't know half the people there. A few of them were musicians and artists, though I suspected a lot of them were just leeches.

I didn't care. As long as it stopped me from agonizing over Leah, that was all I cared about.

Not that I didn't do exactly that. In my worst moments, I brought up her YouTube channel and watched her spinning videos. There were twelve, and I watched them over and over like a stalker. The last video was posted before our breakup, and there hadn't been any new ones since. I felt guilty about that, though I told myself I had nothing to feel guilty about.

I tried not to think about what I'd done to her that night back-stage. The hurt and shock on her face.

That was the worst agony of all.

I didn't want to hurt Leah. Never. It was like stabbing myself, but how could I ever trust her again?

So I poured another drink, rolled another joint, and let one day slip into the next. After a couple of weeks of this, I was waking up in the mornings coughing like some old dude with a pack-a-day habit. I was fucking up my voice.

And for the first time in my life, I didn't care.

Deep inside, an alarm bell sounded.

It told me I was spiraling.

But I didn't give a shit about that either.

Then there were the women. Lots of women always hanging around the house. Tattooed and toned and trying to flirt with me.

Except I didn't want any of them.

All I wanted was a certain dark-haired beauty who laughed at all my dumb jokes. The same beauty who could run as fast as hell, who was badass enough to follow her dreams, and who somehow *got* me. More than any woman I'd ever known. I was always myself with Leah, and she always saw the man first, never the fame or money.

I should have known it was too good to be true.

I'd never been lucky in love.

Jeremy called, and even though it was barely noon, I was already buzzed from the rum-soaked piña coladas Dean made every morning.

"You broke up with *Leah?*" He sounded shocked.

"I had no choice," I said, stewing in my self-righteousness. I told him how she'd given my address to the press. I expected him to be as indignant as I was.

"So she made a mistake. I'll bet she feels like shit about it."

I snorted. "A mistake? It was more than that," I muttered. "She betrayed me."

"It sounds like she barely even knew you when it happened, and that you lied to her to begin with."

"Who the hell's side are you on?"

He laughed. My brother had the gall to *laugh.* "Believe it or not, I'm on *your* side. I just don't think you should throw away the love of your life over a stupid mistake."

"Who says she's the love of my life?"

"You did. It's what you told me."

I went quiet, wishing my rum buzz was stronger. "Well, I was wrong."

"Sometimes people deserve a second chance. Who knows that better than me?"

"This is different."

"No, it isn't. Don't let yourself get hung up on blame."

"What's that supposed to mean?" I asked, pissed off.

He took a deep breath. "Listen, I know you blame yourself that I'm in prison. And the truth is, for a long time, I blamed you too."

I went quiet. Jeremy and I had never discussed this before.

"I blamed you for leaving me behind. For not being there when I needed you. But being in here, I've learned that blame only hurts yourself and the people you love. So I want you to know something. I don't blame you anymore."

"But it *is* my fault," I insisted. As usual, my guilt hung around me like a noose.

"It's not. I'm a grown man responsible for my own actions. It was never your fault."

I didn't know what to say. "Why are you telling me this?"

"Because we all make mistakes, and we all have to own them. It sounds like Leah has owned hers. Blame is just a crutch that stops you from moving forward in life. So stop being stubborn. Let it go."

We talked a little more, but my head was reeling.

I spent the rest of the day wrestling over our conversation. *"Let it go"? Did he really say that to me?* My guilt over Jeremy had been my dark companion for years.

And how could he have defended Leah? My blame toward her is justified. I'm not letting it go.

After taking a shower, I searched through the bag of clothes I'd brought for something to wear. Instead of finding a clean shirt, I nearly had a meltdown when I found the Sasquatch doll Leah had given me.

I stared at it in shock. "What the hell is this doing here?" A memory came to me of when Leah and I first met, and I caught myself smiling. What a crazy beginning we had. But then my smile faded, and I grew outraged. Because there was only one way this could have gotten in my bag.

I marched down to the pool area, where Dean was sitting with Christie in a lounge chair while everyone played Marco Polo in the water. A couple of guys from the Beaver Kings had arrived with a group of people last night. Reggae music blasted from the speakers. It was early evening, and the air smelled like salt water and barbecue.

"You got a lot of nerve," I said, shoving the doll in Dean's face. "Next time mind your own damn business."

"What's this?" He took it from my hand.

"It looks like a Bigfoot," Christie said.

"Don't act like you didn't stick that in my luggage!"

He gave me a strange look. "Why would I stick this in your luggage? I don't even know what it is."

"Then how the hell did it get there?"

"If I had to guess, you put it there yourself. You were pretty out of it when we left Seattle."

I stared at him and knew I sounded unhinged. It felt like I was losing my mind. I grabbed the Sasquatch back.

"Come join us in the water, Josh," somebody called over from the pool. It was one of the women who'd been hanging around a lot. I think her name was Megan. She was an attractive brunette.

I almost didn't reply, then thought, *Why am I still living like a monk?* So I walked over to her.

"Don't you want to play with us?" she asked with a sexy smile as she treaded water.

I grinned a little. "Maybe I will."

"I'd *love* that."

"Let me throw on some swim trunks."

"I'll be waiting," she purred.

I went upstairs and put the Sasquatch on my nightstand while I quickly changed. When I got downstairs, I joined everybody in the water playing Marco Polo. It was a good distraction from thinking about Leah. Except it got a little crazy. Some of the women took their tops off and decided to kiss the person who caught them. I wound up getting kissed so much, I suspected the women weren't even trying to get away when I yelled "Marco."

Eventually we took a breather, and I hoisted myself up on the edge of the pool.

Megan came over with a bong and sat next to me while her friend Alexa sat on my other side. We talked and did bong hits together. It had gotten dark, and the torches were lit. Bob Dylan's "Tangled up in Blue" drifted out from the speakers.

I wasn't sure how it even started, since I was really stoned, but somehow I was kissing both Megan and Alexa, taking turns with each of them.

"Let's go to your room," Megan whispered in my ear.

We got up and headed inside the house. Alexa grabbed a bottle of wine on the way upstairs, and once we were in my bedroom, it didn't take long for the three of us to start making out on the bed.

I hadn't had a threesome in ages.

I was lying on my back, watching the two women kiss each other in front of me. It was an arousing sight. Megan with her long brown hair and slender build, and Alexa with her blonde waves and voluptuous curves.

I tried not to think about Leah, but I was so stoned that, oddly, it wasn't painful. I kept thinking about how much I loved Leah's body and how she always smelled and tasted so good. Those pretty breasts, and her beautiful legs that went on forever. The way she'd pull my hair urgently when I went down on her. I smiled thinking about how she'd sometimes throw her hands in the air after climaxing and laugh with pure joy.

God, I love everything about her.

She always felt so right in my arms.

Fingers slid over the top of my swim trunks, trying to tug them off.

The light in the room was hazy, and my eyes were half-lidded. I kept focusing on that curtain of brown hair, remembering how Leah and I used to have sex in front of the full-length mirror in my bedroom sometimes. I'd stand behind her, and she'd bring all my hair forward, mixing it with her own dark strands. I loved seeing that, the contrast of us.

"Come here, honey," I murmured, dragging her up to me. "I want you so bad. Kiss me, Leah."

CHAPTER FORTY-TWO

~Leah~

For the first week, I kept the breakup to myself. It was too painful to tell everyone what happened, though eventually I'd have to.

The irony was that everybody in my family was now on board with Josh. Lars said that maybe he'd misjudged him, and even my mom decided she'd probably been too harsh in her opinions.

This was mainly because East Echo's show at Walk the Plank had been a smashing success for Shane. Apparently the bar was now booked solid for the next six months. Shane told me he had bands and their managers calling him from all over the country.

"That's great," I said. We were outside in the barn while I fed my girls their dinner. I wasn't surprised my little brother was doing well. Things always seemed to work out for him.

"Are you okay, Leah?"

I sealed up the bin of supplements I added to my alpacas' feed. "Why do you ask that?"

"I haven't seen Josh around. What's going on with you two?"

I didn't reply. It hurt even hearing his name. The only person who knew about our breakup was Salem. She'd called and said how sorry she was. Apparently Dean told Dax what happened and that Josh was staying with him in LA. Salem meant well, but a part of me wished she hadn't told me where he was.

"Josh and I broke up," I said finally.

"Are you serious?" His eyes bugged out. "When?"

"The night of their show at Walk the Plank."

He chewed on this. "Damn, I'm sorry. I had no idea. Are you okay?"

"Not really."

"What happened?"

I sighed to myself and wondered how much I should tell Shane. I didn't want to poison him against Josh, but I didn't see any reason to shelter him either. Obviously none of it would have happened in the first place if I hadn't given his address to the press.

"I did something I shouldn't have," I said. And then I told him the whole story.

Shane seemed shocked when I was done. "He did that to you? Acted like he didn't *know* you? I can't believe he'd be such an asshole."

"It was awful, but in a way, I brought it on myself."

He shook his head. "I agree, what you did was wrong, but that doesn't mean he gets to act like that. It doesn't even sound like Josh. You guys were great together. That shouldn't have been a deal breaker."

I shrugged and finished refreshing the water trough. "Apparently it was for him. You don't have to let this ruin your relationship. I understand if you still want to be friends."

"Are you kidding?" He took a deep breath. "He's helped me a lot, no doubt, but I can't be friends with him anymore. Not after he treated you like that."

"I'm sorry. I wish it hadn't ended this way."

A few days later, I told Claire and Theo about the breakup. They both wanted to come over immediately, but I told them not to, that I was okay.

Most days, I kept as busy as possible, but the nights were rough. I usually cried half the night with a broken heart and by morning switched to being furious at Josh.

All this emotional ping-pong was wearing me out.

I kept remembering something he told me. He'd said that when he finally found out who stabbed him in the back, that person was going to wish they'd never met him.

Did I wish I'd never met him?

I guess that depends on the time of day you ask me.

But deep down I knew the truth. I loved Josh, and I could never regret meeting him.

He'd given me the ride of my life.

One of the quotes he had tattooed on his upper back was from Leonardo da Vinci: "The noblest pleasure is the joy of understanding." I used to trace it with my fingers. It described our relationship so well because we understood each other. I got why he was so upset at what I'd done. It was a betrayal. And for someone as deeply loyal as Josh, betraying him was the worst thing you could do.

Ironically, the other parts of my life were going great. My business was booming. Thanks to Josh, I was so busy that I'd reached out to both the yarn store and sweater store in town. For a percentage, they were each going to fill the holes in my inventory. In fact, it looked like Ellen, the owner of the sweater shop, and I were going into business together producing and selling that sunburst sweater.

It was dizzying to be successful. I was so far in the black that I finally bought some Angora goats. Two kids and two does. I'd read everything I could about them, but it was definitely a learning curve introducing new animals to my farm.

Luckily, the does were sweet and docile. The kids were the cutest things I'd ever seen. So full of life. I named them Annie and Blossom and couldn't wait to send Damian a video. But then my heart clenched when I realized Damian would no longer be a part of my life either.

Salem called regularly to check on me. Apparently Josh was still in LA, and Dean said he wasn't doing so great.

"I can't believe he's being so foolish," Salem said. "I've never known him to be a fool. He needs to get over himself."

I smiled at her bluntness. "I thought you were friends with Josh."

"I *am*. Which is why I'd say the same thing to his face if he were here."

When Saturday night came around, I set myself up with a bottle of wine, a bag of frozen chocolate chips, and a movie to distract me.

But then I heard a car outside. It was Claire and Theo.

"What are you doing here?" I asked, astonished. "I told you I was fine."

Claire waved me off as she walked into the house. "Please. Don't be ridiculous. We're not letting you sit and stew all by yourself."

Theo grinned and held up a bag of groceries. "I brought Oreos and three pints of ice cream to dip them in."

"You brought three pints?" Claire laughed. "So did I."

By the time we were sitting on the couch with our ice cream, cookies, chips, wine, and lemonade for Claire, my heart ached. "You guys are the best," I said, grateful that they'd ignored my attempt at being stoic. "Thank you. This is really nice."

"No thanks necessary." Theo's bright red hair was pulled up in a messy bun, and her tortoiseshell glasses gave her an owlish appearance. "When one of our own is down, we rally."

"And I can't believe how pregnant you look," I said to Claire, who was six months along now. "You're glowing."

"I know." She stroked her baby bump with a smile. "The midwife called it my Jiffy Pop month."

We spent the next few hours talking, eating ice cream, and watching romantic comedies.

"I think the boyfriend sweater curse might be real," I said during a break between movies. "How else do you explain it? That was the second sweater I've knit a boyfriend, and look what happened."

"I still can't believe Josh did that to you." Claire shook her head as she took a sip from her lemonade. "What a jerk. I'm never listening to East Echo again."

Her loyalty touched me. "You don't have to do that. I know they're your favorite band. I don't mind if you listen to them."

"Forget it. They're dead to me."

Theo dipped an Oreo into her vanilla ice cream. "To be honest, after hearing the entire story between you and Josh, I think you both acted like assholes."

"*What?*" Claire threw her hands in the air. She turned to Theo. "How can you say that about Leah?"

"Because she destroyed Josh's privacy." She raised a brow at me. "I'm sorry to say it, but that was an awful thing you did to him and Damian."

"Hmm." Claire glanced at me. "She *does* make a good point."

I leaned back against the couch. "I know it was awful. Believe me, I regret it every day."

"And the way he pretended not to know you in the dressing room? That was awful too. Really harsh." Theo put her ice cream container down. "Hence, you guys are both assholes."

"I'm not sure if I feel better or worse after your analysis," I said.

Theo smiled. "Don't worry. I'm still on your side."

"Me too." Claire patted my leg. "I've always got your back."

Somewhere around eleven, while we were watching our second movie, I heard Shane's truck outside. I was surprised he was home since he usually closed the bar on weekends.

I texted him. *You're home early. Everything okay?*

There was no response, so I put my phone down, but then it pinged. *Martha just dumped me.*

I gasped.

Claire and Theo turned to me.

"What's wrong?" Claire asked.

"Martha just dumped Shane!"

Their mouths fell open.

I'm so sorry, I texted him back. *Claire and Theo are here. Do you want to come over and join us?*

Sure.

Shane showed up, and we hugged and fussed over him. He looked so dejected. It was heartbreaking. We asked if he'd like to indulge in our smorgasbord of breakup food.

"What's with all the ice cream?" he asked, glancing at the containers on the coffee table. "Is that a thing?"

"It's what we do," Claire said with sympathy. "Ice cream is comfort food."

"There are a few more pints in the freezer," Theo offered. "Would you like one?"

Shane shook his head. "No, thanks. I don't want to eat anything."

I couldn't remember the last time my brother turned down food.

He slumped on the couch between Claire and Theo while I took the chair nearby. "I can't believe she dumped me," he said.

"I can't either. What happened?" I asked.

"Martha saw Kayla hugging me after she did the hair for the band tonight. She was happy because the lead singer said he was going to recommend her to some friends."

"Who's Kayla?" Claire asked him.

"She's someone I went out with a while back. She does hair and makeup and has been hanging around the bar a lot lately, hoping to get hired by some of the bands."

"I think I remember her," I said. "She used the shower here once."

"I tried to tell Martha the hug was innocent," Shane went on, pushing his bangs back. "It was nothing. Kayla hugged *me*, not the other way around. But she wouldn't listen. She got really upset and said she'd had enough and that we weren't right for each other, and then she broke up with me."

I leaned back in my chair. "That sucks. I'm really sorry."

Claire and Theo were murmuring their sympathies as well.

He shook his head. "Everything was going so great. I don't know what I'm going to do without her."

OVER THE NEXT WEEK, Shane and I hung out a lot when he wasn't working, both of us commiserating over our broken hearts. My mom and Lars came over a few times, too, since I finally told them what happened with Josh.

Surprisingly, they were both really nice. Lars said Josh was a fool if he thought he'd ever do any better than me, echoing Salem's words, and my mom just shook her head and said she was disappointed in Josh and thought he had more sense than that.

So at least I was getting along better with the two of them. They were even being nice about my farm. My mom said the view from my front porch was picturesque, and they both laughed with delight when I introduced them to Annie and Blossom.

I was glad so many things were coming together in my life, but every night, my heart hurt.

"I think I get the ice cream thing now," Shane said one evening as we sat outside on the front porch despite the cooler weather. He was eating his way through a container of mint chocolate chip. "It is kind of soothing."

I rested my feet on the rail. I had on jeans, a long-sleeved hoodie, and a pair of flip-flops since I'd just taken a shower.

"Do you regret being with Martha even though it ended?" I asked.

"Sometimes," he said. "Sometimes I wonder what the point of all that was if we were just going to break up. But then I'll remember some of the fun we had, and even though I miss her, I'm glad I got to be with her."

"Was that the first time you were ever in love?"

Shane stared into his ice cream. Finally, he nodded. "Yeah," he whispered. He looked at me but didn't say anything more.

I was tempted to call Martha, but what would I say? Try to convince her to make up with Shane? If he found out, he'd be pissed. I wasn't sure if I could deal with anyone else thinking I betrayed them.

He told me Martha had a boyfriend in high school who cheated on her, which explained why she got so upset about Kayla.

"Do you think Kayla purposefully tried to break you and Martha up? Maybe she wants you for herself."

He shrugged. "I don't know. I hope not, but in the end, Martha should trust me. That's what matters."

I nodded in agreement.

"What about you?" He put his ice cream container down. "Do you regret being with Josh?"

I shook my head. "But it's been really hard to get over him." I fingered my spinning wheel necklace as I gazed out at the moonlit pasture and the silhouette of the barn. What I didn't tell Shane was how I'd once worried this relationship could destroy me, and that I now understood why. Because deep down, I suspected I would never get over Josh, that this was it for me.

Shane leaned back in his chair, both of us contemplative.

My phone pinged from where it sat on the small porch table between us. I picked it up and gasped. I blinked at the screen like I was hallucinating. It was a text from Josh.

Leah.

That was all it said.

I stared at the screen, waiting for more.

"What it is?" Shane asked, eyeing me. "Everything okay?"

Before I could tell him about the text, there was a scream in the distance.

My head jerked toward the sound. "That's coming from the barn. It's my alpacas!"

There was another scream, and we both jumped up. Without a second thought, I began running toward it, wishing I had on sneakers instead of flip-flops. Shane followed me. My heart hammered with panic at what could be making them scream. *Some kind of predator? A coyote? A raccoon?* I gulped as I had a terrible thought. *A cougar or a bear?*

I cursed to myself and realized I should have grabbed my shotgun. This was stupid, but now we were almost there.

When we got to the barn, I immediately saw the problem. My alpaca Jade was bucking around, freaking out, and it wasn't because of any predator. One of my Angora kids, Blossom, had gotten out of her pen and was running around the alpacas' area.

"See if you can grab Blossom," I yelled to Shane over the noise of another scream. I decided I would try to calm Jade. She'd always been the most high-strung animal in my herd. The other alpacas and the two llamas had all moved away from her.

I approached her slowly, speaking softly. She was still upset. Luckily, Shane had finally cornered Blossom.

"It's okay, pretty girl," I crooned to Jade as I got closer. She had a beautiful caramel-colored fleece and the softest dark eyes, which were currently in a panic. "Everything is fine, sweetheart. It's just a baby goat. That's all."

Jade snorted and shook her head.

Finally, I was standing beside her. I reached out to stroke her long neck, still speaking gently. She tolerated me and seemed to calm down.

Unfortunately, in that moment, all hell broke loose. Blossom shot out past Shane and ran right toward us. He dove to try and grab her but missed.

Jade screamed again as Blossom streaked in front of her, except this time she reared up on her hind legs. I tried to get out of her way but got knocked to the ground.

Before I knew what was happening, I looked up with alarm to see Jade landing hard on top of me.

CHAPTER FORTY-THREE

~Josh~

"Who's Leah?"

My eyes opened with a jolt.

"Is that your girlfriend?"

I blinked at Megan with confusion. This wasn't Leah. This was just some woman I barely knew.

What the hell am I doing?

I sat up abruptly. My head felt thick and muddled. I was really high. I shouldn't have smoked so much. "Sorry," I told the two women lying on the bed with me, "but I'm not into this. You both have to leave."

"C'mon, you don't mean that." Megan smiled and tried to coax me while Alexa lay on my opposite side. "Let's just relax and have some fun."

"You two are both... very attractive, but I can't do this."

I could tell they were disappointed.

"How about you just watch us?" Alexa offered with a sexy smile, glancing over at Megan. "You wouldn't have to do anything. Unless you change your mind."

"I need to be alone."

The two women finally left. I got up to make sure the door was locked, and then I stood in front of the window. Leaning against the glass, I gazed out at the lights of the Hollywood hills.

I'd never felt so lost.

How was I supposed to get over Leah? It didn't seem possible. It was like cutting out my own heart.

My face was wet, and when I touched it, I realized I was crying. Eventually I lay on the bed again. I didn't know what to do with myself. Music had always been my solace, but even that held no appeal.

I glanced over at the nightstand, and my eyes caught on the Sasquatch. I reached over and picked it up, staring at it, and then I completely lost my shit. I started bawling like a baby.

Jesus, crying over a Sasquatch doll.

I didn't know how long I carried on. At one point, I picked up my phone. More than anything I wanted to talk to her. I wanted to hear her voice. But I'd done a damn good job of ending it between us, hadn't I? Cutting her to the quick. If I knew her, and I did, she was furious.

I began to type a text, and there were a million things I wanted to say. But I just typed her name.

Leah.

I stared at it a long time, my thumbs hovering to add more, but then I hit Send.

———

AFTER THAT NIGHT, I was a mess and hardly left my room. Dean checked on me, brought me food, and tried to convince me to join the others. I woke up coughing and feeling like physical and emotional garbage every morning. You'd think crying would be cathartic, but it wasn't. It was almost a week before I finally emerged and made my way downstairs to the kitchen for my first piña colada of the day. Later I'd switch to whiskey.

The French doors were open, and I could hear people splashing in the pool. Opening the fridge, I searched around for something to eat, still feeling dejected. Dean was sitting at the island talking on his phone.

"He just walked in," Dean said, glancing at me with concern. "I'll tell him. I sure hope Leah's going to be okay."

I jerked my head around. "Did something happen?"

"Leah got trampled on by an alpaca."

"*What?*" My mouth fell open as my blood pressure shot into the stratosphere. "Is she okay?"

Dean shook his head. "She's in the hospital."

"Who are you talking to?" My heart pounded as I strode over to him. "Give me the phone."

"It's Salem," he said, handing it over.

I got on the line. "What's happening? What do you know?"

"All is I know is Leah was trampled by an alpaca, and she's been injured."

I swallowed, sick with panic. "When did this happen? How bad is it?"

"A few days ago. It's not good. I think it might be touch and go," Salem said in a somber tone.

"Touch and *go?*" I went completely still. My heart stopped. The idea of a world without Leah in it was unthinkable. I took a shaky breath and tried to calm myself.

"You should fly up there to her right away," Salem went on. "Don't waste any time."

I shoved the phone back at Dean and ran upstairs. I couldn't believe this happened days ago, and I was only now hearing about it. While I threw stuff into a bag, I called Renata, Kat's assistant, and told her I needed to get on a flight to Seattle immediately.

"You might have to fly commercial," she said. "I don't know if I can get you anything private this fast."

"I don't give a shit about that. Just get me to Truth Harbor."

After stuffing everything into my bag, I took a quick shower. Thank God I hadn't started my spiral of whiskey and weed yet. I felt clearheaded.

In fact, this was the clearest I'd been since I got here.

The soonest flight was commercial first-class, and it left in less than two hours. Thankfully, Renata had already called for a limo to meet me in front of the house.

"Keep in touch. Let me know what's going on, brother," Dean said, pulling me in for a hug before I left. "I hope she's okay."

"Me too."

I hadn't flown commercial in ages. A few people stopped me in the airport for autographs and selfies. I tried not to be an asshole, but obviously I was in a rush. Luckily, once I got on the plane, the flight attendants made sure I was left alone.

I sat near the window and spent most of my time thinking about what an idiot I was and that I should have accepted Leah's apology from the start. She'd done so much for me. Brought so much into my life.

Jeremy was right about everything he said. I'd let my stubbornness get in the way. It wasn't the first time I'd done that, and now the love of my life was fighting for her survival.

If only I'd been there.

How could Leah have gotten trampled? She must have been distracted. Probably because of me.

This whole thing was my fault. I promised myself that if Leah made it through this and was willing to take me back, I'd cherish every single day with her.

ONCE THE PLANE landed in Seattle, I called the hospital in Truth Harbor. They told me they didn't have a patient named Leah Kelly.

I wondered where she could be. Had they flown her out of Truth Harbor? Hell, she could be anywhere.

After checking in at the gate for the short commuter flight, I took a seat and tried calling Shane. He didn't answer, so I texted him.

I heard about Leah. Can you tell me where she is? I'm on my way up there.

No response.

I pushed my panic down. Who else could I call? I didn't have Lars's number, but there was one other person....

I stared down at the steel mama's phone number. *Shit.*

She answered on the first ring. "Hello, Josh. It's about time you took responsibility for yourself."

"Uh... what?" I was confused.

"In case you're wondering, I'm speaking about your treatment of my daughter."

I gripped the phone tighter. "How is Leah? Is she okay? Where is she?"

"Your behavior toward her has been abhorrent. What's your excuse for that? I'd like to hear it."

I opened my mouth.

"Don't bother answering. There *is* no excuse. It won't be tolerated. Do you understand me?"

I felt myself shrink in the chair. It was like I was back in my high school principal's office. She obviously knew what happened at Walk the Plank. "Yes, ma'am. I understand."

"I really thought you had more sense."

"I'm sorry." I didn't know what to say. Sweat broke out on my forehead. Crazily, I wondered if I was getting expelled.

"I'm very disappointed in you, Josh. There's no other way to put it."

I swallowed. The phone felt hot in my hand. "I understand. I know I screwed up."

"You most certainly did."

"Can you just tell me where Leah is? I'm really worried about her."

"She's here on the farm. I've been staying over."

My brows shot up. *Leah's at home? Is this a good thing or a bad one?*

An announcement came over the loudspeakers. My flight to Truth Harbor was boarding. "I have to go," I said quickly. "But I'll be up there shortly."

"This isn't over. I don't care how famous you are or how much money you have. That was no way to treat a person, especially not my daughter."

I grimaced. "I know."

Finally, we hung up, and that was when I realized what Camilla had just said, that she was staying at Clarity Moon Farm. She hated Leah's farm.

My stomach dropped.

If she was there, then things must have been dire.

CHAPTER FORTY-FOUR

~Leah~

For the past week, I'd been living one of the situations I'd always worried about.

Injured and forced to rely on my mom, Lars, and Shane to help take care of my farm. This was the main flaw of a one-woman enterprise—if something happened to me, then the whole thing collapsed.

My mom took some days off work and was actually staying here, sleeping in my guest bedroom. In the past, this would have been unthinkable, but surprisingly, it'd been all right. Today was her last day, since she had to go back to the high school tomorrow.

"I'm going to miss those chickens," she said. "I never knew they had such colorful personalities." We were having lunch in the living room, eating the leftover corn chowder from last night's dinner. "Agnes and Betty are so affectionate."

"They're sweethearts," I agreed from the couch. My foot was propped up on a few pillows to keep it elevated.

"And that rooster is such a charmer, isn't he? He always looks out for his ladies."

It turned out Cary Grant thought my mom was the cat's pajamas. He constantly strutted near her, following her around and clucking flirtatiously in her direction.

My mom's cheeks had a healthy flush from working outside all morning, and after staying here the past week, she seemed softer somehow. Not quite her usual stern self. She told me the other day how invigorating it was working on a farm.

"Thank you again for all your help this week," I said. "I really appreciate it."

"You don't have to thank me. To be honest, I've enjoyed my time here." She gazed out the living room window and then at me. "I'm sorry for the way I doubted you about all this. It's obvious now that you've built something quite wonderful. I'm really proud of you, sweetheart."

I was almost too stunned to speak. "Thank you."

"Spending time here with you has been an eye-opener. I regret that we've grown so distant. I hope we can see more of each other."

"I'd like that."

She motioned down at my foot and ate a spoonful of soup. "Shouldn't you be wearing your cast?"

I had two broken toes from Jade trampling on them. They were buddy-taped together, and I had a removable cast. As frustrating as it was, the doctor told me I needed to stay off my foot for at least a week and that it could take up to six weeks to heal completely.

Being a runner, I was going stir-crazy with pent-up energy.

"I'm just taking a break from it. It makes my leg itchy."

I was spinning earlier—something I could still manage, thankfully. Lars was coming by every morning to pick up packages to be mailed, and Shane was coming home early from the bar every evening to help with chores. I appreciated the way my whole family had come together. We may have had our disagreements, but when it mattered, we were there for each other.

After lunch, Delores arrived, and she and my mom went out to put my garlic bulbs in the ground. It was nice of Delores to help, and they seemed to be having fun. I could hear the two of them laughing through the open window.

Still on the couch, I opened my computer to pay bills and had just finished with the electricity and water when I heard a car pull up outside. A few seconds later, there was a knock on the door, and I yelled, "Come in," figuring it was Lars.

"There's still some leftover corn chowder in the fridge," I said, bringing up my co-op bill. I was on a twelve-month plan to spread out the payments for the winter hay I needed. "Help yourself."

He didn't reply, so I turned my head. To my astonishment, it wasn't Lars but Josh.

He stared at me with wild eyes like he was seeing a ghost. "Leah?"

"*Josh?*" I blinked at him in shock. "What are you doing here?"

He wore jeans and a wrinkled blue hoodie, and his long hair was pulled into a haphazard ponytail. He looked like he'd been through a battle. Despite that, I wanted to drink him in. I couldn't believe he was standing in my living room.

His eyes roamed over me with a freaked-out expression. "I heard you were trampled on by an alpaca."

"I was, but how did you know that?"

"Salem told me." He licked his lips. "She said you were injured. That it was bad."

"Well, I *am* injured." I pointed at my right foot, which sat daintily on a stack of pillows like *The Princess and the Pea*. "Jade broke my big toe and my pointer toe."

He stared down at my foot. "She broke your *big toe*? That's it? That's your injury?"

I nodded. "And my pointer toe."

He gaped at my foot like there were winged monkeys perched on it.

I watched as he walked over to the nearest chair and collapsed.

His leather bag hit the floor with a resounding thud.

"Jesus." He seemed upset. "Salem told me you were seriously injured. That it was 'touch and go.' I rushed to get here as fast as I could!"

"Really?" I tried not to smile. Apparently Salem was a bit of a puppet master. "Well, as you can see, it's not that serious."

He shook his head, and for a long moment, neither of us spoke. Our eyes met, and I remembered I was angry at him. Furious. Except I couldn't seem to summon that fury. It felt too good to see him.

"So what happened?" he asked. "How did you get hurt?"

I rolled my eyes. "By wearing flip-flops and ignoring Barn Safety 101." I told him about Jade's screams and how cute little Blossom—one of my new Angora kids—caused all this havoc. "I've been forced to rest and let my broken toes heal."

His gaze never left my face. "I'm sorry, Leah."

"It's okay. I'll be all right."

"No." He shook his head. His eyes were bright blue and filled with emotion. "I'm *sorry*."

My breath stopped. He was talking about the last time we saw each other.

"I acted like a fucking asshole that night. I don't know what got into me. I was upset, but you didn't deserve that."

I swallowed and tried to bring my breathing under control. "You're right. I didn't deserve it." I went quiet. "But I did an asshole thing too."

"I should have forgiven you. I'm an idiot. I put my pride and anger above you. That was the biggest mistake of my life."

My heart pounded with a tremulous hope.

"I've been furious at you," I said, my eyes stinging. "What you did... that really hurt me."

His expression turned bleak. "I know, Leah. I'm *so* damn sorry. I hope you can forgive me." He leaned forward in his chair with determination. "I promise you this. Nothing like that will *ever* happen again."

I wiped away my tears with annoyance. "I'm angry at myself too. I destroyed your privacy. I put your adoption in danger. Neither of you deserved that either."

Josh got up, then came over and sat next to me on the couch. His musk and lemongrass scent surrounded me—so familiar. I'd missed him. Seeing him up close, I remembered how Dean said he wasn't doing so great, and I could see it was true. He looked tired.

He reached for my hand, and I let him take it. His touch felt good.

"I was thinking about something," he said. "While I was in a deep panic on that flight up here. I thought about everything that happened between us, and I think it all happened that way for a reason. Being forced out of my house is what brought us together."

"In a way, that's true. So you've decided you believe in destiny?"

He nodded and smiled. "When it comes to you and me, honey. I definitely do."

IT DIDN'T TAKE LONG for us to fall in love with each other again, because it turned out we hadn't fallen out of love.

"This white streak in your hair is amazing," he said, looking down at me as we were lying in my bed upstairs. He brushed his fingers along my temple. "I love it."

"You don't think it's weird and witchy?"

"I think it's cool. Definitely sexy."

I rolled my eyes, though I couldn't stop smiling. We'd been in bed with each other nonstop. As soon as my mom left to go back to her house, Josh basically moved in to help take care of me, and he'd definitely been doing that. In every way.

"So, how much did you miss me when we were apart?" he wanted to know. "Tell me again. Was it bad?"

I had my arms around his neck as he lay over me. "You've already asked me that like ten times."

"I know, but I like hearing it."

I couldn't help my laughter. He still tickled my funny bone. "All right, fine. I missed you like crazy. Are you happy?"

"Were you suffering without me?"

"It was agony. I especially missed how endearingly self-centered you are."

He chuckled. "You really *do* get me."

"Did you miss me?"

His laughter quieted. "More than you'll ever know. I even obsessively watched your YouTube videos."

"You did?" This was news.

He nodded. "I couldn't stop myself. As a side effect, I've learned a lot about spinning. I think I'm ready to buy my own wheel."

I played with his hair, gathering it into a ponytail in back. "I'll help you pick it out."

"Sounds good."

We grinned at each other. "You'll be pleased to know I've moved you up in the ranks of my favorite singers."

"Really? What number am I now?"

"Possibly in the top ten."

"Is that so?" he murmured, kissing my neck. "Maybe I can reach number one if I try hard enough."

He gently bit me and then blew on the spot. I gasped at the sensation.

I noticed something else. Something big and stiff pressing against my thigh. "I can't believe you're hard again," I said, trying to catch my breath as I gave in to Josh's seduction.

"Guess I'm still an insatiable beast."

"I know." I slid my leg up the back of his thigh. "I can feel that beast banana."

Josh laughed, and I closed my eyes, enjoying that low rumble. The one that had made my girl parts tingle right from the start.

The past few days had been an emotional roller coaster for both of us. My mom didn't seem surprised at all when, after planting my garlic bulbs, she came into the living room and found Josh sitting on the couch with me. I expected a lecture, but she studied him with a stern expression.

"Do better," she demanded.

"Yes, ma'am," he replied. "I will."

Salem called the next day to check on me. Josh asked if I'd put it on speaker, so I held the phone between us.

The corner of his mouth kicked up. "I think this is the first time I've ever said this to anyone, but thank you for lying to me, Salem. I needed that fire under my ass."

"I felt bad for being dishonest, but I had to do something!" she said. "You weren't thinking clearly. Dax and I are so happy you guys are together again. We just want you to have what we have."

Last night, I invited Shane and Lars over for dinner. And I had to hand it to Josh—he apologized to both of my brothers for what he'd done to me at Walk the Plank. They acknowledged his apology, and also acknowledged that their sister wasn't perfect either.

Josh and I had both learned that you had to own your mistakes and learn from them. Don't waste time looking backwards when you can be looking forward in life.

Lars was still a little standoffish toward Josh, but I could tell Shane was happy and relieved. They'd been friends, so this whole situation was hard on him.

Josh also told me about the phone call with Jeremy, and how Jeremy had told him to let it go and to stop blaming himself.

"Do you think you can you do that?" I asked the next day when he was helping me with chores. I was limping around. My toes were still buddy-taped, but I was wearing my rubber boots and getting back to normal. "Can you really let it go?"

"It's been harder than I thought," he admitted, pushing the wheelbarrow along while I carried the shovels. Unfortunately, today we were cleaning the alpacas' latrine areas. "I've been blaming myself for years. I'm going to keep trying. I think it would help Jeremy a lot if I started seeing him as more than just the source of my guilt."

I was glad to hear it.

"I noticed that rooster is still around." Josh motioned over his shoulder toward Cary Grant, who still glared at him. "I guess there was no chance you would have cooked him in a pot of stew while we were apart. I'm not that lucky."

"Of course not, but guess what? It turns out he's crazy about my mom and follows her everywhere. Can you believe it?"

He rolled his eyes and laughed. "That figures."

At least, being late November, it was cool outside, so the latrine areas didn't smell bad, and scarves weren't necessary. He parked the wheelbarrow at the edge, and we began shoveling piles of alpaca beans into it.

"I've been meaning to ask you something," I said. "Why did you send me that strange text?"

"What strange text?"

"It just said 'Leah' and nothing else."

"Shit." He paused what he was doing and glanced over at me. "You're not going to like this."

Then he told me how he'd almost had a threesome while he was in LA.

My brows shot up. "You *what?*"

He held his hand up. "Hear me out. Nothing happened, except for some kissing. I was so stoned that I got confused and thought *you* were one of the women."

I wasn't sure what to say to this.

"After I sent them away, I had an emotional breakdown. I was a mess." He shook his head, and his expression turned to regret. "I wanted to talk to you so bad, honey, but I figured there was no way you'd want to hear from me. So I sent you that text. Just to feel some kind of connection to you, no matter how small."

"That's kind of sad."

"Pathetic, too, considering I brought it on myself."

I raised a brow. "Just to be clear, I'm never having a threesome with you."

He chuckled. "Don't worry. I couldn't share you. I'd be so jealous it would probably kill me."

I considered everything he'd just said about his time in LA. "I'm glad you told me what happened, but we were broken up, so you didn't have to."

"I know, but that's not who we are. We tell each other everything, right?"

I thought about how I'd hidden something from him in the past and all the trouble it had caused. I was grateful for this second chance. "That's right. We do."

"I figured something else out recently," he said, his expression serious. "I figured out why I lied to you about who I was when we first met."

I stopped what I was doing to listen.

"It was because I wanted you to see me for the man I am, not just somebody famous. I *wanted* that."

"I did see you for the man you are."

"I know. And it's made me realize something about my song, about 'Silver Days.'"

I tilted my head. "What do you mean?"

He was gazing at me, his hands resting on the top of his shovel. "I wrote that song for you, Leah. Before we ever met. Back when you were just a dream."

I went completely still. A torrent of emotion flooded through me, and my eyes filled with tears. "Oh my God, Josh. You can't *do* this to me. You can't tell me something this romantic when we're standing knee-deep in alpaca shit!"

He chuckled and came over to my side. "I love you," he said. "I've always loved you." He leaned down and kissed the tears on my cheek away. His lips were soft.

"I love you, too, you asshole."

"And now here we are together." He glanced around my farm, at the place where it all began for us, and then he smiled gently at me. "These are our silver days."

EPILOGUE

~Leah~

Eight Months Later

It was a warm July evening as I sat alone on my front porch sipping a cold beer. "I'm so grateful for everything," I said, gazing up at the full moon, pale and luminous in the night sky. "My farm is doing well, and my animals are thriving. So is my yarn business."

I could feel those moonbeams sinking into my skin. "I once asked you to bring me a good man, and you did just that. You brought him right to my door."

I smiled to myself.

Talking to the moon might be strange, but I still found it as comforting as when I was a kid.

A sultry breeze blew past. I was glad it was warm out because I was only wearing a thin camisole, white panties, and my tall black rubber boots. My feet rested on the porch rail, crossed at the ankle.

I took another sip of beer. A lot had happened these past months.

For starters, Josh proposed to me while we were in London visiting Damian for the holidays. He gave me an engagement ring as a Christmas present. It was a sweet surprise, and, of course, I said yes. Damian knew about it beforehand and was really excited. The two of them took me around London, and I got to see the tourist attractions as well as their favorite spots. I loved it all. I also briefly met Charlotte again and couldn't believe the change in her. She seemed happy and healthy, and I sensed no animosity toward me. Apparently she'd gotten back into painting again. Josh told me how she was an artist when he first met her.

Damian flew here a couple of weeks ago and will stay with us until after the wedding next month. Josh asked him to be his best man. Damian's already memorizing a short speech to give at the reception. He'll be twelve soon and has grown so much since we last saw him in December.

He was also still a runner and had been joining me every morning with the alpacas. Josh joined us, too, though lately he'd been lazing in bed. "I'll let you two maniacs have your fun while I sleep an extra hour" was what he usually mumbled. It'd given Damian and me a chance to hang out, so I didn't mind at all. I was looking forward to being his stepmom. He was having a sleepover at Eddie's tonight— Martha's younger brother.

Speaking of Martha, I was still friends with her. Unfortunately, she and Shane were still broken up. She told me she had a new boyfriend, though it didn't sound serious. My brother had entertained a string of girlfriends, and none of them had been serious either. To be honest, I thought he was still in love with Martha. At least Walk the Plank was doing well. It was booked out a year in advance now.

The other big news was that Claire had her baby in February! A beautiful little girl with blonde ringlet curls and the bluest eyes. They named her Amelia. So far, I'd enjoyed knitting Amelia a wide variety of hats, sweaters, and booties. Claire was delighted that Josh and I got back together for lots of reasons, one of them being that she got to listen to her favorite band again.

Theo was doing well, though she was still having problems with her new neighbor, "Beauty" Bardales. She hadn't met him yet, but his lawyers were still trying to force her to get rid of her beehives. The latest news was that Bardales were suing her.

Lars had officially announced he was running for sheriff. It was strange to see posters all over town with his name on them. He and Josh had become more friendly lately. I wouldn't call them besties, but it seemed both of them were trying harder since we announced our engagement. Josh knew a lot about being in the public eye and had been giving my brother some pointers.

My mom regularly spent time on my farm these days. She came over for dinner at least twice a month and stopped by occasionally to visit and help with chores. Cary Grant was still crazy about her and followed her everywhere. She'd gone from hating my farm to being its biggest advocate.

She'd also been an advocate for Josh, who took an online philosophy class at college last quarter. My mom helped him with the accommodations for his ADHD, and he'd been thinking about getting a bachelor's degree.

Josh put his house on the market recently since we planned to stay at Clarity Moon Farm. It turned out Dean wanted to buy it, so it looked like he'd be our new neighbor, and we couldn't be happier. Dean had moved on from Nalla but didn't have a serious love interest. In truth, Josh and I worried about him. He was so bighearted but seemed prone to overindulging in a lot of ways.

The other guys in the band were doing all right. Rhys and Terence both lived in Seattle and had been flying or driving up to rehearse and work on new material a lot since East Echo planned to release a new album soon.

"Where is he?" I wondered aloud from my spot on the front

porch. I took another sip from my beer. My ears perked up when I finally heard the roar of a motorcycle approaching.

This should be fun.

The sound grew louder until eventually a bike swept around the corner and parked in the gravel driveway.

I wasn't hiding in the bushes this time, but my heart still pounded.

He turned the engine off and lifted himself off the bike. Just like that first night I saw him, he wore jeans and a faded black motorcycle jacket. There was a riot of blond hair tied back after he removed his helmet.

Josh glanced around at the arborvitae, then noticed me sitting on the porch in the dark.

I didn't say anything, and neither did he. He stood there casually in front of his bike, and I let myself enjoy the sight of his well-made body.

Finally, I put my beer on the table and got up, sauntering down the front steps toward him.

His eyes roamed over me, and I could tell he liked what he saw.

"Can I help you, stranger?" I asked. "Are you lost?"

He rubbed his jaw, still eyeing me with appreciation. "I thought I was lost, but maybe not."

I moved closer. "Well, where is it you're headed?"

"The nearest town. I'm looking for a place to hang my helmet for the night." He motioned down at his motorcycle. "So to speak."

I considered his words. "If you're interested, I could offer you my hayloft." I gave him a little smirk and crossed my arms. "Of course, that depends on what you're willing to do for me. Everything has its price."

"And what might that price be?"

I eyed him slowly from head to toe. The night was warm, but the heat between us was hotter than a rocket on reentry. "A man like yourself... I'll bet there's a lot you can do."

Josh stroked his beard and held my gaze. "I believe we can work something out." He licked his bottom lip, and I felt a tingle between my thighs.

"I only have one question for you," I said. "How fast are you?"

"How fast?"

I nodded. "Because you'll have to catch me first!"

His mouth opened, and I saw the understanding on his face as he reached out to grab me.

Except I was already faster. I laughed. "Too slow." And then I ran.

"Hey! Get back here."

Thankfully, my toes were completely healed, so I had no trouble running. I wasn't as fast as I'd normally be because I was wearing these tall rubber boots.

I could hear Josh behind me. I even felt the tips of his fingers grazing my back.

I raced directly toward the barn, and when I got to the ladder for the hayloft, I knew he was close. Quickly, I climbed each rung, glancing down to see the top of his head.

The hayloft was warm, and the grassy smell filled my nose. I'd already placed a couple of lanterns next to some blankets and pillows earlier. It gave the scene a cozy glow.

I stood and admired it as I caught my breath.

"Now, what have we here?" his voice rumbled behind me.

I spun around, and Josh was right there, grinning like a western gunslinger. He slid his hands over my hips. We kissed, and before I knew it, we were lying on a tangle of blankets.

"I've been thinking about what I would do when I caught you." There was a gleam in his eye. "I've got plans for you, honey."

"Except you didn't catch me," I said with a laugh, wrapping myself around him. I remembered that warm summer night a year ago when I'd been hiding in the bushes, plotting my escape. "*I* caught *you*."

THE NEXT MORNING, Lars showed up at the farm in his uniform. He eyed Josh and me quizzically as we came from the direction of the barn. Me wrapped in a blanket and carrying the pillows while Josh carried his motorcycle jacket and the lanterns.

I was surprised to see my brother. "It's kind of early. Is everything okay?"

"I could ask you two the same question," he said with a grin. "But I think I already know the answer."

Josh laughed, and I elbowed him in the side. "Do you want some coffee?" I asked as Lars followed us up the front steps into the house. "I could put on a pot."

He shook his head. "Actually, I can't stay long. I'm here on official business. It's about your friend Theo."

I dropped the pillows on the couch and turned with alarm. "What about her?"

"Has something happened to Theo?" Josh asked with concern.

Lars shook his head. "She's okay, but how much do you two know about the situation with her new neighbor, that football player— Gabriel Bardales?"

"I know she's having problems with him," I said. "He's trying to force her to get rid of her beehives."

Lars nodded. "She seems to have taken matters into her own hands."

Josh and I glanced at each other.

"What do you mean?" I asked warily.

My brother rubbed the back of his neck. "I'm not sure how to put it. Bardales built a vacation house up here, and Theo has... chained herself to the front of it."

My jaw dropped.

"She's threatening to call the press and refuses to unchain herself," Lars went on. "Not until Bardales meets with her and agrees to leave her bees alone."

"To be fair, the guy's been a real jerk," I said with righteous anger on Theo's behalf. "She's tried to contact him a bunch of times, but he keeps ignoring her."

"Really?" Lars chuckled softly. "Well, it looks like he won't be ignoring her anymore."

The End

TRUTH ABOUT NERDS & BEES

Order the next book in the series! TRUTH ABOUT NERDS & BEES - Theo and Gabe's story.

He's the beauty. She's the beast.

Find out what happens when NFL Quarterback Gabriel "Beauty" Bardales discovers there's a kooky bee biologist chained to his house...

NOTE FROM ANDREA

Thank you for reading Leah and Josh's story! I hope you enjoyed it. I had a lot of fun writing about those two. As you can tell from the ending, the next book will be Theo and Gabe's.

If you enjoyed Leah and Josh's story, I hope you'll be kind enough to leave a review or rating, or tell a friend about it. I appreciate it!

If you have any thoughts or comments you'd like to share, feel free to email me at andrea@andresimonne.com.

With so many books choices out there, thank you for choosing mine.

xo,

Andrea

SOME LIKE IT HOTTER

Did you know Josh's first wife Lindsay has her own book? It's true! It's part of my Sweet Life in Seattle series.

Find out what happens after wild child artist, Lindsay West, has an ill-fated one-night-stand with a surgeon who needs a wife.

Order SOME LIKE IT HOTTER today!

SWEET LIFE IN SEATTLE SERIES

ANDREA SIMONNE

I hope you'll check out the first book from my series Sweet Life in Seattle, YEAR OF LIVING BLONDE.

He's left her for another woman. Could it get any worse? The mistress is thirteen years older.

Order YEAR OF LIVING BLONDE today!

STANDALONE

Read my steamy standalone FIRE DOWN BELOW!

Still single and just turned thirty-five, Kate suddenly finds herself engaged to one man, while obsessing over another...

ACKNOWLEDGMENTS

There are always so many people who help make my books the best they can be. I'm grateful to all of them. I want to thank my beta readers, Jamie, Nancy, and Barb, for all their insights and suggestions. You guys are the best. (And, yes, I'm busy working on Theo and Gabe's story!)

I also want to thank Stephanie and her son Wade for all their help and advice with the chickens and the book's fiber art. They were kind enough to send me advice and even a video of Wade spinning (and creating pretend problems!) which was helpful in sorting out Leah's occasional difficulties at the wheel. Wade is super talented and also makes and sells drop spindles. Damian would definitely approve of that.

My editor Kristin Scearce did an amazing job. I'm grateful to her and everyone at Hot Tree for their skill and support.

My sister-in-law Peg is usually kind enough to read my books and has a knack for finding errors that slip past just about everyone. Thank you, Peg!

As always, I want to thank my wonderful friend Susan for her remarkable proofreading skills. I've never met anyone like her. She's been one of the last set of eyes on nearly every book I've published, and I appreciate her immense talent.

I joined a choir group to research this book. (And, unlike Josh, I'm not much of a singer.) Despite my mediocre singing skills, they were a welcoming bunch. I had fun and learned a lot. Our final concert was a blast! (This was right before the pandemic started.) I also want to thank my husband, John, for being a great sounding board and for always supporting me in following this dream of mine.

Last but not least, I want to thank *you*, my readers. For your emails, messages, and kind words. I appreciate it more than you'll ever know.

xo,

Andrea

ALSO BY ANDREA SIMONNE

Sweet Life in Seattle series

Year of Living Blonde

Return of the Jerk

Some Like It Hotter

Object of My Addiction

Too Much Like Love

About Love series

Truth About Men & Dogs

Truth About Cats & Spinsters

Truth About Nerds & Bees

Other

Fire Down Below

ABOUT THE AUTHOR

Andrea Simonne grew up as an army brat and discovered she had a talent for creating personas at each new school. The most memorable was a surfer chick named "Ace" who never touched a surfboard in her life, but had an impressive collection of puka shell necklaces. Andrea still enjoys creating personas though now they occupy her books. She's an Amazon best seller in romantic comedy and contemporary romance, and author of the series Sweet Life in Seattle and About Love. She currently makes her home in the Pacific Northwest with her husband and two sons.

She loves hearing from her readers! You can find her on the web at www.andreasimonne.com.

Email: authorsimonne@gmail.com.

Made in United States
North Haven, CT
28 September 2023

42088360R00264